A Book Of

IMPORT EXPORT PROCEDURE

For

BBM Semester - VI

As Per New Syllabus w.e.f. 2015

Manisha Paliwal

M.I.B., M.Phil.,
Associate Professor,
Sinhgad Institute of Management,
PUNE.

NIRALI PRAKASHAN
ADVANCEMENT OF KNOWLEDGE

N3476

Import Export Procedure - BBA (Semester - VI) ISBN 978-93-5164-846-8

First Edition : January 2016

© : Author

Published By : Polyplet

NIRALI PRAKASHAN

Abhyudaya Pragati, 1312, Shivaji Nagar,
Off J.M. Road, PUNE – 411005
Tel - (020) 25512336/37/39, Fax - (020) 25511379
Email : niralipune@pragationline.com

☞ **DISTRIBUTION CENTRES**

PUNE

Nirali Prakashan : 119, Budhwar Peth, Jogeshwari Mandir Lane, Pune 411002, Maharashtra
Tel : (020) 2445 2044, 66022708, Fax : (020) 2445 1538
Email : bookorder@pragationline.com, niralilocal@pragationline.com

Nirali Prakashan : S. No. 28/27, Dhyari, Near Pari Company, Pune 411041
Tel : (020) 24690204 Fax : (020) 24690316
Email : dhyari@pragationline.com, bookorder@pragationline.com

MUMBAI

Nirali Prakashan : 385, S.V.P. Road, Rasdhara Co-op. Hsg. Society Ltd.,
Girgaum, Mumbai 400004, Maharashtra
Tel : (022) 2385 6339 / 2386 9976, Fax : (022) 2386 9976
Email : niralimumbai@pragationline.com

☞ **DISTRIBUTION BRANCHES**

JALGAON

Nirali Prakashan : 34, V. V. Golani Market, Navi Peth, Jalgaon 425001,
Maharashtra, Tel : (0257) 222 0395, Mob : 94234 91860

KOLHAPUR

Nirali Prakashan : New Mahadvar Road, Kedar Plaza, 1st Floor Opp. IDBI Bank
Kolhapur 416 012, Maharashtra. Mob : 9850046155

NAGPUR

Pratibha Book Distributors : Above Maratha Mandir, Shop No. 3, First Floor,
Rani Jhanshi Square, Sitabuldi, Nagpur 440012, Maharashtra
Tel : (0712) 254 7129

DELHI

Nirali Prakashan : 4593/21, Basement, Aggarwal Lane 15, Ansari Road, Daryaganj
Near Times of India Building, New Delhi 110002
Mob : 08505972553

BENGALURU

Pragati Book House : House No. 1, Sanjeevappa Lane, Avenue Road Cross,
Opp. Rice Church, Bengaluru – 560002.
Tel : (080) 64513344, 64513355,Mob : 9880582331, 9845021552
Email:bharatsavla@yahoo.com

CHENNAI

Pragati Books : 9/1, Montieth Road, Behind Taas Mahal, Egmore,
Chennai 600008 Tamil Nadu, Tel : (044) 6518 3535,
Mob : 94440 01782 / 98450 21552 / 98805 82331,
Email : bharatsavla@yahoo.com

niralipune@pragationline.com | www.pragationline.com

Also find us on www.facebook.com/niralibooks

Dedication

This book is dedicated to
My Parents
Mrs. & Mr. P.C. Samdani
My Spouse
Mr. Nitin Paliwal
&
My Daughters
Isshita & Annanya

FOREWORD

     Import Export Procedure is subject to frequent changes, amendment and requirements vary from country to country. Export Documentation is one of the most important aspects of overseas trade. Economic activity is globally unified today to an unprecedented degree. Changes in one nation's economy are rapidly transmitted to that nation's trading partners. Any company involved in importing or exporting products or services needs to fully understand the procedurals formalities as well as the incentives related to them to ensure that it is effectively managed.

     The book "Import Export Procedure" by Prof. Manisha Paliwal is indeed an important book. In my view this book will be an addition to the management literature in India. It is a good source of learning, teaching and practicing managers. The book is written in a simple and lucid language and will help to produce export manager's of 21st century, who will make India strong, vibrant and a powerful economy in the world.

Prof. M. N. Navale

President

Sinhgad Technical Education Society

Preface ...

International markets provide a wide range of opportunities compared to the domestic markets. But global business is inherently more risky than domestic business. However, the firm prefers to go international, if the perceived benefits overweigh the anticipated risks.

Companies going global would like to gain from the perceived benefits and minimise the risks or threats to which they are exposed. In the present era of globalisation, many firms do not confine themselves to their domestic market but choose to enter international markets at some point.

Exporting a product is a profitable method that helps to expand the business and reduces the dependence in the local market. It also provides new ideas, management practices, marketing techniques, and ways of competing, which is not possible in the domestic market. Even as an owner of a domestic market, an individual businessman should think about exporting. Research shows that, on average, exporting companies are more profitable than their non-exporting counterparts. The export organisations would have to follow the highly professional managerial approach to meet the emerging challenges and take advantage of the growing opportunities.

The export process is made more complex by the wide variety of documents that the exporter needs to complete to ensure that the order reaches its destination quickly, safely and without problems. Documentation requirements for export shipments also vary widely according to the country of destination and the type of product being shipped. It can help an exporter to reduce the transaction costs by targeting and eliminating common problems. Its wealth of explanations and helpful suggestions is virtually guaranteed to save the firm's time and money in the competitive international arena. An exporter may require finance in order to manufacture or purchase and prepare goods for export. Economic activity is globally unified today to an unprecedented degree. Changes in one nation's economy are rapidly transmitted to that nation's trading partners.

These fluctuations in economic activity are reflected, almost immediately, in fluctuations in currency values. Any company involved in importing or exporting products or services needs to fully understand their foreign exchange risk to ensure it is effectively managed.

This book is intended to provide in one volume various theoretical and managerial aspects of international trade and export import management. The book is organised into six chapters providing a comprehensive coverage of all the vital aspects of export-import procedure and various export benefits under EXIM policy of India. In fact there are two parts of the text: the first deals with exporting, export facilities and incentives, export financing, provides detailed documentation procedural aspect of exports: whereas the second part deals with the import procedure, custom clearance and Procedure for Importing Goods within relevant provisions under various Acts. Special attention has been devoted while presenting the subject matter in a lucid style so that it can be easily understood.

Appropriate case studies along with the sample documents have been included to assist the learning process and give a more comprehensive view of the international trade environment and documentation.

I would like to place on record my gratitude to all those who have helped me, in different ways, in completion of this book. I am very much thankful to Mr. Jignesh Furia, Mrs. Nirja Sharma and the entire staff of Nirali Prakshan, Pune for giving me this opportunity and publishing the book. I would like to thank Prof. M. N. Navale, Founder President, Sinhgad Technical Education Society, my seniors and our colleagues for the inspiration and support.

Finally, I want to thank my husband Nitin Paliwal, and kids Isshita and Ananya for their kind co-operation, continuous support and patience to make this book a reality.

Mrs. Manisha Paliwal

Syllabus ...

1. Essentials for Export

1.1 Registration – IEC, RCMC [Registration cum membership Certificate.] EPC-Export promotion council, central excise.

1.2 Categories of Export

    1.2.1   Physical

    1.2.2   Deemed Export

    1.2.3   Merchant

    1.2.4   Manufacture Export

1.3 Shipping Documents

1.4 Terms used in Shipping

2. Custom Clarence Procedure for Imported Cargo

- Documentation
- Consignment Clearance Procedure
- Payment Procedure
- Concept of Ware Housing
- Procedure for Importing Goods within relevant provisions under various Acts.

3. Export Procedure

3.1 Basic Documentation

3.2 Excise clearance for export

3.3 Quantity – Preshipment inspection

3.4 Packaging, Marketing, Labeling

3.5 Shipment of Goods

3.6 GSP [Generalized System of preferences] Rules & Origin

3.7 Role of overseas agent & remittance of commission.

3.8 Incentives for export from Govt.

3.9 Various modes of transport.

4. Benefits of Export

4.1 Service Tax benefits

4.2 Excise clearance benefits / rebates

4.3 Income Tax benefits

5. Duty Drawback & Remittance Scheme

- Advance License
- Replenishment license
- Special Interest License
- DEPB Scheme [Duty Entitlement Pass Book Scheme]
- DFRC Scheme [Duty Free Replenishment Certificate]

Contents ...

Chapter **1** ...

Essentials for Export

Contents ...

Learning Objectives ...

- To understand the basic procedure of exporting
- To study the registration of export companies with special reference to IEC, RCMC, EPC and central excise
- To learn the various categories of export including, physical, deemed, merchant and manufacture export
- To be able to explain the various shipping documents
- To understand the various terms used in shipping

1.1 Exporting

1.1.1 Meaning

Exports are those goods and services that are made in one country (domestically) and sold to foreign countries. It is of little consequence what the good or service is or how it is sent. It can be shipped, sent by email, or hand-carried in personal luggage on a plane.

Most countries want to increase their exports to gain a competitive advantage and expertise in producing goods and services for overseas markets. This is also done when the local demands are met and surplus goods and services are to be taken care of. Most Countries encourage exports, as it increases jobs, brings in higher wages and raises the standard of living for residents. They are more likely to support their national leaders in this happy frame of mind.

Any company must carefully assess the advantages and disadvantages of exporting into a new market, before committing its resources. Some companies undertake exports unintentionally after receiving an order to purchase from a foreign buyer who liked their product, while others deliberately conduct thorough research before entering an international market. However in both the scenarios companies need to evaluate and carefully assess the advantages and challenges of exporting before committing resources. Entering an export business requires careful planning, some capital, market know-how, access to quality products, competitive pricing strategy, management commitment and realising the challenges and opportunities without which it is almost impossible to succeed in the export business. While there are no hard and fast rules that can help companies make decisions to export and to become successful, understanding the advantages and disadvantages of exporting can facilitate a smooth entry into new markets, keep pace with competition and eventually realise profit.

1.1.2 Advantages of Exporting

The main advantages of exporting include:

1 **Need for Limited Finance:** If the company selects a company in the host country to distribute, the company can either enter international market with no or less financial resources. Alternatively, if the company chooses to distribute on its own, it needs to invest financial resources, but this amount would be quite less compared to that would be necessary under other modes.

2. **Improved Profits and Sales:** Selling items and services in a marketplace which the company has never touched before will boost sales and hence raise revenues. Moreover, overall profitability is enhanced once export development expenses have been covered.

3. Develop Domestic Competitiveness: Most firms become competitive in the local market before they enter the worldwide market. Being competitive in the local market helps companies to obtain some strategies that can assist them in the global market.

4. Increase Worldwide Market Shares and Brand Awareness: By exporting, companies will expand their share in the huge global marketplace. Consider for a moment those brands with which we are most familiar like Coca-Cola, Ford, Microsoft, and McDonald's.

5. Diversification and Risk Minimisation: Exporting involves less risk as the company undertakes the culture, customer and the market of the host country gradually. Selling to numerous markets allows firms to branch out their business and spread their risk. Firms will not be tied to the changes of the trade cycle of a local market or of one specific nation.

6. Minimise Per Unit Overheads: With the help of exporting, firms start capturing an added overseas market that would increase production to meet overseas demand. Improved production can often minimise per unit overheads and lead to bigger use of existing capacities.

7. Balance for Seasonal Demands: Exporting provides an opportunity for firms whose items or services are only used at certain seasons locally and may be competent to sell their items or services in overseas markets during different seasons.

8. Potential for Company Development and Expansion: Companies which venture into the exporting business usually have to have a presence or representation in the overseas market. This venture might need additional personnel support and thus lead to development of the company.

9. Sell Surplus Production Capacity: Companies which have excess production are most likely sell their items in an overseas market with good profit .Otherwise in the absence of exports, they would have been forced to give huge concession or even dispose of their excess production.

10. Expand New Knowledge and Experience: Going worldwide can yield precious ideas and information about new technologies, new marketing methods and overseas competitors. The gains can help a nation's domestic as well as overseas businesses.

11. Currency Benefits: Changes in exchange rates can prove advantageous when selling to a customer whose currency is weaker than others.

12. Expand Life Cycle of Product: Many products go through various cycles namely introduction, growth, maturity and declining stage that is the end of their usefulness in a specific market. Once the product reaches the stage of maturity in a given market, the same product can be introduced in a different market where the product was never marketed before.

1.1.3 Disadvantages of Exporting

While the advantages of exporting by far outweigh the disadvantages, small and medium size enterprises especially face some challenges when venturing in the international marketplace. Multiple disadvantages which must be considered by an exporter are as follows:

1. **Increased Costs:** The costs of travelling abroad to obtain orders could be higher than getting orders domestically. High management fees, shipping charges, agent's fees etc., can sometimes increase the exporter's prices to a level which makes goods and services uncompetitive in overseas markets.

2. **Understanding and Following Import Laws and Regulations:** Import rules and regulations vary between countries, regions, and trading blocs. It is not uncommon for rules to change rapidly and dramatically in some cultures.

3. **Transportation Policy:** Shipping rules and regulations can prove to be complicated and represent a vast body of knowledge, which the exporter will have to be familiar with.

4. **Currency:** The earlier advantage of a strong currency in exchange for a weak dollar might, in alternative circumstances, prove detrimental to the exporter.

5. **Collecting Long-standing Payments and Debts:** This can prove to be a very difficult problem, particularly for the small business, if cultural and social differences are not known and understood.

Apart from the above disadvantages to exporting, small and medium size enterprises especially face some challenges when venturing in the international marketplace. These are discussed below.

(a) Extra Costs: Because it takes more time to develop extra markets, and the payback periods are longer, the up-front costs for developing new promotional materials, allocating personnel to travel and other administrative costs associated to market the product can strain the meagre financial resources of small size companies.

(b) Product Modification: When exporting, companies may need to modify their products to meet the foreign country's safety and security codes, and other import restrictions. At a minimum, modification is often necessary to satisfy the importing country's labelling or packaging requirements.

(c) Financial Risk: Collections of payments using the methods that are available (open-account, prepayment, consignment, documentary collection and letter of credit) are not only more time-consuming than for domestic sales, but also more complicated. Thus, companies must carefully weigh the financial risk involved in doing international transactions.

(d) Export Licenses and Documentation: Though the trend is toward less export licensing requirements, the fact that some companies have to obtain an export license to export their goods makes them less competitive. In many instances, the documentation required to export is more involved than for domestic sales.

(e) Market Information: Finding information on foreign markets is unquestionably more difficult and time-consuming than finding information and analysing domestic markets. In less developed countries, for example, reliable information on business practices, market characteristics, and cultural barriers may be unavailable.

These disadvantages and challenges may justify a decision to forego exporting at the present time. For example, if a company's financial situation is weak, attempting to sell into foreign markets may be ill-timed. On the other hand, some companies have been successful selling abroad even before they have made any sales domestically.

1.1.4 Export Procedure

How to start an export business is a fair question that every first time exporter asks. Export in itself is a very wide concept and lots of preparations are required to be made by an exporter before starting an export business.

A key success factor in starting any export company is a clear understanding and detailed knowledge of products to be exported. In order to be successful in exporting one must fully research its foreign market rather than try to tackle every market at once. The exporter should approach a market on a priority basis. Overseas design and product must be studied properly and considered carefully.

No doubt in this age of globalisation and liberalisation, export has become one of the most lucrative businesses in India. The Government of India is also supporting exporters through various incentives and schemes to promote Indian export for meeting the much needed requirements for importing modern technology and adopting new technology from MNCs through joint ventures and collaboration. Export procedure can be studied under the following heads.

I.   **Registration Stage:** Registration stage involves the following steps.
1.   Registration of the organisation
2.   Opening a bank account – Current A/c
3.   Obtaining an Importer-Exporter Code number (IEC number)
4.   Obtaining a PAN number
5.   Obtaining a sales tax number
6.   Registration with the Export Promotion Council (EPC)

7. Registration with Export Credit and Guarantee Corporation of India (ECGC)

8. Registration with other authorities like FIEO, ITPO, COC, and productivity councils

II. Pre-Shipment Stage: Pre-shipment stage involves the following steps.

1. Approaching foreign buyers

2. Inquiry and offer

3. Conformation of order

4. Opening letter of credit

5. Arrangement of pre-shipment finance

6. Procurement of goods

7. Packing and marking

8. Pre-shipment inspection by Export Inspection Agency

9. Central excise clearance

10. Obtaining insurance cover

11. Appointment of Clearing and Forwarding Agent (C&F agent)

III. Shipment Stage: Shipment stage involves the following steps.

1. Reservation of shipping space

2. Arrangement of internal transportation up to the port of shipment

3. Preparation and processing of shipping documents

4. Customs clearance

5. Obtaining carting order from the port trust authorities

6. Customs examination and issue of "let export order" and "let ship order"

7. Obtaining mate receipt and bill of lading

IV. Post-Shipment Stage: Post-shipment stage involves the following steps.

1. Submission of documents by C&F agents to the exporter

2. Shipment advice to importer

3. Presentation of documents to bank for negotiation

4. Dispatch of documents

5. Letter of indemnity

6. Realisation of export proceeds

7. Processing of the GR form

8. Realisation of export incentives

1.2 Registration

An exporter is required to register with a number of institutions and authorities, which directly or indirectly help the exporter to carry out international trade smoothly. For an Indian exporter some of the registrations include:

1.2.1 Registration with Director General of Foreign Trade (DGFT): Obtaining IEC (Importer Exporter Code) Number

Importers and exporters need to hold a valid IEC number, in the absence of which, Customs will not allow import or export of goods and services into or from India.

An application in duplicate and in the prescribed form is to be made to the Regional Licensing Authority to obtain an IEC number.

- It is necessary to open a bank account in the name of the company/firm with any commercial bank authorised to deal in foreign exchange before applying for an IEC number.

- It is also mandatory for every first time exporter to get registered with the DGFT (Director General of Foreign Trade), Ministry of Commerce, Government of India.

- The DGFT provides an exporter a unique IEC Number. This number is a ten-digit code required for the purpose of export as well as import. However, this IEC number is not required if the goods are exported to Nepal, or to Myanmar through the Indo-Myanmar border or to China through Gunji, Namgaya, Shipkila or Nathula ports provided the CIF value of a single consignment does not exceed Indian amount of ₹ 25,000.

- The application for IEC number can be submitted to the nearest regional authority of DGFT.

- The application form also known as Aayaat Niryaat Form (ANF2A) can also be submitted online at the DGFT web-site: http://dgft.gov.in.

- The following documents are to be provided in support of the duly signed application form:

  1. Bank Receipt (in duplicate)/Demand Draft for payment of the application fee of ₹ 1,000.

  2. Two copies of passport size photographs of the applicant duly attested by the banker to the applicants.

  3. A copy of Permanent Account Number (PAN) issued by the Income Tax Authorities. In the absence of a PAN number, a copy of the application for PAN submitted to Income Tax authorities.

4. A copy of the letter of legal authority may be furnished in case the application is signed by an authorised signatory.

5. In the event of NRI investment with repatriation benefits, a simple declaration indicating whether it is held with the general/specific permission of the RBI on the letter head of the firm should be furnished. A copy may also be furnished in case of specific approval.

6. A declaration by the applicant that the proprietors/partners/directors of the applicant firm/company, as the case may be, are not associated as proprietor/partners/directors with any other firm/company which has been caution-listed by the RBI is required. If the applicant is associated with a caution-listed firm/company the IEC number is allotted with an understanding that he can export only with the prior approval of the RBI.

7. An exporter's profile as per the standard form should be attached. Based on merits, the concerned Regional Licensing Authority will grant an IEC number to the applicant normally within 3 days provided the application is complete in all respects and is accompanied by the prescribed documents. The IEC number thus allotted to an applicant shall be valid for all its branches/divisions as indicated on the number.

An applicant is required to submit his PAN account number while submitting an application form for IEC number. Only one IEC is issued against a single PAN number. Apart from PAN number, an applicant is also required to submit his Current Bank Account number and Bankers Certificate.

An amount of ₹ 1000 is required to be submitted with the application fee in the form of a Demand Draft or payment through EFT (Electronic Fund Transfer) by a bank nominated by DGFT.

1.2.2 Registration with Export Promotion Council (EPC): Obtaining a Registration Cum Membership Certificate (RCMC)

Export Promotion Council or EPC is a non-profit organisation for the promotion of various goods exported from India in international market. Registered under the Indian Company Act, EPC works in close association with the Ministry of Commerce and Industry, Government of India and act as a platform for interaction between the exporting community and the government.

So, it becomes important for an exporter to obtain a Registration Cum Membership Certificate (RCMC) from the EPC. An application for registration should be accompanied by a self certified copy of the IEC number. Membership fee should be paid in the form of cheque or draft after ascertaining the amount from the concerned EPC.

The RCMC certificate is valid from 1st April of the licensing year in which it was issued and shall be valid for five years ending 31st March of the licensing year, unless otherwise specified.

An application for registration should be accompanied by the following documents:

- A self-certified copy of the Importer-Exporter code number issued by the Regional Licensing Authority concerned and
- Bank certificate in support of the applicant's financial soundness.
- Evidence is to be provided in case an exporter desires to get registration as a manufacturer exporter.
- In the case of a manufacturer exporter the licensing authority may seek copy of registration with SSI/any other sponsoring authority in addition to the application in the prescribed form for the Import Export Code Number.

If the application for registration is granted, the EPC or FIEO shall issue the RCMC indicating the status of the applicant as merchant exporter or manufacturer exporter. The RCMC shall be valid for five years ending 31st March of the licensing year. The certificate shall be deemed to be valid from 1st April of the licensing year in which it was issued.

1.2.3 Central Excise

Excise duty is a tax imposed by the central government on goods manufactured in India. It is collected at source before removal of goods from the factory premises. As exports are a valuable means of earning foreign exchange, they are of considerable importance. The Central Excise Rules, 1944 offer several benefits of substantive nature as well as procedural nature for the export of goods outside India. The benefit in respect of duties on inputs used in the manufacture of goods meant to be exported as well as in respect of duty on the finished goods exported is envisaged under the Central Excise law. These benefits are available either in case of

1. Export under rebate,
2. Export under bond.

1. Export under Rebate: Under this system, an exporter is required to pay excise duty initially and can claim it from the Central Excise department after collection of the payment from the importer.

Under Rule 12 of the Central Excise Rules, 1944, rebate of duty paid on the exported goods or the duty paid on materials used in the exported goods, notified for the purpose, is granted to the exporter subject to the conditions laid down in the notifications. However, this leads to blockage of finance.

2. Export under Bond: Under this system, an exporter is required to execute a bond, in favour of excise authorities, for a sum equivalent to the amount of excise chargeable on such goods.

The operations listed below are allowed under Rule 13 of the Central Excise Rules, 1944.

(i) Export of excisable goods under bond;

(ii) Utilisation of raw materials, consumables, components etc. without payment of duty for the manufacture of export goods;

(iii) Removal of excisable goods without payment of duty for the manufacture of specified excisable goods to be exported or for replenishment of duty paid materials used in the manufacture of such export goods, already exported.

Such bond shall be supported by an appropriate bank guarantee to safeguard excise department's financial interest against non-sanctioning of excise refund.

Procedure for Export: The exporter has the option to clear the export goods with or without sealing of the consignment at the place of removal. In case he opts for factory sealing, the goods would be examined by the Central Excise officers at the factory. Otherwise, the goods would be examined by the Customs officer at the port of exportation.

Examination and Sealing of Goods at the Place of Removal:

- The exporter has to file AR-4 application duly filled in, normally 24 hours in advance with the jurisdictional Superintendent in six copies.

- The proper officer after identification and verification of the goods with AR-4, and the duty payment particulars (in case the export is under claim for rebate) or after debiting the running bond account or against the specific bond, shall seal the consignment with the Central Excise seal and make necessary endorsement of the same on the AR-4.

- The original duplicate and the 6th copy of the AR-4 are thereafter handed over to the exporter.

- The exporter desirous of exporting the goods in a container, are required to obtain the permission of the proper officer and shall also present the shipping bill duly processed by the customs authorities of the port of exportation or the ICD as the case may be, along with the AR-4 at the time of sealing of the container.

- The inspector supervising the container's stuffing as well as the Range Superintendent will make an endorsement on the body of the shipping bill.

- The exporter opting for sealing of their consignment or container are required to pay the supervision charges in terms of the provisions of, and at the rates prescribed in the Customs (Fees for rendering services by Customs Officers) Regulation, 1968.

Dispatch of Goods without Examination under Rule 187A

- Clearance of the export goods either on payment of duty under claims for rebate or under bond under the cover of an invoice can be done.

- The original, duplicate and six triplicate copies of the AR-4 are to be provided with the consignment.

- Within 24 hours of clearance of the consignment, the triplicate and quadruplicate and quintuplicate copies of the AR-4 shall be submitted to the Range Superintendent.

- The Jurisdictional Superintendent, after verifying the duty payment particulars shall forward the triplicate copy to the Jurisdictional Assistant Commissioner of Central Excise or the Maritime Commissioner as the case may be, either by post or on request handing over the same to the exporter in a sealed cover.

- The Chief Accounts Officer of the Central Excise Department is provided with the quadruplicate copy of the AR-4.

- Quintuplicate copy is retained by the Range Superintendent for record.

Procedure in respect of Goods not Exported Directly under Rule 187 or 187A

In case goods are not exported directly from the factory of the manufacturer, the triplicate and quadruplicate copies of the AR-4 are sent by the concerned officer to the Superintendent having jurisdiction over the factory of the manufacturer, who upon verification, would forward the triplicate copy to the Maritime Commissioner either by post or by handing over to the exporter in a sealed cover, or the Assistant Commissioner of Central Excise having jurisdiction over the factory, as the case may be. The Superintendent also provides the quadruplicate copy to the Chief Accounts Officer.

Information to be given on AR-4: The following information is to be provided by the exporter on the AR-4 form.

(a) Running serial number of the AR-4 beginning from each financial year;

(b) Scheme under which export has been made, that is, value based advanced licensing scheme/quantity based advanced licensing scheme/under claim for duty drawback etc.;

(c) Whether the exported goods have been manufactured availing/without availing Modvat credit under Rule 57A; and

(d) Particulars of bond executed or the duty debit particulars as the case may be.

1.3 Categories of Export

Exporting is the most traditional and well-established form of operating in foreign markets. Exporting can be defined as the marketing of goods produced in one country into another. In economics, an export is any good or commodity, transported from one country to another country in trade.

Export is an important part of international trade. Export of commercial quantities of goods normally requires involvement of the customs authorities in both the country of export and the country of import.

Export is the appropriate strategy when one or more of the following conditions prevail.

1. Volume of foreign business not large enough to justify production in the foreign market.

2. Higher cost of production in the foreign market.

3. Production bottlenecks like infrastructural problems and problems with materials supplies etc. in the foreign market.

4. Presence of political or other risks of investment in the foreign country.

5. Lack of guarantee of the longer availability of the market or lack of interest by the company in the foreign market.

6. The concerned country does not favour foreign investment.

7. Licensing or contract manufacturing is not a better alternative.

The normal way to get involved in a foreign market is through export. Occasional exporting is a passive level of involvement in which the company exports from time to time, either on its own initiative or in response to unsolicited orders from abroad.

Active exporting takes place when the company makes a commitment to expand into a particular market. The company produces its goods in the home country and might or might not adapt them to the foreign market. Initially companies start with indirect exporting, that is, they work through independent intermediaries like domestic-based export merchants who buy the manufacturer's products and then sell them abroad for a commission. Included in this group are trading companies. Exporting activities on behalf of several producers are carried out and are partly under their administrative control. These export management companies are often used by producers for a fee, primarily in products such as fruits or nuts. Indirect export has two advantages. First, it involves less investment; the firm does not have to develop an export department, an overseas sales force, or a set of foreign contracts. Second, it involves less risk; because international marketing intermediaries bring know-how and services to the relationship. Eventually companies may decide to handle their own exports.

Forms of exporting include direct exporting, indirect exporting and intra-corporate transfers.

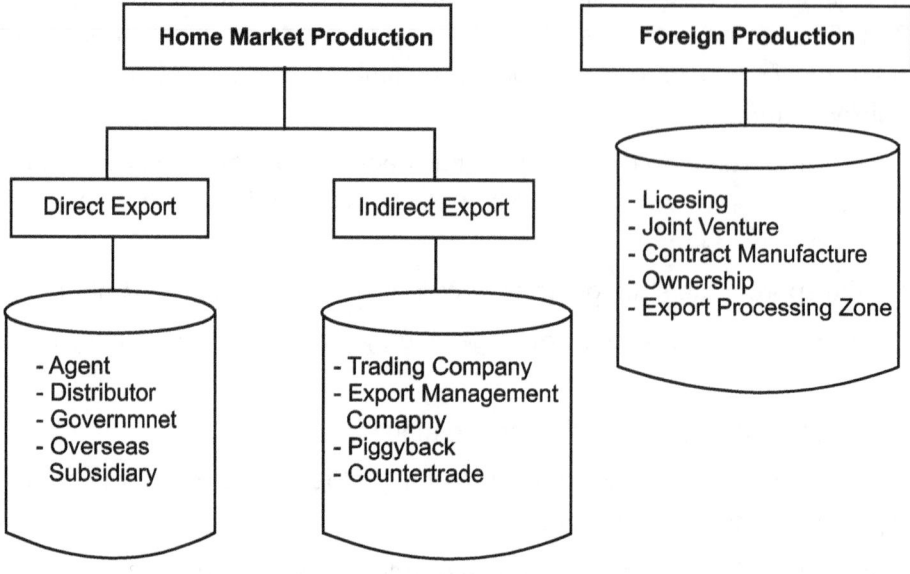

Fig. 1.1

Exports can be classified into the following categories:

1. Physical Export
2. Deemed Export
3. Merchant Export
4. Manufacture Export

1.3.1 Physical Export

Physical export refers to the export of physical goods, for example, readymade garments, engineering goods, furniture, works of art etc. It is selling the product in a foreign country directly through its distribution arrangement or through a host country's company. In physical exporting the organisation may use an agent, distributor, or overseas subsidiary, or act via a government agency. Exporting requires a partnership between exporter, importer, government and transport. Without these four co-ordinating activities the risk of failure is increased. For example, Baskin-Robbins initially exported its ice cream to Russia in 1990 and later opened 74 outlets with Russian partners. Finally in 1995 it established its ice cream plant in Moscow.

Companies make take a more direct, proactive approach to exporting by choosing to transport the goods into a foreign market themselves. This approach enables the company to have greater controls on issues such as the finished product, the selling and marketing methods used and the markets it wishes to enter. This long-term strategy can produce higher profits, as third parties are less involved or not at all. Moreover a great deal of information about the processes involved and the markets is assimilated by the exporter who can therefore quickly adapt products to market changes. It also allows relationships to be built directly with the customer, and maybe even the consumer. With direct exporting the exporter handles every aspect of the exporting process such as market research, foreign distribution, collections etc.

Methods of direct exporting include going through

1. Sales Representatives
2. Distributors
3. Foreign Retailers
4. Direct Sales to End Users

1. Sales Representatives: A sales representative uses the company's product literature and samples to present the product to potential buyers. Sales representatives work on a commission basis; essentially acting as a broker and assume no risk or responsibility for servicing the product after the sale. The representative uses the company's product literature and samples to present the product to potential buyers. A representative usually handles many complementary lines that do not conflict. The sales representative usually works on a commission basis, assumes no risk or responsibility, and is under contract for a definite period of time (renewable by mutual agreement). The contract defines territory, terms of sale, method of compensation, reasons and procedures for terminating the agreement, and other details. The sales representative may operate on either an exclusive or a nonexclusive basis.

2. Distributors: A foreign distributor is a merchant who purchases goods at a substantial discount and resells it for a profit. The main role of a foreign distributor comprises the following.

(a) Foreign distributors generally provide support and service for the product.

(b) Distributors usually carry an inventory of products and a sufficient supply of spare parts.

(c) Distributors maintain adequate facilities and personnel for normal servicing operations.

(e) Distributors usually sell complementary products.

(f) Distributors may resell the product to local dealers and retailers.

The foreign distributor is a merchant who purchases goods from an Indian exporter (often at a substantial discount) and resells it for a profit. The foreign distributor generally provides support and service for the product, thus relieving the Indian company of these responsibilities. The distributor usually carries an inventory of products and a sufficient supply of spare parts and also maintains adequate facilities and personnel for normal servicing operations. Distributors typically handle a range of non-conflicting but complementary products. End users do not usually buy from a distributor; they buy from retailers or dealers.

The terms and length of association between the Indian company and the foreign distributor are established by contract. Some Indian companies prefer to begin with a relatively short trial period and then extend the contract if the relationship proves satisfactory to both parties.

3. Foreign Retailer: A company may sell directly to a foreign retailer effectively in countries that have large retail chains. Sales to foreign retailers can be achieved through

- Travelling sales representatives contacting foreign retailers.
- Direct mailing of catalogues, brochures, or other literature.

A company may also sell directly to foreign retailers, although in such transactions, products are generally limited to consumer lines. The growth of major retail chains in markets such as Canada and Japan has created new opportunities for this type of direct sales. This method relies mainly on travelling sales representatives who directly contact foreign retailers, although results might also be achieved by mailing catalogues, brochures, or other literature. The direct mail approach has the benefits of eliminating commissions, reducing travelling expenses, and reaching a broader audience. For optimal results, a firm that uses direct mail to reach foreign retailers should support it with other marketing activities.

4. Direct Sales to End Users: A company may sell directly to a foreign end user. Selling overseas may incur some added costs. Unless other arrangements are made, the seller is responsible for

- Shipping
- Payment collection
- Product support and service

Companies commonly choose to use a number of different strategies, depending on each market they decide to enter. Most companies will have their own domestic export department, regardless of other methods used.

1.3.2 Deemed Export

'Deemed Exports' as defined in the Export and Import Policy, 1997-2002, means those transactions in which the goods supplied do not leave the country and the supplier in India receives the payment for the goods. It means the goods supplied need not go out of India to treat them as 'Deemed Export'.

Different Categories of Supplies: The following categories of supplying goods manufactured in India shall be regarded as "Deemed Exports".

(a) Supply of goods enabled by licenses issued under the Duty Exemption Scheme;

(b) Supply of goods to various units located in Export Processing Zones (EPZs), Software Technology Parks (STPs), Electronic Hardware Technology Parks (EHTPs) or Export Oriented Units (EOUs);

(c) Supply of capital goods to holders of licenses issued under the Export Promotion Capital Goods (EPCG) Scheme;

(d) Supply of goods to projects financed by multilateral or bilateral agencies/funds as notified by the Department of Economic Affairs, Ministry of Finance under international competitive bidding or under limited tender system in accordance with the procedure of those agencies/funds, where the legal agreements provide for evaluation of tenders without including the customs duty.

(e) Supply of capital goods and spares to fertiliser plants provided the supply is made under the procedure of international competitive bidding.

(f) Supply of goods to any project or purpose in respect of which the Ministry of Finance, by a notification permits the import of such goods at zero customs duty coupled with the extension of benefits to domestic supplies.

(g) Supply of goods to such projects in the power, oil and gas sectors in respect of which the Ministry of Finance, by notification, extends the benefits to domestic supplies.

(h) Supply of marine freight containers by 100% EOU (Domestic freight container manufacturers) to shipping companies including Shipping Corporation of India provided the said containers are exported out of India within 6 months or such further period as permitted by customs.

Benefits available under 'Deemed Exports': The following are the benefits Deemed Exports shall be eligible for with regard to manufacture and supply of goods qualifying as Deemed Exports.

(a) Special Imprest Licence/Advance Intermediate License.

(b) Deemed Exports Drawback Scheme, that is, on the Deemed Exports, drawback at the rate fixed by the Ministry of Finance for the DGFT or his regional officers pay the goods physically exported.

(c) Refund of terminal excise duty, that is, Central Excise duty, if paid, on the goods supplied under Deemed Exports is refunded by the DGFT or his regional officers.

(d) 'Special Import License' at the rate of 6 percent of the FOB value (excluding all taxes and levies).

(e) If the supplier has made the supplies against Advance Release Order (ARO) or Back to Back Letter of Credit, he shall be entitled for the benefits of Deemed Exports Drawback Scheme, Refund or Terminal Excise Duty, and Special Imprest License.

(f) In respect of supply of capital goods to EPCG license holder, the supplier shall be entitled to the benefits stated above. However, the benefit of Special Imprest License or Deemed Export Drawback Scheme shall be available only in case of supplies made to the 'zero duty' EPCG license holder.

1.3.3 Merchant Export

A merchant exporter can export goods either directly from the premises of the manufacturer, with or without sealing the export consignment, or through his premises. Independent people or organisations can take it upon themselves to purchase goods, and take on the task of exporting, marketing and distributing them into a foreign market. In spite of this method not being an export strategy, it helps the company to consider the prospects of exporting and measuring the possibility of success in certain foreign markets. For example, Tesco has indirectly exported Levi Jeans from USA, to resell in the UK. This form of grey marketing degrades branded items, but may be ideal for inexpensive commodities. Some companies may wish to sell excess stock to anyone wishing to purchase it, whether it is sold in Manchester or Mongolia.

This is not a wise long-term strategy as the merchant has the freedom to choose what to buy, where to buy it from and the price of each purchase. Many organisations are multinational, and can bear the loss of trade of one supplier without it being a major blow. These multinationals undertake all marketing and selling costs, but will often limit the types of products they sell. They concentrate on commodities where the manufacturer is not easily identified, specialised knowledge is not required, little or no selling efforts and service are required. It is also ideal for unstable economies such as India, where over 70% of exports are indirectly sold in this manner.

The domestic-based export merchant buys and sells on his own account. Generally engaged in both exporting and importing, it operates in a manner similar to a regular domestic wholesaler.

All aspects of the international marketing tasks are handled by this merchant except for any needed modification in such things as the product itself, its package, or in the quantity included in the unit package to meet any special needs of individual overseas markets.

This also includes selecting the channels within foreign markets as well as activities relating to sales, marketing, merchandising, advertising, delivery, and services.

Limitation: Export merchants may not be available for all markets. Export merchants are principally interested in staple commodities, which are generally open-market items not subject to a high degree of identification by the producer; and they are reluctant to undertake the development details and expense of the introduction and sale of any article that approaches the status of a specialty and which might require a considerable amount of sales effort.

1.3.4 Manufacture Export

"Manufacturer Exporter" means a person who manufactures goods and exports or intends to export such goods.

Procedure for manufacturer exporters:

(i)   A request letter for factory stuffing should be made mentioning the detailed reasons for such request.

(ii) A copy of Central Excise registration attested by the Divisional Authority should be submitted in case of Central Excise assesses. A copy of SSI registration, NOC from jurisdictional AC/DC indicating their willingness to deputise officers for supervising the stuffing, should also be submitted.

(iii) Particulars of export performance should be submitted.

Procedure for merchant exporters

In addition to the above particulars, for warehouse stuffing of non-excisable goods, the merchant exporter should submit a NOC.

1.4 Shipping Documents

Various documents, in addition to commercial and the regulatory documents are used in connection with the shipment of goods in India. A comprehensive list of these documents is as follows.

Commercial Documents

Some significant commercial documents are as follows:

1. Proforma Invoice: The starting point of the export contract is in the form of offer made by the exporter to the foreign customer. The offer made by the exporter is in the form of a proforma invoice. It is a quotation given as a reply to an inquiry. It normally forms the basis of all trade transactions.

It is proposed to conduct training and orientation programmes at all export centres to familiarise the exporting community with the new system.

2. Commercial Invoice: A commercial invoice is an important and basic export document. It is also known as a Document of Contents as it contains all the information required for the preparation of other documents. It is actually a seller's bill of merchandise. It is prepared by the exporter after the execution of the export order giving details about the goods shipped. It is essential that the invoice is prepared in the name of the buyer or the consignee mentioned in the letter of credit.

This is the first basic and the only complete document among all commercial documents for the shipment. Besides fulfilling the obligation under the export contract, the exporter needs this document for a number of other purposes including

(i) Obtaining export inspection certificate,

(ii) Getting excise clearance,

(iii) Getting customs clearance, and

(iv) Securing incentives.

Thus, this document is prepared at both the pre-shipment and post-shipment stages.

In the first place, a Commercial Invoice is a document of contents that describes details of goods sent by the exporter. It is the statement of account, which must contain identification marks and numbers, description of goods and quantity of goods.

1. Packing List/Note: A Packing List/Note contains the date of packing, connecting invoice number, order number, details of shipping such as the name of steamer, bill of lading number and date of sailing, case number to which the list/note relates, the details of goods such as quantity, weight and/or item-wise details. This may be shown on the invoice or separately, and should contain item by item, the contents of cases or containers or of a shipment with its weight and description set forth in such a manner as to permit checks of the contents by the customs on arrival at the port of destination as well as by the recipient. The packing list is a relatively simpler document and the whole of the information can be reproduced from the master by masking information not desired on the packing list. Special information, if any, can be given in the blank space in the lower third portion of the document.

The exporter prepares the packing list to facilitate the buyer to check the shipment. It contains the detailed description of the goods packed in each case, their gross and net weight etc. The difference between a packing note and a packing list is that the packing note contains the particulars of the contents of an individual pack, while the packing list is a consolidated statement of the contents of a number of cases or packs.

2. Shipping Order: A shipping order is issued by the Shipping (Conference) Line which intimates the exporter about the reservation of space of shipment of cargo through the specific vessel from a specified port and on a specified date.

3. Inspection Certification: An Inspection Certificate is required by some purchasers and countries in order to attest to the specifications of the goods shipped. This is usually performed by a third party and often obtained from independent testing organisations.

4. Insurance Documents: Insurance documents also constitute evidence of a contract with a third party namely the insurance company and therefore must be distinguished from the commercial documents. These are used to assure the consignee that insurance will cover the loss or damage to the cargo during transit. These can be obtained from the freight forwarder. The two main insurance documents are: Insurance certificate, Insurance policy.

5. Certificate of Origin: A certificate of origin is a formal official statement issued by either a chamber of commerce or industry indicating where the goods were manufactured. The Ministry of Industry and Trade must certify the certificate of origin before an exporter attaches the certificate to the export declaration upon submitting the latter to the Customs.

6. Mate's Receipt: Mate's Receipt is issued by the Chief of Vessel after the cargo is loaded and it contains the name of the shipping line, vessel, port of loading, port of discharge, place of delivery, marks and numbers, number and kind of packages, description of goods container status/seal number, gross weight, condition of cargo at the time of its receipt on board the vessel and shipping bill number and date. The Mate receipt is of a transferable nature and must be presented immediately at the shipping company's office to be exchanged into a Bill of Lading. The mate's receipt is prima facie evidence that the goods are loaded in the vessel. It is first handed over to the Port Trust Authorities. After making payment of all port dues, the exporter or his agent collects the mate's receipt from the Port Trust Authorities. It is freely transferable. It must be handed over to the shipping company in order to get the bill of lading. Bill of lading is prepared on the basis of the mate's receipt.

7. Bill of Lading: Bill of Lading (B/L) is the traditional transport document for shipping goods by ocean transport. It serves as a contract between the exporter and the shipping line and covers the carriage of goods from the port of loading to the port of discharge. It also serves as a receipt for the goods and confers title of the goods to its holder. Also called a negotiable bill of lading, it is sent to the importer to enable him/her to claim the goods to which it refers. Bill of lading is issued by the shipping company or its agents stating that goods are either being shipped or have been shipped. Essentially a transport document, it serves many purposes in international commerce.

8. Bill of Exchange: Bills of exchange are financial documents that require the individual or business that is addressed in the document to pay a specified amount of money on a date that is cited within the text of the document. Considered to be a negotiable instrument, the date for payment generally ranges from the current date to a date within the next six calendar months. A bill of exchange will also require the authorised signature of the debtor in order to be considered legal and binding.

Regulatory Documents

Some of the regulatory documents are as follows.

1. Exchange Control Declaration Form: As per the exchange control regulations, exporters are required to submit the following declaration forms to the prescribed authority before any export of goods from India is made.

- **Exchange Control Declaration (GR Form)***:* Exports to all countries made otherwise than by post.

- **Form SDF (Statutory Declaration Form):** Used for declaring exports in the case of specified customs offices and specified categories of shipping bills under EDI system.

- **PP Form:** Exports to all countries by parcel post, except when made on 'Value Payable' or 'Cash on Delivery' basis.

- **Form SOFTEX:** Used for declaring software exports through date communication links and receipt of royalty on the software package/products exported.

2. Shipping Bill/Bill of Export: Shipping Bill is the main document required by the Customs authority for allowing shipment. A shipping bill is issued by the shipping agent and represents some kind of certificate for all parties, including ship's owner, seller, buyer and some other parties, for each one represents a kind of certificate document.

A shipping bill is normally prepared in five copies:

(a) Customs copy

(b) Drawback copy

(c) Export promotion copy

(d) Port trust copy

(e) Exporter's copy

3. ARE-1: Application for Removal of Excisable Goods for Exports: This document is used for obtaining approval of the Central Excise authority to remove the goods from the factory for sending the export shipment.

(Please refer to Chapter 3 for a detailed description of shipment documents)

1.5 Terms used in Shipping

A.T.: It stands for American Terms (Marine Insurance). A term used to differentiate between the conditions of American policies with other nations, primarily England.

ABI: It stands for Automated Brokerage Interface; a system available to the US Customs Brokers with the capabilities of computer and customs certification to transmit and exchange the customs entries and other related information, facilitating prompt release of imported cargo.

Admiralty Court: It is a court having jurisdiction over maritime questions related to ocean transport, which includes contracts, charters, collisions, and also cargo damages.

Advance against Documents: It is the loan made on the security of documents covering the shipment.

Advisory Capacity: It is a term, which indicates that the shipper's agent or representative is not empowered to make any definite decisions or adjustments without the approval of the group or the individual being represented.

Air Cargo Agent: A type of freight forwarder specialised in air cargo and acts for airlines that pays a fee. This person is registered with the International Air Transport Association (IATA).

Air Freight Forwarders: They provide pickup and delivery service under their own tariff, consolidate air shipments into larger units, prepare shipping documentation, and also tender shipments to the airlines. Since they do not usually operate their own aircraft, they are also called "Indirect Air Carriers." The airlines consider these forwarders as shippers because they tender the shipment.

Air Waybill: It is a shipping document used for the transportation of air freight that includes conditions, limitations of liability, shipping instructions, description of commodity and the applicable transportation charges. It is usually similar to a non-negotiable bill of lading and is used for similar purposes.

All Risk Insurance: It is a clause in marine insurance policies which covers loss and damage from external causes, like fire, collision, pilferage, etc. excluding innate flaws in the goods, like decay, germination and faulty packaging, improper packing/loading or loss of market, war, strikes, riots and civil commotions.

All Risk Clause: It is an insurance provision providing additional coverage to an Open Cargo Policy. It covers theft, pilferage, non-delivery, fresh water damage, breakage, and leakage. It does not cover inherent vice, loss of market, and losses caused by delay.

Alongside: It is a term used for the side of a ship. The goods to be delivered "alongside" are placed on the dock or barge within the reach of the transport ship's tackle so that they can be loaded aboard the ship.

Belly Cargo: It is a term for freight accommodation below the main deck.

Berth: It is a term for the place beside a pier, quay or wharf where a vessel is loaded or discharged.

Berth Liner Service: It is a regular scheduled steamship line having regular published schedules to and from the defined trade areas.

Berth or Liner Terms: It is the condition of carriage followed by a shipping company. It also states that the costs for loading and unloading are borne by the carrier subject to the customs authority of the port concerned.

Bill of Lading: A contract document agreement between the shipper and the customer that acts as a receipt for the goods delivered to the carrier for shipment; a definition or description of the goods; and evidence of title to the relative goods.

Break Bulk Cargo (B/B): It is a term for cargo being carried in the hold of a vessel rather than in a container.

Cabotage: It is the transportation of goods or persons between ports within the same country.

Cargo: It is a term for merchandise/commodities/ freight carried by means of transportation.

Cargo Receipt: It is a receipt of cargo issued by a consolidator for shipment. It is used in ocean freight.

Carnet: It is a customs document, which permits the holder to carry or send merchandise into certain foreign countries temporarily for display, demonstration, or any other related purpose without paying the duties or posting bonds.

Carrier, Common: It is public or privately owned firm or corporation which transports goods of others over land, sea or air for a predefined freight rate.

Chargeable Kilo: A term used for rate of goods where the volume exceeds six cubic metres to the tonne.

Charter: It is a contract to hire or lease transportation.

Charter Party: It is a contract between the owner of a vessel and a "charterer" who rents use of the vessel or a part of its freight space. It usually includes the freight rates and the ports that are involved in the transportation.

Combi: It is an aircraft having the main deck divided into two sections, one fitted to seats and the other used for cargo.

Consignee: A term for an individual or firm to whom the goods are shipped under a bill of lading.

Container Freight Station (CFS): It is the facility in ocean carrier where the goods are received by carrier for loading into containers or unloading from it and the carrier may also assemble, hold, or store its containers or trailers in the place.

Dead Freight (DF): It is a freight charge, which is paid by the charterer of a vessel for the contracted space only and not for the partial unoccupied space.

Deadweight (DWT): It is the total weight of cargo, stores and bunkers that a vessel can lift when loaded to maximum draught as applicable under the circumstances. It is expressed in tons.

Deck Cargo: It is a cargo carried on deck rather than within the enclosed cargo spaces of a vessel.

Deferred Payment Credit: It is similar to the letter of credit, providing for payment after presentation of shipping documents by exporter.

Delivered Duty Paid (DDP): It is a term that means that the seller pays for all transportation costs and bears all the risks until the goods are delivered and pays the duty. It is also known as "free domicile."

Delivered Duty Unpaid (DDU): It is an term that means the sellers pay for all transportation costs and bear all the risks until the goods are delivered, but do not pay for the duty.

Demurrage: It is a penalty for exceeding the given free time for loading and unloading at a pier or freight terminal.

DEQ: It stands for 'Delivered Ex Quay'/duty paid. It is a term where the title and risk passes to the buyer if the goods are delivered on board the ship at the destination point by the seller who on his part delivers the goods on dock at the destination point cleared for import. It is used for sea or inland waterway transportation.

Dock Receipt: It is a receipt issued by an ocean carrier for a shipment received or delivered at a pier or dock.

FAS (Free Alongside Ship): It is a term which means that the seller pays for the transportation of the goods to the port of shipment. The loading costs, freight, insurance, unloading-costs and transportation from the port of destination to the factory are paid by the buyer. The passing of the risk occurs when the goods have been delivered to the quay at the port of shipment.

FEU: Forty-foot equivalent unit. It is a term used to specify container vessel or terminal capacity.

Two 20-foot containers are equal to one FEU.

FOB (Free On Board): It means that the seller is responsible for inland freight and all other costs until the cargo is loaded on the vessel/aircraft. The buyer is responsible for ocean/airfreight and marine/air insurance.

Free Alongside: A term for the quoted price which includes the cost of delivering the goods alongside a designated vessel.

Free In (F.I.): It is a pricing term in which the charterer of a vessel is responsible for the cost of loading goods onto the vessel.

Free In and Out (F.I.O.): It is a pricing term in which the charterer of a vessel is responsible for the cost of loading and unloading of goods from the vessel.

Free Out (F.O.): It is a pricing term in which the quoted price is inclusive of the cost of unloading goods from the vessel.

Free Port: It is a port in any foreign trade zone where the merchandise is duty-free. It is open to all traders on equal terms.

Gang: It is a term for group of stevedores, generally 4 to 5, with a supervisor assigned to a hold or portion of the vessel being loaded or unloaded.

Gateway: (a) It is a port of entry into a country of origin. (b) It is a point through which the freight moves from one territory to another.

GCR: It stands for General Cargo Rate. It is the rate of the carriage of cargo other than a class rate or specified commodity rate.

Gross Weight: It is the entire weight of goods, packing, and container, which is ready for shipment.

GSA: General Sales Agent who acts on behalf of an airline. They are generally Brokers or Forwarders.

Hatch: It is an opening in a deck that gives access to the internal compartments.

Heavy Lift Vessel: It is a specially designed and equipped vessel for the carriage of heavy cargo.

Heavy Lift: It is a term used for freight too heavy to be handled by regular ship's tackle.

I.C.T.F.: It stands for Intermodal Container Transfer Facility. It is an on-dock facility, which moves containers from ship to rail or truck.

Igloo: It is a container, which has been designed to occupy full main deck width for carrying aircraft.

In-Bond: It is a term under which goods are transported, stored, or handled, prior to clearance and release by customs.

Inland Carrier: It is a transportation line which hauls the export or import traffic between ports and inland points.

Interline Agreement: It is an agreement between two or more airlines co-operating for the carriage over particular routes.

Interline Carriage: It is a term for the carriage over the routes of more than one party of interlines agreement.

Interline Shipping: It is a term used for the movement of a single shipment on more than one carrier.

Jettison: It is the throwing of the cargo or ship's property overboard in a hope of saving the ship from sinking.

Knot (Nautical): It is the unit of speed used in navigation. It is equivalent to one nautical mile, or 6,080.20 feet per hour or 1.85 kilometres per hour.

Lagan: It is a term for goods tied to a buoy and cast into the sea so that it can be recovered.

Lash: It stands for 'Lighter Aboard Ship.' It is a barge carrier that is designed to act as a shuttle between ports, taking on and discharging barges.

Lay Days: It is the number of days permitted in a charter party for loading and discharging of cargo. It can be in consecutive days, working days, weather working days, etc.

Legal Weight: It is the weight of the merchandise along with its own packaging, excluding the exterior containers or packing materials.

Less than Truck Load (LTL): It is a shipment that does not completely fill the truck or it weighs less than the weight required for the application of the truck load freight rate.

Lighter: It is a flat-bottomed boat used in transporting cargo between a vessel and the shore.

Lighterage: It is a term used for the cost of loading or unloading a vessel by means of barges alongside.

Liner: It is a vessel carrying cargo that operates with a fixed schedule on a particular route.

Lo/Lo: It stands for "lift-on, lift-off." It is a method by which the cargo is loaded onto and discharged from an ocean vessel with the use of a crane.

Load Factor: It is the ratio of the average load to the maximum load during a given period of time.

Manifest: It is a document, which lists the specifications of the cargo of a carrier, container or warehouse.

Marine Insurance: An insurance, which compensates the owner of goods transported overseas in the event of loss that cannot be recovered from the carrier.

Marking (for marks): It is the marking on the cargo to indicate the country of origin where the article was produced.

Mate's Receipt: It is a declaration signed by the chief officer of a vessel stating that a certain consignment has been received on board the vessel.

Measurement Ton: It is also known as the cargo ton or freight ton. It is a space measurement, generally 40 cubic feet or one cubic meter.

Mercantile marine: It is the shipping, which is employed in commerce and not in war.

Metric Ton: It is a unit of weight, which is equal to 1,000 kilograms or 2,204.6 pounds.

National Carrier: It is a flag carrier owned or controlled by the state.

National Motor Freight Classification (NMFC): It is the listing of items that contain the class descriptions of a particular item being shipped.

Nested: Packed one within another like paper cups for saving space.

Net Weight: It is the actual net weight of goods alone excluding the packaging.

No Objection Certificate: It is a document provided by the scheduled or national airlines of many countries, which declares no objection to a proposed charter flight operated by another airline.

No Objection Fee: Money paid by a charter airline to a scheduled airline so that it waives its right of objection to its government, allowing a charter to take place.

Open Account: Credit extended to a foreign buyer without guarantee of payment.

Open Policy: It is a marine insurance policy that covers all shipments made by an exporter over a period of time rather than to one shipment only.

Pallet: It is a term used for a load-carrying platform to which the loose cargo is stored before placing aboard the aircraft.

Part Load Charter: It is the chartering of a ship or an aircraft where it agrees that part of the cargo will be discharged at one destination and a part of it at another.

Perils of the Sea: It refers to the damage caused by heavy weather, stranding, striking on rocks or on bottom, contacts with floating agents, collision with other vessels, etc.

Perishables: It is a term when fresh produce is spoiled due to delay in transportation.

Pilferage: It is a petty theft, especially theft of articles in smaller quantities and not in package lots.

Pivot Weight: It is the minimum chargeable weight of a Unit Load Device (air cargo).

Port Authority: It is a government body, which maintains various airports and/or ocean cargo pier facilities, transit sheds, loading equipment warehouses for air cargo, etc. in international shipping. It enjoys the power of levying dockage and wharfage charges, landing fees, etc.

Port Marks: It is an identifying set of letters, numbers and/or geometric symbols being followed by the name of the port of destination. These are placed on export shipments.

Port of Discharge: A port where the vessel is off-loaded and the cargo is discharged.

Port of Entry: A port where foreign goods are admitted into the receiving country.

Prepaid Freight: The freight charges collected in the local currency of the country of export.

Route: It is a path from one network point to another.

Scheduled Flight: Flight operating through a set timetable.

Service Contract: According to the Shipping Act of 1984, it is a contract between a shipper or a shippers' association and an ocean common carrier or conference. In this contract, the shipper commits to provide a certain minimum quantity of cargo or freight revenue over a fixed time period, and the ocean common carrier makes a commitment to a certain rate or rate schedule as well as a defined service level.

Shipment: Property made available by a shipper to a carrier for transportation.

Ships Manifest: It is a written instrument, which contains the shipments list comprising the cargo of the vessel.

Short-Shipped: It is a term used for cargo manifested but not loaded onto the aircraft.

Steamship Agent: It is a term for a representative, duly appointed and authorised in a specified territory to act on behalf of a steamship line or lines and to attend to all matters relating to the vessels owned by his principals.

Stowage: It is the lacing of cargo in a vessel in a manner to provide the utmost safety and efficiency for the ship and the goods it carries.

Sue & Labour Clause: It is a provision in marine insurance, which obligates the assured to do things necessary after a loss in order to prevent any further loss and to act in the best interests of the insurer.

Surety Bond: It is a written document promising to pay damages or to indemnify against losses that are caused by the party or parties mentioned in the document, through non-performance or through defalcation.

Surety Company: It is a term for an insurance company from where a bondholder can obtain a surety bond.

Tare Weight: It is the weight of the container and/or packed materials without considering the weight of the goods inside the container.

Tariff: It is the duty levied on goods transported from one customs area to another, or on imported products.

Temperature Controlled Cargo: It is a term used for any cargo, which requires carriage under controlled temperature.

Third Freedom Right: It is a term where the cargo is carried by an airline, from the base country to a foreign country.

Ton-Deadweight: The term indicates to the carrying capacity of the ship in terms of weight in tons of the cargo, fuel, provisions and passengers, which the vessel can carry.

Tracking: It is a carrier's system of recording movement intervals of shipments from the origin to the destination.

Trade: It is a term for the commercial exchange of goods and services.

Tramp: It is a vessel not operating along a definite route on a fixed schedule. It takes cargo wherever the shippers desire.

Transshipment: It is the transfer of a shipment from a carrier to another, mostly from one ship to another.

ULD: It stands for Unit Load Device, which means pallet or container for freight.

Unitisation: It is a term for the packing of single or multiple consignments into the ULDs or pallets.

Volume Weight: It is a term, which is used while calculating airfreight when the size of the carton is more than the average weight. It is calculated by multiplying the length times, the width times, the height and dividing it by 166.

Warehouse receipt: It is a receipt issued by a warehouse which lists goods received for storage.

Weight Load Factor: It is the payload achieved as against available and is expressed as a percentage.

Weight, Legal: It is net weight of goods along with inside packing. It does not include the weight of the exterior containers or packing materials.

Wet Lease: It is an arrangement for renting of an aircraft under which the owner provides crews, ground support equipment, fuel, etc.

Wharfage: It is a fee charged for the use of a wharf or quay.

With Average: It is a term for marine insurance, which mean that the shipment is protected for partial damage whenever it exceeds a stated percentage.

With Particular Average (W.P.A.): It is an insurance term, which means that a part of loss or damage of goods is insured. Usually it must be caused by seawater. It can also be extended to cover loss by theft, pilferage, delivery, leakage, and breakage.

Without Reserve: It is a term under which the agent or representative of a shipper is empowered to make any decision and adjustments abroad without the approval of the group or individual represented.

1.6 Points to Remember

- Whether companies decide to export indirectly or directly, many companies use exporting as a way to "test the waters" before building a plant and manufacturing a product overseas.

- Any export shipment involves a number of documents required mainly by the Custom/Port Authorities. Mostly the format of these documents is common in most of cases, but may differ in respect to documents used at different ports.

- Documentation requirements vary from product to product and from country to country. The exporter should ensure quality of goods before sending shipment to the foreign buyers. A number of documents must accompany every export shipment.

- Documentation in export business is complex but not difficult to understand if one knows the reasons of making documents at different stages of export transactions. Some of these documents are made or secured at the pre-shipment stage while others are made or secured after the shipment has been made.

- The need for export documents arises due to commercial, legal and incentive perspectives. Commercial perspective helps in protecting the respective interests of the exporter and importer. Regulatory perspective emphasises to follow the regulatory provisions of that particular country. Incentive perspective helps in getting various incentives according to the prevailing policy of the government.

- Some exporters are worried by export documentation because they think it is very complicated. But it can be learnt, and institutions such as the local Ministry of Commerce, Chamber of Commerce or Trade Associations will help the perplexed exporter.

- Furthermore, instead of handling documentation themselves an exporter often uses Shipping and Forwarding agents, who obtain and fill out documents, arrange transportation etc. Having done all the preparatory planning work (no mean task in itself!), the prospective global marketer has then to decide on a market entry strategy and a marketing mix. There are two main ways of foreign market entry either by entering from a home market base, via direct or indirect exporting, or by foreign based production. Within these two possibilities, marketers can adopt an "aggressive" or "passive" export path.

Questions for Discussion

1. Give a short account of shipment documentation.

2. What is the significance of Certificate of Origin?

3. Explain the classification of export. Explain the advantage and disadvantages of exporting.

4. Write short notes on the following:

    (a) Deemed Export

    (b) ICE

    (c) RCME

    (d) Central Excise

Chapter 2

Customers Clearance Procedure for Imported Cargo

Contents ...

Learning Objectives ...

- To study the documentation required for custom clearance of imported goods
- To understand the procedure for customs clearance in general for goods imported in India
- To learn the common methods of payment for imported goods
- To explain the concept of warehousing of imported goods
- To explore the procedure for importing goods within relevant provisions under various acts

2.1 Introduction

Thousands of merchants and business persons consider it a goal to start an import business. Provided an importer proceeds with the right strategies, an import business is also a very profitable business like an export business. A thorough understanding about the international market and foreign market analysis on the part of the importer can ensure the long-term success and profitability of an import business.

Millions of products are bought, sold, represented and distributed somewhere in the world on a daily basis. Today, importing goods from abroad has become a big business. Everything from beverages to cars and other products have now become a part of the global imports.

A fast, rising demand for imports has come about due to increasing middle income groups of consumers in India and their increasing levels on expenditure on various products. Major imports of India include cereals, edible oils, machineries, fertilisers and petroleum products. India is also a bulk importer of edible oil, sugar, pulp and paper, newsprint, crude rubber, iron and steel.

The Directorate General of Foreign Trade (DGFT), a government organisation, that also controls the export business in India, takes care of all the activities associated with imports and exports. DGFT and all its regional offices work under the Ministry of Commerce and Industries, Department of Commerce and Government of India. All the procedures and policies in matters related to importing are announced by the DGFT through its notification, appendices and forms.

2.2 Documentation

There are various documents required for imports. The following section presents in detail the main import documents.

1. Import Order: An import order, besides being a commercial transaction which is important to the importer and exporter, is also of concern to their respective countries, since it affects the balance of payment position of both the countries. The importer is required to produce the copies of the import order to various Government departments/financial institutions; for example, obtaining an import license when the product is covered under the restricted items or canalised items for imports, arranging import finance and dealing with customs offices and exchange control authorities etc. for various purposes.

2. Order Acceptance: Order acceptance is another important commercial document prepared by the exporter confirming the acceptance of an order placed by the importer. The exporter commits the shipment of goods covered at the agreed price during a specified time. The order acceptance normally covers the name and address of the indentor, name and address of the consignee, port of shipment, country of final destination, the description of goods, quantity, price of each order and total amount of the order, terms of delivery, details of freight and insurance, mode of transport, packing and marking details, terms of payment etc.

3. Letter of Credit L/C: A letter of credit also known as documentary credit is a written undertaking by the importer's bank whereby the applicant (the importer) requests and instructs the issuing bank (the importer's bank) or the issuing bank acting on its own behalf to –

- Pay the beneficiary (the exporter) or accept and pay the draft (bill of exchange) drawn by the beneficiary, or

- Authorise the advising bank or the nominated bank to pay the beneficiary or to accept and pay the draft drawn by the beneficiary, or

- Authorise the advising bank or the nominated bank to negotiate, against stipulated document(s), provided that the terms and conditions of the documentary credit are fully complied with.

Procedure for the Issue of Letter of Credit

When payment under a letter of credit is undertaken, the following eight stages can be identified in the documentary credit cycle –

- The exporter and the buyer come to an agreement to terms in the contract of sale for the price, specification, method of transportation, payment of the freight and insurance and that payment shall be made under a letter of credit.

- The buyer's bank at his place of business opens a letter of credit for the exporter on the terms specified by the buyer in his instructions to the issuing bank. The buyer will advise his bank as to what documents must be presented, time and place for presentment, the description of goods, and other conditions to be met by the seller. He will also specify an expiry date at which the documents may be presented to the bank for payment.

  For the bank, the issuance of a letter of credit is similar to supplying short-term finance. It will apply similar criteria to the application, and may demand collateral reduction in other lending limits or even a cash advance before agreeing to issue the letter of credit.

- The issuing bank arranges with the exporter's bank to negotiate, accept, or pay the exporter's draft upon delivery of the transport documents by the seller. This may be done by mail, telex or SWIFT. The advising bank has to authenticate the letter of credit, that is, use authentication codes or books of signatures to assure the beneficiary that the letter of credit is genuine.

- The advising bank assures the exporter that it will negotiate, accept or pay his draft upon delivery of the transport documents. The advising bank may do so either without its own engagement or it may confirm the credit opened by the issuing bank. At this stage the beneficiary should check that the credit terms and conditions match the commercial agreement and can be complied with. The applicant must be contacted and an amendment made if anything in the credit will cause the beneficiary a problem.

- The beneficiary (seller) ships the goods, and then compiles the required documentation.

- Documents must conform to all the terms and conditions laid down in the letter of credit and on presentation, the bank checks the documents and if they are in order, pays the beneficiary according to the method of payment agreed between seller and buyer.

- The documents are then forwarded to the issuing bank who will debit the applicant, remit the funds to the beneficiary's bank and pass the documents to the applicant so that the goods can be claimed from the carrier.

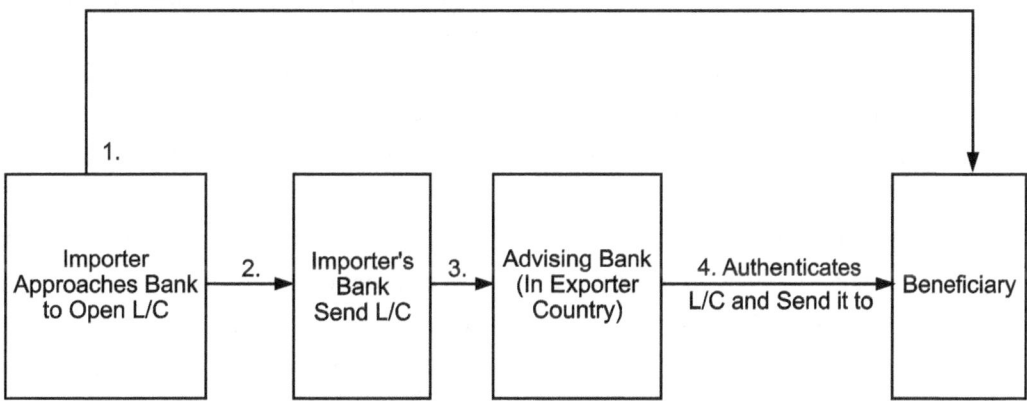

Fig. 2.1: Procedure for the Issue of Letter of Credit

4. Transport Documents: The following documents are used in the export-import trade as transport documents –

(i)	**Ocean Freight**	:	Various types of Bills of Lading
(ii)	**Air Freight**	:	Airway Bills/Air Consignment Notes
(iii)	**Rail/ Road**	:	Railway Receipts/Consignments Notes
(iv)	**Post**	:	Waybill issued by Foreign Post Office
(v)	**Courier**	:	Courier Receipt/Waybill

5. Bill of Exchange: Bills of exchange are negotiable financial documents that require the individual or business that is addressed in the document to pay a specified amount of money on a date that is cited within the text of the document. The date for the demand to pay generally ranges from the current date to a date within the next six calendar months. Moreover, bills of exchange also require the authorised signature of the debtor in order to be considered legal and binding.

The bill of exchange can take on many different forms. One of the most common examples of the bill of exchange is the common bank cheque. A cheque specifies the exact amount of the payment, the recipient of the funds, with the order to pay the face value of the cheque to the order of the creditor. The date specified on the cheque is often the issue date for the cheque, but may also be the date that the bank is to honour the payment. This post dating of a cheque ensures the creditor will physically receive the cheque at some time before it will be honoured.

A bill of exchange can also be in the form of a bank draft. Similar to the bank cheque, drafts are normally set up with a fixed sum of payment, and with specific instructions of when to issue the payment to the creditor.

The bill of exchange can be a simplistic document or detailed one. In most countries around the world, the common means of conducting business is the usage of a bill of exchange. This is often accompanied by an 'allonge' (a paper attached to a negotiable instrument to enable writing endorsements when the back of the bill is full). When the bill of exchange is not honoured, the holder of the document is free to take legal action against the debtor according to local laws, or to sell the bill of exchange at a discounted rate of exchange. The maker of a bill of exchange or draft is called the "drawer", the person who is directed to pay is called the "drawee" and the person who is entitled to receive payment is called the "payee."

When a bill of exchange is drawn on a foreign firm it is termed as a 'foreign draft' or 'foreign bill of exchange'. It is prepared either in an international currency or Indian rupees depending on the terms of the contract. Hence, the bill is known by the name of currency in which it is drawn; for example, a bill drawn in US dollars is known as a 'dollar bill' and when prepared in rupees, it is termed as a 'rupees bill'.

In the event of the goods being shipped by sea, the bills are drawn in sets and two sets of documents, including drafts are mailed to the foreign correspondent through an authorised dealer for presentation to the 'drawee' (importer).

A bill of exchange or draft is of two types –

(i)   'Sight Draft' or 'Draft at Sight' and

(ii) 'Usance Draft' or 'Usance Bill'.

When the exporter (drawer) expects the importer (drawee) to make payment immediately after the draft is presented to him, it is called a 'sight draft'. Unless and until the draft is received, the negotiating/collecting bank does not hand over the shipping documents and the buyer cannot take delivery of goods.

2.3 Customs Clearance Procedure of Imported Goods

All goods imported into India have to pass through the procedure of customs for proper examination, appraisal, assessment, and evaluation. This helps the customs authorities to charge the proper tax and check the goods against illegal imports. Also it is important to note that no import is allowed in India if the importer doesn't have the IEC number issued by the DGFT. There is no requirement of the IEC number if the goods are imported for personal use. Under the Ministry of Finance (Department of Revenue), there are two independent Boards of Revenue, namely, Central Board of Direct Taxes and Central Board of Excise and Customs. The custom administrations come under the latter which shape the policy and decide the functions of the custom formations in the country, as per the provisions of the Customs Act 1962.

All the goods imported in India have to pass through the customs clearance after they cross the Indian border. The goods so imported are examined, appraised, assessed, evaluated and then allowed to be taken out of customs charge for use by the importer.

The procedure for customs clearance in general for goods imported in India is as follows –

1. Import Manifest: In terms of Section 30 of the Customs Act 1962, the persons in charge of a conveyance carrying imported goods should hand over, within 24 hours of the arrival of the conveyance, an import manifest to the customs. The manifest is the complete list of all items the conveyance carries on board, including those to be transhipped and those to be carried to the subsequent ports of call.

2. Entry in the Import Department of the Customs House: On receipt of the information regarding the arrival of the goods, the importer or the agent have to make an entry by filing a bill of entry, in the prescribed form in the Import department of the Customs House. The date of presentation of Bill of Entry is an important date as the rate of duty applicable to the imported goods will be the rate which is in force on the date of presentation.

3. Presentation of Bill of Entry for Approval: The importer clearing the goods for domestic consumption has to file bill of entry in four copies; original and duplicate are meant for customs, third copy for the importer and the fourth copy is meant for the bank for making remittances. If the goods are cleared through the EDI system, no formal bill of entry is filed as it is generated in the computer system, but the importer is required to file a cargo declaration having prescribed particulars required for processing of the entry for customs clearance.

In the non-EDI system along with the bill of entry filed by the importer or his representative, the following documents are also generally required –

(a) Signed invoice

(b) Packing list

(c) Bill of Lading or Delivery Order/Airway Bill

(d) GATT declaration form duly filled in

(e) Importer/CHA declaration

(f) License wherever necessary

(g) Letter of Credit/Bank Draft wherever necessary

(h) Insurance document

(i) Import license

(j) Industrial License, if required

(k) Test report in case of chemicals

(l) Ad hoc exemption order

(m) DEEC Book/DEPB in original

(n) Catalogue, technical write up, literature in case of machineries, spares or chemicals as may be applicable

(o) Separately split up value of spares, components, and machineries

(p) Certificate of Origin, if preferential rate of duty is claimed

(q) No Commission declaration.

When the information/documents furnished by the importer is adequate for the classification and acceptance of ITC license, the Bill of Entry is completed by the Appraiser, countersigned by the Asst. Collector and sent to the license section with an order to the dock staff for examination of goods before clearance.

4. Amendment of Bill of Entry: Whenever mistakes are noticed after submission of documents, amendments to the bill of entry are carried out with the approval of the Deputy/Assistant Commissioner.

5. Clearance of Goods: After payment of duty (the original copy of the bill of entry is retained in the customs house) the importer should obtain the duplicate copy of the bill of entry on which the order for examination of the goods is given by Customs and get the goods examined. If the description of goods is found to be correct, on the basis of declared and accepted particulars, clearance of goods is allowed by the appraiser. This procedure where assessment is completed and duty recovered, prior to the examination of goods is known as "Second Check" procedure. In what is known as "First Check" procedure the Appraiser after initial scrutiny of documents returns the bill of entry to the importers with an order for examination of goods before assessment of duty. This could be for checking up description, type, quantity, size for the purpose of determining value, classification for correctness of the Import License or for chemical tests, etc.

6. Warehousing the Goods: Under the Customs Act provision has been made to allow importers to warehouse the goods pending clearance. For this purpose importers have to present a bill of entry termed "Bill of Entry for Warehousing". The bill of entry for warehousing is required to be presented to the Bonds Department along with a bond for twice the amount of duty payable. Warehousing is initially allowed for a period of 3 months which may be extended up to a period of not more than one year. When the clearance is sought, the importers have to present what is known as Ex Bond Bill of Entry for the quantity required. The warehoused goods can be cleared in one or more instalments.

7. Classification of Goods for Import Policy and Assessment of Duty: Goods imported are assessed for duty provided they are imported in terms of the Import Policy and evaluated for calculation of customs duty by virtues of the nature of goods or by virtue of its end use. The goods which are not falling in the parameter of the Import Policy are normally confiscated or allowed to be cleared only on payment of heavy penalty.

8. Customs Duties: The various types of Customs duties levied on goods imported into or exported out of India are as follows –

(a) **Basic Duty:** Basic duty is levied on all goods imported into India as prescribed in First Schedule of Customs Tariff Act. This schedule is amended from time to time to modify, alter or vary the nature of duty. This duty is levied as a percentage of value of goods imported or at a specified rate.

(b) **Auxiliary Duty:** This duty is levied in addition to the basic duty prescribed under the Finance Act every year. But, now auxiliary duty is not levied as it is withdrawn with effect from 28th February, 1993.

(c) **Specific Duty:** This duty is levied in order to counter balance the excise duty leviable on the imports going into the production of such goods produced into India.

Mode of Levy of Customs Duty

Customs duties are levied in the following three ways.

(a) **Specific Duty:** At the rate prescribed per unit of item, that is, on weight or length

(b) **Ad-valorem Duty:** On value

(c) **Specific and Ad-valorem duty:** Levied in both ways.

9. Valuation of Goods: Valuation of goods is done as per principles laid down in Customs Valuation (Determination and Prices of Imported Goods) Rules, 1988.

10. Assessment and Rates of Customs Duty: The assessment of goods for duty is done on the following basis.

(i) Whether the goods covered by the bill of entry are such as are regularly imported, or

(ii) The goods are required to be tested by the Customs House Laboratory for fulfilment of license conditions, or

(iii) The customs appraiser wants to see the representative sample before completing the Bill of Entry for the purpose of verification of the value/description etc.

11. Demurrage Charges: The goods imported and discharges in the Customs are stored in the warehouses of CWC or Port Trusts or other designated authority. A few days "free period" is allowed for storage of such goods and thereafter the following demurrage or storage charges are levied.

(a) **Commercial and Non-commercial cargo:** 7 calendar days from date of landing.

(b) **Unaccompanied baggage:** 14 calendar days from date of landing.

12. Direct Delivery Facility for Imports by Air: The facility of "direct delivery" of goods imported by air is allowed to certain goods like fresh fruits, frozen food, life saving drugs and appliances, TV films, any cargo requiring special handling/storage and any other cargo in respect of which order of the Deputy Collector of Customs, Air Cargo Unit has been obtained in advance permitting direct delivery.

Payment of Duty: Import duty may be paid in the designated banks or through TR-6 challans. Different customs houses have authorised different banks for payment of duty and it is necessary to check the name of the bank and the branch before depositing the duty.

For faster clearance of the goods, provision has been made in section 46 of the Act, to allow filing of bill of entry prior to arrival of goods. This bill of entry is valid if vessel/aircraft carrying the goods arrives within 30 days from the date of presentation of bill of entry.

Import of goods under specialised schemes such as DEEC and EOU etc. is required to execute bonds with the custom authorities. In case of failure of the bond, the importer is required to pay the duty leviable on those goods. The amount of bond would be equal to the amount of duty leviable on the imported goods. The bank guarantee is also required along with the bond. However, the amount of bank guarantee depends upon the status of the importer like Super Star Trading House/Trading House etc.

A separate form of bill of entry is used for clearance of goods for warehousing. Assessment of this bill of entry is done in the same manner as the normal bill of entry and then the duty payable is determined.

2.4 Payment Procedure

There is no predefined definition of personal import. In general a personal import is a direct purchase of foreign goods from overseas mail order companies, retailers, manufacturers or by an individual for the purpose of personal use.

The most common methods of payment are as follows –

    (1) Consignment Purchase   (2) Cash in Advance (Pre-Payment)

    (3) Down Payment   (4) Open Account

    (5) Documentary Collections   (6) Letters of Credit

1. Consignment Purchase: The most beneficial method of payment for the importer is consignment purchase. In this method of purchase, the importer makes the payment only once the goods or imported items are sold to the end user. In case of no sale, the same item is returned to the foreign supplier. Consignment purchase is considered the most risky and time consuming method of payment for the exporter.

2. Cash in Advance (Pre-Payment): Receiving payment by cash in advance of the shipment might seem ideal. In this situation, the exporter is relieved of collection problems and has immediate use of the money. A wire transfer is commonly used and has the advantage of being almost immediate. Payment by cheque may result in a collection delay of up to six weeks. Therefore, this method may defeat the original intention of receiving payment before shipment.

Cash in Advance is a pre-payment method in which, an importer makes the payment for the items to be imported in advance prior to the shipment of goods. The importer must trust the supplier will ship the product on time and that the goods will be as advertised. Cash in Advance method of payment creates a lot of risk factors for the importers. However, this method of payment is inexpensive as it involves direct importer-exporter contact without commercial bank involvement.

In international trade, Cash in Advance methods of payment is usually done when:

- The Importer has not been long established.
- The Importer's credit status is doubtful or unsatisfactory.
- The political risks are very high in the importer's country.
- The product is in heavy demand and the seller does not have to accommodate an importer's financing request in order to sell the merchandise. For the buyer, however, advance payment tends to create cash flow problems, as well as increase risks. Furthermore, cash in advance is not as common in most of the world as it is in the United States. Buyers are often concerned that the goods may not be sent if payment is made in advance. Exporters who insist on this method of payment as their sole method of doing business may find themselves losing out to competitors who offer more flexible payment terms.

3. Down Payment: In this method of payment, the importer pays a fraction of the total amount of the items to be imported in advance. The method has both advantages and disadvantages. The advantage is that it prompts the exporter or seller to begin performance without the importer or buyer paying the full agreed price in advance. The disadvantage is that there is a possibility the seller or exporter may never deliver the goods even though it has the buyer's down payment.

4. Open Account: In this method, the importer takes the delivery of goods and promises to the supplier to make the payment at some specific date in the future. Moreover, the importer is also not required to issue any negotiable instrument showing his legal commitment to pay at the appointed time. This type of payment method is mostly seen when the importer/buyer has a strong credit history and is well-known to the seller. However, this method of payment offers no protection in case of non-payment to the seller.

Open account terms have many advantages and disadvantages. In an open account payment method, title to the goods usually passes from the seller to the buyer prior to payment and exposes the seller to risk of default by the buyer. The quicker documents are exchanged between the seller and the buyer also determines the time of payment. While this payment term has the fewest restrictions and the lowest cost for the buyer, it also subjects the seller to payment risk and is used only between a buyer and a seller who have a trusting, long-term relationship. In a foreign transaction, an open account can be a convenient method of payment if the buyer is well established, and has credit worthiness. With an open account, the exporter simply bills the customer, who is expected to pay under agreed terms at a future date. Many firms abroad make purchases only on an open account.

Needless to say there are risks to open account sales. The absence of documents and banking channels hinder pursuance of claims in case of legal issues. The exporter might also have to pursue collection abroad, which can be expensive and time consuming. Another problem is that receivables may be harder to finance, since drafts or other evidence of indebtedness are unavailable. However, export credit insurance and factoring are some of the several means of reducing credit risk.

Exporters contemplating a sale on open account terms should thoroughly examine the political, economic, and commercial risks. They should also consult with their bankers if financing will be needed for the transaction before issuing a pro forma invoice to a buyer.

5. Documentary Collections: Documentary collection is an important bank payment method under which the sale transaction is settled by the bank through an exchange of documents. In this process the seller instructs his bank to forward documents related to the export of goods to the buyer's bank with a request to present these documents to the buyer for payment, indicating when and on what conditions these documents can be released to the buyer.

Documentary Drafts

A draft, sometimes also called a bill of exchange, is analogous to a foreign buyer's cheque. Like cheques used in domestic commerce, drafts carry the risk that they will be dishonoured. However, in international commerce, title does not transfer to the buyer until he pays the draft, or at least engages a legal undertaking that the draft will be paid when due.

(A) Sight Drafts: A sight draft is used when the exporter wants to retain title to the shipment until it reaches its destination and payment is made. The original ocean bill of lading must be endorsed by the buyer and surrendered to the carrier to effect release of shipment to the buyer. It is worthy of notice that airway bills of lading do not need to be presented in order for the buyer to claim the goods. Hence, risk increases when a sight draft is being used with an air shipment.

In actual practice, the sight draft, invoices, and other documents like packing lists, consular invoices, insurance certificates accompany the exporter-endorsed ocean bill of lading and sent via the exporter's bank to the buyer's bank. On receipt of these documents the foreign bank notifies the buyer when it has received these documents and as soon as the draft is paid, the foreign bank turns over the bill of lading thereby enabling the buyer to obtain the shipment.

In any case, there is some risk when a sight draft is used to transfer the title of a shipment. The buyer's ability or willingness to pay might keep changing from the time the goods are shipped until the time the drafts are presented for payment. Moreover, there is no guarantee of payment from the bank. Additionally, the policies of the importing country could also change. If the buyer cannot or will not pay for and claim the goods, returning or disposing of the products becomes the problem of the exporter.

(B) Time Drafts and Date Drafts: When the exporter extends credit to the buyer, a time draft is used. The draft states that payment is due by a specific time after the buyer accepts the time draft and receives the goods (for example, 30 days after acceptance). By signing and writing "accepted" on the draft, the buyer is formally obligated to pay within the stated time. This trade acceptance as it is called can be kept by the exporter until maturity or sold to a bank at a discount for immediate payment.

The difference between a date draft and a time draft is that the date draft specifies a date on which payment is due, rather than a time period after the draft is accepted. Buyers sometimes delay payment by delaying acceptance of a sight draft or a time draft. A date draft can prevent this delay in payment.

A bank on accepting a draft becomes obligated whereby the said draft becomes a negotiable instrument known as a banker's acceptance. This acceptance can also be sold to a bank at a discount for immediate payment.

The buyer is in a position to get possession of goods and clear them through customs, if he has the shipping documents such as original bill of lading, certificate of origin, etc. However, the documents are only given to the buyer after payment has been made ("Documents against Payment") or a payment undertaking has been given. The buyer has accepted a bill of exchange issued by the seller and payable at a certain date in the future (maturity date) ("Documents against Acceptance").

Documentary collections make import-export operations easier within a low cost. However, a letter of credit provides more protection as documentary collections do not involve any kind of bank guarantee like the letter of credit.

6. Letter of Credit: It is the most well known method of payment in international trade and plays an intermediary role to help complete the trade transaction. Under this method, the importer's bank guarantees to the supplier that the bank will pay the mentioned amount in the agreement, once the supplier or exporter meets the terms and conditions of the letter of credit. The bank however, deals only in documents and does not inspect the goods themselves. The International Chamber of Commerce and Industries (CII) has laid down rules in the Uniforms Customs and Practice for Documentary Credits (UCPDC) (UCP) by which letters of credit are issued.

2.5 Concept of Warehousing

The Customs Act, 1962 permits the facility of warehousing of imported goods in Customs Bonded Warehouses, without payment of customs duty otherwise leviable on import. Apart from specific provisions in the said Act (Chapter IX), certain regulations have been also framed and provisions of Warehoused Goods (Removal) Regulations, 1963 and Manufacture and other Operations in Warehoused Regulations, 1966 could be referred to in this context. In practicality, goods after landing are permitted to be moved to a warehouse without payment of duty and duty is collected at the time of clearance from the warehouse. The law lays down the time period up to which the goods may remain in a warehouse, without incurring any interest liability and with interest liability.

Warehousing Stations

The Central Board of Excise and Customs declares the appointment and licensing of warehouses at specific places only. The Board has delegated its power for declaring places to be warehousing stations to the Chief Commissioners of Customs. In the case of 100% EOUs, the powers to declare places to be warehousing stations have been delegated to the Commissioners of Customs.

The Assistant/Deputy Commissioner of Customs may appoint a Public Bonded Warehouse where imported dutiable goods may be deposited. Under Section 58, the Assistant/Deputy Commissioner of Customs can licence Private Bonded Warehouses where goods imported by or on behalf of the licencee or other imported goods where facility for public warehouse is not available, may be deposited. The following guidelines are generally kept in mind for ensuring uniformity in the practice in the declaration of warehousing stations.

(i) The industrial development of the proposed area and the need for warehousing of imported goods should be assessed.

(ii) Only those places are notified as warehousing stations where adequate facilities are available for appointing public bonded warehouses. This condition can however be relaxed in case of 100% EOUs, subject to use by 100% EOUs only.

(iii) Adequate customs/central excise staff should be available in the vicinity of the proposed warehousing stations and necessary arrangements for training of the staff should be made. The Board decides cases not fulfilling the aforesaid criteria.

Appointing of Public Bonded Warehouse

In respect of Public Bonded Warehouses, other than the Central Warehousing Corporation and the State Warehousing Corporations, private operators can also be appointed as custodians. Applications for custodianship are to be carefully scrutinised with due consideration given to factors such as the feasibility and financial viability of the warehouse operator, his credibility, his financial status, his past record to comply with Customs & Excise laws, expertise in warehousing field, etc. The applicant should pay cost-recovery charges on payments of Merchant Overtime/Supervision Charges for obtaining services of Customs officers.

Licensing of Private Bonded Warehouses

In case of private bonded warehouses, the applications for such licences have been classified into two categories, namely, storage of sensitive goods such as liquor, cigarettes, foodstuffs, consumables, etc. and other non-sensitive goods.

Under the Board's circular no. 99/95 dated 20.9.1995, the following guidelines in case of storage of sensitive goods have been provided.

(i) Applicants should produce a 'solvency certificate' from a 'scheduled bank' of repute for a value not less than ₹ 50 lakhs.

(ii) Such warehouses are not to be located in residential areas.

(iii) The premises should be secure, possess fire-fighting provisions and easily accessible to the Customs Officers.

(iv) Goods deposited should be fully insured for a value at least equal to the customs duty.

(v) The proprietor/partner/director must not be involved in any customs or excise offence. In case of any involvement in such offences, the licence may be terminated after following the prescribed procedure.

(vi) When individual consignments are to be warehoused, a double duty-bond as prescribed under Section 59 should be given by the licencee. In case of sensitive goods, a cash deposit/ bank guarantee equal to 25% of the duty liability (effective duty foregone) will be taken for each consignment. A revolving bond with a single bank guarantee for a higher amount can be accepted if so requested for a number of consignments.

In the case of non-sensitive goods, applicants for private bonded warehouses have to abide by all provisions as pertaining to sensitive goods discussed above, except that the requirement of furnishing a 'solvency certificate' has been waived. The applicant, however, should possess an impeccable record and be solvent for ₹ 10 lakhs. A double-duty bond with surety would suffice for storage of non-sensitive bonded goods. In case the Customs are not satisfied about the transactions, the applicant may be asked to furnish a bank guarantee.

A licence granted by the Customs under Section 58 may be cancelled or suspended under certain conditions after observing the procedure prescribed under Section 58 of the Customs Act.

Bonding of Import Goods

Where the bonding facility is desired on importation, the importer or his representative is required to present to the Customs a Warehousing Bill of Entry (also known as Into Bond Bill of Entry) in the prescribed form along with the relevant documents required. The duties liable are assessed but not required to be paid. A suitable bond has to be executed with the bond section before Customs allow bonding. The Customs may order the deposit of the goods in the warehouse once the warehousing bond has been executed by the importer. The goods are normally escorted to the bonded warehouse if it is at the same port/airport station where the goods landed or allowed to be moved under a transit bond without escort. Once all the goods brought under any bond have been accounted for to the satisfaction of the Customs officer, after payment of all duties etc., the Customs officer cancels and returns the bond executed as discharged in full.

Storage Period of Warehoused Goods

A bonded warehouse may store deposited goods up to a period of one year. In the case of capital goods intended for use in any 100% EOU, such goods can however be stored up to a period of five years. Extension of the warehousing period is undertaken by the Commissioner of Customs for a period of six months and by the Chief Commissioner of Customs for such further period as is deemed fit by him. The importers should file their applications for extensions well before the expiry of the initial/extended period of warehousing.

Before granting extensions, officers have to examine the condition of the goods to see that they are not likely to deteriorate during the extended period. A somewhat liberal approach in extending warehousing period in the following categories of cases is considered, if the interests of revenue are not likely to be endangered.

(i)   Goods supplied as ship stores/aircraft stores.

(ii) Goods supplied to diplomats.

(iii) Goods used in the units operating under manufacture under bond scheme.

(iv) Goods imported by 100% EOUs.

(v)   Goods warehoused and sold through duty free shops.

(vi) Machinery, equipment and raw materials imported for building and fitment to ships.

It is to be noted however that extensions in warehousing period are not meant to be granted often but only in such cases where the goods have to be kept in the warehouse under circumstances beyond the importer's control. It is not valid to quote 'lack of finance' to pay the duty as a reason for seeking extensions which are otherwise given for short periods.

In case the warehoused goods are likely to deteriorate, the Commissioner of Customs may reduce the one year's period of warehousing to such shorter period as he may see fit.

Rate of Interest on Customs Duty in case of Bonded Goods

In cases where the capital goods for 100% EOUs remain in a warehouse beyond a period of 5 years, interest at the rate of 24% per annum, as currently applicable under notification No. 10/2001 - Cus. (N.T.) dated 1.3.2001, shall be charged on the customs duty payable at the time of clearance of the goods for the period from the expiry of the said warehousing period till the date of payment of duty on the warehoused goods. In the case of all other goods, with effect from 1.6.2001, interest at the rate of 24% per annum is payable after the expiry of thirty days in the warehouse under notification No. 23/2001 - Cus. (N.T.) dated 22.5.2001.

Waiver of Interest

Under Section 61(2) of the Customs Act the Board may by order and under circumstances of an exceptional nature, waive the whole or a part of any interest payable in respect of warehoused goods. In this regard, the power to grant waiver of interest up to an amount of ₹ 15 lakhs has been delegated to the Chief Commissioners of Customs, and guidelines framed by the Board, specifying cases where the interest waiver would be considered. The types of such cases are –

(i) Goods supplied as ship stores/aircraft stores.

(ii) Goods supplied to diplomats.

(iii) Goods used in the units operating under 'manufacture under bond' scheme.

(iv) Goods imported by 100% EOUs.

(v) Goods warehoused and sold through duty free shops.

(vi) Machinery, equipment and raw materials imported for building and fitment to ships.

(vii) Petroleum products.

(viii) Plant and machinery imported for projects.

(ix) Machinery, equipment and raw materials imported for manufacture and installation of power generation units.

(x) Goods imported under OGL and warehoused for subsequent clearance against valid advance licences, Import-Export Pass Book scheme or any similar scheme.

(xi) Goods imported in bulk by canalising agencies/public sector trading or service agencies and warehoused for subsequent release for export production.

(xii) Goods warehoused and subsequently re-exported under Section 69 of the Customs Act, 1962 subject to the conditions that –

(a) The re-export realises the full foreign exchange spent in import in hard currency (in case the import is paid for in that currency) and

(b) The import in the first instance was not unauthorised or in contravention of the Import-Export Policy.

In all the above categories of export related cases Customs officers are required to raise the demand for interest due, without enforcing them immediately. Clearance of goods and other activities are allowed to continue and only after the goods have been cleared or at the time of de-bonding of 100% EOUs, the request for waiver of interest is to be decided. Only under exceptional circumstances 100% EOUs which have not fulfilled their export obligations and have been allowed to debond their warehoused goods prematurely, are granted waiver of interest. These cases of waiver of interest not covered under the aforesaid guidelines have to be referred to the Board for decision.

Vide notification No. 67/95 - Cus. (N.T.) dt. 1.11.1995, interest accrued on customs duties payable on certain specified bonded goods like capital goods, components/spares, office equipments, captive power plants, tools etc. have been exempt at the time of clearance in the following cases.

(i)   Goods imported by 100% EOUs under notification No. 13/81 - Cus.

(ii) Goods imported by 100% EOUs in EHTPs under various notifications.

(iii) Goods imported by 100% EOUs in STPs under certain notifications.

Operations on Warehoused Goods

Customs officers control all warehoused goods. The owner of the warehoused goods may inspect, sort, show for sale, draw samples etc., from the bonded warehouse with the permission of the concerned officer. The owner of the bonded goods shall also pay the warehouse keeper rent and warehouse charges at the rates fixed under law.

Manufacture under Bond Operations

The owner of any bonded goods may carry on any manufacturing process or other operations in the bonded warehouse in relation to such goods with the permission of the Assistant/Deputy Commissioner of Customs.

As a policy, it has been decided to extend in-bond manufacture facility under Section 65 of the Customs Act mainly to EOUs or to units which are primarily engaged in exports. Customs supervision on a cost-recovery basis is required to carry out manufacture under bond operations. The license to carry out these activities is granted by Customs under Section 65 after scrutinising the application and satisfying itself that the applicant is financially secure, has good credibility and has not been involved in Customs or Excise duty evasion in the preceding five years. Observance of the provisions of Manufacture and Other Operations in Warehouse Regulations, 1966 is important. Moreover, the premises should be adequately secure.

Movement under Bond

The owner of bonded goods may remove the said goods from one warehouse to another either under the supervision of the Customs officer or by executing a bond equal to the amount of import duty leviable on such goods if the goods are to be removed to a warehouse in another town. The procedural details and terms of the bond to be executed are provided under Warehoused Goods (Removal) Regulations, 1963. Under circular No. 99/95 - Cus. dt. 20.9.1995, customs duty is to be secured by a transit bond backed by a bank guarantee/cash security for 50% of the duty involved in case the goods are of sensitive nature. In respect of non-sensitive goods, transit bonds would be covered by a bank guarantee or a cash security for 25% of the duty involved. Commissioners of Customs may demand greater guarantee/security if felt necessary in certain cases. In the case of 100% EOU/EHTP/STP and EPZ units, the requirement of bank guarantee for transfer of imported goods has been waived vide the Board's circular no. 41/97 - Cus. dt. 19.9.1997, subject to the conditions prescribed in the said circular.

Clearance of Imported Goods

In terms of Section 68 of the Customs Act the importer of any warehoused goods can clear the goods for home consumption by filing an ex-bond Bill of Entry and after payment of duties.

Rate of Duty/Value for Assessment

The applicable rate of duty is as per provisions of Section 15 of the Customs Act, that is, on the date on which the goods are actually removed from the warehouse. If the warehousing period or the extended warehousing period has expired, the duty payable is with respect to the date when the warehousing/extended warehousing period expired and not the actual date of removal. The value for assessment of duty for warehoused goods is not required to be re-determined and it is the original value as determined at the time of filing of into Bond Bill of Entry and assessments before warehousing.

Transfer of Bonded Goods

Transfer of bonded goods to another person is possible under Section 59 (3) of the Customs Act, 1962. The sale of the warehoused goods to holders of duty exemption or duty concession license for the goods is permitted under the law as per the Board's circular issued from F. No. 473/43/94 dt. 22.9.1994.

Export of Bonded Goods

Warehoused goods may also be exported out of India without payment of duty after the filing of a Shipping Bill/Bill of Export and the payment of relevant export duties etc. However, in the event warehoused goods exported from India to certain neighbouring countries are likely to be smuggled back to India, the Government has directed vide notification no. 45 - Cus. dt. 1.2.1963 (as amended) that warehoused goods shall not be exported without payment of import duty to any place in Bhutan or Nepal. Similar restrictions are placed in the case of warehoused goods to be exported by land to any place in Myanmar, Xikang, Tibet or Xinjiang. A ban has also been placed on export from bond of vessels of less than 1000 tons. The following items, namely, alcoholic liquors, cigarettes, cigars and pipe tobacco are also not permitted to be taken on board any foreign-going vessel of less than 200 tons without payment of import duty leviable vide notification No. 47 - Cus. dt. 1.2.1963.

Recovery of Duty on Bonded Goods

The full amount of duty chargeable on bonded goods, along with all the penalties, rent, interest and other charges payable may be demanded by Customs officers in the following cases –

(i) Where any warehoused goods are removed in contravention of the Customs Act, 1962.

(ii) Where such goods have not been removed from a warehouse at the expiry of the period permitted under Section 61.

(iii) Where any warehoused goods have been taken under Section 64 as samples without payment of duty.

(iv) Where any bonded goods have not been cleared for home consumption or exportation or are not duly accounted for to the satisfaction of the Customs.

In case the owner fails to pay the amount as demanded above, Customs may detain and sell, after notice to the owner, such portion of the bonded goods as may be selected.

2.6 Procedure for Importing Goods within Relevant Provisions under Various Acts

2.6.1 Introduction

All goods imported into India have to pass through the procedure of customs for proper examination, appraisal, assessment, and evaluation. This helps the customs authorities to charge the proper tax and check the goods against illegal import. In addition it is important to note that no import is allowed in India if the importer doesn't have the IEC number issued by the DGFT. There is no requirement of an IEC number if the goods are imported for personal use. Under the Ministry of Finance (Department of Revenue), there are two independent Boards of Revenue, namely, Central Board of Direct Taxes and Central Board of Excise and Customs. The customs administrations come under the latter which shapes the policy and decides the functions of the Customs formations in the country, in terms of the provision of the Customs Act 1962.

All the goods imported in India have to pass through customs clearance after they cross the Indian border. The goods so imported are examined, appraised, assessed, evaluated and then allowed to be taken out of customs charge for use by the importer.

2.6.2 Various acts relating to Procedure for Importing

I. Foreign Trade (Development) Regulation Act 1992 (FTDRA, 1992): This law governs imports into India and deals with the development and regulation of foreign trade by facilitating imports into, and augmenting exports from, India and for matters connected therewith or incidental thereto. The FTDRA, 1992 provides for obtaining of importer-exporter code number from the Director General of Foreign Trade (DGFT), which is essential to the

Indian buyer for importing goods as well as relevant licence for importing or exporting. The DGFT is responsible for the execution of the Import-Export policy and the Ministry of Commerce is the overall in charge of foreign trade in India.

II. Foreign Trade (Regulation) Rules, 1993: Foreign Trade (Regulation) Rules, 1993, which inter alia, provide for grant of special licence, application for grant of licence, fee, conditions for licences, refusal of licence, amendment of licence, suspension of a licence, cancellation of licence, declaration as to the value and quality of imported goods, declaration as to the Importer-Exporter Code number, utilisation of imported goods, provisions regarding making, signing of any declaration/statement or documents, power to enter the premises and inspect, search and seizure of goods, documents, things and conveyance, settlement, confiscation and redemption and confiscation of conveyance.

III. Foreign Trade Policy (2009-14): It is a policy framed from time to time by the DGFT functioning under the Ministry of Commerce for 5 years at a stretch. It contains the procedure in respect of import of various commodities/categories of importers. The Indian importer has to comply with the provisions herein for valid import of goods into India. The present import policy and procedures in respect of various commodities/category of importers, are, inter alia, contained in the following publications issued by the Ministry of Commerce and revised from time to time such as –

- Foreign Trade Policy 2009-2014
- Foreign Trade Policy 2004-2009
- New Exim Policy 2003 Highlights
- Exim Policy 2002-2007
- Exim Policy 2001-2002
- Highlights of Exim Policy 2001-2002
- Import-Export Policy, 1997-2002 as modified up to 31.03.1999
- Handbook of Import-Export Procedures (Volume 1), 1997-2002 as modified up to 31.03.2000.
- Handbook of Import-Export Procedures (Volume 2)
- ITC (HS) Classification of Import and Export items

IV. Procedure for Import of Goods into India the Customs Act 1962 (CA 1962)

This law deals with inter alia clearance of imported/exported/re-exported goods at notified places such as coastal ports, airports, routes, warehousing stations, etc. It also provides for matters relating to customs duties. It regulates import of goods into India at the notified places. The CA 1962 lays down the procedure of customs after the goods cross the Indian border where goods are examined, appraised, assessed, evaluated by the customs administration and then allowed to be taken out of customs charge for use by the importer.

One of the most important issues while negotiating cross-border sale and purchase of goods is the contract, which may be governed by the Indian Contract Act 1872. The terms and conditions of sale and purchase of goods have to be clearly laid down in order to effectuate payment, relief, compensation or remedies available to a foreign exporter against the Indian importer in the event of default or breach of contract. Purchase order, transaction value, payment provisions such as letters of credit, escrow agreements, specification of goods, documentary requirements, packaging, port of shipment, delivery schedule, expenses and taxes, force majeure, dispute resolution are some other essential terms that need to be covered in a contract.

Normally, the mode of pricing is based on Inco Terms, which are the terms prevailing in international trade transactions. The mode of payment must conform to FEMA, which basically allows three modes of payments/remittances that is, advance payment, bills drawn under letters of credit and bills received from abroad for collection against imports into India.

(A) Procedure for Import of Goods into India

Generally, the procedure for import of goods into India is as follows.

1. The vessel (conveyance) containing imported goods arrives at the notified place. The concerned person of the vessel produces before the custom authorities an import manifest (as stipulated under the CA 1962).

2. Thereafter, pursuant to examination by the customs authorities, payment of duties by the importer and other requisite formalities (discussed below), the goods may be removed by the importer. The importer is required to present the below mentioned documents to the customs authority as soon as he/she receives intimation of arrival of goods at the notified place. These documents may also be filed in advance before the customs authority for the speedy removal of imported goods from the port.

If any goods brought into India from a place outside India are not cleared for home consumption or warehoused or transhipped within 30 days from the date of the unloading thereof at a customs station or within such further time as the proper officer may allow or if the title to any imported goods is relinquished, such goods may, after notice to the importer and with the permission of the concerned officer, be sold by the person having the custody thereof subject to provisos therein.

The importer has certain duties and obligations under the CA 1962 and prevailing EXIM Policy for clearance of goods from the notified place. The import manifest and the bill of entry are the important documents. Depending upon the nature of goods to be imported, there are several other documentary requirements such as the import manifest, bill of entry, invoice, bill of lading, etc.

Goods are imported in India or exported from India through sea, air or land. Goods can come through post parcel or as baggage with passengers. Procedures naturally vary depending on mode of import or export. Procedures discussed in this chapter are applicable for imports by sea, air or land, but not as baggage or postal dispatch.

3. Entry: 'Entry' in regard to goods means an entry made in a Bill of Entry, Shipping Bill or Bill of Export. It includes –

(a) A label or declaration accompanying the goods which contains the description, quantity and value of the goods.

(b) An entry to be made in case of goods to be exported.

(c) An entry in respect of goods imported which are not accompanied by a label or declaration made as per provisions of Section 84.

4. Amendment to Documents: Importer, exporter or the 'person in charge' has to submit various documents to the customs authorities like bill of entry, import manifest, export manifest etc. Amendments to these documents may become necessary due to various reasons like change in classification, clerical mistakes in document, change in unloading/loading plan of vessel etc. Permission to amend these documents have to be obtained from customs authorities [Section 149]. Such permission is granted only if there are no fraudulent intentions.

Bill of entry, shipping bill or bill of export can be amended only after clearance on the basis of documentary evidence which was in existence at the time the goods were cleared, warehoused or exported, and not on the basis of any subsequent document [Proviso to Section 149].

5. Customs Station: Imported goods are permitted to be unloaded only at specified places. Similarly, goods can be exported only from specified areas. Customs area means all the areas of the Customs Station and includes any area where imported goods or export goods are ordinarily kept pending clearance by Customs authorities. Customs Area could include some areas even outside the Customs Station. In other words, Customs Station means (a) customs port (b) inland container depot (c) customs airport and (d) land customs station.

Section 7 of the Customs Act empowers CBEC (Board) to appoint customs ports, customs airports, places for inland container depots, and coastal ports under notification. Section 8 authorises Commissioner of Customs to approve ideal places in any customs port, customs airport or coastal port for unloading and loading of goods or for any class of goods and specify the limits of the customs area. Thus, the place (city/town/village) is approved by CBEC, while exact location within that city/town/village is approved by the Commissioner of Customs.

(B) Procedure to be followed by Person-in-Charge of Conveyance as well as the Importer:

1. Person-in-charge: As per section 2(31), a person-in-charge means (a) In case of vessel – its master (b) In case of aircraft – its commander or pilot-in-charge (c) In case of train – its conductor or guard and (d) In case of vehicle or other conveyance – its driver or other person-in-charge.

The meaning of this definition is

- He is responsible for submitting Import Manifest and Export Manifest

- His responsibility is to ensure that the conveyance comes through approved routes and at approved places only.

- He has to make sure that goods are unloaded at a proper place. Loading also has to be only after permission.

- His responsibility is to make sure that conveyance does not leave without the written order of Customs authorities.

- He can also be penalised for (a) giving false declaration and statement (b) shortages or non-accounting of goods in conveyance.

2. Procedure to be followed by the Carrier: The person-in-charge of conveyance (carrier of goods) has to follow the stipulated procedures:

- **Arrival at Customs Port/Airport Only:** Section 29 provides that the person-in-charge of a vessel or an aircraft entering India shall call or land at customs port or customs airport only. It can land at other places only in the event of accidents, weather conditions or other unavoidable causes. In such cases, he should report to the nearest police station or Customs Officer. While arriving by a land route, the vehicle should come by approved route to 'land customs station' only.

- **Import Manifest/Report:** Person-in-charge of vessel, aircraft or vehicle has to submit an Import Manifest/Report, also known as IGM (Import General Manifest). In case of a vessel or aircraft, it is called an import manifest, while in the case of a vehicle it is called an import report. This import manifest is to be submitted prior to the arrival of a vessel or aircraft. Import report (in case of vehicle) has to be submitted within 12 hours of arrival at the customs station. If the report/manifest could not be submitted within the prescribed time, person-in-charge or any person specified as responsible by a notification is liable to a penalty up to Rs. 50,000. As per Section 30(1) such penalty will not be imposed if the excise officer is satisfied that there was sufficient cause for the delay.

  IGM can be submitted electronically through floppy where EDI facility is available.

- **Import Manifest is required to be submitted before Arrival of Aircraft or Vessel:** Section 30(1) of Customs Act stipulates that Import Manifest should be filed before arrival of ship or aircraft. Normally, the agents submit the Import Manifest before arrival, so that maximum possible formalities are completed before vessel or aircraft arrives. This also enables importers to file the Bill of Entry in advance.

- **Grant of Entry Inwards by Customs Officer:** Unloading of cargo can start only after the Customs Officer grants 'Entry Inwards'. Such entry inwards can be granted only when berthing accommodation is granted to a vessel. If there is heavy congestion at port, shipping berth may not be available and in such case, 'Entry Inwards' cannot be granted. This date is highly relevant for determining the applicable rate of customs duty.

- **Carrier responsible for Shortages during Unloading:** If the goods are short landed, the carrier is liable to pay penalty up to twice the amount of duty payable on such short landed goods. It has been held that tally sheet prepared by Port Trust authorities on unloading of goods is a statutory document and should be accepted in preference to steamer survey.

(C) Procedure by Importer

The importer importing the goods has to follow prescribed procedures for import by ship/air/road. There is a separate procedure for goods imported as a baggage or by post.

1. Bill of Entry: This is a very vital and important document which every importer has to submit under Section 46. The Bill of Entry should be in the prescribed form. The standard size of Bill of Entry is 16"×13". However, for computerisation purposes, 15"×12" size is permitted as per Mumbai Customs Public Notice No. 142/93 dt. 3-11-93.

2. Bill of Entry should be submitted in Quadruplicate: Original and duplicate for customs, triplicate for the importer and the fourth copy for the bank to make remittances.

Under EDI system, Bill of Entry is actually printed on computer in triplicate only after 'out of charge' order is given. Duplicate copy is given to importer.

3. Types of Bill of Entry: Bills of Entry are of three types. Two types are for clearance from customs while the third is for clearance from the warehouse.

  (i) **Bill of Entry for Home Consumption:** This form is used when the imported goods are to be cleared on payment of full duty. Home consumption means use within India. It is often called a 'white bill of entry' as it is white in colour.

  (ii) **Bill of Entry for Warehousing:** In case there is no urgency in the requirement of the imported goods, the importer may like to store the goods in a warehouse under a bond without payment of duty and then clear the same from the warehouse when required on payment of duty. This will enable him to defer payment of customs duty till goods are actually required by him. This bill of entry is printed on yellow paper and often called 'yellow bill of entry'. It is also known as 'Into Bond Bill of Entry' as the bond is executed for transfer of goods in warehouse without payment of duty.

(iii) **Bill of Entry for Ex-Bond Clearance:** The third type is for ex-bond clearance. This is used for clearance from the warehouse on payment of duty and is printed on green paper. Since the goods are classified and value is assessed at the time of clearance from customs port, the same are not required to be determined in this bill of entry. The columns in this bill of entry are similar to other bills of entry.

4. **Rate of Duty for Clearance from Warehouse:** It must be understood that rate of duty applicable is as prevalent on the date of removal from warehouse. In case the rate has changed after the goods are cleared from customs port, customs duty as assessed on yellow bill of entry and as paid on green bill of entry will not be same.

5. **Mention of BIN on Bill of Entry:** A BIN (Business Identification Number) is allotted to each importer and exporter with effect from 1.4.2001. It is a 15-digit code based on PAN of Income Tax (PAN is a 10-digit code). Earlier an EC (Import Export Code) number issued by DGFT was required to be mentioned on Bill of Entry.

6. **Filing of Bill of Entry:** Normally, Bill of Entry is filed by CHA on behalf of the importer. Customs work at some ports has been computerised. In that case, the Bill of Entry has to be filed electronically, that is, through Customs EDI system. The procedure for the same has been prescribed vide Bill of Entry (Electronic Declaration) Regulations, 1995.

7. **Documents to be submitted by Importer:** Documents required by customs authorities are required to be submitted to enable them to:

(a) Check the goods;

(b) Determine value and classification of goods; and

(c) Ensure that the import is legally permitted.

The documents that are essentially required are:

(i)   Invoice

(ii) Packing list

(iii) Bill of lading/Delivery order

(iv) GATT declaration form duly filled in

(v)   Importers/CHA's declaration duly signed

(vi) Import licence or attested photocopy when clearance is under licence

(vii) Letter of credit/Bank draft wherever necessary

(viii) Insurance memo or insurance policy

(ix) Industrial license if required

(x)   Certificate of country of origin, if preferential rate is claimed

(xi) Technical literature

(xii) Test report in case of chemicals

(xiii) Advance license/DEPB in original where applicable

(xiv) Split up of value of spares, components and machinery

(xv) No commission declaration

A declaration in prescribed form about correctness of information should be submitted.

The noting is now done electronically in large ports, while it is done manually in small ports. A 'thoka number' or serial number is given while noting the bill of entry.

8. Electronic Submission under EDI System: Where an EDI system is in place, formal submission of Bill of Entry is not required. Importer can submit declaration in an electronic format to the service centre. A signed paper copy of declaration for non-repudiation should be submitted. The bill of entry number is generated by the system which is endorsed on a printed check list. Original documents are to be submitted only at the stage of examination.

9. Prior Entry of Bill of Entry: On unloading the goods they are to be cleared within three working days to avoid high demurrage charges. Hence, the importer is compelled to complete as many formalities as possible before the ship arrives. Proviso to Section 46(3) of the Customs Act allows the importer to present bill of entry up to 30 days before the expected date of arrival of the vessel. In such a case, duty will be payable at the rate applicable on the date on which 'entry inward' is granted to the vessel and not the date of presentation of bill of entry, but rate of exchange will be as prevalent on date of submission of bill of entry.

10. Appraising the Goods: The appraiser has to (a) correctly classify the goods (b) decide the value for purpose of customs duty (c) find out the rate of duty applicable as per any exemption notification and (d) verify that the goods are not imported in violation of any law. He can call for any further documents that may be required for assessment. If he is of the opinion that goods have to be examined for appraisal, he will issue an examination order, usually on the reverse of the bill of entry. If such order is issued, the bill of entry is presented to appraising staff at docks/air cargo complexes, where the goods are examined in presence of importer's representative. Assessment is finalised after getting the report of examination.

11. Valuation of Goods: As per Rule 10A(1) of Customs Valuation Rules, the importer has to file declaration about full value of goods. If the assessing officer has doubts about the truth and accuracy of value as declared, he can ask the importer to submit further information, details and documents. If the doubt persists, the assessing officer can reject the value declared by importer. As per Rule 10A(2) of Customs Valuation Rules if the importer requests, the assessing officer has to give reasons for doubting the value declared by importer. If the value declared by importer is rejected, the assessing officer can value imported goods on other basis for example value of identical goods, value of similar goods etc. as provided in Customs Valuation Rules. This amendment has been made with effect from 19.2.98, as per WTO agreement. However, it has been held that burden of proof of under valuation is on department. The assessing officer should not arbitrarily reject the declared value and increase the assessable value. He should follow due process of law and issue the appealable order.

12. Approval of Assessment: The assessment has to be approved by the Assistant Commissioner, if the value is more than ₹ One lakh. In cases covered under 'fast track clearance for imports', the appraiser is also authorised to approve valuation. After the approval, duty payable is typed by a "pin-point typewriter" so that it cannot be tampered with. The assessing officer should sign in full in bill of entry followed by his name, preferably by rubber stamp.

EDI Assessment: In the EDI system, the cargo declaration is transferred to the assessing officer in the groups electronically. Processing is done on the screen itself. All calculations are done by the system itself. If the assessing officer needs clarification, he can raise a query. The query is printed at the service centre and the importer replies through the service centre. Facility of tele-enquiry about status of documents is provided in major customs stations. Under EDI, normally, documents are inspected only after assessment. After assessment, copy of bill of entry is printed at service centre. The final bill of entry is printed only after 'Out of Charge' order is given by customs officer.

13. Payment of Customs Duty: After assessment of duty, the necessary duty is paid. Regular importers and Customs House agents keep current account with Customs department. The duty can be debited to such current account, or it can be paid in cash/DD through TR-6 Challan in designated banks.

After payment of duty, if goods were already examined, delivery of goods can be taken from custodians (port trust) after paying their dues. If goods were not examined before assessment, these have to be submitted for examination in the import shed to the examining staff. After the shed appraiser gives a 'out of charge' order, delivery of goods can be taken from the custodian.

14. First and Second System of Assessment: There are two systems of assessment. Section 17(2) provides for assessment after examination of goods and Section 17(4) provides for assessment on basis of documents, followed by inspection and testing of goods.

- **First appraisement system** or **first check procedure** is undertaken if the appraiser is not able to make assessment on the basis of documents submitted and feels that inspection is necessary. Goods are assessed after first examining them. The importer himself may also request 'first check procedure', if he cannot give all the required details regarding description/value of goods. He has to make a request for first check examination at the time of filing of bill of entry or at data entry stage in case of EDI. He has to state the reason for seeking first appraisement. The examination order is recorded on bill of entry and then returned to importer/CHA. It is then presented to the import shed for examination. The shed appraiser/dock examiner examines the goods as per examination order and records his findings. If samples are required, they are taken out. In case of EDI system, the report of examination is given in the computer itself. The goods are then assessed for duty by the appraiser.

- **Second Appraisement System** or **second check procedure** is normally followed, wherein assessment is done on the basis of documents and then the goods are examined. Though not mandatory, it is done on a selective basis on the premise of 'risk assessment' or specific intelligence report. Section 17(4) of Customs Act specifically provides that if initially assessment is done on the basis of documents, re-assessment can be done after examination or testing of goods or otherwise, if it is found subsequent to examination or testing or otherwise, that any statement made on bill of entry or any information supplied is not true in respect of matter relevant to assessment of duty.

- First appraisement is generally carried out in the following cases –
  (i)   If complete documents are not submitted
  (ii)   Goods are to be tested for correct classification
  (iii) Goods are re-imported
  (iv)   Goods are damaged or deteriorated and abatement is claimed
  (v)   Goods are abandoned and remission of duty is applied for
  (vi)   When goods are provisionally assessed
  (vii) When importer himself requests for examination of goods before payment of duty

15. Examination of Goods: This entails examiners carrying out physical examination and quantitative checking like weighing, measuring etc. Packages are selected randomly, opened and examined on a sample basis in the 'customs examination yard'. The examiner then prepares a report.

Accelerated Clearance of Imports and Exports Scheme (ACS): In his budget speech on 28-2-2003, the Finance Minister had announced a 'self assessment scheme' for importers and exporters. As per this scheme, the importer will himself determine classification of goods including claim for exemption benefits on a computer system that will calculate the duty based on his declaration. Physical inspection of imported goods will be done by risk-assessment and management techniques on a computer-based system and not on the orders of the customs examining staff. Audit of import documents will not be by existing system of concurrent audit but will be done by post-clearance audit, as prevalent in developed countries.

Subsequently, an Accelerated Clearance of Import and Export Scheme (ACS) was announced. The scheme was announced through administrative instructions, without making any change in statutory provisions. Hence, the scheme is not the same as 'self removal' under Central Excise. Presently, the scheme is introduced on a trial basis at Air Customs, Sahar (Mumbai), ICD (New Delhi) and Sea-Port Customs (Chennai).

In case of imports, the scheme will be open to all status holders under EXIM policy, Central and State Government PSUs and other importers who have been importing for at least two years and have filed at least 25 bills of entry in the preceding year. In case of exports, the scheme will be open to all status holders under EXIM policy, EOU/STP/EHTP units whose goods have been sealed in the presence of customs/excise officers. Certain sensitive items have been excluded from the provisions. Importers/exporters intending to avail this facility have to make an application to the Commissioner. The clearances will be subjected to post clearance audit.

16. Provisional Assessment: Section 18 of Customs Act, 1962 provides that provisional assessment can be done in cases when (a) Customs Officer is satisfied that importer or exporter is unable to produce documents or furnish information required for assessment; (b) It is deemed necessary to carry out chemical or other tests of goods; (c) When the importer/exporter has produced all documents, but the Customs officer still finds it mandatory to make further enquiry. In such situations, assessment is done on a provisional basis. The importer/exporter has to furnish guarantee/security as required for payment of difference if any. Goods can be cleared after payment of duty provisionally assessed and after providing the security. After final assessment, difference is paid by importer or refunded to him as the case may be. As per Section 18(2)(a) if the imported goods were warehoused after provisional assessment, the Customs officer may require the importer to execute a bond for twice the difference in duty, if duty finally assessed is higher. This bond is known as PD Bond (Provisional Duty Bond). The bond is with security or surety. Moreover, a bank guarantee can also be given as a security.

17. Checking of Duty Drawback/License Documents: Documents in respect of Duty Entitlement Pass Book (DEPB), advance license, duty drawback etc. will be checked.

18. Execution of Bond and Payment of Duty: The bill of entry is returned to the importer once the duty is assessed. The bill of entry is presented to a comptist for calculation and pinpointing of the duty. If a bond has to be executed, it will be taken in the bond section.

19. Payment of Duty: Duty payment is not required if the goods are to be moved to a warehouse. The goods can be shifted to a warehouse under bond, without payment of duty. However, payment of customs duty is essential if goods are to be removed for home consumption. Large importers and CHAs have PD (Provisional Duty) accounts with customs, similar to PLA accounts in central excise. Duty can be paid either in cash or through the PD account. Payment effected using a PD account is quick and convenient. The importer or CHA pays a lump sum amount in the account and gets credit on the amount paid. By debiting the amount in PD account he can pay customs duty. If the importer does not have an account, he can pay duty by cash using TR-6 challan. As per Section 47(2) of Customs Act, 1962, the duty should be paid within five working days, that is, within five days excluding holidays, after the bill of entry is returned to the importer for payment of duty.

20. Interest for Late Payment: If duty is not paid within five working days as aforesaid, interest is payable. As per Section 47(2) of Customs Act, 1962, interest can be from 10% to 36%, as may be notified by the Central Government. Interest rate is 15% with effect from 3-5-2002. Earlier the interest rate was 24% per annum.

21. Disposal if Goods are not cleared within 30 Days: As per Section 48 of the Customs Act, the goods must be cleared within 30 days after unloading. However, the customs officer can grant an extension. Goods can also be sold after giving notice to the importer. Animals, perishable goods and hazardous goods can be sold any time before 30 days. Arms and ammunition can be sold only with the permission of the Central Government.

22. Out of Customs Charge Order: After goods are examined, it is verified that import is not prohibited and after customs duty is paid, Customs officer will issue an 'Out of Customs Charge' order under Section 47. Goods can be cleared from customs area only on receipt of such order. This is an adjudicating order and can be passed by the Appraiser and not by the Assistant Commissioner.

Demurrage if Goods not cleared: Not clearing the goods from the port within three days will attract heavy demurrage.

(D) Import of Software through Data Communication

Import of software through data communication/tele-communication is allowed. However, proper accounting in books should be done since such imports are not available for physical verification. An estimated annual requirement is to be intimated to the Development Commissioner of EOU/Director of STP by a unit intending to import software through data link. After the import of software through the internet, written information should be submitted to the Director of STP/Development Commissioner of EOU and the importer shall get a certificate. This certificate should be submitted to Assistant/Dy. Commissioner of Customs within 48 hours, along with the bill of entry and a certificate from the Development Commissioner of EOU/Director of STP. He will issue an 'out of charge' order. The documents such as invoice etc. will be routed through the bank.

- **Relevant Date for Rate and Valuation of Customs Duty:** Section 15 of Customs Act stipulates that the rate of duty and tariff valuation applicable to imported goods shall be the rate and valuation in force at one of the following dates – (a) if the goods are entered for home consumption, the date on which bill of entry is presented (b) in case of warehoused goods, when bill of entry for home consumption is presented under Section 68 for clearance from warehouse and (c) in other cases, date of payment of duty.

- Goods must be mentioned in import manifest or import report submitted by person-in-charge of conveyance. Such goods should not be 'prohibited goods' under Section

11 of Customs Act. The conveyance may be a vehicle, ship or aircraft. After transit, the goods may go to another customs station. As per Section 55 on arrival at the customs station, the goods will be liable for customs duty as if it is first importation in India.

- **Transhipment of Goods:** Goods imported in any customs station can be transhipped without payment of duty, under Section 54 of Customs Act. Transhipment means transfer from one conveyance to another. The conveyance may be a vehicle, ship or aircraft. Such transhipment may be to any major port or airport in India. The goods can be transhipped to any other customs station in India if customs officer is satisfied that the goods are bona fide intended for transhipment to any customs station. The facility is available at all customs ports and Inland Container Depots (ICDs).

- Goods to be transhipped must be specified in the Import Manifest or Import Report and a 'Bill of Transhipment' should be submitted to the customs officer. In case of goods being transhipped under an international treaty or bilateral agreement between the government of India and the government of a foreign country, a Declaration of Transhipment shall be submitted instead of Bill of Transhipment.

(E) Import through Courier:

Though considered as 'baggage' imports and exports through couriers are treated as imports or exports as any other mode with no restriction whatsoever on the value of goods. The duty payable is normal duty as applicable to all other goods normally imported by ship or air transport. Duty concessions are also permissible. Courier Imports and Exports (Clearance) Regulations, 1998 specify the procedures, which are summarised in Chapter 17 of CBEC's Customs Manual, 2001.

The salient features of the regulations are as follows.

- Import through courier is permitted by air from Mumbai, Delhi, Chennai, Bangalore, Hyderabad, Ahmedabad, Jaipur and Kolkata or from any land customs station, except two land stations in West Bengal.

- The weight of the individual package should not exceed 70 kgs.

- Goods requiring any specific condition to be fulfilled under any other Act, rule or regulations are not permitted.

- Items like animals or its parts, plants, perishables, publications containing maps depicting incorrect boundaries of India, precious stones, gold, silver and chemicals and chemical products are not permitted to be brought through couriers. However, life-saving drugs are permitted.

- An 'authorised courier' must be registered with the Commissioner of Customs. His financial viability should be authenticated by a certificate from a bank. He has to execute a bond and furnish security to the Commissioner of Customs. Failure to comply with regulations or misconduct can lead to the cancellation of the courier's registration.

- An 'authorised courier' should diligently advise his clients about the provisions of the Customs Act and should disclose all information to the Assessing Officer in connection with the imported goods. It is important he maintain proper records.
- It is not essential that goods must be carried by the on-board courier himself. The person-in-charge of aircraft or authorised agent of courier service may also carry the consignment.
- The courier bags are stored separately and shall be dealt with only as per directions of the Commissioner of Customs.
- Goods like documents, free samples and free gifts up to a prescribed value limit, duty or commercial goods can be sent through courier. These should be packed separately with appropriate labels. These goods must be accompanied by a declaration by sender in respect of contents of the package and its value.
- Free gifts and samples up to ₹ 10,000 (exclusive of freight and insurance) can be imported per consignment.
- Import of gem and jewellery of EOU/SEZ and export of cut and polished diamond, gems and jewellery is permitted if value of each consignment does not exceed ₹ 25 lakhs.
- The authorised courier has to submit declaration in the prescribed form. He will present all the imported goods brought by the on-board courier or the person-in-charge of aircraft to the customs officer. The goods will be disposed of if the goods are not cleared within 30 days.
- The authorised courier also has to file a 'Courier Bill of Entry' in the prescribed form.

(F) Exemption from Duty

Some exemptions from duties are provided in the Customs Act, while some are provided in the Customs Tariff Act. Besides, under Section 25, the Central Government can grant partial or full exemption from duty. These exemptions are summarised below.

- **Exemptions by Notification:** Section 25 (1) of Customs Act, 1962 authorises the Central Government to issue notifications granting exemptions from duty. Exemptions may be unconditional or subject to conditions. Such conditions may be required to be fulfilled before or after clearance. The government can also grant exemption by a special order in exceptional circumstances. The exemption notification is issued only in 'public interest' and should be published in the gazette.

- **Imports by Privileged Persons and Organisations:** Import by UN agencies, Governors, Ford Foundation, Vice President of India, specified equipment by foreign news agency, personal effects of deceased persons, gifts imported by CARE have been granted various exemptions.

- Foreign Privileged Persons (Regulation of Customs Privileges) Rules, 1957 make provisions for privileges to specified foreign privileged persons like the High Commissioner, Ambassador, and Consul General etc. Goods for official or personal use are allowed duty free on producing an exemption certificate in the prescribed form signed by the Head of Diplomatic Mission. Goods, generally, are not checked, but can be if there is suspicion. Cars can be imported and sold to another privileged person. These cars can also be sold to non-privileged persons after payment of customs duty, subject to certain restrictions. The car can also be sold duty free after four years of import. If the car is totally damaged in an accident or stolen, the amount of insurance claim will be treated a 'scum-duty' price and duty so calculated will be payable.

- **Import for Repairs, Reconditioning etc.:** Goods can be imported for repairs, reconditioning or re-engineering. These have to be re-exported within three years of imports. After imports, the repairs, reconditioning or re-engineering has to be in a bonded warehouse under customs bond. Moreover, it is not essential that goods must have been manufactured in India.

- **Ad hoc Exemptions:** In exceptional cases, Section 25 (2) of Customs Act permits the Government to issue ad hoc exemption from customs duty. The order should specify the exceptional circumstances for granting ad hoc exemption. Such an exemption can be granted even after the duty is paid which is refundable.

- **Exemption of Imports for Export:** Various schemes like FTZ, 100% EOU, STP, EHTP, Advance Licences etc. have been formed to allow duty free imports of raw materials and components for exports.

Other Methods of Customs Clearance for Imported Goods

1. Green Channel Procedure: This procedure has been introduced in major Custom Houses on an experimental basis to expedite clearance of imported goods. Only certain specified imports are applicable for this procedure and they are:

(a) Goods imported by government departments and public sector undertakings, which do not require physical identification for the purpose of either ITC classification/ restrictions or customs classification.

(b) Imports under Project Import Regulations.

(c) Bulk imports sourced directly from reputed suppliers.

(d) Consignments which consist of a single product of a well-known brand or specification, tested earlier and covered by a valid test report of the earlier import.

(e) Imports by importers with proven identity and unblemished record of past conduct.

The bills of entry under this procedure are processed and assessed for duty under the second appraisement system, that is, assessment and duty collection is done first and then the consignment is examined. In such cases the Assessing Officer indicates on the reverse of the duplicate bill of entry to the Appraiser in charge of examination to 'inspect the lot and check marks and numbers on the packages'. After inspection of the lot and marks and numbers of the packages with reference to the declaration in the bill of entry and other connected documents, the Docks Appraiser gives 'Passed out of Customs' order. The Docks Appraiser, in the presence of the Assistant Commissioner may examine the goods in exceptional cases. Any discrepancy on examination with regard to description, quantity, weight, declaration made with regard to value, etc. will bar the importer from utilising this scheme in future. The facility of 'green channel' clearance is not extended in cases of goods sought to be cleared under the 'self assessment' procedure.

2. Self Assessment Procedure: The Government of India introduced the procedure of 'Self Assessment' of bills of entry in major Custom Houses to simplify import procedures and expedite clearances. In this procedure the importers of repetitive imports can assess their own bills of entry by producing previous clearances and assessment of the same goods. The bill of entry under this procedure will have a 'green coloured band' at the edges to distinguish it from other bills of entry. Such bills of entry after self-assessment are presented to the noting clerk in the Custom House who assigns a serial number and affixes the date stamp with initials. The amount of duty payable is mentioned on the bill of entry. Thereafter, the importers/their agents should pay the duty in the Customs Treasury (Cash Section). After collecting duty the cash section detaches the original copy of bill of entry and the remaining copies with other documents are sent to the appraiser in charge of examination who will complete the assessment of the bill of entry with reference to the documents submitted along with a copy of bill of entry for the same goods assessed and cleared earlier. The goods are then examined as usual and clearance is allowed if the goods are found to agree with the declaration.

Such bills of entry are subjected to the post clearance audit. This 'self assessment' procedure is now extended only in the major Custom Houses in respect of the following cases.

(i)   Imports made by (a) Government departments (b) Public sector undertakings and other importers with proven identity and unblemished record of past conduct.

(ii) Import license/customs clearance permit are not required for the goods in question nor are they subject to any restriction/prohibition.

(iii) Acceptance of bond including test bond and end use bond is not essential for the assessment and release of goods.

(iv) Original examination of the goods in question is also not required.

Points to Remember

- Consequent upon a comfortable balance of payment position of the country, increasing necessity of imports for export production and globalisation of the Indian economy, the government of India has liberalised the import regime from time to time and practically all controls on imports have been lifted.

- In the initial years of planning the main emphasis was on "export promotion and import substitution". After the process of globalisation and liberalisation, the Government of India followed a Free Trade policy. India has opened its economy by liberalising the import-export regime. This implies the conversion of quantitative restrictions to low and uniform tariffs and the use of the exchange rate for bringing balance of payment equilibrium.

- The EXIM policy and Foreign Trade Policy shifted the focus to the export market. It was also necessary to simplify the tariff system and reduce the administrative forms of intervention substantially.

- The exporters are eligible for various benefits under different laws governing the exports from and imports into India. Duty drawback is the most sought after and popular benefit with the exporting community.

- The Directorate General of Foreign Trade (DGFT), a government organisation, that also controls the export business in India, takes care of all the activities associated with imports and exports.

- There are various documents required for imports.

- All goods imported into India have to pass through the procedure of customs for proper examination, appraisal, assessment, and evaluation. This helps the customs authorities to charge the proper tax and check the goods against illegal imports. Also it is important to note that no import is allowed in India if the importer doesn't have the IEC number issued by the DGFT.

- The most common methods of payment are as follows –
    a. Consignment purchase
    b. Cash in advance (pre-payment)
    c. Down payment
    d. Open account
    e. Documentary collections
    f. Letters of credit

- The Customs Act, 1962 permits the facility of warehousing of imported goods in Customs Bonded Warehouses, without payment of customs duty otherwise leviable on import.

- The Central Board of Excise and Customs declares the appointment and licensing of warehouses at specific places only. The Board has delegated its power for declaring places to be warehousing stations to the Chief Commissioners of Customs.

- In respect of Public Bonded Warehouses, other than the Central Warehousing Corporation and the State Warehousing Corporations, private operators can also be appointed as custodians.

- In case of private bonded warehouses, the applications for such licences have been classified into two categories, namely, storage of sensitive goods such as liquor, cigarettes, foodstuffs, consumables, etc. and other non-sensitive goods.

- Where the bonding facility is desired on importation, the importer or his representative is required to present to the Customs a Warehousing Bill of Entry (also known as Into Bond Bill of Entry) in the prescribed form along with the relevant documents required. The duties liable are assessed but not required to be paid.

- A bonded warehouse may store deposited goods up to a period of one year. In the case of capital goods intended for use in any 100% EOU, such goods can however be stored up to a period of five years. Extension of the warehousing period is undertaken by the Commissioner of Customs for a period of six months and by the Chief Commissioner of Customs for such further period as is deemed fit by him. The importers should file their applications for extensions well before the expiry of the initial/extended period of warehousing.

- There are various acts relating to procedure for importing.

- In his budget speech on 28-2-2003, the Finance Minister had announced a 'self assessment scheme' for importers and exporters. As per this scheme, the importer will himself determine classification of goods including claim for exemption benefits on a computer system that will calculate the duty based on his declaration.

- Import of software through data communication/tele-communication is allowed. However, proper accounting in books should be done since such imports are not available for physical verification.

Questions for Discussion

1. What are the legal dimensions of the import procedure? Explain.
2. Explain the customs clearance procedure for imported goods.
3. "Payment procedure in international business is much different than domestic trade". Comment on this statement.
4. Discuss the customs clearance procedure for imported cargo in India.
5. What is the procedure for importing goods with relevant provisions under various acts in India?
6. Write short notes on:
   (a) Bill of Entry
   (b) Letter of Credit
   (c) Concept of warehousing
   (d) Accelerated Clearance of Imports and Exports Scheme (ACS)
   (e) Import of Software through Data Communication
7. Discuss the various documents required for imports.
8. Discuss the common methods of payment procedure.
9. Discuss the methods of Customs Clearance for imported goods.

Export Procedure

Contents ...

Learning Objectives ...

- To study the basic documentation for export
- To understand the excise clearance for export
- To learn the pre-shipment inspection of product quality
- To explain the concepts of packaging, marketing, labelling
- To elaborate the process of shipment of goods
- To study the rules and origin of GSP [Generalised System of preferences]
- To understand the role of overseas agent and remittance of commission
- To learn the various incentives for export from government
- To explain the various modes of transport

3.1 Introduction

Export procedure consists of several commercial and regulatory formalities, which an exporter is required to complete during the course of export trade transactions. These formalities are very time consuming, complex and involve considerable documentation.

Any export shipment involves a number of documents required mainly by the Customs/Port authorities. Mostly, the format of these documents is common in the majority of cases, but may differ in respect to documents used at different ports. While trading in domestic markets the issue of documents does not concern the parties, as the only documents required are those relevant to the nature of the transaction and usually only entail documents are required by the buyer. International trade, however, extends the demand for documents to a range of aspects related to the transaction. International transactions engage activities not encountered in domestic trade, and these activities place their own demands on documentary requirements and content.

It is, however, important that exporters are fully familiar with the export documentations and procedures so that unnecessary delay in getting the goods cleared from the ports can be avoided and the goods can be delivered as per the time schedule. Export documentation work constitutes a heavy charge on any export activity. It is complex, cumbersome and costly. This is partly due to the nature of export trade itself, involving as it does a number of intermediary organisations and authorities at different stages of export activity between the seller and the buyer. All these, in turn, generate a lot of paperwork and procedural formalities. The documents that are to be submitted to an export sales contract are not many in number. However, the problem is complicated due to the heavy paperwork and the procedural formalities that are required to be complied with before the essential documents can be procured.

3.2 Basic Documentation

Documentation is one of the most important aspects of overseas trade. Correct documentation is very important because it alone can secure the swift passage of goods resulting in prompt payment of goods exported.

The exporter has to prepare and submit various documents at different stages of sending the shipment of goods to the importer once the goods are ready. These documents are important for two reasons –

1. As an evidence of shipment and title of goods.

2. For obtaining payments.

Hence, the various documents are of vital interest to the exporter and the bank which is the usual means of payment. The documentary requirements are different for different types of products. Moreover, the documents are both regulatory and operational in nature and have to comply with the rules and regulations of the Indian government as well as the importing country. The documents required for the product concerned are to be known by the buyers when exporting for the first time.

Documents pertaining to export shipments have to be accurate and complete in all respects. Regardless of whether two or twenty copies of the invoice are required by the buyer, the same should be supplied as the buyer probably has some reasons for it. Even minor discrepancies either in the date itself or in the typing in the documents, though looking harmless may create serious complications. Erasures, overwritten text, changes or additions made in ink are likely to arouse suspicion that the documents have been tampered with. All alterations or additions made by an authority issuing the documents must be endorsed properly, with the signatures of the person issuing the documents only. Incorrect documents can result in the importer not being able to get the goods when the ship carrying the docks at the port. It is to be remembered that both the requirements and penalties are greater in export than in domestic trade.

The main purpose of the documents accompanying a shipment is to provide a specific and complete description of the goods so that they can be assessed correctly for duty purpose and meet the Import Licensing requirements or Import Quota Restrictions imposed on the goods for clearance purpose. If there are any discrepancies in the documents and/or if the required documents are not produced, the shipment may not be allowed for import or may even be confiscated by the Customs of the importing country. There is a plethora of documents in the export trade – different forms, applications and documents are required to be filled in for obtaining export licences, completing pre-shipment Inspection, for customs clearance and shipping, for obtaining payment and export finance and for claiming export benefits like duty drawback, etc.

The experienced exporter, because of the complexity of documentation, will find it a good idea to have the various documents prepared for him by a Shipping and Forwarding Agent or should take advice from a fellow exporter. The exporter should also develop a habit of thoroughly scrutinising the documents for any possible errors or discrepancies and if any errors or discrepancies are found, must rectify them immediately before dispatching them to the bank of the buyer.

The major documents that any exporter must be familiar with include the following:

✓ Bill of Lading
✓ Export Licence
✓ Customs Entry Form
✓ Commercial Invoice
✓ Customs Invoice
✓ Legalised Invoice
✓ Consular Invoice
✓ Bill of Exchange
✓ Certificate of Origin and GSP Certificate
✓ Certificate of Value
✓ Certificate of Inspection
✓ Packing List
✓ Weight Note
✓ Manufacturer's Quality Inspection
✓ Certificate of Insurance
✓ Shipping Advice
✓ Antiquity Certificate
✓ Certificate of Export
✓ Shipping Bill
✓ Lorry Ticket

Not all the above documents are required by all countries and not for all goods. The exporter must find out which ones are necessary in each case.

3.2.1 Aligned Documentation System

Aligned Documentation System (ADS) is based on the UN layout key. Under this system, different forms used in the international trade transactions are printed on the paper of the same size and in such a way that the common items of information are given relative slots in each of the documents. The ADS methodology involves the preparation of documents on a uniform and standard A4 size paper. The documents are aligned to one another in such a way that, the common items of information are given the same relative slots in each of the documents included in the System. This makes it possible to prepare one Master document embodying the information common to all the documents included in the aligned series and to run off all the aligned documents from the same Master document with the help of suitable marking reproduction techniques. The pre-shipment documents on a standard layout were first introduced by Sweden in 1956 followed by Denmark, Finland and Norway. It was later that most of the European countries and the USA, Australia, etc., have adopted this ADS system.

Advantages

The ADS system offers the following advantages –

1. Dispenses with the conventional documentation practices.
2. Brings in uniformity in documentation.
3. Ensures economy, speed, accuracy and convenience.
4. Facilitates expeditious checking and processing of documents at different stages.
5. Generates as many copies as required of commercial and regulatory documents from their respective master copies through photocopying machines.

For the purpose of an Aligned Documentation System documents have been classified as under.

(a) Commercial Documents: Commercial documents are required for effecting physical transfer of goods and their title from the exporter to the importer and the realisation of export sale proceeds. Out of the 16 commercial documents in the export documentation framework, as many as 14 have been standardised and aligned to one another. These are performance invoice, commercial invoice, packing list, shipping instructions, intimation for inspection, certificate of inspection of quality control, insurance declaration, certificate of insurance, mate's receipt, bill of lading or combined transport document, application for certificate of origin, certificate of origin, shipment advice and letter to the bank for collection or negotiation.

However, shipping order and bill of exchange could not be brought within the fold of the Aligned Documentation System.

The following are the 16 Commercial documents generally involved at the pre-shipment stage:

1. Proforma Invoice
2. Commercial Invoice

3. Packing List
4. Shipping Instruction
5. Intimation of Inspection
6. Certificate of Inspection
7. Insurance Declaration
8. Certificate of Insurance
9. Shipping Order
10. Mate's Receipt
11. Bill of Lading/Combined Transport Document
12. Application for Certificate of Origin
13. Certificate of Origin
14. Bill of Exchange
15. Shipment Advice
16. Letter to the Bank for Collection/Negotiation of Documents

(b) Regulatory Documents: Regulatory pre-shipment export documents are prescribed by the different government departments and bodies in order to comply with various rules and regulations under the relevant laws governing export trade such as export inspection, foreign exchange regulation, export trade control, customs, etc. Out of 9 regulatory documents four have been standardised and aligned. These are shipping bill or bill of export, exchange control declaration (GR form), export application dock challan or port trust copy of shipping bill and receipt for payment of port charges.

The regulatory documents associated with the pre-shipment stage of an export transaction are given below –

1. Gate Pass-I/Gate Pass-II (now deleted)
2. AR-4 Form
3. Shipping Bill/Bill of Export
4. Export Application/Dock Challan/Port Trust Copy of Shipping Bill
5. Receipt for Payment of Port charges
6. Vehicle Chit
7. Exchange Control Declaration (GRIPP) Forms
8. Freight Payment Certificate
9. Insurance Premium Payment Certificate

Out of the above 9 regulatory documents, four have been standardised. In fact, these four documents have been reduced to only three. The receipt for payment of port charges has been incorporated in the Export Application/Dock Challan/Port Trust Copy of Shipping Bill, thus one document has been completely eliminated.

3.2.2 Functions of Export Documentation

Documentation is used to keep shipment and delivery on schedule, to describe cargo, for customs clearance, to indicate the ownership of goods for collection purposes or in the event of dispute, and to obtain payment.

Export documentation may serve any or all of the following functions:

(a) An attestation of facts, such as a certificate of origin.

(b) Evidence of the terms and conditions of a contract of carriage, such as in the case of an airway bill.

(c) Evidence of ownership or title to goods, such as in the case of a Bill of Lading.

(d) A promissory note that is, a promise to pay.

(e) A demand for payment, as with a bill of exchange.

(f) A declaration of liability, such as with a customs bill of entry.

(g) A receipt for goods received.

3.2.3 Need for Preparing Export Documents

Export documents have to be prepared for various purposes, namely –

(a) Declaration of exports as per exchange control regulations of the country.

(b) Transportation of the goods.

(c) Customs clearance of the goods.

(d) Other purposes.

Some of the forms for preparing documents have been standardised under the Aligned Documentation System introduced with effect from 1st October 1991.

3.2.4 Documents for Declaration of Goods under Foreign Exchange Regulations

The Statutory Regulation: Notification No. F1/67/EC/73-1 dated 1st January, 1974, as amended, deals with export otherwise than by post and prohibits the export of all the goods either directly or indirectly to any place outside India, other than Bhutan and Nepal, unless the exporter furnishes a declaration in the prescribed form and affirms in the said declaration that the full export values of the goods has been or will be paid in the prescribed period and manner.

Declaration Forms: There are four main declaration forms which are prescribed. These are called GR, PP, and SOFTEX Forms.

GR/PP/SOFTEX PROCEDURE

As per the exchange control regulations, exporters are required to submit the following declaration forms to the prescribed authority before any export of goods from India is made.

(a) Exchange Control Declaration (GR Form): Exports to all countries made otherwise than by post.

(b) Form SDF (Statutory Declaration Form): Used for declaring exports in the case of specified customs offices and specified categories of shipping bills under EDI System.

(c) PP Form: Exports to all countries by parcel post, except when made on 'Value Payable' or 'Cash on Delivery' basis.

(d) Form SOFTEX: Used for declaring software exports through date communication links and receipt of royalty on the software package/products exported.

Export declaration forms have utmost importance and are binding on the exporter. It is therefore necessary, that enough care is taken while declaring exports on these forms with special reference to the following points –

(i)   Name and address of authorised dealer through whom proceeds of exports have been or will be realised should be specified in the relevant column of the form.

(ii)   Details of commission and discount due to foreign agent or buyer should be correctly declared otherwise difficulties may arise at the time of remittance of such commission.

(iii) It should be clearly indicated in the form whether the export is on 'outright sale basis' or 'on consignment basis' and irrelevant clauses must be struck out.

(iv)   Under the item 'analysis of full export value', a breakup of the full export value of goods under FOB value, freight and insurance should be furnished in all cases, irrespective of the terms of the contract.

- GR Form is an exchange control document required by the Reserve Bank of India (RBI). As per the exchange control regulations, an exporter has to realise the proceeds of the goods, he has exported within 180 days of their shipment from India. In order to ensure this, the RBI has introduced the GR procedure.

- GR form is to be submitted in duplicate to the Customs at the port of shipment along with the shipping bill. Customs will give their running serial number on both the copies after admitting the customs shipping bill. Customs authorities will certify the value declared by the exporter on both the copies of the GR form at the space earmarked and will also record the assessed value. They will then return the duplicate copy of the form to the exporter and retain the original for transmission to the RBI.

- Within 21 days from the shipment of goods, the exporter must lodge the duplicate copy of GR together with relative shipping documents with the authorised dealer named in the GR form for negotiation of export bills.

- After the documents have been negotiated, the authorised dealer will report the transaction to the RBI. The duplicate copy of GR form together with a copy of invoice will be retained by the authorised dealer till full export proceeds have been realised and thereafter submitted to the RBI.

- On account of introduction of the Electronic Data Interchange (EDI) system at certain customs offices where shipping bills are processed electronically, the existing declaration in the GR form has been replaced by a declaration in Form SDF (Statutory Declaration Form).

Copies of export declaration forms should be disposed of as under –

(a) The GR forms are to be completed in duplicate and both the copies are to be submitted to the Customs at the port of shipment along with the shipping bill. After admitting the corresponding shipping bill, Customs will give their running serial number on both the copies. This serial number will have ten numerals denoting the code number of the port of shipment, the calendar year and a six-digit running serial number. The value declared by the exporter on both the copies of the GR form will be certified by Customs at the space earmarked and the assessed value will also be given. The duplicate copy of the form is returned to the exporter and the original will be retained for handing over to the Reserve Bank. The duplicate copy of the GR form is again submitted to Customs by the exporters along with the cargo to be shipped. After examination of the goods and certifying the quantity passed for shipment on the duplicate copy, it is returned by the Customs to the exporter for submission to the Authorised Dealer for negotiation or collection of export bills.

(b) The exporter should lodge the duplicate copy together with relative shipping documents and an extra copy of the invoice with the Authorised Dealer named in the GR form within twenty-one days from the date of export,. After the documents have been sent for collection, the Authorised Dealer should report the transaction to the Reserve Bank in statement ENC under cover of the appropriate R-Supplementary Return. However, the duplicate copy of the form together with a copy of invoice etc. will henceforth be retained by the Authorised Dealer and may not be submitted to the Reserve Bank.

3.2.5 Documents for Transportation of Goods

Transport documents are distinguished from the commercial documents in which they represent a contract of carriage with a third party. Transport documents are fundamental to the payment and delivery process in an import transaction.

The purpose of all transport documents is to:

- Provide proof that the carrier has received the goods
- Show evidence of a contract of carriage, and
- Produce a freight bill (information on transport details and costs)

There are certain main types of transport documents that can be used in international transport. They are –

1. Bill of Lading
2. Airway Bill/Air Consignment Note
3. Mate's Receipt
4. Consignment Note

1. Bill of Lading (B/L)

The Bill of Lading (B/L) is the traditional transport document for shipping goods by ocean transport.

- It serves as a contract between the exporter and the shipping line and covers the carriage of goods from the port of loading to the port of discharge.
- It also serves as a receipt for the goods and confers title to the goods to its holder.
- Also called a negotiable Bill of Lading, it is sent to the importer to enable him/her to claim the goods to which it refers.
- Bill of Lading is issued by the shipping company or its agents stating that goods are either being shipped or have been shipped. Essentially, a transport document it serves many purposes in international commerce.
- The Bill of Lading is a document issued by the shipping company or its agent acknowledging the receipt of goods on board the vessel, and undertaking to deliver the goods in the like order and condition as received, to the consignee or his order, provided the freight and other charges as specified in the bill have been duly paid.
- It is also a document of title to the goods and, as such, is freely transferable by endorsement and delivery.
- A Bill of Lading serves three main purposes:

(i) This document evidences the contract of affreightment (transport) between the shipping company and the shipper (exporter or importer).

(ii) It is a receipt given by the shipping company for cargo received by it.

(iii) It is a document of title (the most significant function of the Bill of Lading).

- From the legal point of view, a Bill of Lading is:

(i) A formal receipt by the ship-owner or the master of the ship acknowledging that the goods of the stated specifications, quantity and condition in a ship or at least received in the custody of the ship-owner for the purpose of shipment.

(ii) A memorandum of the contract of carriage, repeating in detail, the terms of the contract which was in fact concluded prior to the signing of the bill.

(iii) A document of title of the goods enables the consignee to dispose the goods by endorsement and delivery of the Bill of Lading.

- Bill of Lading is a receipt issued by the shipping company on its agents. Law requires that as a receipt, it must contain leading identification marks, number of packages or quantity or weight or any other unit of account, and apparent order and condition of the goods.

- Bill of Lading is the only evidence to file a claim against the shipping company in the event of non-delivery, defective delivery or short-delivery of the cargo at the destination. As a result, this document indicates that the contracted goods have been either given into the charge of the shipping companies or shipped by the exporter by the named ship on the date specified on the Bill of Lading. If shipment is according to the contract terms, the exporter gets the right to demand the sale amount from the importer while the importer is entitled to get delivery of the goods at the destination.

For the Bill of Lading to be negotiable in fact three requirements must be fulfilled –

(1) It must be made out to the order to the shipper.

(2) It must be signed by the steamship company.

(3) It must be endorsed in blank by the shipper.

Other documents are usually attached to the carrier's copy of the Bill of Lading, some of which are –

- Copy of the Commercial Invoice
- Copy of the Certificate of Origin
- Packing List
- Weight List
- Certifications from the exporting country if any
- Prior entry authorisations in the importing country if any

Main Types of Bill Of Lading

(a) **Clean Bill of Lading:** A Bill of Lading acknowledging receipt of the goods apparently in good order and condition and without any qualification is termed as a clean Bill of Lading.

(b) **Claused Bill of Lading:** A Bill of Lading qualified with certain adverse remarks such as, "goods insufficiently packed in accordance with the Carriage of Goods by Sea Act," is termed as a Claused Bill of Lading.

(c) **Through Bill of Lading:** It covers goods being transhipped en route but where the first carrier has the responsibility as the principal carrier for all stages of the journey. For example, goods may be shipped from Mumbai to Dubai and transhipped from Dubai to a port in Latin America.

(d) **Trans-shipment Bill of Lading:** It has similar characteristics as the Through Bill of Lading (B/L) except that in this case the first carrier acts only as an agent for effecting trans-shipment of cargo.

(e) **Stale Bill of Lading:** A Bill of Lading that has been held too long before it is passed on to a bank for negotiation or to the consignee is called a Stale Bill of Lading.

(f) **Freight Paid Bill of Lading:** When freight is paid at the time of shipment or in advance, the Bill of Lading is marked, Freight Paid. Such a Bill of Lading is known as Freight Bill of Lading.

(q) Freight Collect Bill of Lading: When the freight is not paid and is to be collected from the consignee on the arrival of the goods, the Bill of Lading is marked, freight collected and is known as Freight Collect Bill of Lading.

Example: An exporter sent off his goods but forgot to send the Bill of Lading to the customer. Without this document the customer was unable to obtain the goods at the port of destination, so the goods had to be stored at the docks until the bill arrived. The customer sent the storage charges to the exporter, maintaining that because of the exporter's fault, the charges had been incurred. He sued the exporter for the costs of the storage, and won the case.

Contents of Bill of Lading

    (a) Name and logo of the shipping line.

    (b) Name and address of the shipper.

    (c) Name and the number of the vessel.

    (d) Name of the port of loading.

    (e) Name of the port of discharge and place of delivery.

    (f) Marks and container number.

    (g) Packing and container description.

    (h) Total number of containers and packages.

    (i) Description of goods in terms of quantity.

    (j) Container status and seal number.

    (k) Gross weight in kilograms; volume in terms of cubic metres.

    (1) Amount of freight paid or payable.

    (m) Shipping bill number and date.

    (n) Signature and initials of the Chief Officer.

Sending of Bill of Lading to Importer

B/Ls are made out in sets and any number of copies may constitute the set according to the requirements of the particular transaction and the importer. The number of copies to be made out will be indicated by the importer before the shipment takes place. In case there is no such indication, normally, two copies are made. One set of documents is sent by first class airmail and the second by the following mail, so that if one is lost, delivery of the goods can be taken by the importer because of the second set.

Significance of Bill of Lading for Exporters

    (a) The Bill of Lading is a contract between the shipper and the shipping company for the carriage of goods to the port of destination.

(b) The Bill of Lading indicates that the goods mentioned in the document have been received on board for the purpose of shipment.

(c) Certification that the goods are in order and good condition is assured by a Clean Bill of Lading.

(d) Incentives offered by the government to exporters can be claimed.

(e) In the event goods are lost or damaged, the exporter can claim damages from the shipping company after the issue of a Clean Bill of Lading.

Significance of Bill of Lading for Importers

(a) It acts as a title to goods, that is transferable by endorsement and delivery.

(b) The Bill of Lading is sent by the exporter to the bank of the importer so as to enable him to take the delivery of goods.

(c) An advance intimation to the importer about the shipment of goods is provided by the exporter by sending him a non-negotiable copy of the Bill of Lading.

Significance of Bill Of Lading for Shipping Company

(a) It is useful to the shipping company for collection of transport charges from the importer if not collected from the exporter.

2. Airway Bill/Air Consignment Note

Airway Bill or Air Consignment Note is the receipt issued by the airline company for the carriage of goods, in terms of the conditions of the contract of carriage of goods. An Airway Bill or Air Consignment Note is not treated as a document of title and is not issued in negotiable form.

Contents of Airway Bill

The contents of an Airway Bill are as follows.

(a) Name of the airport of departure and destination.

(b) The names and addresses of the consignor, consignee and the first carrier.

(c) Marks and container number.

(d) Packing and container description.

(e) Total number of containers and packages.

(f) Description of goods in terms of quantity.

(g) Container status and seal number.

(h) Amount of freight paid or payable.

(i) Signature and initials of the issuing carrier or his agent.

Importance of Airway Bill

(a) It is a contract between the airlines or his agent to carry goods to the destination.

(b) It is the document of instructions for the airline handling staff.

(c) It acts as a customs declaration form.

(d) Since, it contains details about freight it also represents freight bill.

3. Mate's Receipt

Mate's Receipt is issued by the Chief of Vessel after the cargo is loaded and it contains the name of the shipping line, vessel, port of loading, port of discharge, place of delivery, marks and numbers, number and kind of packages, description of goods, container status/ seal number, gross weight, condition of cargo at the time of its receipt on board the vessel and shipping bill number and date. The mate's receipt is of a transferable nature and must be presented immediately at the shipping company's office to be exchanged for a Bill of Lading. The Mate's Receipt is *prima facie* evidence that the goods are loaded in the vessel. The mate's receipt is first handed over to the Port Trust Authorities. After making payment of all port dues, the exporter or his agent collects the mate's receipt from the Port Trust Authorities. The mate's receipt is freely transferable. It must be handed over to the shipping company in order to get the Bill of Lading. Bill of Lading is prepared on the basis of the mate's receipt.

Types of Mate's Receipts

(a) **Clean Mate's Receipt:** The commanding officer of the ship issues a Clean Mate's Receipt, if he is satisfied that the goods are packed properly and there is no defect in the packing of the cargo or package.

(b) **Qualified Mate's Receipt:** The commanding officer of the ship issues a Qualified Mate's Receipt, when the goods are not packed properly and the shipping company does not take any responsibility of damage to the goods during transit.

Contents of Mate's Receipt

(a) Name and logo of the shipping line.

(b) Name and address of the shipper.

(c) Name and number of the vessel.

(d) Name of the port of loading.

(e) Name of the port of discharge and place of delivery.

(f) Marks and container number.

(g) Packing and container description.

(h) Total number of containers and packages.

(i) Description of goods in terms of quantity.

(j) Container status and seal number.

(k) Gross weight in kilograms and volume in terms of cubic meters.

(l) Shipping bill number and date.

(m) Signature and initials of the Chief Officer.

Significance of Mate's Receipt

(a)   It is an acknowledgement of goods received for export on board the ship.

(b)   It is a transferable document. It must be handed over to the shipping company in order to get the Bill of Lading.

(c)   Bill of Lading, which is the title of goods, is prepared on the basis of the mate's receipt.

(d)   It enables the exporter to clear port trust dues to the Port Trust Authorities.

Distinction between Mate's Receipt and Bill of Lading

Mate's Receipt	Bill of Lading
1. Meaning: Mate's Receipt is a receipt by the Commanding Officer of the ship when the cargo is loaded on the ship.	Bill of Lading is the official document issued by the shipping company acknowledging the receipt of goods on board the vessel.
2. Purpose: It is issued in order to enable the exporter or his agent to secure a Bill of Lading from the shipping company.	It is issued in order to enable the importer to take the delivery of goods at the port of destination.
3. Evidence: It is an evidence of goods having been loaded on board the ship.	It is a contract between the shipper and the shipping company for the carriage of goods from the port of loading to the port of destination.

4.   Types: It is of two types –
• Clean Mate's receipt
• Qualified Mate's receipt
	It is of several types –
	  • Clean and Claused Bill of Lading
	  • Transhipment Bill of Lading
	  • Stale Bill of Lading
	  • Freight Paid & Collect Bill of Lading

5. Details of Freight: It does not specify whether the freight is paid on goods or not.	It does specify whether Bill of Lading of freight is paid or not.
6. Issuing Authority: It is issued by the Commanding Officer of the ship or his mate.	It is issued by the shipping company or its agent.
7. Title of Goods: It is not a title of goods.	It is a document of title of goods.
8. Negotiability: It is not a negotiable document.	It is a negotiable instrument.
9. Sequence: It is prepared before the Bill of Lading.	It is prepared on the basis of the Mate's Receipt.

4. Consignment Note

It is a document prepared by a consignor and countersigned by the carrier as a proof of receipt of consignment for delivery at the destination. Used as an alternative to Bill of Lading (especially in inland transport), it is generally neither a contract of carriage nor a negotiable instrument.

3.2.6 Documents for Custom Clearance of Goods

In India, customs clearance is a complex and time consuming procedure that every exporter faces in his export business. Physical control is still the basis of customs clearance in India, where each consignment is manually examined in order to impose various types of export duties. High import tariffs and multiplicity of exemptions and export promotion schemes also contribute in complicating the documentation and procedures. So, a proper knowledge of the customs rules and regulation becomes important for the exporter.

Shipping Bill/Bill of Export: Shipping Bill/Bill of Export is the main document required by the Customs authority for allowing shipment. A shipping bill is issued by the shipping agent and represents some kind of certificate for all parties, included ship's owner, seller, buyer and some other parties, for each one represents a kind of certificate document.

Shipping Bill/Bill of Export is the main document required by the Customs authority for allowing shipment. A Shipping bill is normally prepared in five copies:

(a) Customs copy   (b) Drawback copy

(c) Export promotion copy   (d) Port trust copy

(e) Exporter's copy

Free Shipping Bill is used for export of goods which neither attracts any duty/cess nor is entitled to duty drawback on their exportation. Dutiable Shipping Bill is used in case of goods subject to export duty/cess but might or may not be entitled to duty drawback. Drawback Shipping Bill or Bill of Exports is used in the case of goods which are entitled to drawback. Shipping Bill for Shipment Ex-bond is for use in case of imported goods for re-exports and which are kept in bond.

The following documents are required for the processing of a Shipping Bill –

(a) GR Forms in duplicate for shipments to all countries.

(b) Four copies of packing list giving contents, quantity, gross and net weight of each package.

(c) Four copies of invoices indicating all relevant particulars such as number of packages, quantity, unit rate, total FOB/CIF value, correct and full description of goods, etc. (One copy of this invoice is to be pasted on the duplicate copy of Shipping Bill).

(d)   Contract, Letter of Credit, Purchase Order.

(e)   Inspection/Examination Certificate.

The formats presented for the Shipping Bill are as given below –

1.   White Shipping Bill in triplicate for export of duty-free of goods.

2.   Green Shipping Bill in quadruplicate for the export of goods which are under claim for duty drawback.

3.   Yellow Shipping Bill in triplicate for the export of dutiable goods.

4.   Blue Shipping Bill in 7 copies for exports under the DEPB scheme.

Types of Shipping Bill

Based on the incentives offered by the government, customs authorities have introduced three types of shipping bills:

(a)   **Drawback Shipping Bill:** Drawback shipping bill is useful for claiming the customs drawback against goods exported.

(b)   **Dutiable Shipping Bill:** Dutiable shipping bill is required for goods which are subject to export duty.

(c)   **Duty-free Shipping Bill:** Duty-free shipping bill is useful for exporting the goods on which there is no export duty.

In order to facilitate easy recognition and quick processing, the following colours have been provided to different kinds of shipping bills.

Types of goods	By Sea	By Air
Drawback Shipping Bill	Green	Green
Dutiable Shipping Bill	Yellow	Pink
Duty-free Shipping Bill	White	Pink

Contents of Shipping Bill

The various contents of a shipping bill are as follows –

(a)   Name and address of the exporter.

(b)   Name and address of the importer.

(c)   Name of the vessel, master or agents and flag.

(d)   Name of the port at which goods are to be discharged.

(e)   Country of final destination.

(f)   Details about packages, description of goods, marks and numbers, quantity and details of each case.

(g)   FOB price and real value of goods as defined in the Sea Customs Act.

(h)   Whether Indian or foreign merchandise to be re-exported.

(i)   Total number of packages with total weight and value.

Significance of Shipping Bill

(a)   Shipping bill is the main customs document, required by the customs authorities for granting permission for the shipment of goods.

(b)   The cargo is moved inside the dock area only after the shipping bill is duly stamped, that is, certified by the customs.

(c)   Duly endorsed shipping bill is also necessary for the collection of export incentives offered by the government.

(d)   It is useful to the Customs Appraiser while determining the actual value of goods exported.

3.2.7 Other Documents

1. Certificate of Origin

A certificate of origin is a formal official statement issued by either a chamber of commerce or industry indicating where the goods were manufactured. The Ministry of Industry and Trade must certify the certificate of origin before an exporter attaches the certificate to the export declaration upon submitting the latter to the Customs.

Types of Certificate of Origin

(a)   **Non-preferential Certificate of Origin:** All countries in general require the Non-preferential certificate of origin for clearance of goods by the importer, on which no preferential tariff is given. It is issued by –

- The authorised Chamber of Commerce of the exporting country.
- Trade Association of the exporting country.

(b)   **Certificate of Origin for availing Concessions under GSP:**   For availing of concessions under the Generalised System of Preferences (GSP) extended by certain countries such as France, Germany, Italy, BENELUX countries, UK, Australia, Japan, USA, etc. a certificate of origin is required. This can be obtained from specialised agencies, namely –

- Export Inspection Agencies.
- Director General of Foreign Trade.
- Commodity Boards and their regional offices.
- Development Commissioner, Handicrafts.
- Textile Committees for textile products.

- Marine Products Export Development Authority for marine products.
- Development Commissioners of EPZs.

(c) Certificate for availing Concessions under Commonwealth Preferences (CWP): Certificate of Origin for the purpose of Commonwealth Preference is also known as 'Combined Certificate of Origin and Value'. Two member countries, Canada and New Zealand of the Commonwealth, require it. For concession under Commonwealth preferences, the certificates or origin have to be submitted in special forms obtainable from the High Commission of the country concerned.

(d) Certificate for availing Concessions under other Systems of Preference: Certificate of origin is also required for tariff concessions under the Global System of Trade Preferences (GSTP), Bangkok Agreement (BA) and SAARC Preferential Trading Arrangement (SAPTA) under which India grants and receives tariff concessions on imports and exports. The Export Inspection Council (EIC) is the sole authority to print blank Certificates of Origin under BA, SAARC and SAPTA which can be issued by such agencies as EPCs, DCs of EPZs, EIC, APEDA, MPEDA, FIEO, etc.

Contents of Certificate of Origin

(a) Name and logo of Chamber of Commerce.

(b) Name and address of the exporter.

(c) Name and address of the consignee.

(d) Name and the number of vessel.

(e) Name of the port of loading.

(f) Name of the port of discharge and place of delivery.

(g) Marks and container number.

(h) Packing and container description.

(i) Total number of containers and packages.

(j) Description of goods in terms of quantity.

(k) Signature and initials of the concerned officer of the issuing authority.

(l) Seal of the issuing authority.

Significance of the Certificate of Origin

(a) To avail of concessions under Generalised System of Preferences (GSP) as well as Commonwealth Preferences (CWP) a certificate of origin is essential.

(b) The customs will have to submit this for the assessment of duty and clearance of goods with concessional duty.

(c) Goods produced in a particular country and banned for import in the foreign market will require the certificate of origin.

(d)   It ensures the buyer adheres to the import regulations of the country.

(e)   A certificate of origin is also required sometimes in order to ensure that goods bought from some other country have not been reshipped by a seller.

2. Export Invoice

The invoice is a basic document of content. It's the exporter's bill for goods and sets forth the terms of sale. As a document of contents it must fully identify the overseas shipment and serve as a base for the preparation of all other documents. With regard to invoicing the exporter should strictly follow the requirements of the importer.

The United Nations Key Layout has been accepted as the basis of this document in many entries. By examining a number of forms of invoices used by leading export organisations and after series of discussions with the representatives of the Department of Customs and Central Excise and the Federation of Customs House Agents' Associations in India the information requirements of this document have been determined.

Invoices based on this suggested design will be acceptable in many countries and will also help facilitate processing of documents at various stages. The declaration given at the bottom (left hand) of the invoice is based on the UN recommendation. The standard invoice can be reproduced from the master by masking only three columns, that is, Notify Party, Insured Value and Number of Original B/L Number and Date on the invoices. However, under the present system for customs clearance and shipment of export cargo, this information, particularly in respect of the B/L No. and date, will be available to exporters only after the shipment has been effected. Moreover, banks will be needed for negotiation where such information is required under letter of credit. The rest of the information can be reproduced from the master document.

The information referred to in the preceding lines can be given above the columns for Country of Origin and Final Destination in the order of name of shipping line, ETD (port of shipment), ETA (destination port) and B/L No. and Date. Unused space, in the Buyer's column and below the Consignee's column can be utilised for incorporation of any other information which may be special to a transaction. Value and Origin clauses are printed on the back side of the standard invoice.

In the cases where exports are required to give detailed descriptions or specifications of the various items forming part of the consignment exported in one lot, exporters are advised to use continuation sheets to the invoice.

(A) PROFORMA INVOICE

The starting point of the export contract is in the form of offer made by the exporter to the foreign customer. The offer made by the exporter is in the form of a proforma invoice. It is a quotation given as a reply to an inquiry. It normally forms the basis of all trade transactions.

It is proposed to conduct training and orientation programmes at all export centres to familiarise the exporting community with the new system.

Contents of Proforma Invoice

(a)   Name and address of the exporter.

(b)   Name and address of the importer.

(c)   Mode of transportation, such as sea or air or multimodal transport.

(d)   Name of the port of loading.

(e)   Name of the port of discharge and final destination.

(f)   Provisional invoice number and date.

(g)   Exporter's reference number.

(h)   Buyer's reference number and date.

(i)   Name of the country of origin of goods.

(j)   Name of the country of final destination.

(k)   Marks and container number.

(l)   Number of packing descriptions.

(m)   Description if goods given detailed terms of internationally accepted price quotation.

(n)   Signature of the exporter with date.

Importance of Proforma Invoice

(a)   It forms the basis of all trade transactions.

(b)   It may be useful for the importer in obtaining import licence or foreign exchange.

(B) COMMERCIAL INVOICE

Commercial Invoice is an important and basic export document. It is also known as a Document of Contents as it contains all the information required for the preparation of other documents. It is actually a seller's bill of merchandise. It is prepared by the exporter after the execution of the export order giving details about the goods shipped. It is essential that the invoice is prepared in the name of the buyer or the consignee mentioned in the letter of credit.

This is the first basic and the only complete document among all commercial documents for the shipment. Besides fulfilling the obligation under the export contract, the exporter needs this document for a number of other purposes including –

1.   Obtaining export inspection certificate

2.   Getting excise clearance

3.   Getting customs clearance, and

4.   Securing incentives

Thus, this document is prepared at both the pre-shipment and post-shipment stages.

In the first place, a Commercial Invoice is a document of contents that describes details of goods sent by the exporter. It is the statement of account, which must contain identification marks and numbers, description of goods and quantity of goods.

Functions of the Commercial Invoice

1.   The quantity described on the commercial invoice should neither be less nor more than the contracted quantity. In other words, the exporter should not ship less than the contracted quantity, unless the contract permits part shipment.

2.   The second function of the commercial invoice is that it is the seller's bill given to the buyer. As a bill, it must contain the name and address of the buyer, the unit price, the amount and the authorised signatures with designation. Unless required by the buyer, the total invoiced value should be net of any commission or discount; in other words, it should be the realisable amount of goods as per the trade terms. Sometimes, a contract requires a detailed breakup of the amount to be recorded on the invoice for enabling the customs authority in the importing country to calculate import duty.

3.   The commercial invoice also sets forth the terms of sale, that is, FOB/CIF/C & F etc., mode and date of shipment and terms of payment. It can also serve as a packing list and a certificate of origin. A packing list shows details of goods contained in each pack of shipment. When the law in an importing country does not specifically require a separate certificate of origin issued by a third party, it can be self-certified by the exporter on the commercial invoice. Exporters themselves according to the requirements of their business devise the format of the commercial invoice.

The name and address given in the commercial invoice should be the same as given in the export contract or the letter of credit, as the case may be. Under a letter of credit, unless otherwise specified, the commercial invoice must be made out in the name of the applicant of the credit. As in the case of quantity to be recorded on the invoice, the amount should neither be less nor more than the stipulated amount in the contract or the letter of credit. The only exception is that if the contract or the letter of credit permits part-shipment, an individual invoice can be less than the total amount.

Contents of Commercial Invoice

(a) Name and address of the exporter.

(b) Name and address of the consignee.

(c) Name and the number of vessel or flight.

(d) Name of the port of loading.

(e) Name of the port of discharge and final destination.

(f) Invoice number and date.

(g) Exporter's reference number.

(h) Buyer's reference number and date.

(i) Name of the country of origin of goods.

(j) Name of the country of final destination.

(k) Terms of delivery and payment.

(l) Marks and container number.

(m) Number and packing description.

(n) Description of goods giving details of quantity, rate and total amount in terms of internationally accepted price quotation.

(o) Signature of the exporter with date.

Significance of Commercial Invoice

(a) It is the basic document useful in preparation of various other shipping documents.

(b) It is used in various export formalities such as quality and pre-shipment inspection, excise and customs procedure etc.

(c) It is also useful in negotiation of documents for collection and claim of incentives.

(d) It is useful for accounting purposes to both exporters as well as importers.

3. Bill of Entry

Clearance of imported goods can be made on the strength of the Bill of Entry, a document prepared by the importer or his clearing agent in the prescribed form under Bill of Entry Regulations, 1971.

The Bill of Entry is a document, which states that the goods of the stated values and description in the specified quantity have entered into the country from abroad. This bill of entry is drawn in triplicate. The customs authorities may ask the importer to supply other documents like invoice, broker's note and insurance policy, etc. in order to verify the correctness of the information supplied in the Bill of Entry form.

In the Bill of Entry form, goods are classified into three categories namely –

(i) Bill of Entry for Home Consumption (white in colour): Where an importer wants to get his goods cleared in one lot, he has to present the Bill of Entry for home consumption.

(ii) Bill of Entry for Warehousing 'Into Bond' (yellow in colour): Where an importer wants to shift goods to a warehouse and thereafter gets his goods. Cleared in small lots, he has to present a 'into bond' Bill of Entry. Reason may be that he is unable to pay duty leviable on all goods at one instance or may be because of storage problem.

(iii) Ex-Bond Bill of Entry (green in colour): When an importer wants to remove goods from the warehouse, he has to present an Ex-bond Bill of Entry which is green in colour.

Bill of Entry is not required in the following cases –

(a) Passengers' baggage

(b) Favour parcels

(c) Mail box and post parcels

(d) Boxes, kennels and cargos containing live animals or birds.

(e) Unserviceable stores, for example, dunning wood, empty bottles, drums etc. of reasonable value.

(f) Ship's stores in small quantities for personal use.

(g) Cargo by sailing vessels from customs ports when landed in open bundles only.

The importer has to fill up a separate Bill of Entry form for different classes of goods. In India, separate forms are not used but all the entries are made in one form. The free goods are marked as free in the entry form itself. The importer has to pay the duty before securing the possession of the goods.

Contents of Bill of Entry

(a) Name and address of the importer.

(b) Name and address of the exporter.

(c) Import licence number of the importer.

(d) Name of the port/dock where goods are to be cleared.

(e) Description of goods.

(f) Value of goods.

(g) Rate and amount of import duty payable.

(h) Other relevant documents.

4. Insurance Documents: Insurance documents also constitute evidence of a contract with a third party, namely the insurance company and therefore must be distinguished from the commercial documents. These are used to assure the consignee that insurance will cover the loss of or damage to the cargo during transit. These can be obtained from the freight forwarder.

The two main insurance documents are:

• Insurance certificate

• Insurance policy

5. Boat Notes: Sometimes, a vessel instead of actually docking at a port may unload cargo in a smaller boat which will bring the cargo onto the shore. In such cases, the small boat must be accompanied by a Boat Note. Such Boat Notes will be issued by a Customs officer in the prescribed form in duplicate.

Similarly, in case of exports, a boat may carry the export cargo to a waiting ship at sea. In such cases, a Boat Note is required. However, a Boat Note is not required if the cargo is accompanied by a shipping list.

A Boat Note is also required for trans-shipment of cargo that is transfer from one ship to another for reshipment.

6. Transit Goods: Any goods imported in a vessel or aircraft will be allowed to remain on board of the vessel or aircraft and to be transited without payment of custom duty. However, all these goods must be mentioned in the import manifest submitted by the person in charge of the conveyance.

7. Trans-shipment of Goods means transfer of goods from one vessel to another for transport to any port. Goods can be trans-shipped without payment of any customs duty provided they are mentioned in the Import Manifest. In such cases, a Bill of Trans-shipment must be submitted to the Customs officer. However, such trans-shipment is not allowed in case of certain prohibited goods.

8. Coastal Goods mean goods transported from one port in India to another port in India but do not include imported goods. Though no import or export is involved in case of coastal goods, adequate control procedures are required in order to ensure that these goods are not illegally exported. Trade and transport of coastal goods by sea can be carried out only on approved coastal ports. The consignor must file a Bill of Coastal Goods to the Customs authorities in the prescribed form giving the prescribed details. The goods will be loaded by the master of vessel only after the Bill of Coastal Goods is approved by the Customs authorities. The master of vessel must carry an advice book where entries will be made by the Customs officer. This advice book can be inspected by a Customs officer at a coastal port. On completion of loading, entry outwards is granted by the Customs officer after which the vessel may leave the port. The coastal goods can be unloaded on a Coastal Port or a Custom Port. The relevant documents and goods will be inspected by the Customs authorities. Unloading can be done only after obtaining permission from the Customs officer.

9. Customs Invoice: Customs invoice is mainly needed for countries like USA, Canada, etc. It is prepared on a special form being presented by the Customs authorities of the importing country. It facilitates entry of goods in the importing country at a preferential tariff rate.

10. Consular Invoice: Consular invoice is a document required mainly by countries like Kenya, Uganda, Tanzania, Mauritius, New Zealand, Myanmar, Iraq, Australia, Fiji, Cyprus, Nigeria, Ghana, Guinea, Zanzibar, etc. This invoice is the most important document, which needs to be submitted for certification to the Embassy of the importing country concerned. The main purpose of the consular invoice is to enable the authorities of the importing country to collect accurate information about the volume, value, quality, grade, source, etc. of the goods imported for the purpose of assessing import duties and also for statistical purposes.

In order to obtain a consular invoice, the exporter is required to submit three copies of invoice to the Consulate of the importing country concerned. The Consulate of the importing country certifies them in return for fees. One copy of the invoice is given to the exporter while the other two are dispatched to the customs office of the importer's country for the calculation of the import duty. The exporter negotiates a copy of the consular invoice to the importer along with other shipping documents.

Significance of Consular Invoice for the Exporter

(a) It facilitates quick clearance of goods from the customs in the exporter's as well as the importer' country.

(b) Certification of goods by the Consulate of the importing country indicates that the importer has fulfilled all procedural and licensing formalities for import of goods.

(c) It also assures the exporter of the payment from the importing country.

Significance of Consular Invoice for the Importer

(a) It facilitates quick clearance of goods from the customs at the port of destination and therefore, the importer gets quick delivery of goods.

(b) The importer is assured that the goods imported are not banned for imports in his country.

Significance of Consular Invoice for the Customs Office

(a) It makes the task of the customs authorities easy.

(b) It facilitates quick calculation of duties as the value of goods as determined by the Consulate is considered for the purpose.

11. Inspection Certification: An Inspection Certificate is required by some purchasers and countries in order to attest to the specifications of the goods shipped. This is usually performed by a third party and often obtained from independent testing organisations.

12. Dock Receipt and Warehouse Receipt: Used to transfer accountability when the export item is moved by the domestic carrier to the port of embarkation and left with the ship line for export.

13. Legalised/Visaed Invoice: This shows the seller's genuineness before the appropriate consulate or chamber of commerce/embassy.

14. Certified Invoice: It is required when the exporter needs to certify on the invoice that the goods are of a particular origin or manufactured/packed at a particular place and in accordance with a specific contract. Sight Draft and Usance Draft are available for this. Sight Draft is required when the exporter expects immediate payment and Usance Draft is required for credit delivery.

15. Certificate of Inspection: It is a type of document describing the condition of goods and confirming that they have been inspected.

16. Black List Certificate: It is required for countries which have strained political relations. It certifies that the ship or the aircraft carrying the goods has not touched those country(s).

17. Manufacturer's Certificate: It is required in addition to the Certificate of Origin for few countries to show that the goods shipped have actually been manufactured and are available.

18. Certificate of Chemical Analysis: It is required to ensure the quality and grade of certain items such as metallic ores, pigments, etc.

19. Certificate of Shipment: It signifies that a certain lot of goods have been shipped.

20. Health/Veterinary/Sanitary Certification is required for export of foodstuffs, marine products, hides, livestock etc.

21. Certificate of Conditioning: It is issued by the competent office to certify compliance of humidity factor, dry weight, etc.

22. Antiquity Certificate: The certificate is issued by the Archaeological Survey of India in the case of exports of antiques. The Government of India has authorised the Export Inspection Council of India and its various agencies to issue the Certificate of Origin. The Export Promotion Offices at Mumbai, Kolkata, Chennai and Cochin and the heads of the Licensing Offices have also been authorised to issue the Certificate of Origin.

23. Shipping Order: Issued by the Shipping (Conference) Line which intimates the exporter about the reservation of space of shipment of cargo through the specific vessel from a specified port and on a specified date.

24. Cart/Lorry Ticket: It is prepared for admittance of the cargo through the port gate and includes the shipper's name, cart/ lorry number marks on packages, quantity, etc.

25. Shut Out Advice: It is a statement of packages which are shut out by a ship and is prepared by the concerned shed and is sent to the exporter.

26. Short Shipment Form: It is an application to the customs authorities at port which advises short shipment of goods and is required for claiming the return.

27. Bill of Exchange: Bills of exchange are negotiable financial documents that require the individual or business that is addressed in the document to pay a specified amount of money on a date that is mentioned in the document. The date for the demand to pay generally ranges from the current date to a date within the next six calendar months. However, a bill of exchange will also require the authorised signature of the debtor in order to be considered legal and binding.

The bill of exchange can take on many different forms. One of the most common examples of the bill of exchange is the common bank cheque wherein it is mentioned who is to receive the funds, with the order to pay the face value of the cheque to the order of the creditor. The exact amount of the payment is specified. The date specified on the cheque is often the issue date for the cheque, but may also be the date that the bank is to honour the payment. This process is referred to as post-dating a cheque, since the creditor will physically receive the cheque at some time before it will be honoured.

A bill of exchange can also be in the form of a bank draft. Similar to the bank cheque, drafts are normally set up with a fixed sum of payment, and with specific instructions of when to issue the payment to the creditor.

The bill of exchange can be a very simplistic document or a detailed one. In most countries around the world, the bill of exchange is a common means of conducting business, and is often accompanied by an 'allonge' (a paper attached to a negotiable instrument to add additional endorsements when the back of the bill is full). The holder of the document is free to take legal action against the debtor according to local laws, or to sell the bill of exchange to a collector at a discounted rate of exchange in situations where the bill of exchange is not honoured. A bill of exchange also known as draft contains an order from the credit to the debtor to pay a specified amount to a person mentioned therein. The maker of a bill is called the "Drawer", the person who is directed to pay is called the "Drawee" and the person who is entitled to receive payment is called the "Payee."

When it is drawn on a foreign firm it is termed as a Foreign Draft. It is prepared either in an international currency or Indian rupees depending on the terms of the contract. For example, a bill drawn in US dollars is known as 'Dollar Bill' and when prepared in rupees, is termed as a 'Rupee Bill'.

When the goods are shipped by sea, the bills are drawn in sets and two sets of documents, including drafts are mailed to the foreign correspondent through an authorised dealer for presentation to the Drawee (importer). Each set bears a reference to the other.

A Bill of Exchange or Draft is of two types – (i) 'Sight Draft' or 'Draft at Sight' and (ii) "Usance Draft" or "Usance Bill".

When the exporter (Drawer) expects the importer (Drawee) to make payment immediately after the draft is presented to him, it is called a 'Sight Draft'. Unless and until the draft is received, the negotiating/collecting bank does not hand over the shipping documents and the buyer cannot take delivery of goods. As there is no aligned document for the draft, the same can be prepared by the exporter in the usual format.

28. Weight Note: This document is used to confirm that the packets/bales, etc., are of a particular weight and not more than the stipulated weight as per contract. It may at times give gross weight and net weight of the whole consignment.

29. Manufacturer's/Supplier's Quality/Inspection Certificate: This is a certificate to the effect that the goods which have been manufactured/supplied are as per the requirement of the Contract of Sale.

30. Manufacturer's/Supplier's Quality/Inspection Certificate: Manufacturer's Certificate: It is required in addition to the Certificate of Origin for a few countries to show that the goods shipped have actually been manufactured and are available.

31. Export Order: An order is a commercial transaction which is not only important to the exporter and importer, but it is also of concern to their respective countries, since it affects the balance of payment position of both the countries. The exporter is required to produce copies of export order to various government departments/financial institutions, for example, obtaining export licenses when the product is covered under the restricted items or canalised items for exports.

32. Order Acceptance: The Order Acceptance is another important commercial document prepared by the exporter confirming the acceptance of order placed by the importer. The exporter commits the shipment of goods covered at the agreed price during a specified time. Order Acceptance normally covers the name and address of the indenter, name and address of the consignee, port of shipment, country of final destination, the description of goods, quantity, price of each order and total amount of the order, terms of delivery, details of freight and insurance, mode of transport, packing and marking details, terms of payment etc.

33. Letter of Credit: Letter of Credit is a negotiable document issued by the importer's bank in favour of the exporter giving him the authority to draw bills up to a particular amount, covering a specified shipment of goods and services and assuring him of payment against the delivery of shipping documents. The basic features of a letter of credit are –

(a)   It is an undertaking given by a bank to honour a financial commitment.

(b)   It is an undertaking given by a bank on behalf of its importer client.

(c)   It is an undertaking given by the bank to an exporter who may not be a client of the bank.

(d)   The undertaking will be honoured subject to fulfilment of certain conditions by the exporter.

(e)   There is another bank being involved for collection of the sum promised in the letter of credit.

34. Post Parcel Receipt: Post Parcel Receipt evidences the receipt of goods for exports by the post offices and it is also not treated as a document of title. If the post parcel is sent directly in the name of the buyer, the buyer can take immediate possession of the goods sent by the exporter sometimes without paying for it.

36. Packing List/Note: A Packing List/Note contains the date of packing, connecting invoice number, order number, details of shipping such as the name of steamer, Bill of Lading number and date of sailing, case number to which the list/note relates, the details of goods such as quantity and weight and/or item-wise details. This may be shown on the invoice or separately, and should contain item by item, the contents of cases or containers or of a shipment with its weight and description set forth in such a manner as to permit checks of the contents by the customs on arrival at the port of destination as well as by the recipient.

The packing list is a relatively simpler document and the whole of the information can be reproduced from the master by masking information not desired on the packing list. Special information, if any, can be given in the blank space in the lower third portion of the document.

The exporter prepares the packing list to facilitate the buyer to check the shipment. It contains the detailed description of the goods packed in each case, their gross and net weight etc. The difference between a packing note and a packing list is that the packing note contains the particulars of the contents of an individual pack, while the packing list is a consolidated statement of the contents of a number of cases or packs.

Contents of Packing List

(a)   Name and address of the exporter.

(b)   Name and address of the consignee.

(c)   Name and the number of vessel or flight.

(d)   Name of the port of loading.

(e)   Name of the port of discharge and final destination.

(f)   Invoice number and date.

(g)   Name of the country of origin of goods.

(h)   Name of the country of final destination.

(i)   Marks and container number.

(j)   Number and packing description.

(k)   Description of goods in terms of quantity and special remarks, if any.

(l)   Signature of the exporter with date.

Normally, ten copies of the packing note/list should be prepared. The first is to be sent with the shipping documents, two copies in advance to the buyer, one to the shipping agent and the remaining retained by the exporter.

3.3 Excise Clearance for Export

All excisable goods exported out of India are exempt from payment of Central Excise Duties, for which two different procedures have been approved.

1.   Rebate of Duty on Goods Export Procedure

Under the 'Rebate of Duty on Goods Export' procedure the manufacturer has first to pay the excise duty on goods meant for export and then claim refund of the same after exportation of such goods to countries except Nepal and Bhutan. This is done under Rule 12 of Central Excise Rules which states rebate of duty is granted for the finished stage as well as input stage. However, rebate of duty in respect of the excisable materials used in the manufacture of the exported goods shall not be allowed if the exporter avails of the drawback allowed under the Customs and Central Excise Duties Drawback Rules, 1995 or Modvat. The following procedure should be followed while exporting under the rebate of duty:

1. Removal of goods under claim of rebate from a factory or warehouse without examination by the Central Excise Officers. The exporters are allowed to remove the goods for export on their own without getting the goods examined by the Central Excise Officers.

2. In such cases Form AR4 should be prepared in sixtuplicate giving all particulars and declarations. The exporter shall deliver triplicate, and quadruplicate, quintuplicate and sixtuplicate copies of AR4 to the Superintendent of Central Excise having jurisdiction over the factory or the warehouse, within 24 hours of the removal of the consignment and would retain the original and duplicate copies for presenting along with the consignment to the Customs officer at the point of export.

3. The information contained in AR4 is examined by the jurisdictional superintendent of Central Excise who verifies the facts of payment of duty and other certificates/declarations made by the exporter.

4. After confirming the information contained in the AR4 is true, he signs at appropriate places in the four copies of AR4 submitted to him and plus his stamp with his name and designation below his signature. He would then dispose of the triplicate, quadruplicate, quintuplicate and sixtuplicate copies of AR4 as under –

(i) **Original and Duplicate:** To the exporter for presenting to Customs officer at the point of export along with the export consignment.

(ii) **Triplicate:** To the rebate sanctioning authority, that is, Maritime Commissioner of Central Excise or the jurisdictional Assistant Commissioner of Central Excise, as declared by the exporter on the AR4. The Central Excise officer may hand over this copy under the sealed cover on exporter's request.

(iii) **Quadruplicate:** To the Chief Accounts Officer at his Commissionerate Headquarters.

(iv) **Quintuplicate:** To be retained for records by the Central Excise Officer.

(v) **Sixtuplicate:** To be given to the exporter.

2. Export under Bond Procedure: Under the second procedure known as "Exports Under Bond" goods can be exported out of India except to Nepal or Bhutan without prior payment of duty subject to the execution of the Bond with security for a sum equivalent to the duty chargeable on the goods to be exported. This is done under Rule 13 of Central Excise Rules which deals with export of goods in bond as well as utilisation of raw materials etc. without payment of duty for manufacture and export of excisable goods.

Such a bond should be supported by an appropriate bank guarantee to safeguard excise department's financial interest against non-sanctioning of excise refund.

Information to be given on AR-4: The exporter is required to give the following information on the AR-4 form:

(a) Running serial number of the AR-4 beginning from each financial year.

(b) Scheme under which export has been made, that is, value based advanced licensing scheme/quantity based advanced licensing scheme/under claim for duty drawback etc.

(c) Whether the exported goods have been manufactured availing/without availing Modvat credit under Rule 57A, and

(d) Particulars of bond executed or the duty debit particulars as the case may be.

3.4 Quality Control and Pre-shipment Inspection

In order to promote exports of quality goods as per the international standards, the government of India has introduced compulsory Quality Control and Pre-Shipment Inspection for 90% of the items of export under one or the other system as per the Export (Quality Control and Inspection) Act, 1963. An important aspect about the goods to be exported is compulsory quality control and pre-shipment inspection. Under the Export (Quality Control and Inspection) Act, 1963, about 1000 commodities under the major groups of Food and Agriculture, Fishery, Minerals, Organic and Inorganic Chemicals, Rubber Products, Ceramic Products, Pesticides, Light Engineering, Steel Products, Jute Products, Coir and Coir Products, Footwear and Footwear Products/Components are subject to compulsory pre-shipment inspection.

At times, there may be a conflict when foreign buyers lay down their own standards/specifications which may or may not adhere to the Indian standards. They may also insist upon inspection by their own nominated agencies. These issues should be sorted out before confirmation of order. Specific provisions have also been made for compulsory inspection of textile goods.

Products having ISI Certification mark or Agmark are not required to be inspected by any agency as these products do not fall within the purview of the export inspection agencies network. The Customs Authorities allow export of such goods even if not accompanied by any pre-shipment inspection certificate, provided they are otherwise satisfied that the goods carry ISI Certification or the Agmark. Goods meant for export, depending upon the nature of the products, are inspected for quality in the following manner –

Consignment to Consignment Inspection: Each individual consignment is inspected by the Export Inspection Agency, Commodity Board and certificate of inspection is issued. The application for inspection for goods has to be submitted well in advance before the expected date of shipment of the consignment. Inspection of the consignment is generally carried out either at the premises of the exporter or at the port of shipment by the export inspection agency with a right to exercise supervision of inspected consignment(s) at any place or time.

The application should be made in duplicate in the new prescribed form 'Intimation for Inspection' as per standardised pre-shipment export documents to the nearest office of the respective export inspection agency accompanied by the following documents:

1. Particulars of the consignment intended to be exported.
2. A crossed cheque/draft for the amount of requisite inspection fees.
3. Copy of the commercial invoice.
4. Copy of letter of credit.
5. Details of packing specifications.
6. Copy of the export order/contract, indicating the buyer's requirement of goods are strictly according to the prescribed specifications, or as per samples etc.

The inspection agency, after verification that the consignment of exportable goods meets the requirements laid down in the export contract/order, issues within four days of receipt of intimation for inspection, the necessary certificate of inspection to the exporter in the prescribed proforma in five copies.

This certificate is issued in the standardised form which is aligned pre-shipment export document. (Three copies for exporter – original copy for customs use, the second copy for the use of the foreign buyer and the third copy for the exporter's use, fourth copy for Data Bank, Export Inspection Council, New Delhi and the fifth copy is retained with the agency for their own office record).

3.4.1 Methods of Quality Control and Pre-shipment Inspection

Export Inspection Council (EIC) has recognised three systems of pre-shipment inspection, namely:

1. In-Process Quality Control (IPQC): Under this system certain products like chemicals or engineering goods are subject to this control stage by stage inspection. This is done during the various stages of production as follows –

(i) The exporter has to get his unit registered as "export worthy" and keep record of processing and production. Inspection by the officers of Export Inspection Agency is done from time to time.

(ii) The certification of inspection on the end-products is then given without in-depth study at the shipment stage. Under this system, export is allowed on the basis of adequacy of in-process quality control and inspection measures carried out by the manufacturing units themselves.

(iii) The certificates of inspection in favour of the units approved under the scheme are issued by the Export Inspection Agencies (EIAs) in the normal course subject to random spot checks of the consignments.

(iv) The units approved under this system of in-process quality control may themselves issue the certificate of inspection, but only for the products for which they have been granted IPQC facilities. Consequently, the manufacturer-exporters of products approved under the IPQC have been recognised as agencies for pre-shipment inspection for export of engineering products as approved by the Export Inspection Agencies at Mumbai, Kolkata, Cochin, Delhi and Chennai.

2. **Self Certification Scheme:** Large manufacturers/exporters, export houses/trading houses are allowed the facility of self-certification on the assumption that the exporter himself is the best judge for the quality of his products and will not allow his reputation to be spoiled in the international market by compromising on quality. The means to avail the facility of self certification scheme is as follows –

(i) Industrial units having a proven reputation and adequate testing facilities have to apply to the Director (Inspection and Quality Control), Export Inspection Council of India, New Delhi.

(ii) They are granted a certificate valid for a period of one year, allowing them self-certification facility. The facility is available to manufacturers of engineering products, chemical and allied products and marine products.

(iii) During this period, the exporter can issue a certificate signed by himself or by a person authorised by him. The certificate has to indicate the number and date of EIA's reference for registration under self-certification scheme and has to be issued in the aligned format as per new standardised pre-shipment documents.

(iv) The approval of an industrial unit under this scheme is notified in the Gazette of India and the exporter has to pay a lump sum fee to the export inspection agencies depending upon his export turnover.

(v) Minimum Quality Norms prescribed by the Export Inspection Council should be maintained and achieved for the grant of facility under Self-Certification Scheme.

3. **Consignment-wise Inspection:** Under this system, each individual consignment is subject to compulsory inspection by the EIA. The procedure to have consignment-wise inspection is as follows –

(i) The exporter has to apply in the prescribed form to EIA at least 7 days before the expected date of shipment.

(ii)   After getting the "intimation for inspection", the EIA deputes an inspector to conduct the pre-shipment inspection at the exporter's factory.

(iii) After the inspection, the goods are packed with EIA seal and the inspector submits a report to the Deputy Director of EIA.

(iv)   Deputy Director of EIA issues the Inspection Certificate in triplicate, if the inspection report is favourable. Otherwise, he issues a rejection note.

3.4.2 Units Exempted from the Inspection Procedure

1. Approved 100% EOUs and EPZs.
2. Export houses, Trading houses, Star Trading houses and Super Star Trading houses.
3. Exporters who are registered with the Textile Committee.
4. Goods marked with ISI, AGMARK, BIS-14000, ISO-9000.

3.4.3 ISO 9000

The discussion on quality control and pre-shipment inspection will be incomplete without saying a few words about ISO 9000. The ISO-9000 series of standards evolved by the International Standards Organisation has been accepted worldwide as the norm assuring high quality of goods. The ISO-9000 is also the hallmark of a good quality-oriented system for suppliers and manufacturers. It identifies the basic principles underlying quality, and specifies the procedures and criteria to be followed to ensure that what leaves the manufacturer/supplier's premises fully meets the customer requirements. The ISO-9000 series of standards are basically quality assurance standards and not product standards. ISO-9000 spells out how a company can establish, document and maintain an effective and economic quality control system which will demonstrate to the customer that the company is committed to quality. The series of standards aims at the following:

- Increased customer confidence in the company.
- Shift from a system of inspection, to one of quality management.
- Removing the need for multiple assessments of suppliers.
- Gaining management commitment.
- Linking quality to cost-effectiveness.
- Giving customers what they need.

The implementation of ISO-9000 Standards involves –

- Management education.
- Writing quality policy.
- Nominating a quality representative.
- Identifying responsibilities.

- Identifying business processes.
- Writing a quality manual.
- Writing procedures.
- Writing work instructions.

It is thus clear that the ISO-9000 series of standards constitute the concept of Total Quality Management (TQM).

3.5 Packaging, Marking, Labelling

An important stage after manufacturing of goods or their procurement is their preparation for shipment. This involves labelling, packaging, packing and marking of export consignments.

3.5.1 Packaging

Packaging is an important part of the branding process as it plays a role in communicating the image and identity of a company. According to Phillip Kotler, *"packaging refers to all the activities of designing and producing the container for a product."* Packaging can be defined as the wrapping material around a consumer item that serves to contain, identify, describe, protect, display, promote, and otherwise make the product marketable and keep it clean. Packaging is the outer wrapping of a product. It is the intended purpose of the packaging to make a product readily sellable as well as to protect it against damage and prevent it from deterioration while storing. Furthermore the packaging is often the most relevant element of a trademark and is conducive to advertising or communication.

Packaging is the enclosing of a physical object, typically a product that will be offered for sale. It is the process of preparing items of equipment for transportation and storage and which embraces preservation, identification and packaging of products. It should not be confused with packing. Packing refers to the external protective covering used for the safe transportation of the goods to the importer. For example, plastic box used to pack a set of handkerchiefs is an example of packaging. On the other hand, the corrugated fibre board boxes which are used for packing the plastic box for their safe transportation to the importer in the foreign country would represent packing.

Packing is recognised as an integral part of modern marketing operation, which embraces all phases of activities involved in the transfer of goods and services from the manufacturer to the consumer. Packaging makes the product more valuable and offers more 'value' to the customer. For instance, an expensive chess board offered to a customer wrapped in the old newspaper is very likely to lose out to an identical chess board set neatly presented in a nice matching box. Thus, packaging refers to a container in which the product reaches the end use consumer. It is a part of the presentation of the product and stays right till the customer takes it from the store.

Packaging Design: The primary packaging of the product performs the function of the silent salesman. It should appeal to the prospective consumer and satisfy his desire to use a better quality product. The exporter should also keep in mind the product and the target group of customers while designing the primary packaging of the product. The total packaging design (comprising of material, size, shape, colour, text, graphics and logo) should be such that it provides proper perception and expectations about the product, convenience and efficiency in use and should be faultless.

The packaging design should be developed very carefully to ensure that –

1. Proper protection is provided to the product.
2. The product is environment friendly to produce and dispose off.
3. It is safe to handle during transportation.
4. It is economical to produce, handle and store.
5. It is very attractive when displayed.
6. It is convenient and safe to use in compliance with the relevant standards of the target export market.

Packaging Materials: Considering that there are various types of materials like paper, plastics, wood, cardboard etc. available for packaging of the goods, selection of the packaging materials should be made keeping in mind the specifications given by the importer because he has to plan further for consumer packaging of the goods. Paper and board are the most widely used packaging materials in terms of weight. Aluminium is used in packaging beverages and food. It has a high value as a scrap metal and can be recycled economically. The selection of the packaging materials would depend upon the following factors –

1. Characteristics of the product.
2. Transportation and storage methods.
3. Climate and culture.
4. Standards and environmental considerations.
5. Market position.

The type and quality of the packaging is specific to the given product. For example, products such as garments, shoes, textiles etc. are sold to the consumers without any packaging. These products are usually displayed without any packaging at the stores. The exporters often package products in polyethylene bags to ensure products from getting dirty.

Cardboard boxes are used for packing items such as sets of glasses or tableware, decorations with several delicate parts, pairs of candle holders, glass vases etc., to ensure that they are not damaged and their appearance is not spoiled during handling and display.

Expensive products and gift items such as jewellery require a high standard of packaging. In fact, the more expensive or exclusive the product is, the more expensive the packaging is.

Packaging Types: Packaging for export products can be classified into the following types –

1. Plastic packaging

2. Paper-based packaging

3. Combined plastic and cardboard packaging

4. Miscellaneous packaging

1. Plastic Packaging

Numerous types of plastic materials are used for export packaging. The commonly used plastic materials are polyethylene (PE) and polypropylene (PP). Polyethylene film has two main varieties of consumer packaging namely, low density polyethylene (PE-LD) film and high density polyethylene (PE-HD).

PE-LD film is used in the manufacture of plastic bags, shrink wrapping and stretch wrapping. This film, though very useful for protection against moisture and dirt, does not however, provide any mechanical protection.

(a) Plastic Bags: Exporters use plastic bags made of PE-LD films for wrapping articles like T-shirts, table cloths, napkins, leather handbags etc. These plastic bags are transparent and are suited for retail display.

(b) Shrink Wrapping: Shrink film solves a wide variety of retail and industrial packaging needs, as it is versatile and popular. Completely enclosing the product, shrink wrapped packaging provides tamper-resistant protection. Moreover, the shrink film is transparent enough to reveal the details and graphics of the product, or it can be custom printed, a new and increasingly popular choice with bundled items. A specially treated film is loosely wrapped around the products and then shrunk with heat to form a tight package. This kind of wrapping is suitable for solid products like sets of drinking glasses, a group of egg-cups or a set of table mats.

(c) Stretch Wrapping: A thin film is tightly wound around the product, often in several layers. On completion of the wrap, the stretched film tries to return to its original size, holding the product or group of products tightly in place.

Both PE-HD and PE-LD are used for making plastic bags. However, PE-HD, though more expensive, provides better resistance against moisture and fats than PE-LD. Both forms of plastic films are environment friendly as they are easily recyclable.

It is advisable to use PP films as they are stronger than PE films. Bags made of PP films are used for packaging textiles and garments as these can be printed or can be used in plain form as well. PP films, though expensive, are better than PE films in terms of providing better moisture protection. Another alternative to PP films is polyvinylchloride (PVC) material. But from the environmental point of view, PVC materials should not be used as these are not recyclable.

(d) **Plastic Boxes** can be used as retail packages especially for jewellery and other small, precious products. They are also well suited to add appeal to products such as embroidered handkerchiefs or tablecloths etc. They come in various shapes and sizes.

2. Paper-based Packaging

Paper-based materials produced from virgin wood fibres or recycled fibres are used as wrapping, as paperboard cartons or corrugated fibre board boxes. Various types of paper can be coated with plastics, waxed or treated with anticorrosion agents. The virgin wood fibres are stronger than recycled fibres. Paper wrapping provides protection against dust and light, but does not provide mechanical protection.

Paper absorbs moisture when the surrounding air is more humid than the paper, and it gives up moisture when the surroundings are drier. Thus, paper wrappings can be used to some extent as moisture protection inside the packages. One may use tissue paper instead of newspaper to protect the surface of the products.

(a) **Paperboard Folding Cartons:** Folding cartons made of different paperboard qualities can be used as retail packaging for a variety of reasons. Folding cartons are fairly economical; they can be shaped in numerous ways; they can be printed very decoratively; properly designed cartons provide mechanical protection to products; they protect products against dust and light and are easy to handle in shops. 'Stiffness' is the most important property of such cartons.

(b) **Paperboard Cans:** The paperboards can is a form of paper-based retail packaging which is quite inexpensive and is used to pack different types of products. These cans can be lined inside with aluminium foil or plastic films to provide additional protection against humidity. Such cans are used for packaging toys, puzzles, games, tennis balls and other sports goods.

3. Combined Plastic and Cardboard Packaging

In this type of packaging the product is visible through the plastic. Hence, these packages are used mainly for retail packaging of pens, small toys, gift items, light weight souvenir articles. The paperboard card can be printed to provide information and to add sales appeal. This form of packaging ensures small products do not get lost or stolen easily. The following are the types of packaging in this category.

(a) **Skin Packaging:** Skin packaging is that form of packaging where the product is first placed on a paperboard card with heat seal coating. It is suitable for products which need a light and inexpensive protection against moisture. Skin packaging ensures the appearance and safety of the product. It is however, not suitable for products which are sensitive to heat. Needless to say, this form of packaging cannot be reused again.

(b) Blister and Clamshell Packaging: Blister and clamshell packaging are perfect for small products that require a high level of security and product visibility. Also known as carded packaging, blister packaging is backed by a printed card for product descriptions and instructions. Clamshell packaging gives the product visibility from the front and the back of the package. Blister packaging can be used for a variety of products such as fruits, pens, textiles, articles and decorations etc. and not for those products which are too delicate as there is always some space for movement inside the blister which might damage the delicate product.

(c) Plastic Bag with Paperboard Card: In this form of packaging, a paperboard card is attached to the plastic bags through a hole in the bag. Besides adding sales appeal to plain plastic bags, it is also very cost effective. The paperboard card can be printed on adding information. Though the plastic bags can be made of any materials, PP film is desirable for better product presentation.

3. Miscellaneous Packaging

Besides the above-mentioned forms of packaging, the exporter can make use of wood, textiles, straw, leaves or any other locally available materials for packaging of the goods. Specially made wooden boxes can be used to package traditional ceramics, wood carvings, various gift items, pieces of jewellery etc. If wooden packaging is used as a gift or retail package, it has to be smooth, clean, and dry with any hinges or locks well made and functioning. Packing the product with sufficient cushioning material in a wooden package is important to avoid damage to the product during transportation. However, before using wood as packaging material, one should always find out if there are any regulations concerning the treatment or certification of wooden materials.

In order to provide a more decent appearance paperboard cartons or boxes can be covered or lined with cloth. Bags made of jute, cotton, velvet or other fabric could be used for packaging of products which do not need much protection. Handicraft products can be attractively packed using baskets made of local materials.

Functions of Packaging: Packaging should be such that it is capable of protecting the product at minimum cost. The important functions of packaging are given below.

(a) Protection: Packaging can protect the product during transport and distribution from climatic effects like heat and cold, moisture, vapour and drying atmospheres. It will also protect it from hazardous substances, contaminants and infestation. Protection is required against transportation hazards, spillage, dirt, ingress and egress of moisture, insect infection, contamination by foreign material, tampering, pilferage etc.

A package should preserve the contents in 'factory fresh' condition during the period of storage and transportation, ensuring protection from bacteriological attacks, chemical reactions etc. Packaging should preserve the quality of the product. The interaction between the product and packaging should be totally eliminated. This is specifically important in case of food and pharmaceutical products.

(b) Controls Cost: Packaging provides agglomeration of small objects into one package for reason of efficiency and cost factor. For example it is better to put 1000 pens in one box rather than putting each pen in separate 1000 boxes.

(c) Communication: A major function of packaging is the communication of the product. A package must communicate what it sells. When international trade is involved and different languages are spoken, the use of unambiguous, readily understood symbols on the distribution package is essential. Packaging protects the interests of consumers. Information includes quantity, price, inventory levels, lot number, distribution routes, size, and elapsed time since packaging, colour, and merchandising and premium data.

(d) Marketing: Proper and attractive packaging plays an important role in encouraging a potential buyer. Packages can have features which add convenience in distribution, handling display, sale, opening, use and reuse.

(e) Security: Packaging can play an important role in reducing the security risk of shipment. It also provides authentication seals to indicate that the package and contents are not counterfeit. Packages also can include anti-theft devices, such as dye-packs, RFID tags or electronic article surveillance tags, that can be activated or detected by devices at exit points and require specialised tools to deactivate. Using packaging in this way is a means of loss prevention.

(f) Create excitement: Packaging should not be dull. Novel shapes and designs can be used to stimulate interest and create excitement among buyers. For example, to satisfy the Japanese preference for beautiful packaging, Avon upgraded its inexpensive plastic packaging to crystalline glass.

Significance of Packaging

The significance of packaging has come to be increasingly recognised in export as well as in marketing of a wide range of consumer goods and industrial products within the country. Packaging decisions are important for several reasons including:

1. Protection: Packaging is used to protect the product from damage during transportation and to deter spoilage if the product is exposed to air or other elements.

2. Visibility: Packaging design is primarily to attract the customers' attention when they are shopping or browsing through a catalogue or website. This is particularly important for customers who are not familiar with the product and mainly in cases where a product must stand out among thousands of other products in order to catch the eyes of the buyers.

3. Added Value: Packaging design and structure can add value to a product. For example, package structures that make the product easier to use and more attractive to display in the customer's home can enhance the value of the product.

4. Distributor Acceptance: Packaging decisions, besides acceptance by the final customer, also have to be accepted by distributors who sell the product for the supplier. Retailers will be reluctant to accept packages if they do not conform to requirements they have for storing products on their shelves.

5. Cost: A significant portion of a product's selling price is represented by packaging. It is estimated that in the cosmetics industry the packaging cost of some products may be as high as 40 percent of the product's selling price. Reductions in cost possibly leading to higher profits can be brought about by smart packaging decisions.

6. Expensive to Create: It is quite expensive to develop new packaging methods. The costs involved in creating new packaging includes graphic and structural design, production, customer testing, possible destruction of leftover old packaging, and possible advertising to inform customer of the new packaging.

7. Long-term Decision: When companies create a new package, it is most often a long-term decision with the intention of having the design on the market for an extended period of time. Changing a product's packaging too frequently, in fact, can have a negative effect on customers as they have become conditioned to locate the product based on its package and may be perplexed if the design is altered.

8. Environmental or Legal Issues: Packages that are not easily bio-degradable or environment friendly could attract customer and possibly governmental concern. Hence packaging decisions must include an assessment of its environmental impact especially for products with packages that are frequently discarded. Also, care must be taken in creating packages that do not infringe on intellectual property held by others, such as copyrights, trademarks or patents.

9. Mode of Transport: Transportation also influences packaging. For example, bulk ocean shipments of liquids, grain and ores do not need any packaging. Goods transported by air generally need less protective packaging than those sent by ship.

10. Waste Legislation: Many markets abroad have waste regulations that favour packaging which can be easily recycled or has a minimal impact on the environment when disposed of. In many export markets, there are stricter rules on packaging waste and collection, for example, the 'green dot system' in Germany.

Steps to prepare for Packaging

Exporter should ensure the use of quality packaging material for packaging of the product. Quality packaging plays a very important role in creating the image of a country. The transformation of the image of Japan as a supplier of industrial goods owes to quality packaging, so is true for South Korea, Singapore and Hong Kong.

Packaging has two components namely, technical and promotional. The technical aspect of packaging is concerned with protection of the product from moisture, heat, scratches, and mechanical shocks and so on. The exporter can ensure technical protection by using appropriate plastic materials, paper and the cushioning materials. The promotional aspect of packaging is concerned with creating sales appeal through packaging by making use of traditional patterns/designs of the country and by way of illustration of the item using a combination of two or three colours.

1. Clean all the products so that they are completely free of dust, dirt or fingerprints. It is important to remove fingerprints from polished metal surfaces, as fingerprints may cause decay and stains.

2. Dry those products which are stains affected by humidity. The drying should be done just before packing so that the humidity in the air cannot penetrate the products again. For example articles made of wood, straw, paper, leather and all textiles and garments.

3. Make sure that all parts of the product are there and that articles in sets are complex.

4. Make sure that possible stickers or other product labels are correct and that they are fastened so that removal of the labels by the end consumer does not damage the product.

Factors Influencing Packaging Decisions

The following special factors to be considered in export packaging decisions.

1. **Government Regulations in Foreign Countries:** Government regulations abroad have an impact on packaging and labelling. Some countries have specified packaging standards for certain commodities. The popular trend of labelling in a country's native language is growing. Regulations for dangerous goods are very specific on acceptable inner and outer packaging. Hence if such regulations are not strictly followed, the goods may be confiscated or may attract some other stringent action.

2. **Importer's Specifications:** In some cases, importers may want the exporters to give the packaging specifications. While incorporating such specifications, it is imperative to satisfy other statutory requirements.

3. **Socio-cultural Factors:** Socio-cultural factors relating to the importer's country like customs, traditions, beliefs, religion etc. should also be considered while designing the packaging for a product.

4. **Retailing Characteristics:** The nature of retail outlets is a very important consideration for the packaging decision. In some foreign markets due to the spread of supermarkets and discount houses, a large number of products are sold on a self-service basis. In such cases the package has to perform many of the salesmen's tasks like attracting attention, describing the product's features, giving the consumer confidence and making an overall favourable impression.

5. **Environmental Factors:** Environmental factors like weather and climate influence packaging decisions. The impact of such factors in the place where the product originates, while the product is in transit and while in the market should be considered. In other words the package should be capable of withstanding the hazards of handling and transportation, stacking, storing etc. under diverse conditions.

6. **Disposability:** Attention should also be paid to the aspects relating to the disposal of the packaging. One of the qualities required for a good package is that it should be easily disposed of or recycled. Unlike other countries where the disposal of packaging materials is causing environmental problems, in India many packaging materials easily find some alternate use or are recycled. Moreover, reusable packages may be used for selling bogus products.

3.5.2 Marking

Marking is essential for identification purpose and should provide information on exporters' mark, port of destination, place of destination, order number and date, gross, net and tare weight and handling instructions, the address, number of packages etc. on the packets. It should also be ensured that while putting the marks, the laws of the buyer's country are duly complied with.

Marking a number with special symbols, selected by the exporters or the importers, on all shipping cases will ensure the competitors cannot find out the details of the customers and the country of destination or supplier's country of despatch. This marking should confirm to those written in the invoice, insurance certificate, Bill of Lading and other documents. The International Cargo Handling Co-ordination Association has laid out a number of recommendations for the marking of goods carried by ships. These markings are equally useful for sending goods by other modes of transportation.

Suggestions for Good Marking

*   The marks should appear in a certain order. Essential data should be placed in oblong frames with 1.5 centimetre thick lines, and subsidiary information should be placed in another type of frame.

- Declaration on large packages should be placed on two continuous sides, and for consignments bound together on a pallet, the declaration should also be on the top.

- Handling instructions should be placed on all four sides. Similar packages like goods in sacks should be marked on two opposite sides.

- Lettering should be at least 7.5 centimetres high for essential data, and at least 3.5 centimetres for subsidiary data. In case of small packages, other sizes may be used, but in the same ratio. The sizes of the symbols should also be in proportion to the size of the package and of the other markings.

- Only fast dyes should be used for lettering. The main data should be in black and subsidiary data in a less conspicuous colour; red and orange lettering should be reversed for dangerous goods only. Only harmless dyes should be used for food packed in sacks, and the dye should not seep through the packing as to affect the goods.

- Individual packages or parcels should only have stick-on labels and all old labels should be removed. Marking may be made by stencil or by branding or by pencil or brush without a stencil. When stencils are used, utmost care should be taken to ensure letters and figures are perfectly legible to prevent confusion, especially letters and figures – B.R.P, O, G-G-D-C, H.N; 3-8: 6-9 and 1-7.

- The surface should be smooth and clean in order to be marked. If packages are to be bonded, they can be marked before bonding; the hoops should not cover the markings.

- The figure should indicate the total number of packages making up the consignment and the consecutive number of the individual packages. For example: 1520/15/1 identifies the first package of a total number of 15 packets and 1520/15/15 the last one.

- The name of the ship and the Bill of Lading number should be shown when this is possible. Handling instructions must appear in the language of the exporter and importer, and when possible, in the language of the countries where goods are to be handled en route or transhipped.

3.5.3 Labelling

Labelling is the process of fixing labels on the export product. Its main purpose is to inform the consumer essential details in respect of the product as regards its quantity, quality, how to use and maintain it. Many a times, the foreign buyers insist on inclusion of a particular type of label to comply with the regulations of their countries. Different countries have different regulations as regards labelling of the product. One of the most common regulations is in respect of origin of the goods that is a product must carry the label to indicate the country in which it has been manufactured. For example, in Germany the label must indicate the quality of the material used. Thus, if a garment is made of 100% cotton fabric, then the label fixed on the garment should state that it is made of 100% cotton. In Oman, use of adhesive labels is prohibited by law. Each label has to be printed both in English and Arabic language.

Thus, the exporter must ascertain the legal requirements as regards labelling of the product as applicable in different countries.

List of Information on a Label: Every label should contain the following information:

1. Information to satisfy the legal requirements of a particular country.
2. Instructions for taking care of the product.
3. Dimensions of the product that is size, weight, thickness etc.
4. Inputs used that is the contents of the materials used in the manufacture of the product.
5. Instructions for the use of the product.
6. Country of origin.
7. Name and address of the manufacturer.
8. Lot number of the consignment.
9. Date of manufacture and date of its expiry.
10. Brief information about those who made it. It is particularly relevant in the case of items of handicrafts or other creative items.

Forms of Labels: Labels on the products may assume any of the following forms –

1. Strip of cloth
2. Card label
3. Adhesive sticker
4. User's manual

Importance of Labelling Decisions: For consumer products, labelling decisions are extremely important for the following reasons:

1. Labels serve to capture the attention of shoppers. The use of catchy words may cause strolling customers to stop and evaluate the product.
2. The label is likely to be the first thing a new customer sees and thus offers their first impression of the product.

3. The label provides customers with product information to aid their purchase decision or help improve the customer's experience when using the product (for example, recipes).

4. Labels generally include a Universal Product Codes (UPC) and, in some cases, Radio Frequency Identification (RFID) tags, that make it easy for resellers, such as retailers, to check out customers and manage inventory.

5. For companies serving international markets or diverse cultures within a single country, bilingual or multilingual labels may be needed.

6. In some countries many products, including food and pharmaceuticals, are required by law to contain certain labels such as listing ingredients, providing nutritional information or including usage warning information.

Features of a Good Quality Label: A good quality label has the following features:

1. It includes all the relevant information.

2. It is printed in the language of the importer's country.

3. It is appropriate to the product. For instance, a label in the form of an adhesive sticker on the leather purse or on a wooden article would not be appropriate as it would damage the product.

4. It should be developed taking into consideration the colour and shape preferences of the prospective buyers.

Labels for Textile Products

The exporters should devise the labels depending upon the requirement of the product. As far as garments and textiles are concerned, there is a need for special type of labels which should include the symbol for textile care. The Federal Trade Commission of USA has specified in the care labelling rule in regard to textiles and garments that each care label should include the instructions with regard to how to take care of garments, appropriate temperature settings and the warnings with regard to the use of the garments and the textiles. The Federal Trade Commission of USA introduced the new labelling system, which gives option to the manufacturer of garments and textiles to make use of symbol on care label instead of written instructions. These labels have been developed by the American Society for Testing and Materials. These symbols relate to washing, bleaching, drying, ironing and dry cleaning.

The International Association for Textile Care Labelling known as GINETEX had also developed a set of textile care symbols which have been in use with effect from 1st January, 1986. These symbols for textile care adopted by the 13 member countries of GINETEX have come to be accepted as International Symbol for Textile Care. These countries are Austria,

Belgium/Luxembourg, Finland, France, Great Britain (UK), Italy, Israel, New Zealand, Portugal, Spain, Switzerland, The Netherlands and Germany. These international symbols for textile care are given below:

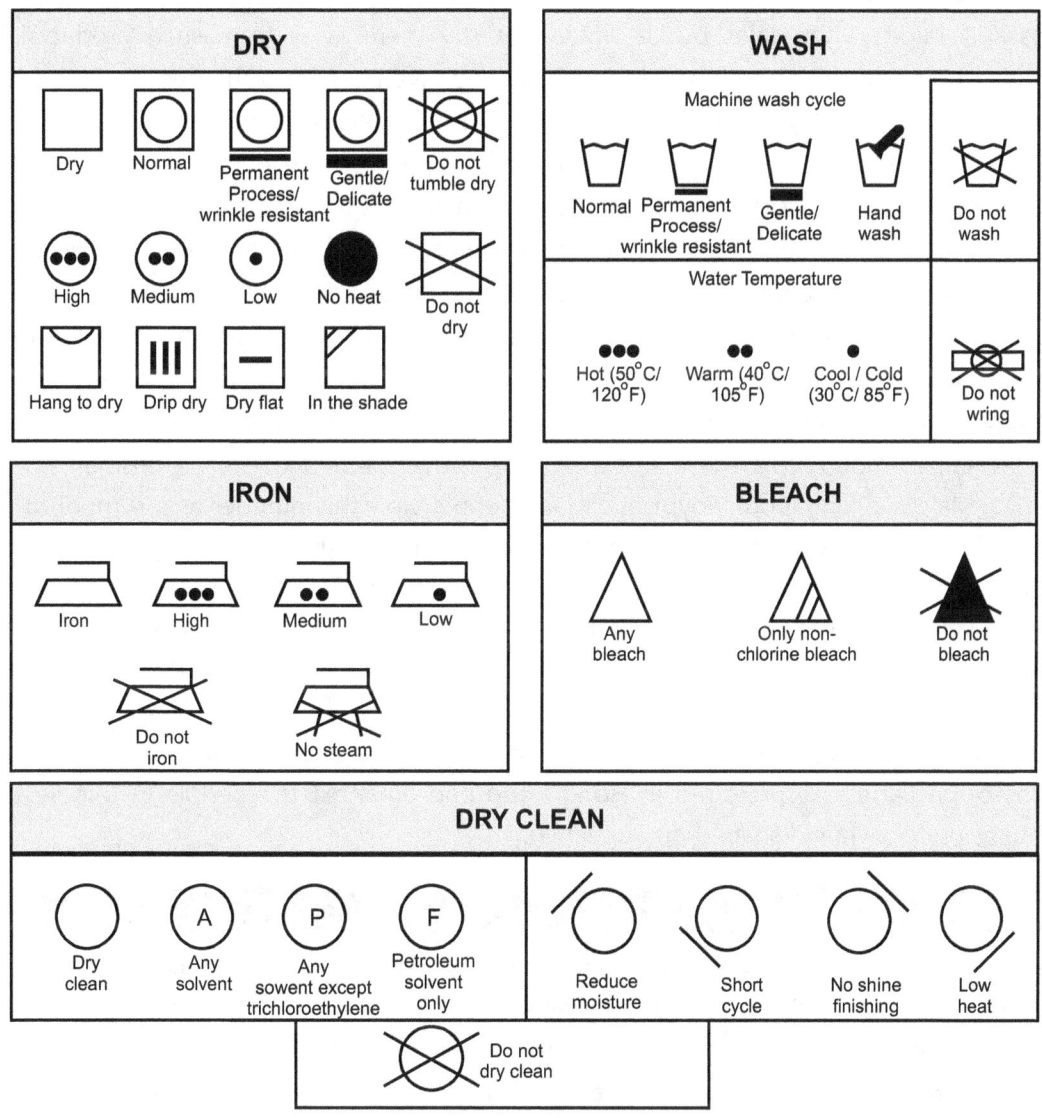

Fig. 3.1

Colours, Numbers and Shapes of Labels preferred in Various Countries

While designing the labels, the exporters should keep in mind the preferences of the consumers with regard to colours, numbers and shapes. People in different countries have their preferences with regard to the impact of colours, numbers and shapes with regard to labels and packages. Fig. 3.1 explains the various types of symbols used for labelling textile products. Though it sounds superstitious yet it is a fact that people across different parts of the world shy away from those products, which are made of shapes or colour schemes which they think have 'negative effect' on their minds. The use of colours, labels or numbers on the product/packages which people think have a 'positive effect' on their minds would not necessarily improve the sales but it would not shy them away from such products. For example, the colour black is considered to have negative impact on the people in countries such as Singapore, Malaysia, Libya, Japan, Middle East, Greece, Argentina and other countries in Latin America. The colour purple has negative impact on the minds of people in Italy whereas colours with soft tones are considered to have positive impact. The colour green is welcomed across the countries in Muslim communities, combinations of red and white and gold and silver are preferred colours in Japan. Red colour is perceived to have negative impact on the minds of people in the African region. Bright colours have positive impact on the minds of the people in Peru, Surinam, Hong Kong, Taiwan, Greece and Malaysia.

The number 13 is perhaps the most hated number across different countries of the world such as Japan, Hong Kong, Korea, Taiwan, Germany, Denmark, Greece, Romania, Latin America, Malaysia, Singapore, Egypt etc. Many people view this number as a symbol of bad luck and the exporters should avoid this number while numbering the packages. Number 17 is considered to have negative impact in Italy and number 7 or any other number ending with 7 is considered to be number of bad luck in Kenya. The even numbers are preferred in Hong Kong, Korea and Taiwan whereas some of the numbers like 1, 3, 5 and 8 are viewed as numbers with positive effect in Japan.

Triangular shapes of packages are not preferred in Korea and Taiwan. Round and square shapes of packages are preferred in Hong Kong and amongst the people in Middle East. Egyptians prefer pyramid shaped packages.

3.6 Shipment of Goods

The exporter should arrange for the shipment of the goods as soon as they have been cleared by the inspection agency. The process of shipment of goods would involve essentially their clearance by the Central Excise and the Custom Authorities.

Part I: Central Excise Clearance Procedure: In the previous section of this chapter the procedure for Central Excise has already been explained.

Part II: Custom Clearance of Export Shipment: Every exporter is required to seek custom clearance of the export goods before sending them to the importer. The exporter can send the shipment through any one of the following modes of transportation:

1. Shipment by air
2. Shipment by sea

3. Shipment by post
4. Shipment by road

The procedure for custom clearance is the same whether the shipment is sent by air/sea/post/road. However, there are some minor variations too.

For clearance of export goods, the export or his agents have to undertake the following formalities.

(a) Registration

- The exporters have to obtain PAN based Business Identification Number (BIN) from the Directorate General of Foreign Trade prior to filing of shipping bill for clearance of export goods. Under the EDI System, PAN based BIN is received by the Customs System from the DGFT online.

- The exporters are also required to register authorised foreign exchange dealer code (through which export proceeds are expected to be realised) and open a current account in the designated bank for credit of any drawback incentive.

(b) Registration in the case of export under export promotion schemes

- All the exporters intending to export under the export promotion scheme need to get their licences/DEEC book etc. registered at the Customs Station. For such registration, original documents are required.

(c) Processing of Shipping Bill – Non-EDI

- Under manual system, shipping bills or, as the case may be, bills of export are required to be filed in format as prescribed in the Shipping Bill and Bill of Export (Form) regulations, 1991. The bills of export are being used if clearance of export goods is taken at the Land Customs Stations. Different forms of shipping bill/bill of export have been prescribed for export of duty-free goods, export of dutiable goods and export under drawback etc.

- Shipping Bills are required to be filed along with all original documents such as invoice, AR-4, packing list etc. The assessing officer in the Export Department checks the value of the goods, classification under Drawback schedule in case of Drawback Shipping Bills, rate of duty/cess where applicable, exportability of goods under EXIM policy and other laws enforce. The DEEC/DEPB Shipping bills are processed in the DEEC group. In case of DEEC Shipping bills, the assessing officer verifies that the description of the goods declared in the shipping bill and invoice match with the description of the resultant product as given in the DEEC book. If the assessing officer has any doubts regarding value, description of goods, he may call for samples of the goods from the docks. He may also call for any other information required by him for processing of shipping bill. He may assess the shipping bill after visual inspection of the sample or may send it for tests and pass the shipping bill provisionally.

- Once the shipping bill is passed by the Export Department, the exporter or his agent presents the goods to the shed appraiser (export) in docks for examination. The shed appraiser may mark the document to a Custom officer (usually an examiner) for examining the goods. The examination is carried out under the supervision of the shed appraiser (export). If the description and other particulars of the goods are found to be as declared, the shed appraiser gives a 'let export' order, after which the exporter may contact the preventive superintendent for supervising the loading of goods on to the vessel.

(d) Processing of Shipping Bill – EDI

- Under EDI System, declarations in prescribed format are to be filed through the Service Centres of Customs.

- A checklist is generated for verification of data by the exporter/CHA. After verification, the data is submitted to the System by the Service Centre operator and the System generates a Shipping Bill Number, which is endorsed on the printed checklist and returned to the exporter/CHA.

(e) Octroi procedure, Quota allocation and other certification for Export Goods

- The quota allocation label is required to be pasted on the export invoice. The allocation number of AEPC is to be entered in the system at the time of shipping bill entry.

- The quota certification of export invoice needs to be submitted to Customs along with other original documents at the time of examination of the export cargo. For determining the validity date of the quota, the relevant date needs to be the date on which the full consignment is presented to the Customs for examination and duly recorded in the computer system.

- In EDI system at Delhi Air cargo, the quota information is automatically verified from the AEPC/TEXPROCIL system.

- Since the shipping bill is generated only after the 'let export order' is given by Customs, the exporter may make use of export invoice or such other document as required by the Octroi authorities for the purpose of Octroi exemption.

(f) Arrival of Goods at Docks

- The goods brought for the purpose of examination and subsequent 'let export' is allowed entry to the dock on the strength of the checklist and other declarations filed by the exporter in the Service Centre. The port authorities have to endorse the quantity of goods actually received on the reverse of the Check List.

(g) System Appraisal of Shipping Bills

- In many cases the Shipping Bill is processed by the system on the basis of declarations made by the exporters without any human intervention. In other cases where the Shipping Bill is processed on screen by the Customs officer, he may call for the samples, if required for confirming the declared value or for checking classification under the Drawback schedule. He may also give any special instructions for examination of goods, if felt necessary.

(h) Status of Shipping Bill

- The exporter/CHA can check up with the query counter at the Service Centre whether the Shipping Bill submitted by them in the system has been cleared or not, before the goods are brought into the docks for examination and export. The Customs officer may pass the Shipping Bill after all the queries have been satisfactorily replied to.

(i) Customs Examination of Export Cargo

- After the receipt of the goods in the dock, the exporter/CHA may contact the Customs officer designated for the purpose present the check list with the endorsement of port authority and other declarations as aforesaid along with all original documents such as Invoice and Packing List, AR-4, etc.

- Customs officer may verify the quantity of the goods actually received and enter into the system and thereafter mark the Electronic Shipping Bill and also hand over all original documents to the Dock Appraiser of the Dock, who may assign a Customs officer for the examination and intimate the officers' name and the packages to be examined, if any, on the check list and return it to the exporter or his agent. The Customs officer may inspect/examine the shipment along with the Dock Appraiser.

- The Customs officer enters the examination report in the system. He then marks the Electronic Bill along with all original documents and check list to the Dock Appraiser. If the Dock Appraiser is satisfied that the particulars entered in the system conform to the description given in the original documents and as seen in the physical examination, he may proceed to allow "let export" for the shipment and inform the exporter or his agent.

(j) Variation between the Declaration and Physical Examination

- The check list and the declaration along with all original documents are retained by the appraiser concerned.

- In case of any variation between the declaration in the Shipping Bill and physical documents/examination report, the appraiser may mark the Electronic Shipping Bill to the Assistant Commissioner/Deputy Commissioner of Customs (Exports). He may also forward the physical documents to Assistant Commissioner/Deputy Commissioner of Customs (Exports) and instruct the exporter or his agent to meet the Assistant Commissioner/Deputy Commissioner of Customs (Exports) for settlement of dispute.

- In case the exporter agrees with the views of the department, the Shipping Bill needs to be processed accordingly. Where, however, the exporter disputes the view of the department natural justice is required to be followed before finalisation of the issue.

(k) Stuffing/Loading of Goods in Containers

- The exporter or his agent should hand over the exporter copy of the shipping bill duly signed by the Appraiser permitting "Let Export" to the steamer agent who may then approach the proper officer (Preventive Officer) for allowing the shipment.

- In case of container cargo the stuffing of container at the dock is done under preventive supervision. Loading of both containerised and bulk cargo is done under preventive supervision. The Customs Preventive Superintendent (Docks) may enter the particulars of packages actually stuffed into the container and the bottle seal number particulars of loading of cargo container on board into the system, and endorse these details on the exporter copy of the shipping bill presented to him by the steamer agent.

- If there is a difference in the quantity/number of packages stuffed in the containers/goods loaded on vessel, the Superintendent (Docks) may put a remark on the shipping bill in the system and that shipping bill requires amendment or changed quantity. Such shipping bill also may not be taken up for the purpose of sanction of Drawback/DEEC logging, till the shipping bill is suitably amended for the changed quantity. The Customs Preventive Officer supervising the loading of container and general cargo in to the vessel may give "shipped on board" endorsement on the exporter's copy of the shipping bill.

(l) Drawal of Samples

- Where the Dock Appraiser (export) orders for samples to be drawn and tested, the Customs officer may proceed to draw two samples from the consignment and enter the particulars thereof along with details of the testing agency in the ICES/E system. There is no separate register for recording dates of samples drawn. Three copies of the test memo are prepared by the Customs officer and are signed by the Customs officer and Appraising officer on behalf of Customs and the exporter or his agent. The disposal of the three copies of the test memo are as follows:

  (i)Original – To be sent along with the sample to the test agency.

  (ii) Duplicate – Customs copy to be retained with the 2nd sample.

  (iii) Triplicate – Exporter's copy.

(m) Amendments

- Any correction/amendments in the check list generated after filing of declaration can be made at the service centre, provided, the documents have not yet been submitted in the system and the shipping bill number has not been generated.

- Where corrections are required to be made after the generation of the shipping bill number or after the goods have been brought into the Export Dock, amendments are carried out in the following manner.

(n) Export of Goods under Claim for Drawback

- After actual export of the goods, the Drawback claim is processed through EDI system by the officers of Drawback Branch on first come first served basis. There is no need for filing separate drawback claims.

- The status of the shipping bills and sanction of DBK claim can be ascertained from the query counter set up at the service centre. If any query has been raised or deficiency noticed, the same is shown on the terminal. A printout of the query/deficiency may be obtained by the authorised person of the exporter from the service centre.

- The exporters are required to reply to such queries through the service centre. The claim will come in the queue of the EDI system only after replies to queries/deficiencies are entered by the service centre.

- All the claims sanctioned on a particular day are enumerated in a scroll and transferred to the bank through the system. The bank credits the drawback amount in the respective accounts of the exporters. The bank may send a fortnightly statement to the exporters of such credits made in their accounts.

(o) Generation of Shipping Bills

- After the "let export" order is given on the system by the Appraiser, the Shipping Bill is generated by the system in two copies, that is, one customs copy, one exporter's copy (EP copy is generated after submission of EGM).

- After obtaining the printout, the appraiser obtains the signatures of the Customs officer on the examination report and the representative of the CHA on both copies of the shipping bill and examination report. The Appraiser thereafter signs and stamps both the copies of the shipping bill at the specified place.

3.7 ECGC Services [Export Credit Guarantee Corporation]

Export Credit Guarantee Corporation of India Limited was established in the year 1957 by the Government of India to strengthen the export promotion drive by covering the risk of exporting on credit. Being essentially an export promotion organisation, it functions under the administrative control of the Ministry of Commerce and Industry, Department of Commerce, Government of India. It is managed by a Board of Directors comprising of representatives from the Government, Reserve Bank of India, banking, insurance and exporting community.

Functions of ECGC: The functions of ECGC are as follows:

1. Provides a range of credit risk insurance cover to exporters against loss in export of goods and services.

2. Offers guarantees to banks and financial institutions to enable exporters to obtain better facilities from them.

3. Provides overseas investment insurance to Indian companies investing in joint ventures abroad in the form of equity or loan.

4. Offers insurance protection to exporters against payment risks.

5. Provides guidance in export-related activities.

6. Makes available information on different countries with its own credit ratings.

7. Makes it easy to obtain export finance from banks/financial institutions.

8. Assists exporters in recovering bad debts.

9. Provides information on credit-worthiness of overseas buyers.

Need for export credit insurance: Payments for exports are open to risks even at the best of times. The risks have assumed large proportions today due to the far-reaching political and economic changes that are sweeping the world. An outbreak of war or civil war may block or delay payment for goods exported. A coup or an insurrection may also bring about the same result. Economic difficulties or balance of payment problems may lead a country to impose restrictions on either import of certain goods or on transfer of payments for goods imported. In addition, the exporters have to face commercial risks of insolvency or protracted default of buyers. The commercial risks of a foreign buyer going bankrupt or losing his capacity to pay are aggravated due to the political and economic uncertainties. Export credit insurance is designed to protect exporters from the consequences of the payment risks, both political and commercial, and to enable them to expand their overseas business without fear of loss.

Objectives of ECGC

- To protect the exporters against credit risks, that is non-repayment by buyers
- To protect the banks against losses due to non-repayment of loans by exporters

Covers Issued by ECGC

The covers issued by ECGC can be divided broadly into four groups –

1. **Standard Policies:** Issued to exporters to protect them against payment risks involved in exports on short-term credit.

2. **Specific Policies:** Designed to protect Indian firms against payment risk involved in (i) exports on deferred terms of payment (ii) service rendered to foreign parties, and (iii) construction works and turnkey projects undertaken abroad.

3. **Financial Guarantees:** Issued to banks in India to protect them from risk of loss involved in their extending financial support to exporters at pre-shipment and post-shipment stages; and

4. **Special Schemes** such as Transfer Guarantee meant to protect banks which add confirmation to letters of credit opened by foreign banks, insurance cover for buyer's credit, etc.

(A) Standard Policies

ECGC has designed 4 types of standard policies to provide cover for shipments made on short-term credit –

1. **Shipments (comprehensive risks) Policy:** To cover both political and commercial risks from the date of shipment.

2. **Shipments (political risks) Policy:** To cover only political risks from the date of shipment.

3. **Contracts (comprehensive risks) Policy:** To cover both commercial and political risk from the date of contract.

4. **Contracts (political risks) Policy:** To cover only political risks from the date of contract.

Risks Covered under the Standard Policies

1. **Commercial Risks**

   - Insolvency of the buyer.

   - Buyer's protracted default to pay for goods accepted by him.

   - Buyer's failure to accept goods subject to certain conditions.

2. **Political Risks**

   - Imposition of restrictions on remittances by the government in the buyer's country or any government action which may block or delay payment to exporter.

   - War, revolution or civil disturbances in the buyer's country. Cancellation of a valid import license or new import licensing restrictions in the buyer's country after the date of shipment or contract, as applicable.

   - Cancellation of export license or imposition of new export licensing restrictions in India after the date of contract (under contract policy).

   - Payment of additional handling, transport or insurance charges occasioned by interruption or diversion of voyage that cannot be recovered from the buyer.

   - Any other cause of loss occurring outside India, not normally insured by commercial insurers and beyond the control of the exporter and/or buyer.

Risks not covered under Standard Policies

The losses due to the following risks are not covered:

1. Commercial disputes including quality disputes raised by the buyer, unless the exporter obtains a decree from a competent court of law in the buyer's country in his favour.

2. Causes inherent in the nature of the goods.

3. Buyer's failure to obtain import or exchange authorisation from authorities in his county.

4. Insolvency or default of any agent of the exporter or of the collecting bank.

5. Loss or damage to goods which can be covered by commercial insurers.

6. Exchange fluctuations.

7. Discrepancy in documents.

(B) Specific Policies

A continuing insurance for the regular flow of exporter's shipment of raw materials, consumable durables for which credit period does not normally exceed 180 days requires a standard policy.

ECGC insures on a case-to-case basis, under specific policies, contracts for export of capital goods, turnkey projects, construction works or rendering services abroad as they are not of a repetitive nature.

1. Specific Policy for Supply Contracts

Specific policies for supply contracts are issued in case of export of capital goods sold on deferred credit. These can be of any of the four forms mentioned below.

- **Specific Shipments (Comprehensive Risks) Policy** to cover both commercial and political risks at the post-shipment stage.

- **Specific Shipments (Political Risks) Policy** to cover only political risks after shipment stage.

- **Specific Contracts (Comprehensive Risks) Policy** to cover political and commercial risks after contract date.

- **Specific Contracts (Political Risks) Policy** to cover only political risks after contract date.

2. Service Policy

Indian firms would be exposed to payment risks similar to those involved in export of goods as they provide a wide range of services like technical or professional services, hiring or leasing to foreign parties (private or government). Such risks are covered by ECGC under the service policy.

Specific Services (political risks) Policy can be obtained if the service contract is with overseas government, overseas private parties, and especially those contracts not supported by bank guarantees. Normally, cover is issued on a case-to-case basis. The policy covers 90 percent of the loss suffered.

3.   Construction Works Policy

This policy covers civil construction jobs as well as turnkey projects involving supplies and services contracts both with private and foreign governments.

It covers 85 percent of the loss suffered on account of contracts with government agencies and 75 percent of loss suffered on account of construction contracts with private parties.

(C) Financial Guarantees

Adequate financial support from banks is required by exporters to carry out their export contracts. The lending programmes of banks are supported by ECGC who issue financial guarantees which protect the banks from losses on account of their lending to exporters. Six guarantees are in place for this purpose –

   (i)   Packing Credit Guarantee

   (ii)   Export Production Finance Guarantee

   (iii) Export Finance Guarantee

   (iv)   Post Shipment Export Credit Guarantee

   (v)   Export Performance Guarantee

   (v)   Export Finance (Overseas Lending) Guarantee.

These guarantees give protection to banks against losses due to non-payment by exporters on account of their insolvency or default. A premium is charged by ECGC for its services that may vary from 5 paise to 7.5 paise per month for ₹ 100. If ECGC desires, the premium charged depends upon the type of guarantee and is subject to change.

(i) Packing Credit Guarantee: This is a guarantee given to the exporter for the manufacture, processing, purchasing or packing of goods meant for export against a firm order of L/C.

Pre-shipment advances towards preliminary expenses are given by banks to firms who enter contracts for export of services or for construction works abroad. These advances are also eligible for cover under this guarantee. ECGC bears two thirds of the loss.

(ii) Export Production Finance Guarantee: This guarantee enables banks to provide finance at pre-shipment stage to the full extent of the domestic cost of production and subject to certain guidelines.

The guarantee covers some specified products such as textiles, woollen carpets, ready-made garments, etc. and the loss covered is two thirds.

(iii) Export Finance Guarantee: Banks grant this guarantee over post-shipment advances to exporters against export incentives receivable such as DBK. However, in case the exporter does not repay the loan, the banks suffer loss. The loss insured is up to three fourth or 75 percent.

(iv) Post-Shipment Export Credit Guarantee: This guarantee covers post-shipment finance given to exporters by the banks, and purchase or discounting of export bills. The ECGC confirms that the exporter has obtained a Shipment or Contract Risk Policy. The loss covered under this guarantee is 75 percent.

(v) Export Performance Guarantee: Exporters are often required to execute bid bonds supported by a bank guarantee, and on the contract being secured by the exporter, he has to furnish a bank guarantee to foreign parties to ensure due performance or against advance payment or in lieu of retention money. Needless to say, it is very frustrating when the exporter's bank is unwilling to issue the guarantee.

This guarantee protects the bank against 75 percent of the losses that it may suffer on account of guarantee given by it on behalf of exporters.

(vi) Export Finance (Overseas Lending) Guarantee: When a bank financing overseas projects provides a loan to the contractor in foreign currency, it can protect itself from risk of non-payment by the contractor by obtaining this guarantee. The loss covered under this policy is to the extent of three fourth (75 percent).

(D) Special Schemes

Apart from providing policies (standard and specific) and guarantees, ECGC provides special schemes to the banks and to the exporters. The schemes are –

1. **Transfer Guarantee:** The transfer guarantee is provided to safeguard banks in India against losses arising out of risk of confirmation of L/C. The risks can be either political or commercial or both. Loss due to political risks is covered up to 90 percent and that due to commercial risks up to 75 percent.

2. **Insurance Cover for Buyer's Credit and Lines of Credit:** Today Indian financial institutions have started direct lending to the buyers or financial institutions in developing countries for importing machinery and equipment from India. This sort of financing facilitates immediate payment to exporters and frees them from the problem of credit management. ECGC has introduced this scheme to protect Indian financial institutions which extend export credit to overseas buyers or institutions.

3. **Overseas Investment Insurance:** The involvement of exporters in capital anticipation in overseas projects has assumed importance with the increasing exports of capital goods and turnkey projects from India. ECGC through this scheme provides protection for such investment. Ideally the insurance cover is for 15 years.

3.8 GSP [Generalised System of Preferences] Rules and Origin

3.8.1 Introduction

GSP is a non-contractual instrument by which industrialised (developed) countries unilaterally and on the basis of non-reciprocity extend tariff concessions to developing countries. It involves reduced MFN tariffs or duty-free entry of eligible products exported by beneficiary countries to the markets of donor countries.

The following countries extend tariff preferences under their GSP Scheme.

- United States, European Union, Canada, Australia (only to LDCs), New Zealand, Japan, Norway, Switzerland, Bulgaria, Poland, Hungary, Belarus, Slovakia, Russia, Czech Republic.
- Most imports eligible under the GSP programme are free of duty. There are over 20 industrialised countries – donor countries (country of destination) which maintain GSP programmes and over 100 least developed countries – beneficiary countries (country of origin) which are eligible under the GSP programme.

In order to meet the general conditions to qualify for preference, products must –

- Fall within a description of products eligible for preference in the country of destination.
- The description entered on the form must be sufficiently detailed to enable the products to be identified by the Customs officer examining them.
- Comply with the rules of origin of the country of destination.
- Comply with the consignment conditions specified by the country of destination.
- In general, products must be consigned directly from the country of exportation to the country of destination but most preference-giving countries accept passage through intermediate countries subject to certain conditions (for Australia, direct consignment is not necessary).

The main objectives of granting trade preferences to developing countries are to:

- Enhance their export earnings;
- Promote industrialisation, and
- Encourage the diversification of their economies.

3.8.2 Origin of the GSP

The idea of tariff preferences for developing countries was the subject of considerable discussion within the United Nations Conference on Trade and Development (UNCTAD) in the 1960s.

The Generalised System of Preferences was introduced at the first meeting of the UNCTAD with a view to assisting the developing countries in their exports and development efforts.

In 1971, the GATT enacted two waivers to the MFN that permitted tariff preferences to be granted to developing country goods. Both these waivers were limited in time to ten years.

In 1979, as part of the Tokyo Round, the GATT established a permanent exemption to the MFN obligation by way of the enabling clause. This exemption allowed contracting parties to establish systems of trade preferences for other countries, with the warning that these systems had to be 'generalised, non-discriminatory and non-reciprocal' with respect to the countries they benefited. Countries were not supposed to set up GSP programs that benefited just a few of their 'friends'.

The enabling clause has thus created a permanent legal basis for trade preferences provided by developed countries, both generally for all developing countries under GSP regimes, and also for specific more preferential treatment of the least-developed countries.

One important aspect of the enabling clause is that it did not impose any legal obligation on GATT countries to extend such trade preferences.

In other words, developed countries can provide trade preferences for developing countries, but they are not legally bound to do so. As a result, trade preferences under the GSP continue to be granted unilaterally by the developed countries concerned, and so can always be changed or even withdrawn completely, without violating GATT/WTO commitments.

3.8.3 Rules of Origin

The Rules of Origin are an essential element of all schemes and clearer understanding of them and their proper application is of utmost importance for the implementation of any GSP.

The main purpose of rules of origin is to ensure that the benefits of preferential tariff treatment under the Generalised System of Preference (GSP) are limited to products which have bona fide been taken from harvested, produced or manufactured in the preference-receiving countries of export.

The rules of origin include the origin details, consignment conditions and documentary evidence. The origin criteria is normally defined in terms of the goods that are wholly produced and manufactured in a beneficiary country, or goods that have been sufficiently worked, processed and transformed into a new and different article. The main consignment condition is that the originating products must be directly imported from the beneficiary country into the preference-giving country. The main documentary evidence is the provision of an originating certificate known as the Form A.

3.8.4 Product Coverage

Most of the GSP product coverage includes agricultural and industrial exports with a few but often notable exceptions. The exceptions established by the United States GSP include textiles and apparel, certain footwear, certain leather products (handbags, luggage), certain watches and watch parts, canned tuna, and petroleum and petroleum products.

3.8.5 Countries that Extend GSP Benefits

Presently, 29 preference giving countries are extending GSP concession through their respective schemes. These are Australia, Canada, Czech Republic, European Union, Japan, New Zealand, Norway, Bulgaria, Hungary, Poland, Russian Federation, Slovakia, Switzerland, and USA.

It is to be noted that the GSP schemes offered by the various donor countries and their rules of origin differ fundamentally. Goods complying with the conditions of the GSP of the USA, for example, will not necessarily comply with the EU GSP.

3.8.6 Beneficiaries of GSP

The beneficiaries of non-reciprocal preferential schemes have to meet certain, often non-economic conditions to be designated and to maintain the beneficiary status. For example, United States GSP states that a country will not be designated as a beneficiary if it is a communist country or lacks adequate and effective protection of intellectual property rights.

In May 1998, the EU introduced a special incentive scheme providing additional preferential GSP margins (between 10 to 35 percent) for beneficiaries that voluntarily comply with the International Labour Office conventions on the right to organise and to bargain collectively.

In addition, graduation or the withdrawal of GSP preferences rests on the argument by preference-giving countries that preferences comprise special treatment that should be reserved only for the needy developing countries. Hence, those developing countries which have attained a sufficient degree of competitiveness in the production of a particular product or sector should have their GSP benefits terminated for that product or sector. The full country graduation is applied to developing countries that have become economically more advanced. For example, Switzerland has withdrawn GSP benefits for Bahamas, Bermuda, Brunei, Darussalam, Caiman Islands, Cyprus, Falkland Islands, Hong Kong, Kuwait, Mexico, Qatar, Republic of Korea, Singapore and the United Arab Emirates.

3.8.7 Economic Effects

In general GSP programs have been a mixed success. On one hand, most rich countries have complied with the obligation to generalise their programs by offering benefits to a large number of beneficiaries, generally including nearly every non-OECD member state.

However criticism has been raised that most GSP programs are not completely generalised with respect to products. That is, they don't cover products of greatest export interest to low-income developing countries lacking natural resources. In the United States and many other rich countries, domestic producers of "simple" manufactured goods, such as textiles, leather goods, ceramics, glass and steel, have long claimed that they could not compete with large quantities of imports. Thus, such products have been categorically excluded from GSP coverage under the U.S. and many other GSP programs. Critics assert that these excluded products are precisely the kinds of manufactures that most developing countries are able to export, the argument being that developing countries may not be able to efficiently produce things like locomotives or telecommunications satellites, but they can make shirts.

However, supporters note that even in the face of its limitations, it would not be accurate to assume that GSP has failed to benefit developing countries, though some say GSP has benefited developing countries unevenly. Some insist that, for most of its history, GSP has benefited "richer developing" countries while providing virtually no assistance to the world's least developed countries, such as Haiti, Nepal, and most countries in sub-Saharan Africa. The U.S. however, has closed some of these gaps through supplemental preference programs like the African Growth and Opportunity Act.

3.9 Role of Overseas Agent and Remittance of Commission

If a supplier has some success in personal selling to visiting buyers or during sales visits abroad, he may feel that the next step is to have someone selling for him in a selected export market. He may also feel that he needs on-the-spot help in establishing the marketing channels, for example, in finding and working with distributors or wholesalers.

The supplier cannot spend a great deal of time on export selling himself because of his responsibilities to the business at home. The idea of a full-time travelling sales person may seem attractive at first. But it is probably not economical to make such an appointment as a first step in exporting. Furthermore, if the supplier appoints one of his sales executives to handle this, it would take this executive time before he or she gets to know the export market well enough to sell successfully.

In such situations, it is usual to appoint an agent. An agent is a person of the firm that handles negotiations on the supplier's behalf. An export agent is simply an agent who is active in the export market. Agents work on the basis of commissions and do not assume any risks. In contrast, a distributor being a direct customer pays for the goods that are supplied and takes over the risk of further marketing.

The following box compares the advantages of using an agent with those of employing the company's export sales staff.

Advantages of an Agent	Advantages of a Sales Executive
Cost is variable; No expenses unless sales are achieved.	100% commitment of time.
Agent has local knowledge.	Can carry out research and other activities.
An agent's sales of an already established product can help in the introduction of a new and unknown product.	Will not fear that success will bring about his/her replacement.
Highly motivated, is paid only if he/she sells.	Staff development. Customers impressed by commitment. Knows details of production and origin.

Finding an Agent

There are good agents and bad ones, and even some good ones may not be suitable for the products or for the prospective customers. When selecting, check that:

- They are respectable business representatives.

- They are not representing a competing producer.

- They have the organisational structure and the facilities necessary to do the job.

- They have serious long-term interest in the product and are not handling too many other products.

- They are experienced in the type of product and market area and have established connections.

Finding, appointing and using an agent needs careful planning. First a list of the possible agents for this particular product is needed. The suppliers own embassy abroad or local chambers of commerce can probably supply that list. Then the supplier can write to these possible agents, explain his requirements and ask if they are available to handle the product.

From the replies received, a short list of the most suitable agents can be prepared. If possible, each of them can be visited personally. In any case, references should be obtained from others, particularly from other firms that the agent represents and if possible, from some customers.

It is customary for exporters to have agents (the distributor or sales representative) located in the importing country. The distributor imports, stocks and distributes the product. The sales representative solicits order from the distributor and collects a commission and/or a fee from the exporter and/or the distributor. Selling a product through an overseas agent is a very successful strategy. Sales agents are available on commission basis for any sales they make. The key benefit of using an overseas sales agent is that you get the advantage of their extensive knowledge of the target market. A sales agent also provides support to an exporter in the matter of transportation, reservation of accommodation, appointment with the government as and when required. It is, therefore, essential that one should very carefully select an overseas agent.

The decision to have a distributor or a sales representative depends on the product, market size, distribution patterns, and business practices of the importing country. For a small market like United Arab Emirates, a distributor is preferred. For a huge market like U.S.A. or China, several distributors and/or sales representatives is necessary. The domestic market is widely spread across the states in U.S.A. or provinces in China. It is difficult for one agent to effectively handle the entire U.S.A. or China.

Exclusive Agency versus Non-Exclusive Agency

When one agent represents the exporter in an importing country it is known as an exclusive agency. An exclusive agency usually requires an annual quota, that is, a required annual import volume, and prohibits the agent from representing competitors.

Non-exclusive agency means any agent can represent the exporter in an importing country or can buy from the exporter at anytime without an annual quota. Both the exclusive agency and the non-exclusive agency normally require a minimum amount in a shipment.

It is important to let the agent have a trial sales period, for example six months, in order to gauge the performance before granting exclusive agency. It is necessary to deal on a non-exclusive agency basis for a large market like U.S.A. At times an agent from the U.S.A. may request exclusive agency covering a specific state. This arrangement rarely works to the benefit of the agent. It is difficult for the exporter to prevent its distributors in other states from selling to that specific state.

Company Exclusivity versus Product Exclusivity

Exclusivity or exclusive representation normally refers to company exclusivity, which means that the agent exclusively represents the exporter and all its products and services in an importing country.

Product exclusivity means that the agent exclusively represents the selected product(s) of the exporter or the product(s) made by the exporter under contract from the agent. Product exclusivity is common in the OEM (Original Equipment Manufacturer) arrangement between the buyer and the export-manufacturer. The exporter supplies the proprietary product made under contract to the buyer and the exporter is prohibited from selling this product to other buyers.

Agency Contract

In certain countries agency contracts are regulated by the government. Agency contracts may be required by some exporting countries in commission sales abroad, even on a non-exclusive agency basis. The agency contract and supporting shipping documents are used by the exporter to apply for the remittance to pay the overseas agent's commission.

The exporter must be cautious in selecting an agent and in preparing the agency contract. The agency contract in certain countries is quite onerous. It can cost the exporter a fortune to rescind the contract due to the agent's poor performance or non-compliance to the terms of the contract. At times, it is impossible to rescind the contract under the national laws and regulations. The international litigation is costly.

The agency contract issued and signed is binding and it must be respected by the exporter and the agent. The export-manufacturer who is exclusively represented in a country must not intentionally sell its products to that country through any export-traders in the exporter's country or in a third country. This malpractice is exercised by some exporters in the hope of selling more. The malpractice usually ends in a price war between the exporter's own products in the importing country. The agent's loss of profit may end in the agent's loss of confidence in the product and the exporter.

Agency Inquiry

Quite often, an exporter exclusively represented in a country may still receive inquiries from other agents in that country. Some agency contracts may stipulate a procedure to follow in the event of receiving such inquiries. Otherwise, the exporter may send a reply indicating that it is being represented already in that country and give the name, address and contact number of the agent, and then forward a copy of both the reply and the inquiry to the exclusive agent for reference. Or, the exporter may forward a copy of the inquiry to the exclusive agent, without directly replying to the inquiry.

Methods of Paying Agents

Agents are usually paid on a commission basis and hence are known as 'commission agents'. The commission is normally a percentage of the value of the goods sold and for which, payments have been received from the customer.

It is difficult to arrive at specific rates of commission. They may vary from less than 1% to more than 15% according to the nature of the market and the sales problems. In other words contracts for a large volume of commodities to be delivered over a fairly long period may give the agent a commission of 1 percent and small orders may give a commission of up to 15 percent.

Sometimes there might be an agreement with the agents to pay them a commission on all orders received from customers in their territory regardless of whether orders are actually placed through them. Whatever type of agreement is there, agents should always be told about orders received direct from customers so that they can follow up and possibly obtain repeat orders. The supplier and the agent should also let each other have copies of all correspondence with customers.

Del credere agents: Agents receive higher than usual payments when they act del credere. In other words this means that they take risk of payment for the orders if the customer fails to do so. Del credere agents are normally paid a higher commission than ordinary agents. The extra commission may be anything from 5 percent to 15 percent, to compensate them for the credit risk they assume. However, Del credere agents are not very common, but where they exist they help exporters to sell with great confidence in markets where it is difficult for them to judge the creditworthiness of prospective customers.

3.10 Incentives for Export from Government

The facilities and incentives presently available to the Indian exporters include the following.

(A) Import Facilities for Exporters

1. Advance License: An advance licence is granted for the import of inputs without payment of basic customs duty. Such licences shall be issued in accordance with the policy and procedure in force on the date of issue of the licence and shall be subject to the fulfilment of a time-bound export obligation, and value addition as may be specified. Advance licences may be either value based or quantity based.

As per the latest amendments to the EXIM Policy, the facility of back to back inland Letter of Credit has been introduced, to enable an Advance Licence holder to source his inputs from domestic suppliers.

Value-based Advance License: Under a value-based advance licence, any of the inputs specified in the licence may be imported within the total CIF (Cost Insurance and Freight) value indicated for those inputs, except inputs specified as sensitive items.

Under a value-based advance licence, both the quantity and the FOB value of the exports to be achieved shall be specified. It shall be obligatory on the part of the licence holder to achieve both the quantity and FOB value of the exports specified in the licence.

Advance licence can be issued for (i) Physical exports, (ii) Intermediate supply and (iii) Deemed exports.

The licences are issued to the manufacturer exporter or the merchant exporter. The licences and/or materials imported there under shall not be transferable even after completion of export obligation. The licences are issued to make a positive value addition. The licences are subject to the fulfilment of a time bound export obligation as specified in the policy.

Advance Licence for Intermediate Supply: Advance licence may be issued for intermediate supply to a manufacturer-exporter for the import of inputs required in the manufacture of goods to be supplied to the ultimate exporter/deemed exporter holding another advance licence.

Advance Licence for Deemed Export: Advance licence can be issued for deemed export to the main contractor for import of inputs required in the manufacture of goods to be supplied to the categories mentioned in the policy. An advance licence for deemed export can also be availed by the sub-contractor of the main contractor to such project. The licences shall be exempted from basic customs duty, surcharge and additional customs duty only.

2. Duty Entitlement Pass Book Scheme (DEPB): Duty Entitlement Pass Book Scheme, in short DEPB, is an export incentive scheme. Notified on 1st April, 1997, the DEPB Scheme consisted of (a) Post-export DEPB and (b) Pre-export DEPB. The pre-export DEPB scheme was abolished with effect from 1st April, 2000. Under the post-export DEPB, which is issued after exports, the exporter is given a Duty Entitlement Pass Book Scheme at a pre-determined credit on the FOB value. The DEPB rates allow import of any items except the items which are otherwise restricted for imports. Items such as gold nibs, gold pen, gold watches etc. though covered under the generic description of writing instruments, components of writing instruments and watches are thus not eligible for benefit under the DEPB scheme.

3. Duty-free Replenishment Certificate (DFRC): DFRC scheme was first announced in EXIM Policy 2000-2001 with effect from 1st April 2000. DFRC scheme was continued in EXIM Policy 2002-07 with some minor changes. The earlier DFRC scheme announced in the 2000-01 EXIM Policy required that for the purpose of allowing DFRC benefit to imported inputs used in the resultant export product, the quality, technical characteristics and specifications of the inputs under import should be the same as those used in the resultant export product. For this purpose the quality, technical characteristics and specifications of each input used in the resultant export product were required to be specified on the shipping bill and at the time of import. Customs was required to co-relate it with the input under import so as to allow DFRC benefit to those inputs which were of the same quality, technical characteristics and specifications.

Export Promotion Capital Goods Scheme (EPCG): EPCG scheme was introduced by the EXIM policy of 1992-97 in order to enable the manufacturer exporter to import machinery and other capital goods for export production at concessional or no custom duties at all. The scope of the Export Promotion Capital Goods Scheme (EPCG) has been enlarged and various amendments have been done (ref. Chapter 5 for details).

(B) Fiscal Incentives

Financial sufficiency is core to export competitiveness. New exporters face significant start-up costs as they gather information on foreign markets, develop marketing channels, adapt products and packaging to foreign tastes, and learn to deal with new bureaucratic procedures. Market and government failures mean that these 'sunk costs' bar firms from joining the export markets.

The exporters are eligible for fiscal incentives such as Sales Tax Exemption and Income Tax Exemption. Exporters can claim exemption from the levy of sales tax on the supplies taken by them for manufacture of goods meant for production of export product or supplies of goods for exports against specific export orders. This facility is available to the exporters both under the Central Sales Tax Act 1956 and under the Local Sales Tax Acts of the specific states. The exporters are required to give Form H to the suppliers of goods/ materials from another state and the exemption for prescribed by the Sales Tax Department of the state. The 100% export-oriented units and the units in export processing zones, Special Economic Zones (SEZs), Electronic Hardware Technology Park (EHTP) and Software Technology Parks (STP) are entitled to full reimbursement of Central Sales Tax paid by them on the purchases made by them from within the State in which they are located, for the purpose of production of goods meant for exports.

The export firms are eligible for deduction under Section 80 HHC in respect of income from export turnover on their incomes earned in the previous year in a phased manner. Deduction is available to the units engaged in the export of computer software. Under Section 10A, tax holiday has been provided for 10 years beginning assessment year 2000-2001 for the newly established industrial undertakings in Free Trade Zones, SEZs, EHTP or STP as well as 100% Export Oriented Units (EOUs). One of the basic conditions is that the exports proceeds must be realised in free foreign exchange, that is, freely convertible foreign currency.

A fiscal and financial policy incentive for export competitiveness is an unfolding area of research. Current literature covers topics such as exchange rates and tax-based policy incentives, duty drawbacks and bonded warehouse facilities, and smart subsidies like export loan subsidies, export credit guarantees and matching grants.

(C) Marketing Assistance

1. Market Development Assistance (MDA): The Ministry of Commerce and Industry has a scheme of MDA, which was launched in 1963 with a view to stimulate and diversify the export trade, along with the development of marketing of Indian products and commodities abroad. The MDA is utilised for market research, commodity research, area survey and research, participation in trade fairs and exhibitions, export publicity and dissemination of information, trade delegation and study teams, establishment of offices and branches abroad, grant-in-aid to Export Promotion Councils and other approved organisations for the development of exports and the promotion of foreign trade, and any other scheme which is generally aimed at promoting the development of markets for Indian products and commodities abroad. The salient points of revised guidelines of MDA scheme (with effect from 1.4.2006) are reproduced below.

Export promotion continues to be a major thrust area for the government. In view of the prevailing macroeconomic situation with emphasis on exports and to facilitate various measures being undertaken to stimulate and diversify the country's export trade, Marketing Development Assistance (MDA) scheme is under operation through the Department of Commerce to support the under mentioned activities.

(i)   Assist exporters for export promotion activities abroad.

(ii) Assist Export Promotion Councils (EPCs) to undertake export promotion activities for their product(s) and commodities.

(iii) Assist approved organisations/trade bodies in undertaking exclusive non-recurring innovative activities connected with export promotion efforts for their members.

(iv) Assist focus export promotion programmes in specific regions abroad like FOCUS (LAC), Focus (Africa), Focus (CIS) and Focus (ASEAN + 2) programmes.

(v) Residual essential activities connected with marketing promotion efforts abroad.

Assistance to individual exporters for export promotion activities abroad – Participation in EPC led Trade Delegations/BSMs/Trade Fairs/Exhibitions –

(i) Exporting companies with an FOB value of exports of up to ₹ 15 crores in the preceding year will be eligible for MDA assistance for participation in trade delegations/BSMs/fairs/exhibitions abroad to explore new markets for export of their specific product(s) and commodities from India in the initial phase. This will be subject to the condition that the exporter has completed 12 months membership with the concerned EPC and filing of returns with concerned EPC/organisation regularly. However, this condition would not apply in case of a new EPC for a period of 5 years from the date of its creation.

(ii) Assistance would be permissible on travel expenses by air, in economy excursion class fair and/or charges of the built-up furnished stall. This would, however, be subject to an upper ceiling mentioned in the table per tour.

Sl. No.	Area/Sector No. Of visits eligible	,Maximum Financial ceiling per event
1	Focus LAC 1	Rs. 1,80,000
2	Focus Africa (Including WANA countries)1	Rs. 1,50,000
3	Focus CIS 1	Rs. 1,50,000
4	Focus ASEAN +2 1	Rs. 1,50,000
5	General Areas 1	Rs. 80,000*
TOTAL	5 General (Areas)	

The participation of individual companies in the above activities shall be subject to the following conditions:

(1) For EPC led Trade Delegations/BSMs only air-fare by Economy Excursion class up to a maximum of ₹ 70,000 (₹ 1,00,000 in case of Focus LAC) shall be permissible. For participation in Trade Fairs/Exhibitions reimbursement shall be permissible subject to ceilings mentioned in column 4 in the above table.

(2) Maximum number of permissible participations shall be five in a financial year as indicated in the above table (No travel grant is permissible for visit to General Areas).

However, for priority sectors, having large employment generation potential, namely agriculture including food items, handicrafts, handlooms, carpets, leather and minor forest produce including LAC, 2 (two) participations in General Areas would be admissible with the assistance of ₹ 1,50,000 for each participation. The exporters availing of assistance under this provision would, however, be in addition to these participations, eligible for only any 2 Focus Area participations.

(3) Assistance shall be permissible to one regular employee/director/ partner/ proprietor of the company. Assistance would not be available to exporter of foreign nationality or holding foreign passport.

(4) Intimation application must be received in the concerned EPC with a minimum of 14 days clear advance notice excluding the date of receipt of application in the office of the concerned organisation and the date of departure from the country.

(5) The company shall not be under investigation/charged/prosecuted/debarred /black listed under the Foreign Trade Policy of India or any other law relating to export and import business.

(6) Member exporters of EPCs would also be eligible for MDA assistance for participation in events organised by ITPO (India Trade Promotion Organisation) abroad. Their applications/claims would be routed/reimbursed through the concerned EPC.

(7) Maximum MDA assistance shall be inclusive of MDA assistance received from all Government bodies/FIEO (Federation of Indian Export Organisations)/EPCs (Export Promotion Councils)/Commodity Boards/Export Development Authorities/ITPO etc.

(8) A maximum of three participations in a particular trade fair/exhibition would be eligible for MDA assistance and exporting companies after availing assistance three times including past cases for a particular fair/exhibition, have to participate in that fair, if any, on a self-financing basis.

2. Market Access Initiative (MAI): Market Access Initiative scheme is intended to provide financial assistance for medium term export promotion efforts with a sharp focus on country and product. The MAI scheme is a 'plan' scheme that is intended to act as a catalyst in promoting India's exports on a sustained basis. The scheme is based upon 'focus' concept that is, 'focus product' and 'focus market'. Under the scheme, assistance is extended to the Departments of Central Government and Organisations of Central/State Governments, Export Promotion Councils, Registered Trade Promotion organisations, Commodity Boards, recognised Apex Trade Bodies, recognised Industrial Clusters and Individual Exporters. Assistance is given for supporting the following activities:

(i)   Export potential survey of the states.

(ii) Market studies.

(iii) Studies on WTO related matters.

(iv) Marketing projects like opening of showrooms, participation in trade fairs abroad, publicity campaigns, display in departmental stores abroad, opening of show rooms, opening of warehouses, research and product development.

(v) Registration charges for product registration abroad for pharmaceuticals, biotechnology and agro-chemicals.

(vi) Reverse visits of the prominent foreign buyers from the project focus countries.

(vii) Testing charges for engineering products abroad.

Assistance is also given to cottage and handicrafts units for similar activities and for developing a website for virtual exhibition, industrial clusters for marketing study, participation in trade fairs abroad and any project/study which would further the objectives of the schemes.

The Ministry of Commerce and Industry has introduced the MAI in April 2001 with the idea that the Government shall assist the industry in R&D, market research, specific market and product studies, warehousing and retail marketing infrastructure in selected countries and direct market promotion activities through media advertising and buyer-seller meets. Financial assistance shall be available under the scheme to EPCs, industry and trade associations and other eligible activities, as may be notified from time to time.

3.11 Various Modes of Transport

The exporter can send the shipment of goods using any one of the following modes of transport as specified in the export contract.

1. Air Transport
2. Sea Transport
3. Multimodal Transport
4. Road Transport
5. Rail Transport.

The choice of the mode of transport by industries will depend on the nature of a good whether perishable or non-perishable, whether bulky or light weight, cost of the mode of transport, custom duties by the export or import duties, the source and destination of the good.

1. Perishable and Non-perishable Goods: For perishable goods like flowers, fruits and other agricultural products the mode of transport is usually by air. Time is of the essence here. For non perishable goods the industries will use other modes.

2. Bulk or light weight goods: Transportation by air is very expensive. Hence bulky goods are usually transported by road, rail or ship. For light weight goods, the mode of transport will be air transport.

3. Custom and exercise duties: Determination of the mode of transport is dependent on the existence of duties by the government. Some transportation modes experience high taxation levels and therefore most industries avoid them.

4. Source and destination of goods: The source and destination of the goods will also determine the mode of transport to be chosen by the industries. Rail transport is normally used for short distance transportation and if the distance is long then the mode of transportation would be rail, air or even the sea.

Various Modes of Transport

1. Air Transport: This mode of transport is used for perishable goods, fragile goods and goods that are not bulky. This is a very fast mode of transportation used for goods that need fast delivery. The bulk per value ratio will determine the choice of this mode of transportation.

Advantages

- It is a fast mode of transportation.
- It has an advantage of time saving for delivery of goods.
- It is a reliable means of transport.

Disadvantages

- There may be freight delays and cancellation in case of extreme weather conditions.
- Good delivered through these means attract high duties.
- This method of transportation is very expensive.

2. Sea Transport: This mode of transportation is ideal when bulky goods are to be delivered over large distances.

Advantages

- It is the ideal mode of transportation for bulky goods.
- It is ideal for transportation of goods over large distances.
- It is less expensive than other modes of transportation.

Disadvantages

- It takes a longer time to deliver goods from the source to their destination.
- Perishable commodities cannot be transported using this means.
- Monitoring the location of goods being transported or the time period the goods will be under transit is difficult.

3. Road Transport: This is the most common and widely used mode of transportation. This mode of transport is very reliable as there exists a transport network which is extensive to every part of a region.

Advantages

- It is the most cost-effective mode of transportation.
- Its reliability lies in the fact that it offers fast delivery of goods.
- It is the ideal means of transport over short distances.
- Today's communication networks make it easy to monitor goods in transit.

Disadvantages

- There could be delays due to traffic congestion.
- Breakage of fragile goods could occur as a result of careless driving.
- Delays could also be caused due to traffic regulations on speed.

4. Rail Transport: This is the most reliable mode of transportation for bulky goods, especially coal and iron.

Advantages

- This mode of transport is fast.
- It can be used to transport heavy and bulky goods.
- It is a safer mode of transportation when compared to transportation by air or sea.
- This mode of transport offers the best reliability.

Disadvantages

- There may be inevitable delays in the transportation of goods.
- It may be problematic when the destination of the goods is not covered by the rail network and therefore there is a need to switch the mode of transport.

5. Multimodal Transport can be viewed as *"the chain that interconnects different links or modes of transport – air, sea, and land into one complete process that ensures an efficient and cost-effective door-to-door movement of goods under the responsibility of a single transport operator, known as a Multimodal Transport Operator (MTO), on one transport document"*. Over the past decade the world has witnessed considerable strategic developments. The movement towards globalisation and trade liberalisation paralleled by the revolution in information and communications technologies is continually advancing and significantly altering existing markets and triggering a race for the future. Apparently, a new economic era is materialising and driving more countries towards global economic integration. The massive growth in containerisation which introduced the modern concept of Multimodal Transport has shifted the cargo delivery system from "port-to-port" to "door-to-door". Moreover, several industrial and agricultural companies have changed their production methods to be able to use containers for export and capture the advantages of MT. A good example is the Japanese square melons.

Fig. 3.2: Japanese Square Melons Being Prepared for Transport to the USA Source: Die Welt, June 15, 2001

Table 3.1: Advantages and Disadvantages of various modes of transport

Method	Advantages	Disadvantages
Road	Cheap, convenient, flexible, private.	Noisy, pollutes the environment, less safe than alternatives, stressful for drivers, potential delays, can be expensive where there are congestion or road charges.
Rail	Fast, safe, more environmentally friendly than alternatives, does not add to congestion.	Limited routes, inflexible routes and timetables, expensive, sometimes unreliable.
Air	Fast for long distance deliveries, safe.	Expensive, unsuitable for some goods, limited routes, inflexible timetables, pollutes the environment, airport taxes.
Sea	Cheap for large volumes	Very slow, higher costs, inflexible routes and timetables, port duty or taxes - requires inland transportation for door-to-door delivery.
Courier	Fast, reliable, secure.	Very slow, relatively few ports, inflexible routes and timetables, port duty or taxes - requires inland transportation for door-to-door delivery
Electronic delivery	Instant, cheap, for international and domestic deliveries.	Insecure due to viruses and hackers, limited to certain goods and services.

Points to Remember

- Any export shipment involves a number of documents required mainly by the Custom/Port Authorities. Generally, the format of these documents is common in most of cases, but may differ in respect to documents used at different ports. Documentation requirements vary from product to product and from country to country . The exporter should ensure quality of goods before sending shipment to the foreign buyers. A number of documents must accompany every export shipment.

- A key success factor in starting any export company is clear understanding and detail knowledge of products to be exported. In order to be successful in exporting, one must fully research its foreign market rather than try to tackle every market at once. The world is made up from billions of buyers with their own sets of needs and behaviour. To be a successful exporter one has to be very well versed as far as the preliminaries of exports are concerned. The registration process is very essential in the export procedures; the exporter has to register with some authorities such as, RBI, Regional licensing authority, Export Promotion Council, Sales Tax Dept. etc. In the international trade the role of clearing and forwarding agent is very important. At the last part of the chapter, various modes of transportation have been explained.

- Export procedure consists of several commercial and regulatory formalities, which an exporter is required to complete during the course of export trade transactions. These formalities are very time consuming, complex and involve considerable documentation.

- Any export shipment involves a number of documents required mainly by the Customs/Port authorities. Mostly, the format of these documents is common in the majority of cases, but may differ in respect to documents used at different ports.

- Documentation is used to keep shipment and delivery on schedule, to describe cargo, for customs clearance, to indicate the ownership of goods for collection purposes or in the event of dispute, and to obtain payment.

- There are four main declaration forms which are prescribed. These are called GR, PP, and SOFTEX Forms.

- In India, customs clearance is a complex and time consuming procedure that every exporter faces in his export business. Physical control is still the basis of customs clearance in India, where each consignment is manually examined in order to impose various types of export duties. High import tariffs and multiplicity of exemptions and export promotion schemes also contribute in complicating the documentation and procedures. So, a proper knowledge of the customs rules and regulation becomes important for the exporter.

- All excisable goods exported out of India are exempt from payment of Central Excise Duties, for which two different procedures have been approved.

- In order to promote exports of quality goods as per the international standards, the government of India has introduced compulsory Quality Control and Pre-Shipment Inspection for 90% of the items of export under one or the other system as per the Export (Quality Control and Inspection) Act, 1963.

- An important stage after manufacturing of goods or their procurement is their preparation for shipment. This involves labelling, packaging, packing and marking of export consignments.

- The exporter should arrange for the shipment of the goods as soon as they have been cleared by the inspection agency. The process of shipment of goods would involve essentially their clearance by the Central Excise and the Custom Authorities.

- Export Credit Guarantee Corporation of India Limited was established in the year 1957 by the Government of India to strengthen the export promotion drive by covering the risk of exporting on credit. Being essentially an export promotion organisation, it functions under the administrative control of the Ministry of Commerce and Industry, Department of Commerce, Government of India. It is managed by a Board of Directors comprising of representatives from the Government, Reserve Bank of India, banking, insurance and exporting community.

- GSP is a non-contractual instrument by which industrialised (developed) countries unilaterally and on the basis of non-reciprocity extend tariff concessions to developing countries. It involves reduced MFN tariffs or duty-free entry of eligible products exported by beneficiary countries to the markets of donor countries.

- If a supplier has some success in personal selling to visiting buyers or during sales visits abroad, he may feel that the next step is to have someone selling for him in a selected export market. He may also feel that he needs on-the-spot help in establishing the marketing channels, for example, in finding and working with distributors or wholesalers.

- The exporter can send the shipment of goods using any one of the following modes of transport as specified in the export contract.
    1. Air Transport
    2. Sea Transport
    3. Multimodal Transport
    4. Road Transport
    5. Rail Transport.

Questions for Discussion

1. Give a short account of export documentation?

2. Discuss briefly the facilities and incentives provided for an export business.

3. Write in detail the procedure of shipment of goods.

4. What are the various modes of transportation available to an export?

5. Write short notes on:

    (a) Role of overseas agent

    (b) ECGC Services

    (c) Packaging of export goods

6. Discuss the excise clearance for export.

7. Explain the pre-shipment inspection of product quality in detail.

8. Explain the concepts of packaging, marketing and labelling in detail.

9. Explain the rules and origin of GSP.

10. Discuss the various incentives for export from government.

✍   ✍   ✍

Benefits of Export

Contents ...

Learning Objectives ...

- To study in detail the following benefits of export:
  o   Service Tax benefits
  o   Excise clearance benefits/rebates
  o   Income tax benefits

4.1 Introduction

A comprehensive view needs to be taken for the overall development of the country's foreign trade for India to become a major player in world trade. An increase in exports is of great importance, and also imports which are required to stimulate the economy must be facilitated. In order to maximise the contribution of policies to development consistency among trade and other economic policies is important. Hence, it is necessary to take an integrated approach to the developmental requirements of India's foreign trade. The Foreign Trade Policy is essentially a guide for the development of India's foreign trade. It contains the basic principles and points the direction in which it is proposed to go. By virtue of its dynamic nature, a trade policy cannot be fully comprehensive in all its details and would naturally require modification from time to time. This is to be done through continuous updating, based on the inevitable changing dynamics of international trade.

Trade is a means to economic growth and national development. The primary purpose is the stimulation of greater economic activity and not the mere earning of foreign exchange.

The Foreign Trade Policy is rooted in this belief and built around two major objectives. These are:

- To double the percentage share of global merchandise trade within the next five years;

- To act as an effective instrument of economic growth by giving a thrust to employment generation.

The basic aim of India's EXIM and Foreign trade policy is to promote exports. To achieve this objective, the government of India provides a variety of incentives and facilities. One of the distinctive features of international marketing is that exporters have to deal with different legal systems. An Indian manufacturer operating in the domestic market is well aware of the fact that he is governed by Indian laws and is subject to the jurisdiction of Indian courts. But an Indian exporter exporting his products to an importer, say in the USA, must contend with the fact that US laws may also have influence over their contractual relations as well as settlement of dispute, if any, arising 'out of the contract'. This is technically referred to as the conflicts of laws, which can be settled in advance by incorporating specific provisions in the contract, as to the proper law governing the contract and jurisdiction.

Export incentives are a widely employed strategy of export promotion. The main aim of these incentives is to increase the profitability of export business. Financial sufficiency is the core to export competitiveness. New exporters face significant start-up costs as they gather information on foreign markets, develop marketing channels, adapt products and packaging to foreign tastes, and learn to deal with new bureaucratic procedures.

- The exporters are eligible for fiscal incentives such as Sales Tax Exemption and Income Tax Exemption.

- Exporters can claim exemption from the levy of sales tax on the supplies taken by them for manufacture of goods meant for production of export product or supplies of goods for exports against specific export orders.

- This facility is available to the exporters both under the Central Sales Tax Act, 1956, and under the Local Sales Tax Acts of the specific states.

- The exporters are required to give Form H to the suppliers of goods/materials from another state and the exemption prescribed by the Sales Tax Department of the State.

- 100% Export Oriented Units (EOUs) and the units in export processing zones, Special Economic Zones (SEZs), Electronic Hardware Technology Park (EHTP) and Software Technology Parks (STPs) are entitled to full reimbursement of Central Sales Tax paid by them on the purchases made by them from within the state in which they are located, for the purpose of production of goods meant for exports.

- The export firms are eligible for deduction under Section 80 HHC in respect of income from export turnover on their incomes earned in the previous year in a phased manner. Deduction is available to the units engaged in the export of the computer software.

- Under Section 10A, tax holiday has been provided for 10 years beginning assessment year 2000-2001 for the newly established industrial undertakings in Free Trade Zones, SEZs, EHTP or STP as well as 100% Export Oriented Units (EOUs). One of the basic conditions is that the exports proceeds must be realised in free foreign exchange, that is, freely convertible foreign currency.

4.2 Overview of Export Benefits

Various incentives and facilities are offered by the Government of India to exporters which would help them improve their competitiveness in foreign markets. These incentives and facilities relate to export performance, promotion of exports, fiscal incentives, schemes aimed at facilitation of imports for exports and various subsidies. These schemes can be classified into the following categories.

(I) Incentives for Export Performance

(II) Incentives for Marketing of Export Goods

(III) Fiscal Incentives

(IV) Import Facilitation for Exports

(V) Export Financing

(VI) Foreign Currency Retention

(VII) Recognition of Exporters

Some of the facilities and incentives are already explained with the policies.

(I) Incentives for Export Performance

The facilities provided to improve export performance are –

1. Duty Drawback
2. Duty Free Import Authorisation
3. Duty Entitlement Pass Book Scheme
4. Special Import Licence

   (a) **Duty Drawback:** The scheme of Duty Drawback is governed by the 'Customs and Central Excise Duties Drawback Rules' compiled and notified by 'Drawback Directorate' of the Department of Revenue, Ministry of Finance of the Government of India. Under these rules, customs duties and central excise duties on raw materials, components and packing materials used in export products are refunded back to the exporter, on post-export basis. In other words, import duties and central excise duties on material inputs for export products are allowed to be drawn-back (that is refunded) under the incentive scheme of duty drawback. Thus the drawback refers to the rebate of duty chargeable on any imported or excisable material used in the manufacture of goods exported from India. According to the Drawback Rules 1995, drawback has been permitted not only on materials/inputs used in the manufacture but also processed or subjected to any other operation for export of goods from India. Drawbacks are given both to the manufacturers, exporters or merchant-exporters and export/trading houses, etc. Levy of interest on delayed payment of drawback has also been permitted. Interest at such rate as may be fixed by the Board would be leviable in case payment against a claim for drawback is not made within three months of filing the claim in the prescribed manner. Drawback will not be allowed if the total foreign exchange spent on inputs used in the goods exported is more than the FOB value of the exports or the value addition is negative. Drawback will also not be allowed if the export value of goods is less than the value of the imported material used in the manufacture of the export goods or where the sale proceeds of the exported goods are not received within the specified limit. It will also not be admissible if Modvat is availed of.

(b) **Duty Free Import Authorisation (DFIA):** Effective from 1st May, 2006, Duty Free Import Authorisation or DFIA in short is issued to allow duty free import of inputs which are used in the manufacture of the export product (making normal allowance for wastage), and fuel, energy, catalyst etc. which are consumed or utilised in the course of their use to obtain the export product. Duty Free Import Authorisation is issued on the basis of imports and export items given under Standard Input and Output Norms (SION).

(c) **Duty Entitlement Pass Book (DEPB):** Duty Entitlement Pass Book Scheme, in short DEPB is an export incentive scheme. According to DEPB scheme, an exporter is eligible to claim import duty credit as a specified percentage of FOB value of exports made in freely convertible currency. DEPB provides post export incentives of duty remission on inputs used in export. The exporter can use this credit to pay for the import duty on the import of inputs whether required for the manufacture of the export product or not. The DEPB is valid for a period of 12 months from the date of its issuance. The claim for the import duty credit is admissible only after the realisation of the export proceeds. Both the merchant-exporter and manufacturer-exporter are eligible for the benefit under the DEPB scheme. The import duty credit granted under the DEPB scheme or the materials imported against it are freely transferable. The transfer of DEPB shall however, be for import at the port specified in the DEPB which shall be the port from where exports have been made. An application for grant of import duty credit under DEPB should be made to the licensing authority.

(d) Special Import Licence: Exporters, export-oriented units, units located in STP, EHTP, EPZ are granted recognition for their previous export performance by being certified as export house, trading house, star trading house, super star trading house etc. The eligibility for the different grades depend on the FOB value of goods exported or net foreign exchange earned by the unit in the preceding three/one licensing year.

Exporters who have applied and been granted such certifications are eligible for special import licence which will be valid for import of a number of items mentioned in the ITC (HS) classification of Imports. While this licence is freely transferable, import under this licence is subject to normal customs duty.

(II) Incentives for Marketing of Export Goods

(a) Market Development Assistance (MDA): The Ministry of Commerce and Industry has a scheme of MDA, which was launched in 1963 with a view to stimulate and diversify the export trade, along with the development of marketing of Indian products and commodities abroad. The MDA is utilised for market research, commodity research, area survey and research; participation in trade fairs and exhibitions; export publicity and dissemination of information; trade delegation and study teams; establishment of offices and branches abroad; grant-in-aid to Export Promotion Councils and other approved organisations for the development of exports and the promotion of foreign trade; and any other scheme which is generally aimed at promoting the development of markets for Indian products and commodities abroad. Salient Points of Revised Guidelines of MDA Scheme (with effect from 1.4.2006) are reproduced below.

The major thrust area for the government is export promotion. In view of the prevailing economic situation with emphasis on exports and to support various measures being undertaken to stimulate and diversify the country's export trade, Marketing Development Assistance (MDA) Scheme is under operation through the Department of Commerce to support the under mentioned activities.

   (i)   Assist exporters for export promotion activities abroad.

   (ii) Assist Export Promotion Councils (EPCs) to undertake export promotion activities for their product(s) and commodities.

   (iii) Assist approved organisations/trade bodies in undertaking exclusive non-recurring innovative activities connected with export promotion efforts for their members.

   (iv) Assist focus export promotion programmes in specific regions abroad like FOCUS (LAC), Focus (Africa), Focus (CIS) and Focus (ASEAN + 2) programmes.

   (v)   Residual essential activities connected with marketing promotion efforts abroad.

(b) Market Access Initiative (MAI): Market Access Initiative scheme is intended to provide financial assistance for medium term export promotion efforts with a sharp focus on country and product. The MAI Scheme is a plan scheme that is intended to act as a catalyst in promoting India's exports on a sustained basis. The scheme is based upon 'focus' concept that is, 'focus product' and 'focus market'. Under the scheme, assistance is extended to the Departments of Central Government and Organisations of Central/State Governments, Export Promotion Councils, Registered Trade Promotion organisations, Commodity Boards, recognised Apex Trade Bodies, recognised Industrial Clusters and Individual Exporters. Assistance is given for supporting the following activities.

(i)   Export potential survey of the states.

(ii) Market studies.

(iii) Studies on WTO related matters.

(iv) Marketing projects like opening of showrooms, participation in trade fairs abroad, publicity campaigns, displays in departmental stores abroad, opening of show rooms, opening of warehouses, research and product development.

(v)   Registration charges for product registration abroad for pharmaceuticals, biotechnology and agro-chemicals.

(vi) Reverse visits of the prominent foreign buyers etc. from the project focus countries.

(vii) Testing charges for engineering products abroad.

Assistance is also given to cottage and handicrafts units for similar activities and for developing a website for virtual exhibition, industrial clusters for marketing study, participation in trade fairs abroad and any project/study which would further the objectives of the schemes.

1. Air freight subsidies on export horticulture and floriculture products.

2. Assistance for product promotion and packaging development schemes of the Spices Board.

3. Subsidy schemes of APEDA (Agriculture and Processed Food Products Exports Developing Authority) for agricultural, horticultural and meat products.

4. Subsidy for the marketing of marine products.

1. Air Freight subsidies on Export Horticulture and Floriculture Products

The APEDA provides air freight subsidy on selected fruits, vegetables and floriculture products exports from India. The various items eligible for air subsidy in fresh fruits are mangoes other than alphonso, banana, strawberries, papaya, and water melon. In the fresh vegetable category are asparagus, broccoli and mushroom and in floriculture products are cut flowers, live plants, gladiolas and other live plants. The subsidy is given at different rates for exports to different countries. Application is considered on first come first serve basis. Subsidy is paid only to the direct exporter. It is paid on gross rate actually shipped. Application on the form prescribed by APEDA should be submitted to the Regional Office of APEDA along with the documents within 30 days from the last date of the fortnight.

2. Assistance for Product Promotion and Packaging Development Schemes of the Spices Board

The Spices Board provides various facilities for the marketing of spices to the exporters of spices. Exporters who have Spice House certificate or Spices Board logo are eligible for the grant of financial assistance for various export promotion activities. The various types of financial assistance provided by the Spices Board by way of reimbursement of the expenditure incurred by the exporter are –

(i)   For product promotion of branded goods in foreign markets maximum of ₹ 5 lakhs or 50% of the total expenditure whichever is less.

(ii) For multilingual printing of brochures/folders for distribution among overseas buyers maximum of ₹ 1 lakh or 50% of the total cost of printing whichever is less.

(iii) For packaging development /bar code registration maximum ₹ 2 lakhs or 50% of the actual cost whichever is less.

(iv) For setting up/upgrading of laboratory ₹ 1 lakh or maximum of the 50% of the cost of laboratory equipment whichever is less, provided the exporter has achieved the export turnover of ₹ 5 lakhs.

3. Subsidy Schemes of APEDA (Agriculture and Processed Food Products Exports Developing Authority) for Agricultural, Horticultural and Meat Products

The APEDA provides financial assistance for the development and promotion of export of agricultural, horticultural and meat products. The schemes for which financial assistance is provided are feasibility, study consultancy and data base upgrade, development of infrastructure, market development, packaging development, quality control assistance, upgrading of meat plants, organisation building and human resource development.

4. Subsidy for the Marketing of Marine Products

The Marine Products Export Development Authority (MPEDA) provides financial assistance to the exporters of marine products under various schemes like Infrastructure Development, Prawn Farming, Diversification and Modification, Quality Control and Marketing Services. The financial assistance provided by APEDA/MPEDA is in the nature of reimbursement of expenses incurred by the export firms registered with these agencies. MPEDA offers financial assistance to the exporters of marine products to promote export production and marketing of products. The schemes of financial assistance cover all the stages namely, farming, quality control, development of production infrastructure and equipment, transportation and air freighting of samples. The exporters registered with

MPEDA should apply on the prescribed form for getting their proposals first approved before incurring the expenditure.

(III) Fiscal Incentives

Exporters are eligible for fiscal incentives such as Sales Tax Exemption and Income Tax Exemption. Exporters can claim exemption from the levy of sales tax on the supplies taken by them for manufacture of goods meant for production of export product or supplies of goods for exports against specific export orders. This facility is available to the exporters both under the Central Sales Tax Act, 1956 and under the Local Sales Tax Acts of the specific states. The exporters are required to give Form H to the suppliers of goods/ materials from another state and the exemption as prescribed by the Sales Tax Department of the state. The 100% export-oriented units and the units in export processing zones, Special Economic Zones (SEZs), Electronic Hardware Technology Park (EHTP) and Software Technology Parks (STPs) are entitled to full reimbursement of Central Sales Tax paid by them on the purchases made by them from within the state in which they are located, for the purpose of production of goods meant for exports.

The export firms are eligible for deduction under Section 80 HHC in respect of income from export turnover on their incomes earned in the previous year in a phased manner. Deduction is available to the units engaged in the export of computer software. Under Section 10A, tax holiday has been provided for 10 years beginning assessment year 2000-2001 for the newly established industrial undertakings in Free Trade Zones, SEZs, EHTP or STP as well as 100% Export Oriented Units (EOUs). One of the basic conditions is that the exports proceeds must be realised in free foreign exchange that is, freely convertible foreign currency.

(IV) Import Facilitation for Exports

The facilities provided are Export Promotion Capital Goods Scheme, Duty Exemption Scheme, Advance Licence, DEPB etc.

1. Export Promotion Capital Goods Schemes (EPCG)

An importer of capital goods has to pay the applicable import duty. If an exporter imports capital goods against payment of import duty, then the cost of capital goods will certainly increase by the amount of import duty and it would result in increase in the cost of production. As a consequence, the cost competitiveness of the export products would be adversely affected. Though the primary responsibility of the exporter is to ensure cost effectiveness, yet the Government of India in the EXIM Policy 1997-2002 has introduced Export Promotion Capital Goods Scheme to promote cost competitiveness of India's exports.

Under this scheme, an exporter is allowed to import new capital goods against payment of import duty of 5%. The term 'capital good' includes computer software systems and jigs, dies, fixtures, moulds and spares. If an exporter desires to take advantage of this facility, he has to apply for the grant of licence under this scheme known as the EPCG licence. The import of jigs, dies, moulds and spares is allowed up to 100% of the CIF value of the EPCG licence.

2. Duty Exemption/Remission Scheme

The EXIM Policy has introduced Duty Exemption/Remission Scheme, in addition to the EPCG scheme, to promote the competitiveness of India's exports. The basic aim of the Duty Exemption Scheme is to enable the exporters to import duty free the inputs required for the manufacturer of products for export. The Duty Remission Scheme provides for:

(a) The post export replenishment of the inputs in the export product in the form of Duty Free Replenishment Certificate and

(b) Remission of the duties on the inputs used in the export product under the Duty Entitlement Passbook Scheme.

Import of Replacement of Goods: An exporter can export without any licence the goods or parts thereof which had been imported earlier and are now found to be defective or otherwise unfit for use or which have been damaged after import. The exporter may import without licence the goods representing their replacement supplied free of charge by the foreign suppliers or imported against a marine insurance or marine-cum-erection insurance claim settled by an insurance company. Such goods shall be allowed clearance by the customs authorities without an import licence provided that –

(a) The shipment of replacement goods is made within 24 months from the date of clearance of the previously imported goods through the Customs or within the guarantee period in the case of machines or parts thereof where such period is more than 24 months and

(b) No remittances shall be allowed except for payment of insurance and freight charges where the replacement of goods by foreign suppliers is subject to payment of insurance and/or freight by the importer and documentary evidence to this effect is produced at the time of making the remittance.

Import of Second Hand Capital Goods

(a) Import of second hand capital goods shall be permitted without any age restrictions.

(b) Minimum depreciated value for plant and machinery to be relocated into India has been reduced from ₹ 50 crores to ₹ 25 crores.

3. Advance Licence

An advance licence is granted for the import of inputs without payment of basic customs duty. Such licences shall be issued in accordance with the policy and procedure in force on the date of issue of the licence and shall be subject to the fulfilment of a time-bound export obligation, and value addition as maybe specified. Advance licences maybe either value based or quantity based.

As per the latest amendments to the EXIM policy, the facility of Back to Back Inland Letter of Credit has been introduced, to enable an Advance Licence holder to source his inputs from domestic suppliers.

Value Based Advance Licence: Under a value based advance licence, any of the inputs specified in the licence maybe imported within the total CIF (Cost Insurance and Freight) value indicated for those inputs, except inputs specified as sensitive items.

Under a value based advance licence, both the quantity and the FOB value of the exports to be achieved shall be specified. It shall be obligatory on the part of the licence holder to achieve both the quantity and FOB value of the exports specified in the licence.

Advance licence can be issued for (i) Physical exports, (ii) Intermediate supply and (iii) Deemed exports.

The licences are issued to the manufacturer exporter or the merchant exporter. The licences and/or materials imported shall not be transferable even after completion of export obligation. The licences are issued to make a positive value addition. The licences are subject to the fulfilment of a time bound export obligation as specified in the policy.

(V) Export Financing

The exporters in India have the facility to obtain both the long-term funds and the short-term funds. Export-Import Bank of India and the All India financial institutions as well as state level financial institutions provide long-term funds to the industry. The Export-Import Bank of India is exclusively meant for the promotion of exports from India. The various schemes of the Export Credit and Guarantee Corporation of India (ECGC) facilitate the grant of short-term loans to the exporters. The commercial banks provide funds to the exporter both before sending shipment (pre-shipment finance) and after sending the shipment (post-shipment finance) at concessional rates of interest. Both these types of finance are governed in India by RBI. Pre-shipment finance is a facility to provide working capital finance to an exporter. The basic purpose of granting this facility is to enable the eligibility exporters to procure raw materials, supplies, process or manufacture or warehouse or ship the goods meant for export. Various pre-shipment finances are packing credit, advance against incentives receivables from Government covered by ECGC guarantee and advance against cheques/ drafts received as advance payment. Packing credit refers to the credit granted by a bank to enable an exporter to pack the goods meant for exports. It is granted on the basis of a confirmed export order or an irrevocable letter of credit opened by an importer in favour of exporter from India or any other evidence of an order for export placed by a foreign buyer with Indian exporter. The advance against incentives receivables from the Government of India are granted on the post-shipment stage. But in certain exceptional circumstances when the value of the materials to be procured for the execution of the order is more than FOB value of the export order then the banks may grant packing credit against the amount of incentives available from the Government of India. Advance against cheques/drafts received as advance payment are extended by the banks to only those exporters who have a clear track record of dealings with the bank.

Post-shipment finance is defined as "any loan or advance granted or any other credit provided by an institution to an exporter of goods from India from the date of extending the credit after shipment of the goods to the date of realisation of export proceeds and includes any loan or advance granted to an exporter, in consideration of, or on the security of, any drawback or any other incentive receivable from Government of India." RBI has allowed the commercial banks to grant the facility of post-shipment credit at concessional rates of interest. Post-shipment finance can be extended up to 100% of invoice value of goods. It can be granted up to a period of 180 days at the concessional rate of interest in the case of cash exports.

(VI) Foreign Currency Retention

According to the liberalised exchange rate management system announced in 1994-95, the exporter would be permitted to maintain foreign currency balance in separate foreign currency account known as Exchange Earners Foreign Currency Account (EEFC). EEFC account can be maintained by any exporter with any designated branch of SBI/Public Sector Banks of India. It can be maintained in the form of current or savings account and in any of the permitted currencies. No credit facility is allowed. Funds held in this account can be freely converted into Indian currency at the market determined rates. EEFC account can be used for participation in fairs/exhibitions abroad, travel abroad for business purpose, advertisement for export promotion, market and technical studies conducted abroad, expenses incurred for publication of journals, brochures, pamphlets and more. The facility of retention of foreign exchange in the EEFC account is of great help to the exporters in the management of their requirement for foreign exchange.

(VII) Recognition of Exporters

An export firm can seek recognition as Export House, Trading House, Star Trading House and Super Star Trading House. The criterion for such recognition is the FOB (Free On Board) value of physical exports or Net Foreign Exchange (NFE) earned at the option of the exporter. The exporter can apply for recognition either on the basis of performance in the previous year or on the basis of average of the performance for the three preceding years. Net Foreign Exchange earned on exports is equal to the FOB value of exports minus the value of all the licences including 2.5 times the DEPB credit earned/granted. Export House, Trading House, Star Trading House and Super Star Trading House certificate is valid for a period of three years starting from 1st April of the licensing year. On expiry, renewal of the certificate should be made within a period of six months. The recognised export firms get the benefit of Golden Status Certificate, exempt from the requirement of compulsory pre-shipment inspection; licences are issued automatically to the exporter and are allowed to submit legal undertaking instead of bank guarantee. Export House, Trading House, Star Trading House and Super Star Trading House certificate can be cancelled or refused or suspended if the applicant fails to discharge the export obligation, tampers with licences, has used fraudulent practice to obtain licence and fails to furnish the information required by the DGFT.

4.3 Service Tax Benefits

Service tax benefits are also part of export promotion and incentives for exporters in India. To understand the facilities and benefits an Indian service provider gets, we need to highlight the concept of service tax in India.

4.3.1 Service Tax in India

As per the Finance Act of 1994, all service providers in India, except those in the state of Jammu and Kashmir, are required to pay a service tax in India. The provisions related to service tax came into effect on 1st July, 1994. Service tax in India is regulated and administered by the Central Excise Commissions who work directly under the Department of Revenue, Ministry of Finance, Central Board of Excise and Customs, and the Government of India. Service tax is essentially an indirect tax. Individuals are required to pay the service tax only once in a quarter. Companies can pay service tax for one month by the 25th of the following month. The Finance Act of 2001 launched self assessment for service tax returns so that assessees can be spared the inconvenience of regular scrutiny. Although legal penalties exist for failing to pay service tax, these penalties cannot be imposed if the assessee can prove that there was due cause for failure.

The interesting thing about service tax in India is that the government depends heavily on the voluntary compliance of the service providers for collecting service tax in India. This is expected to foster and sustain faith in Indian citizens regarding the government's tax initiatives.

When the concept of service tax was introduced in India in 1994-95, only three services came under the purview of the tax. Since then, in several phases and instalments, the government has brought nearly 100 categories under the ambit of service tax, including –

- Telephone
- Stock broking
- General insurance
- Advertising agencies
- Courier agencies
- Consulting engineers
- Air travel agents
- Tour operators

- Architects
- Market research agencies
- Management consultants
- Sound recording
- Broadcasting
- Event management
- Beauty parlours
- Fashion designers
- Internet cafés
- Outdoor caterers
- Intellectual property services
- Packaging services

The government charges service tax in India on the gross amount which the service providers charge from their clients. By bringing more and more services within the scope of service tax, the government intends to enhance its revenue earnings manifold.

Service Tax Exemptions

The Central Government can grant partial or total exemption by issuing an exemption notification. The general exemptions are:

- Small service providers whose turnover is less than ₹ 4 lakhs per annum are exempted from service tax.
- There is no service tax on export of services.
- Services provided to UN and international agencies and supplies to SEZ (Special Economic Zones) are exempted from service tax.
- Service tax is not payable on value of goods and material supplied while providing services. Such exclusion is permissible only if Cenvat credit on such goods and material is not taken.

4.3.2 Export of Service

If the services are exported, the Cenvat credit is not required to be reversed. Assessee can utilise credit for payment of service tax on other services.

However, if this is not possible, he can get a refund. However, subsequent rules envisage that rebate can be obtained both by manufacturer as well as service provider. The basic principle of taxation is that 'goods and services should be exported and taxes are not to be exported'. Another principle is that service tax can be levied only if service is provided or received or consumed in India. Exemption/rebate is admissible only if export is as per rules of exports of Service Rule 2005. The new rules are effective from 15-3-2005. The rules make it clear that exemption from services/rebate of service tax and excise duty paid is admissible only if there is 'export of service' as defined in these rules.

Exemption or Rebate of Service tax: Exporter of service has three options –

(a) Export without payment of service tax and utilise Cenvat credit for payment of service tax on other services.

(b) Export without payment of service tax and claim rebate of service tax paid on input services and excise duty paid on inputs (or forget about rebate as procedure is too complicated and impractical)

(c) Pay service tax on exported services and claim rebate (by this, he can utilise his input credit)

Export of Service without Service Tax: As per Rule 4 of Export of Services Rules, any service, which is taxable under section 65(105) of the Finance Act, 1994; may be exported without payment of service tax.

Rebate of Service Tax: Where any taxable service is exported, the Central Government can grant rebate of service tax paid on such taxable service or service tax or duty paid on input services or inputs, as the case may be, used in providing such taxable service. Such rebate will be granted by issuing a notification. The rebate shall be subject to such conditions or limitations, if any, and fulfillment of such procedure, as may be specified in the notification.

Meaning of Export of Taxable Service

Rule 3 of Export of Service Rules classifies the taxable services in three categories.

(a) Immovable property is situated abroad

(b) Service performed outside India

(c) Recipient is located outside India

(a) Immovable property situated abroad: In case of first category, the service will be treated as 'export of taxable service' only if the immovable property is situated abroad. These services will be eligible for exemption as 'export of service' only when following conditions are satisfied – (i) The immovable property is situated abroad (ii) The service is delivered outside India and used in business or for any other purpose outside India and (iii) Payment for such service is received in convertible, that is, free foreign exchange.

(b) Services performed outside India: In case of some specified services, the service will be treated as 'export of service' if following conditions are satisfied (i) It should be at least partly performed outside India. (ii) The service is delivered outside India and used in business or for any other purpose outside India and (iii) Payment for such service is received in convertible that is, free foreign exchange.

Even if such a taxable service is partly performed outside India, it shall be considered to have been performed outside India. Thus, part performance of service in India will be permissible. Since no percentage has been specified, it should be sufficient if just 1% of service is provided outside India and balance is provided from India.

However, payment should be received in foreign exchange. Thus, services of courier who deliver mail abroad will not be 'export of service' if they do not get paid in foreign exchange.

(c) Service provided from India, but recipient of service outside India: Remaining services, which fall in the third, that is, residual category, will be treated as 'export of service' if recipient is located abroad. These can be treated as 'export of service', even if the service is provided from India.

In case of services falling under the third category, there are certain conditions and restrictions if the recipient has a commercial or industrial establishment or any office relating thereto, in India. These are discussed in the next paragraph.

- **Recipient abroad but has establishment in India:** As explained above, in case of certain specified services falling under the third category, service provided will be treated as 'export of service' even if service is provided from India, if the recipient of service is out of India. However, if the recipient has office or establishment in India, the service will be treated as 'export of service' subject to certain restrictions and conditions.

- **Taxable services provided and used in or in relation to commerce or industry:** If the taxable service is provided and used in relation to commerce and industry and the recipient is located outside India, the service will be treated as 'export of service' only if the following conditions are satisfied in order for provision of such service is made by the recipient of such service from any of his commercial or industrial establishment or any office located outside India.

Service so ordered is delivered outside India and used in business outside India; and payment for such service provided is received by the service provider in convertible foreign exchange.

Note that these restrictions are applicable only if – (a) the recipient has any commercial or industrial establishment or any office relating thereto, in India and (b) the taxable service is used in relation to commerce and industry.

Rebate of service tax paid on exported services or tax paid on inputs/input services: Subsequent to issue of Export of Service Rules, 2005; two notifications have been issued making provisions for rebate.

(a) Notification No. 11/2005-ST dated 19-4-2005, providing for rebate of service tax and education cess paid on taxable services exported, that is, tax paid on output services.

(b) Notification No. 12/2005-ST dated 19-4-2005, providing for rebate of excise duty paid on inputs and service tax paid on input services, which are used in providing exported taxable services.

- **Export of service without payment of service tax:** As per Rule 4 of Export of Service Rules, any service, which is taxable under section 65(105) of the Finance Act, 1994; may be exported without payment of service tax. Thus, payment of service tax on export of services is optional.

- **Services provided abroad to be taxed in India:** An explanation has been added to Section 65(105) with effect from 16-6-2005 to provide that service provided from outside India to a person in India will be taxable, if such service is received by a person who has a place of residence or establishment in India. Even services provided and consumed abroad come under the net of service tax.

- **Services provided and consumed abroad:** It says, even if a service is received abroad by a person who has his place of residence in India, the service will be taxable. For example, if a construction company having an office in India is undertaking some construction work in Dubai and if some taxable service is availed there, it will be taxable in India.

  If a branch of Indian company like Infosys, Air India, State Bank of India has office abroad, the services like telephones, courier, security, construction etc. received abroad will be taxable in India.

- **Services received by an individual abroad:** An individual who goes abroad may use some services like telephone, beauty treatment, travel agent etc. Abroad. Such services are exempted from service tax, if the services are not in the course or furtherance of commerce or industry of any other business – Notification No. 25/2005-ST dated 7-6-2005.

  Thus, if a person goes abroad on private or personal visit, services received and consumed by him abroad will not be taxable. However, if he goes on a business trip, the services received and consumed by him abroad will be taxable and tax will be payable in India.

- **Person liable to pay service tax:** If a person providing service is a non-resident and does not have an address or place of business in India, service tax is payable by person receiving taxable service in India [Rule 2(1)(d)(iv)].

  The exact wording of rule 2(1)(d)(iv) (as amended with effect from 16-6-2005) is as follows – Person liable for paying the service tax means - In relation to any taxable service provided or to be provided by a person, who has established a business or has a fixed establishment from which the service is provided or to be provided, or has his permanent address or usual place of residence, in a country other than India, and such service provider does not have any office in India, the person who receives such service and has his place of business, fixed establishment, permanent address or, as the case may be, usual place of residence, in India.

Thus, a person receiving service in India will be liable to pay service tax. He will have to register under service tax provisions and submit returns.

4.4 Sales Tax Exemption

Goods meant for export, if purchased, are exempted from sales tax. However, only a registered dealer of goods meant for export can be the purchaser of tax-exempt goods. He will be required to furnish a satisfactory proof of export of goods to the seller of goods, along with Form-H. The proof of export can be in the form of an export-invoice and bill of lading (non-negotiable copy) or airways bill or postal receipt etc. On receipt of any of these, the seller will submit the proof of export along with Form-H to the sales tax authorities.

The Form-H is to be filled in triplicate by the exporter and the original and duplicate copies are to be issued to the supplier. He must retain the triplicate copy for his own record. The supplier submits the original of Form-H and proof of export to the sales tax authority. In order to avail the benefit of sales tax exemption, the exporter should first get the items concerned covered under his local sales tax registration certificate and apply for issuance of Form-H. The exporter should enclose the following documents for issuance of Form-H.

(i)   Copy of shipping bill, duly certified by the customs authority.

(ii) Copy of invoice duly certified.

(iii) Copy of letter of credit.

(iv) Copy of confirmed export order.

4.5 Excise Clearance Benefits/Rebates

Excise duty is a tax imposed by the Central Government on goods manufactured in India. This duty is collected at source, that is, before removal of goods from the factory premises. Export goods are totally exempted from central excise duty. However, necessary clearance has to be obtained in one of the following ways.

- Export under rebate.
- Export under bond.

In relation to Central Excise and Customs, the following are the concessions/incentives for exports: (1) Exemption from duty on final products (or refund of duty paid) and (2) Exemption/Refund of excise and customs duties paid on inputs.

Inputs Free of Duty: Exporting units need raw materials without payment of customs/excise duty, to enable them to compete in the world market. The government has devised the following schemes for this purpose – (a) Special Economic Zones (SEZs) at various places where inputs are allowed to be imported without payment of duty and finished goods are exported; (b) Export Oriented Undertakings; (c) Permission to avail Cenvat (Central Value Added Tax) on inputs for other similar products; (d) Refund of duty on inputs if Cenvat credit cannot be used and (e) Duty Drawback Scheme.

Exports Free of Duty on Finished Product: Exports of almost all excise goods except hides, skin and leather and salt and exports to all countries except to Nepal and Bhutan are exempted from central excise duties. Exports to Nepal and Bhutan do not qualify for export incentives as payment is received in Indian rupees. However, export rebate can be obtained if export to Nepal is made (a) on payment of free convertible foreign exchange or (b) for specified capital goods to Government of Nepal against global tender, even if payment is received in Indian currency.

Rule 18 or Rule 19 of the Central Excise Rules 2002 governs exports under central excise. Rule 18 provides for two types of rebates, namely –

1. Rebate of duty paid on the manufactured excisable goods which are exported (final product rebate) and
2. Rebate of the duty paid on the materials which are used in the manufacture of such export goods (input stage rebate).

Rule 19 comprises of three sub-rules: Under Rule 19(1) export of manufactured excisable goods without payment of duty from a factory of manufacture/warehouse/any other approved premises is permitted and

1. Rule 19(2) states the procedure for removal of any materials from a factory/ warehouse/approved premises, without payment of duty, for use in the manufacture of goods earmarked for exports.
2. Rule 19(3) prescribes the conditions/safeguards/procedures for the above said sub-rules. In other words, Rule 19(1) governs the clearance of excisable goods (final products) without payment of duty and Rule 19(2) provides for clearance of excisable goods (inputs) without payment of duty for use in the manufacture of export goods.

As discussed above, Rule 19 deals with two situations. As Rule 19(1) deals with the export of excisable goods without payment of duty under a bond, Rule 19(2) governs the procurement of raw materials without payment of duty for use in the manufacture of export goods (governed by Notification 43/2001, as amended). Interestingly the embargo imposed vide paragraph (v) of the Notification (supra) is only to the availment of facility under Rule 19(2) and not under Rule 19(1). In other words, the Notification prohibits only the procurement of raw materials without payment of duty under Rule 19(2). This has to be read in consonance with the bar under Rule 18 also. As stated above, Rule 18 is akin to Rule 19, wherein, it provides for grant of rebate of excise duty on two situations, one on the duty paid on the input stage and the other on the duty paid on the final products. Though no separate sub-rules are present in Rule 18, as provided for in Rule 19, they are in *pari materia*. The contents of Rule 18 and 19 may be tabulated as below, for easy understanding.

Rule 18	Rule 19
Deals with export of final products on payment of duty and subsequent claim for rebate of such duty paid.	Deals with export of final products without payment of duty.
Deals with procurement of inputs for manufacture of export goods, on payment of duty, and claim for rebate of such input stage duty.	Deals with procurement of inputs for manufacture of export goods, without payment of duty.

In other words, the rebate of duty paid on final products (final product rebate) is similar with Rule 19(1) and the rebate of duty paid on input materials used in the manufacture of export goods (input stage rebate) is similar with Rule 19(2). Going by the above, it can be reasoned out that there is no blanket prohibition as to the availment of Rule 18 under the Advance Licence scheme but the prohibition is restricted only to the availment of input stage rebate. In other words, there is no restriction for exporting the resultant products under an Advance Licence scheme in discharge of the export obligation under the claim of final product rebate.

As discussed above, Rule 19(2) provides for procurement of input materials without payment of duty for the manufacture of export goods. If a manufacturer avails the facility under Rule 19(2) and procures his input materials without payment of duty and also imports the materials under Advance Licence without payment of duty and if he is allowed to discharge the export obligation both under the Advance Licence as well as under Rule 19(2), then, it will confer an undue double benefit to the exporter. For a single export, the exporter would be entitled to two benefits, namely, discharge of obligation under the Advance Licence as well as the obligation under Rule 19(2), which is sought to be curbed by the said condition. Input stage rebate under Rule 18, being similar to Rule 19(2), shall also be prohibited on the same lines, to create a level playing field.

4.6 Income Tax Benefits

As a measure of export promotion, various tax incentives are granted under the Income Tax Act. The major incentives are –

1. The part of the profits derived from export of specified goods or merchandise of exporters and/or the supporting manufacturers is deducted from the total profit.

2. A specified amount of profits of companies engaged in the business of hotel or of a tour operator or a travel agent is deducted from the total profit.

3. There is a provision for the tax relief on export of computer software and for the import of system.

4. The profits from export or transfer of film NT software, TV news software, telecast rights are partially deducted.

5. There is a provision for tax relief to an Indian company or resident taxpayer by giving a specified deduction of 50% of the profits from project exports in computing the taxable income.

6. There is a provision for a ten-year tax holiday to units in FTZ/EPZ/100% EOU ending with the year 2010-11.

7. There is a provision for tax exemption of plantation subsidy.

8. Rebate on royalties, commissions, dividends etc. from certain foreign enterprises are granted.

9. Tax relief is provided on remuneration received from abroad by teachers, professors, etc.

10. Tax relief is provided to playwrights, artists, sportsmen, etc.

11. Tax rebate is given on remuneration received on services rendered outside India.

There is a provision for deduction of the profit from business of export or transfer of film software, television software, etc.

Points to Remember

- Exporters are eligible for various benefits under different laws governing the exports from and imports into India.

- The latter part explains in detail the fiscal incentives available to exporters such as income tax benefits, service tax benefits, and rebate on excise duty.

- The Foreign Trade Policy is rooted in this belief and built around two major objectives. These are:

- a.)To double the percentage share of global merchandise trade within the next five years;

- b.) To act as an effective instrument of economic growth by giving a thrust to employment generation.

- Various incentives and facilities are offered by the Government of India to exporters which would help them improve their competitiveness in foreign markets. These incentives and facilities relate to export performance, promotion of exports, fiscal incentives, schemes aimed at facilitation of imports for exports and various subsidies.

- Under the rules of Duty Drawback, customs duties and central excise duties on raw materials, components and packing materials used in export products are refunded back to the exporter, on post-export basis.

- Duty Free Import Authorisation or DFIA in short is issued to allow duty free import of inputs which are used in the manufacture of the export product (making normal allowance for wastage), and fuel, energy, catalyst etc. which are consumed or utilised in the course of their use to obtain the export product.

- According to DEPB scheme, an exporter is eligible to claim import duty credit as a specified percentage of FOB value of exports made in freely convertible currency.

- Exporters, export-oriented units, units located in STP, EHTP, EPZ are granted recognition for their previous export performance by being certified as export house, trading house, star trading house, super star trading house etc. Exporters who have applied and been granted such certifications are eligible for special import licence which will be valid for import of a number of items mentioned in the ITC (HS) classification of Imports.

- The MDA is utilised for market research, commodity research, area survey and research; participation in trade fairs and exhibitions; export publicity and dissemination of information; trade delegation and study teams; establishment of offices and branches abroad; grant-in-aid to Export Promotion Councils and other approved organisations for the development of exports and the promotion of foreign trade; and any other scheme which is generally aimed at promoting the development of markets for Indian products and commodities abroad.

- Market Access Initiative scheme is intended to provide financial assistance for medium term export promotion efforts with a sharp focus on country and product.

- The APEDA provides air freight subsidy on selected fruits, vegetables and floriculture products exports from India.

- The Spices Board provides various facilities for the marketing of spices to the exporters of spices. Exporters who have Spice House certificate or Spices Board logo are eligible for the grant of financial assistance for various export promotion activities.

- The APEDA provides financial assistance for the development and promotion of export of agricultural, horticultural and meat products.

- The Marine Products Export Development Authority (MPEDA) provides financial assistance to the exporters of marine products under various schemes like Infrastructure Development, Prawn Farming, Diversification and Modification, Quality Control and Marketing Services.

- Exporters are eligible for fiscal incentives such as Sales Tax Exemption and Income Tax Exemption.

- The facilities provided are Export Promotion Capital Goods Scheme, Duty Exemption Scheme, Advance Licence, DEPB etc.

- Service tax benefits are also part of export promotion and incentives for exporters in India.

- The government charges service tax in India on the gross amount which the service providers charge from their clients.

- If the services are exported, the Cenvat credit is not required to be reversed. Assessee can utilise credit for payment of service tax on other services.

- Goods meant for export, if purchased, are exempted from sales tax. However, only a registered dealer of goods meant for export can be the purchaser of tax-exempt goods.

- Excise duty is a tax imposed by the Central Government on goods manufactured in India. This duty is collected at source, that is, before removal of goods from the factory premises. Export goods are totally exempted from central excise duty.

- As a measure of export promotion, various tax incentives are granted under the Income Tax Act.

Questions for Discussion

1. Briefly describe the export promotional measures and schemes available to the Indian exporters.

2. Give a brief account of fiscal incentives provided by the Government of India for export promotion.

3. Write short notes on:

    (a) Service tax benefits.

    (b) Rebate on excise duty in India.

    (c) Income Tax benefits

    (d) Sales Tax exemption

4. Give an overview of export benefits.

Chapter **5**...

Duty Drawback and Remittance Scheme

Contents ...

5.1   Introduction

5.2   Duty Exemption Schemes

5.3   Advance Licence

5.4   Replenishment Licence

5.5   Special Import Licence

5.6   Duty Entitlement Pass Book (DEPB) Scheme

5.7   Duty-free Replenishment Certificate (DFRC) Scheme

5.8   Highlights from Foreign Trade Policy 2014-19

•   Points to Remember

•   Questions for Discussion

Learning Objectives ...

•   To study in detail the following schemes for exporters and importers in India.

    o   Advance license

    o   Replenishment license

    o   Special interest license

    o   DEPB Scheme (Duty Entitlement Pass Book Scheme)

    o   DFRC Scheme (Duty-free Replenishment Certificate)

5.1 Introduction

The Government of India offers many incentives to Indian exporters and importers under special schemes. These schemes are mostly available on those imported products, which will later be used for manufacturing of goods meant for export. This not only stimulates industrial growth and development but also brings in foreign currency after the final export process. The following are some of the important import incentives offered by the Government of India, which significantly reduce the effective tax rates for the import companies:

•   Preferential Rates

- DEPB
- Duty Drawback
- DFRC
- DFIA
- Deemed Exports
- Agri Export Zones
- Served from India
- Manufacture under Bond
- Export Promotion Capital Goods Scheme (EPCG)

It is an internationally accepted principle that goods exported out of a country are relieved of the duties borne by them at various stages of their manufacture so that they become competitive in the international market. This is done through duty drawback schemes.

5.2 Duty Exemption Schemes

Duty Exemption Schemes enable duty-free import of inputs required for export production. Duty Exemption Schemes consist of:

1. Advance Authorisation
2. Duty-free Import Authorisation (DFIA).

A Duty Remission Scheme enables post-export replenishment/remission of duty on inputs used in export products. Duty remission schemes consist of –

   (a) Duty Entitlement Pass Book Scheme

   (b) Duty Drawback Scheme

Duty Exemption Scheme comprises of imports under duty-free licences.

Duty-free Licences: These licences are of three types – *the advance licence*, the *advance intermediate licences* and the *special imprest licences*. Goods like raw materials, intermediates, components, consumables, parts, accessories, mandatory spares (less than 5% of the value of the licence) and packing material (referred to as inputs) can be imported under these licences.

- An advance licence is given to an exporter for the import of inputs required for the manufacture of goods without payment of basic customs duty. An additional customs duty equal to the excise duty applicable for the product at the time of import will have to be paid. Exemption from payment of this additional customs duty is granted under certain conditions to certain categories (for example, a manufacturer exporter). Advance licences are subject to the fulfilment of a time bound export obligation/value addition. Such export obligation can be met either directly or by export through third parties.

- An advance intermediate licence is granted to a manufacturer for the import of inputs required for the manufacture of goods to be supplied to an exporter holding an advance licence/special imprest licence.

- A special imprest licence is given to manufacturer exporters for the import of inputs required in the manufacture of goods to be supplied to the following deemed export categories –

  (a) Export-oriented units, units located in software technology parks and export processing zones, electronic hardware technology parks.

  (b) Zero duty EPCG licence holders.

  (c) Projects financed by multilateral/bilateral agencies/funds notified by the Department of Economic Affairs, Ministry of Finance under international competitive bidding or under limited tender system in accordance with the procedures of those agencies/funds, where the legal agreements provide for tender evaluation without including customs duty.

  (d) Fertiliser plants.

  (e) Other projects notified by the Ministry of Finance as eligible for deemed exports.

  (f) United Nations programmes under the aid programme of the UN or multilateral agencies and paid for in foreign exchange.

A duty-free licence unless otherwise specified has a minimum value addition requirement of 33%. However, requests for grant of these licences on lower value additions of 25% or lower may be granted in exceptional cases. Value addition is calculated as per the formula given below.

$$\text{Value addition} = \{(A - B)/B \times 100$$

where A is the FOB value of the goods exported and B is the CIF value of the imported inputs covered by the licence plus any other imported materials.

The period for fulfilment of export obligation under duty-free licences will commence on the date of issue of the licence. The export obligation has to be met within 18 months except in the case of import under the special imprest licence for supply of goods under a project. Here the export obligation has to be completed during the contracted duration of the project.

Exporters who have an export performance record for the previous three years are eligible for advance licence and advance intermediate licence (as well as special intermediate licence for supply of goods to EHTPs, STPs, and EPZs etc.) without an export order.

Goods falling under the prohibited section of the negative list of imports cannot be imported under these duty-free licences.

Duty Drawback

The scheme of Duty Drawback is governed by the 'Customs and Central Excise Duties Drawback Rules' compiled and notified by **'Drawback Directorate'** of the Department of Revenue, Ministry of Finance of the Government of India.

Under these rules, customs duties and central excise duties on raw materials, components and packing materials used in export products are refunded back to the exporter, on post-export basis. In other words, import duties and central excise duties on material inputs for export products are allowed to be drawn back, that is, refunded under the incentive scheme of duty drawback. Thus, the drawback refers to the rebate of duty chargeable on any imported or excisable material used in the manufacture of goods exported from India.

According to the Drawback Rules 1995, drawback has been permitted not only on materials/inputs used in the manufacture but also processed or subjected to any other operation for export of goods from India. Drawbacks are given both to the manufacturers, exporters or merchant-exporters and export/trading houses, etc. Levy of interest on delayed payment of drawback has also been permitted. Interest at such rate as may be fixed by the Board would be leviable in case payment against a claim for drawback is not made within three months of filing the claim in the prescribed manner.

Drawback will not be allowed if the total foreign exchange spent on inputs used in the goods exported is more than the FOB value of the exports or the value addition is negative. Drawback will also not be allowed if the export value of goods is less than the value of the imported material used in the manufacture of the export goods or where the sale proceeds of the exported goods are not received within the specified limit. Drawback will also not be admissible if Modvat is availed of.

Drawback Rates

Two types of drawback rates are available. They are –

(i) **All Industry Rates:** These are published in the form of notification by the government every year and are normally valid for one year.

(ii) **Brand Rates or Special Brand Rates:** These are fixed on the individual request of an exporter/manufacturer.

The rates at which the incentive of duty drawback will be granted to an individual exporter have been specified product-wise in the drawback schedule specified under the drawback rules. Sometimes the amount or rates of drawback are not determined in respect of export goods. In such cases the manufacturer or exporter of such goods may apply in the prescribed form.

Application for Fixation of Drawback Rates: The application should be submitted to the Department of Revenue, Ministry of Finance or with the Customs House/Central Excise Collectorate in whose jurisdiction their manufacturing unit is located. The application must be submitted within 60 days from the date of export.

The documents prescribed for such an application are –

(i)   Application for Fixation of Drawback Rates

(ii)   OBI Statement I

(iii)   DBK Statement II

(iv)   DBK Statement III

(v)   Relevant facts including the proportion in which the material or components are used in the production or manufacture of goods and duties paid on such material or components.

A copy of such application should be sent directly to the Director (Drawback), Ministry of Finance, New Delhi. On receipt of the application, the customs/central excise officer will verify the application and forward it to the Director (Drawback), Ministry of Finance, Government of India, New Delhi for fixation of Brand Rate. If satisfied, he will determine the amount or rate of drawback in respect of such goods. The Government has also provided simplified procedure of brand rate fixation without insisting on pre-verification of data by the Drawback Department.

Procedure for Claiming Duty Drawback: Based on the relevant information given in the drawback copy of the shipping bill, the claim of Duty Drawback (DBK) is processed and passed for payment.

- The exporters are required to submit the drawback copy of the shipping bill in triplicate, in quadruplicate if any export assistance is applicable, well in advance to the Export Department or Central Registration Unit at the port or ICD Container Freight Station/Air Cargo Complex, etc.

- The DBK shipping bill must indicate the DBK schedule number of the export product, product description, DBK rate and total amount of drawback claim. In addition, it should also have a declaration that exports are being made under a claim of duty drawback.

- Simultaneously a declaration has to be made that the duties of customs and central excise have been paid in respect of the material inputs used in manufacture of export goods as also in respect of container or packing materials.

- Under the central excise rules exporters have to make sure that no separate claim is being made for rebate of central excise duties.

- The concerned customs officer scrutinises and examines the shipping bills and other documents. The exporters receive the duplicate and triplicate copies of the shipping bills with the suitable examination order for presenting them to the Docks Appraising Officer.

- An examination report on both the copies of shipping bills is given by the customs officer who returns the duplicate and triplicate copies to the exporters while the original copy is retained.

- The exporters in turn present the duplicate and triplicate copy of the shipping bills duly received from the customs officer to the Docks Appraising Officer along with the export goods. On finding the documents in order, the Docks Appraising Officer endorses 'Let Export' order on both copies of the shipping bills. The triplicate copy of the shipping bill is considered to be the claim for drawback.

- If claims are found admissible an 'in order' sanction is then given. The amount is credited in the ledger account of the exporter maintained in the Drawback section.

Documents: The claim for duty drawback is submitted along with the following documents.

(i)   Copy of export contract or letter of credit, as the case may be.

(ii)   Copy of packing list.

(iii)   Copy of AR4 form, wherever applicable.

(iv)   Insurance certificate wherever necessary.

(v)   Copy of communication regarding rate of drawback (if applicable).

(vi)   Copy of test report (if required).

(vii)   Declarations (if required).

(viii)   Declaration regarding not availing Modvat (Modified Value Added Tax).

(ix)   Certificate from the Jurisdictional Excise Superintendent (if applicable).

(x)   Any other documents.

An exporter desiring the incentives of drawback provisionally may, after making the application, apply in writing to the Drawback Directorate. He may request for a provisional amount to be granted to him towards export of such goods, pending determination of the amount or rate of drawback. In order to achieve this, an exporter may be required to execute a general bond for the amount of drawback claim with the Collector of Customs at the port from where the goods are exported.

If the rate of drawback is less than three-fourths of the duties paid on the materials or components used in the production or manufacture of the said goods the exporter may make an application in writing to the Drawback Directorate for fixation of appropriate amount or rate of drawback within sixty days from the date of export. The procedure and documents required for such application is similar for fixation of drawback rates.

Duty Drawback Credit Scheme: The Government of India has authorised the Reserve Bank of India to instruct the commercial banks (Authorised Dealers in Foreign Exchange) to grant interest-free credit to the exporters as an export promotional measure. The credit is given against their duty drawback entitlements pending investigation, sanction and payment by the Custom House. This interest-free credit is being made available to exporters in India for a period of 90 days. However, the scheme is applicable only for export of such products for which drawback rates have already been determined either on all-industry rate basis or on brand-rate basis.

Drawback on Export by Post: When goods are to be exported by post under a claim of drawback, 'Drawback-Export' must be marked on the outer surface of the packing.

Moreover, the exporters will submit to the postal authorities a drawback claim form instead of a shipping bill giving details regarding drawback schedule number, product description, drawback rate and amount.

Refund of Central Excise: An important incentive for export promotion is the refund of central excise. Ideally, exports should not bear the burden of indirect taxes. For this reason, export goods are either exempted from such taxes or these taxes are refunded, if exemption is not possible. In India, excisable goods are free from excise duty, both on finished products and raw materials, as indicated by Section 37 of the Central Excise and Salt Act, 1944. This act has been amended on September 22, 1995. Only Rule 12 of the Central Excise Rules operates for exports under claim for rebate of duty. The rebate is granted on the duty levied on finished products and on inputs for this finished product. Rule 13, 191-B, and 91-BB of Central Excise Rules have been integrated into Rule 13 and are applied for exports of goods in bond and utilisation of non-duty paid raw material for manufacture and export of excisable goods.

A Personal Ledger Account (PLA) is required to be opened by manufacturers of export products in order to register their factories with the local Central Excise Authorities. The credit balance of the deposit account opened by individual manufacturers with the Central Excise Authority is shown in the PLA. At the time of removal of a consignment, the amount of duty actually levied on the consignment is shown as debit entry. On receipt of proof of exportation, the equivalent amount is again entered on the credit side. Exporters under bond do not need PLA because the duty has not been actually paid.

Documents: The major excise documents are:

1. Invoices: Invoices are prepared in four copies wherein the original copy is for the buyer, duplicate for the transporter, triplicate for the Central Excise Officer and fourth copy for manufacturer's record.

2. AR4/AR5 Forms: These are prepared in sixtuplicate. Both these forms can be used for export in bond or under rebate of central excise duty.

AR4 form is to be used where either finished stage duty is not paid or its rebate is to be claimed later on. It can be elaborated as under.

(i)   Form AR4 is to be used in case of exports in bond, of all goods without payment of duty on finished item (not on inputs).

(ii) AR4 form is also used where the finished stage duty is paid and a rebate thereof is to be claimed after export.

Form AR5 is used where goods are manufactured/exported without the payment of duty or inputs (input stage duty). In other words –

(i)   AR5 form is used where no duty is paid on production inputs and the finished stage duty is also not paid on account of their export being made in bond.

(ii) AR5 form is also used where inputs stage duty is not paid but duty on finished goods is paid and the rebate thereof is to be claimed after export.

Form C: It is an application for refund of excise duty. It contains details like AR4 form number and date of shipping bill, name and address of the factory and its licence number, tariff classification of the goods exported and shipment details.

5.3 Advance Licence

In case of import of inputs without payment of basic customs duty an advance license is issued. These licences are issued in accordance with the policy and procedure in force on the date of issue of the licence. They are also subject to the fulfilment of a time-bound export obligation, and a specified value addition. Such licences maybe either value based or quantity based.

Value Based Advance Licence: Any of the inputs specified in the license maybe imported under a value based advance licence within the total CIF (Cost Insurance and Freight) value indicated for those inputs, except for specified sensitive items.

It is obligatory on the part of the licence holder to achieve both the quantity and the FOB value of the exports specified in the licence under a value based advance licence.

Advance licence can be issued for:

1. **Advance Licence for Physical Export:** The licences are issued to the manufacturer exporter or the merchant exporter. The licences and/or materials imported thereunder shall not be transferable even after completion of export obligation. The licences are issued to make a positive value addition. The licences are subject to the fulfilment of a time bound export obligation as specified in the policy.

2. **Advance Licence for Intermediate Supply:** Advance licence may be issued for intermediate supply to a manufacturer-exporter for the import of inputs required in the manufacture of goods to be supplied to the ultimate exporter/deemed exporter holding another advance licence.

3. **Advance Licence for Deemed Export:** Advance licence can be issued for deemed export to the main contractor for import of inputs required in the manufacture of goods to be supplied to the categories mentioned in the policy. An advance licence for deemed export can also be availed by the sub-contractor of the main contractor to such project. The licences shall be exempted from basic customs duty, surcharge and additional customs duty only.

Amendments to the Advance Licence Scheme: The Advance Licence Scheme has been expanded and liberalised with the amendments made to the EXIM Policy, announced on 31st March 1995.

5.4 Replenishment Licence

Replenishment (REP) licenses are the earliest and still the principal methods of giving incentives to exporters. Combined with duty drawback and Cash Compensation (CCS), REP licences permit the exporter to import certain restricted raw materials and components, that is, raw materials and components appearing on the lists of limited permissible and canalised items in the Import-Export Policy. Refunds can be claimed through the Duty Drawback Scheme. The exported products for which REP licences can be obtained, along with the foreign exchange value of the REP license, expressed as a percentage of the FOB value of the export are listed in the Import-Export policy.

During the 1960s and 1970s, because of import controls and foreign exchange rationing, REP licences often could be sold at premium prices in the open markets. These provided an adequate export incentive, provided the materials incorporated in the exports actually could be obtained at reasonable cost. However, REP premiums declined during the 1980s and particularly after 1985, most probably due to the steadily increasing level of customs duties, some relaxation of import controls and the increased domestic production of many raw materials.

5.5 Special Import Licence

Exporters, export-oriented units, units located in STP, EHTP, EPZ are granted recognition for their previous export performance by being certified as an export house, trading house, star trading house, super star trading house etc. The eligibility for the different grades depend on the FOB value of goods exported or net foreign exchange earned by the unit in the preceding three/one licensing year.

Exporters who have applied and been granted such certifications are eligible for special import licence which will be valid for import of a number of items mentioned in the ITC (HS) classification of imports. While this licence is freely transferable, import under this licence is subject to normal customs duty.

Table 5.1: Entitlement Rates for Special Import Licence

Category	Entitlement Rate FOB Basis	Entitlement Rate NFE Basis
Export house	6.0%	7.5%
Trading house	8.0%	10.0%
Star trading house	10.0%	12.0%
Super star trading house	12.0%	15.0%

Such recognised units are also permitted to import cars under the special import licence and subject to certain quantity restrictions ranging from one car for export houses to five cars for super star trading houses.

Import Licence Application Forms

There are different application forms for imports under various licences as well as imports of certain specific product categories. A comprehensive set of these forms is available in the appendix section of the Handbook of Procedures (Volume 1).

5.6 Duty Entitlement Pass Book (DEPB) Scheme

Duty Entitlement Pass Book Scheme, in short DEPB is an export incentive scheme.

- According to the DEPB scheme, an exporter is eligible to claim import duty credit as a specified percentage of FOB value of exports made in freely convertible currency.

- DEPB provides post export incentives of duty remission on inputs used in export. The exporter can use this credit to pay for the import duty on the import of inputs whether required for the manufacture of the export product or not.

- The DEPB is valid for a period of 12 months from the date of its issuance. The claim for the import duty credit is admissible only after the realisation of the export proceeds. Both the merchant-exporter and manufacturer-exporter are eligible for the benefit under the DEPB scheme.

- The import duty credit granted under the DEPB scheme or the materials imported against it are freely transferable. The transfer of DEPB shall however, be for import at the port specified in the DEPB which shall be the port from where exports have been made.

- An application for grant of import duty credit under DEPB should be made to the licensing authority. The applicant may file one or more applications subject to the condition that each application shall not contain more than 25 shipping bills.

- The DEPB shall be issued with single port of registration, which will be port from where the exports have been affected. Notified on 1st April, 1997, the DEPB Scheme consisted of:

  (a) Post-export DEPB and

  (b) Pre-export DEPB

The pre-export DEPB scheme was abolished with effect from 1st April, 2000. Under the post-export DEPB, which is issued after exports, the exporter is given a Duty Entitlement Pass Book Scheme at a pre-determined credit on the FOB value. The DEPB rates allow import of any items except the items which are otherwise restricted for imports. Items such as gold nibs, gold pens, gold watches etc. though covered under the generic description of writing instruments, components of writing instruments and watches are thus not eligible for benefit under the DEPB scheme.

The DEPB rates are applied on the basis of FOB (free-on-board) value or value cap whichever is lower. For example, if the FOB value is ₹ 700 per piece, and the value cap is ₹ 500 per piece, the DEPB rate shall be applied on ₹ 500.

The DEPB scheme is issued only on post-export basis and pre-export DEPB scheme has been discontinued. Some core points related to DEPB are as follows.

1. Benefits of DEPB Rates: The benefit of DEPB scheme is available on the grounds that export products may have extraneous material up to 5% by weight. In such cases, extraneous material up to 5% shall be ignored and the DEPB rate as notified for that export product is to be allowed.

2. Review of DEPB Rates: The Government of India reviews the DEPB rates after getting the appropriate export import data on FOB value of exports and CIF (Cost, Insurance and Freight) value of inputs used in the export product, as per SION. Such data and information is usually obtained from the concerned Export Promotion Councils.

3. Implementation of the DEPB Rates: For better implementation of the DEPB rates some additional facilities have been provided. DEPB rates are rationalised to account for the changes in customs duties. Caps are fixed on certain items but there would be no verification of Present Market Value (PMV) on such items. A number of ports have been added for availing facilities under the Duty Exemption Scheme, including DEPB. The threshold limit of ₹ 200 million for fixing new DEPB rates was removed.

4. **Provisional DEPB Rate:** Encouragement of diversification and promotion of exports of new products is the main objective behind the provisional DEPB rates. However, provisional DEPB rates would be valid for a limited period of time during which an exporter would furnish data on export and import for regular fixation of rates.

5. **Maintenance of Record:** It is mandatory for Customs Houses at ports to maintain a separate record of details of exports made under DEPB schemes.

6. **Port of Registration:** The exports/imports made from specified ports like Mumbai, Kolkata, Cochin, Dahej, Kakinada, Kandla, Mangalore, Marmagoa, Mundra, Chennai, Nhava Sheva, Paradeep, Pipavav, Sikka, Thoothukudi, Visakhapatnam, Surat (Magdalla), Nagapattinam, Okha , Dharamtar and Jamnagar are entitled for DEPB.

Airports: Ahmedabad, Bengaluru, Bhubaneswar, Mumbai, Kolkata, Coimbatore Air Cargo Complex, Kochi, Delhi, Hyderabad, Jaipur, Srinagar, Thiruvananthapuram, Varanasi, Nagpur and Chennai.

ICDs: Agra, Ahmedabad, Bengaluru, Bhiwandi, Coimbatore, Daulatabad, (Wanjarwadi and Maliwada), Delhi, Dighi (Pune), Faridabad, Guntur, Hyderabad, Jaipur, Jallandhar, Jodhpur, Kanpur, Kota, Ludhiana, Madurai and the land Customs station at Ranaghat, Mullanpur, Moradabad, Meerut, Nagpur, Nasik, Guwahati (Amingaon), Pimpri (Pune), Pitampur (Indore), Rudrapur (Nainital), Salem, Singanalur, Surat, Tirupur, Udaipur, Vadodara, Varanasi, Waluj, Bhilwara, Puducherry, Garhi-Harsaru, Bhatinda, Dappar, Chheharata (Amritsar), Karur, Miraj and Rewari.

LCS: Ranaghat, Singhabad, Raxaul, Jogbani, Nautanva (Sonauli), Petrapole and Mahadipur.

The exports made to the following Special Economic Zones (SEZ) are also entitled to DEPB.

SEZ: Santacruz , Kandla, Kochi, Vishakhapatnam, Chennai, Falta, Surat, and Noida.

(a) **Credit under DEPB and Present Market Value:** When the rate of credit entitlement under DEPB scheme comes to 10% or more, amount of credit against each such export product shall not exceed 50% of Present Market Value (PMV) of the export product. During export, exporter shall declare on shipping bill that benefit under DEPB scheme would not exceed 50% of PMV of export product.

   However, PMV declaration shall not be applicable for products for which value cap exists irrespective of DEPB rate of product.

(b) **Utilisation of DEPB Credit:** Payment of Indian customs duty including capital goods is done by utilising credit given under DEPB schemes.

(c) **Re-export of Goods Imported under DEPB Scheme:** In case of defective exported goods being returned, these may be again exported according to the EXIM guidelines as mentioned by the Department of Revenue.

In such cases 98% of the credit amount debited against DEPB for the export of such goods is generated by the concerned Commissioner of Customs in the form of a certificate, on the basis of which a fresh DEPB is issued by the concerned DGFT Regional Authority. It is important to note that the issued DEPB has the same port of registration and shall be valid for a period equivalent to the balance period available on the date of import of such defective/unfit goods.

5.7 Duty-free Replenishment Certificate (DFRC) Scheme

DFRC Scheme was first announced in EXIM Policy 2000-2001 with effect from 1st April 2000. DFRC scheme was continued in EXIM Policy 2002-07 with some minor changes. The earlier DFRC scheme announced in the 2000-01 EXIM Policy required that for the purpose of allowing DFRC benefit to imported inputs used in the resultant export product, the quality, technical characteristics and specifications of the inputs under import should be the same as those used in the resultant export product. For this purpose the quality, technical characteristics and specifications of each input used in the resultant export product were required to be specified on the shipping bill and at the time of import, Customs was required to co-relate it with the input under import so as to allow DFRC benefit to those inputs which were of the same quality, technical characteristics and specifications.

Under the new DFRC scheme such co-relation of quality, technical characteristics and specifications has been done away except in the case of items which are listed in paragraph 4.31 of the Hand Book of Procedure Volume 1 as amended by DGFT/ Notice No. 4/2002-07 dated 1st April, 2002. In respect of such items, customs shall continue to ascertain the quality, technical characteristics and specifications of the inputs under import with reference to the quality, technical characteristics and specifications of the inputs used in the export product as declared on the shipping bill. Quantity of each input shall be permitted in the DFRC licence in terms of SION for the relevant export product as earlier. Licences issued under DFRC scheme are freely transferable as earlier.

Other procedural requirements of DFRC Scheme as specified in DOR's earlier Circular Nos. 33/2000-Cus. dated 2.5.2000, 42/2000-Cus. dated 2.5.2000 and 59/2000-Cus. dated 11.5.2000 shall continue to be followed with the aforesaid modifications. Customs Notification No. 46/2002-Cus. dated 22.4.2002 has been issued to put into operation this scheme.

- The duty-free replenishment certificate is a facility extended to both the merchant exporter and manufacturer exporter for the duty-free import of inputs used in the manufacture of goods for their replenishment.

- The term duty-free here means that the exporter is exempt from the payment of basic customs duty and special additional duty at the time of customs clearance of the import consignment. The exporter who wants to avail this facility should give a declaration in the export promotion copy of the shipping bill indicating the serial number and the product group of the standard input output norms of the export products at the time of seeking customs clearance of the export shipment.

- The exporter can file application for the grant of DFRC within a period of 90 days from the date of realisation of the export proceeds. The application for the grant of DFRC should be submitted to the Regional Licensing Authority having jurisdiction over the firm in the prescribed form along with documents.

- The CIF value of imports that can be made against DFRC is arrived at on the basis of the international price of the inputs as given under standard input output norms. The DFRC and the material imported against it are freely transferable.

- It should be ensured that the imports under DFRC should be made from the same port from where the exports have been made. Import of fuel under DFRC entitlement shall be allowed to be transferred to marketing agencies authorised by the Ministry of Petroleum and Natural Gas.

Duty-free Replenishment Certificate (DFRC) shall be available for exports only up to 30.04.2006 and from 01.05.2006: this scheme is being replaced by the Duty-free Import Authorisation (DFIA).

Duty-free Import Authorisation (DFIA)

Effective from 1st May, 2006, Duty-free Import Authorisation or DFIA in short is issued to allow duty-free import of inputs which are used in the manufacture of the export product (making normal allowance for wastage), and fuel, energy, catalyst etc. which are consumed or utilised in the course of their use to obtain the export product. Duty-free Import Authorisation is issued on the basis of inputs and export items given under Standard Input and Output Norms (SION).

5.8 Highlights from Foreign Trade Policy 2014-19

With an aim to make India a significant partner in global trade by 2020, the government unveiled a new Foreign Trade Policy (FTP). The Foreign Trade Policy (FTP) 2015-20 was unveiled by Ms Nirmala Sitharaman, Minister of State for Commerce & Industry (Independent Charge), Government of India on April 1, 2015. Talking about the new policy, which aims at boosting India's exports, 'Make in India' and 'Digital India' will be integrated with the new Foreign Trade Policy. The government is pitching India as a friendly destination for manufacturing and exporting goods, and the new policy is being seen as an important step towards realising that goal.

Following are the highlights of the Foreign Trade Policy 2015-2020:

- Foreign Trade Policy 2015-20 offers a framework for increasing exports of goods and services, at the same time creating employment opportunities, increasing value addition in the country, within 'Make in India' programme.

- The Policy intends to enable India to counter the challenges of the external environment, keeping pace with the rapidly evolving international trading architecture and making trade a major provider to the country's economic growth and development.

- Foreign Trade Policy 2015-20 launches two new schemes, namely 'Merchandise Exports from India Scheme (MEIS)' for export of particular goods to particular markets and 'Services Exports from India Scheme (SEIS)' for increasing exports of notified services.

- Duty credit scrips subjected under MEIS and SEIS and the goods imported against these scrips are entirely transferable.

- For the grant of rewards under MEIS, the countries have been classified into 3 Groups, where the rates of rewards under MEIS vary from 2 percent to 5 percent. Under SEIS the chosen services would be rewarded at the rates of 3 per cent and 5 per cent.

- Actions have been taken to nudge procurement of capital goods from original manufacturers under the EPCG scheme by shrinking specific export obligation to 75 per cent of the normal export obligation.

- Steps have been taken to provide a boost in the exports of defense and hi-tech objects.

- E-Commerce exports of handloom products, books/periodicals, leather footwear, toys and customised fashion garments via courier or foreign post office would also gain benefit of MEIS (for values up to INR 25,000).

- Manufacturers, who are also status holders, will now be able to self-certify their manufactured goods in phases, as initiating from India with a view to succeed for preferential treatment under different forms of bilateral and regional trade agreements. This 'Approved Exporter System' will assist manufacturer exporters greatly in getting rapid access to international markets.

- Measures have been taken for promoting manufacturing and exports under 100 per cent EOU/EHTP/STPI/BTP Schemes. The steps comprise of a fast track clearance facility for these units, allowing them to share infrastructure facilities, allowing inter unit transfer of goods and services, allowing them to launch warehouses near the port of export and to make use of duty free equipment for training reason.

- 108 MSME clusters have been recognised for focused interventions to improve exports. Accordingly, 'Niryat Bandhu Scheme' has been galvanised and repositioned to attain the aims and goals of 'Skill India'.

- Trade facilitation and enhancing the ease of doing business are the other major focus areas in this new FTP. One of the major objectives of new FTP is to move towards paperless working in 24×7 environment.

Points to Remember

- In the initial years of planning the main emphasis was on "export promotion and import substitution". After the process of globalisation and liberalisation, the Government of India followed a Free Trade Policy. India has opened its economy by liberalising the import-export regime. This implies the conversion of quantitative restrictions to low and uniform tariffs and the use of the exchange rate for bringing balance of payment equilibrium.

- The EXIM Policy and Foreign Trade Policy shifted the focus to the export market. It was also necessary to simplify the tariff system and reduce the administrative forms of intervention substantially.

- The exporters are eligible for various benefits under different laws governing the exports from and imports into India. Duty drawback is the most sought after and popular benefit with the exporting community.

- Duty Exemption Schemes enable duty-free import of inputs required for export production. Duty Exemption Schemes consist of:

    1. Advance Authorisation

    2. Duty-free Import Authorisation (DFIA).

- A Duty Remission Scheme enables post-export replenishment/remission of duty on inputs used in export products. Duty remission schemes consist of:

    (a) Duty Entitlement Pass Book Scheme

    (b) Duty Drawback Scheme

- Duty Exemption Scheme comprises of imports under duty-free licences.

- The scheme of Duty Drawback is governed by the 'Customs and Central Excise Duties Drawback Rules' compiled and notified by 'Drawback Directorate' of the Department of Revenue, Ministry of Finance of the Government of India.

- The application for fixation of drawback rates should be submitted to the Department of Revenue, Ministry of Finance or with the Customs House/Central Excise Collectorate in whose jurisdiction their manufacturing unit is located. The application must be submitted within 60 days from the date of export.
- Based on the relevant information given in the drawback copy of the shipping bill, the claim of Duty Drawback (DBK) is processed and passed for payment.
- In case of import of inputs without payment of basic customs duty, an advance license is issued. These licences are issued in accordance with the policy and procedure in force on the date of issue of the licence. They are also subject to the fulfilment of a time-bound export obligation, and a specified value addition. Such licences maybe either value based or quantity based.
- Replenishment (REP) licenses are the earliest and still the principal methods of giving incentives to exporters. Combined with duty drawback and Cash Compensation (CCS), REP licences permit the exporter to import certain restricted raw materials and components, that is, raw materials and components appearing on the lists of limited permissible and canalised items in the Import-Export Policy. Refunds can be claimed through the Duty Drawback Scheme.
- Exporters, export-oriented units, units located in STP, EHTP, EPZ are granted recognition for their previous export performance by being certified as an export house, trading house, star trading house, super star trading house etc.
- Duty Entitlement Pass Book Scheme, in short DEPB is an export incentive scheme.
- Under the new DFRC scheme such co-relation of quality, technical characteristics and specifications has been done away except in the case of items which are listed in paragraph 4.31 of the Hand Book of Procedure Volume 1 as amended by DGFT/ Notice No. 4/2002-07 dated 1st April, 2002. In respect of such items, customs shall continue to ascertain the quality, technical characteristics and specifications of the inputs under import with reference to the quality, technical characteristics and specifications of the inputs used in the export product as declared on the shipping bill. Quantity of each input shall be permitted in the DFRC licence in terms of SION for the relevant export product as earlier. Licences issued under DFRC scheme are freely transferable as earlier.
- Effective from 1st May, 2006, Duty-free Import Authorisation or DFIA in short is issued to allow duty-free import of inputs which are used in the manufacture of the export product (making normal allowance for wastage), and fuel, energy, catalyst etc. which are consumed or utilised in the course of their use to obtain the export product.

Questions for Discussion

1. Define the concept of duty exemption schemes as regards to India's foreign trade.

2. Discuss how advance licence schemes facilitate exporters for smooth international trade.

3. Write short notes on:

    (a) DEPB

    (b) DFRC

    (c) Special Import Licence

    (d) Advance Licence

    (e) Replenishment Licence

4. Discuss the highlights from Foreign Trade Policy 2014-19.

Appendices

Format of Important Import-Export Documents

APPENDIX - 1

FORMAT OF IMPORTER - EXPORTER CODE NUMBER

GOVERNMENT OF INDIA

MINISTRY OF COMMERCE & INDUSTRY

O/O JT./DY.DIRECTOR GENERAL OF FOREIGN TRADE

(Full Address)

CERTIFICATE OF IMPORTER - EXPORTER CODE (IEC) NUMBER

----

1. Name   ....

2. Address   ....

               ....

               ....

PIN ☐☐☐☐☐☐

3.   Address of the Branches/Division/

....

Units/factories, if any.

....

....

PIN ☐☐☐☐☐☐

4. IEC Number

....

5. Date of issue

....

6. PAN Number

....

(Signature of the Issuing Authority)

Name   ....

Designation   ....

(Official Stamp)

Place ....

Date ....

(Issued from File No. ....)

Note : In case of any change in the name/address or constitution of IEC holder, the IEC holder shall cease to be eligible to import or export against the IEC number after expiry of 60 days from the date of such change unless in the meantime, the consequential changes are effected in the IEC by the concerned licensing authority.

APPENDIX - 2

STATEMENT OF PARTICULARS OF IEC NUMBERS ISSUED FOR THE PERIOD

Sr. No.	Name	Address	IEC No.	Date of Allotment
[1]	[2]	[3]	[4]	[5]

Note : The periodicity of the submission of the above information by the IEC issuing authorities shall be on fortnightly basis and the information shall be submitted to the concerned office of RBI by the end of the week succeeding the fortnight.

APPENDIX - 3

LETTER OF CREDIT PROFORMA

- - - - - - - - - - - - - - - - Transmission - - - - - - - - - - - - - - - - -	
Received from SWIFT	
Network priority : Normal	
Message output Reference : 6543 010126	
Message input Reference : 6543 010125	
- - - - - - - - - - - - - - - - Message Header - - - - - - - - - - - - - - -	
SWIFT output delivery status : Open Asked	
FIN 701 Issue of a documentary credit	

Sender :	The Sun Bank Sunlight City Import-Country
Receiver :	The Moon Bank 5 Moonlight Blvd. Export-City and Postal Code Export-Country

SB-87654	Banking priority : Normal

- - - - - - - - - - - - - - - Message Text - - - - - - - - - - - - - - - -		
20	:	Documentary credit number SB-87654
23	:	Issuing bank's reference SBRE-777
31C	:	Date of Issue January 26, 2001
31D	:	Date and place of expiry March 26, 2001 Export-City, Export-Country
32B	:	Currency code amount Twenty Five Thousand U.S. Dollars (USD 25,000.00)
39B	:	Maximum credit amount Not exceeding Twenty Five Thousand U.S. Dollars (USD 25,000.00)

40A	:	Form of documentary credit Irrevocable
41D	:	Available with ... by ... Draft(s) drawn on The Moon Bank, by payment
42C	:	Drafts at At sight for full invoice value
42D	:	Drawee - Name and Address The Moon Bank, 5 Moonlight Blvd., Export-City and Postal Code, Export-Country
43P	:	Partial shipments Prohibited
43T	:	Transhipments Permitted
44A	:	On board/disp/taking charge Moonbeam Port, Export-Country
44B	:	For transportation to Sunny Port, Import-Country
44C	:	Latest date of shipment March 19, 2001
45A	:	Description of goods and services 100 Sets 'ABC' Brand Pneumatic Tools, 1/2" drive, complete with hose and quick couplings, CIF Sunny Port
46A	:	Documents required 1. Signed commercial invoice in five (5) copies indicating the buyer's Purchase Order No. DEF-101 dated January 10, 2001. 2. Packing list in five (5) copies. 3. Full set 3/3 clean on board ocean bill of lading, plus two (2) non-negotiable copies, issued to order of The Sun Bank, Sunlight City, Import-Country, notify the above accountee, marked "freight Prepaid", dated latest March 19, 2001, and showing documentary credit number. 4. Insurance policy in duplicate for 110% CIF value covering Institute Cargo Clauses (A), Institute War and Strike Clauses, evidencing that claims are payable in Import-Country.

47A	:	Additional conditions 1. All documents indicating the Import License No. IP/123456 dated January 18, 2001. 2. Draft(s) drawn under this credit must be marked : "Drawn under documentary credit No. SB-87654 of The Sun Bank, Sunlight City, Import-Country, dated January 26, 2001". 3. This credit is subject to the Uniform Customs and Practice for Documentary Credits, 1993 Revision, International Chamber of Commerce Publication No. 500.
48	:	Period of presentation Documents must be presented for payment within 15 days after the date of shipment.
49	:	Confirmation instructions Add your confirmation
50	:	Applicant DEF Imports, 7 Sunshine Street, Sunlight City, Import-Country
52A	:	Issuing bank The Sun Bank, Sunlight City, Import-Country
57D	:	Advise through bank The Moon Bank, 5 Moonlight Blvd., Export-City and Postal Code, Export-Country
59	:	Beneficiary UVW Exports, 88 Prosperity Street East, Suite 707, Export-City and Postal Code, Export-Country
71B	:	Charges All charges outside the Import-Country are on beneficiary's account
72	:	Sender to receiver information This is an operative instrument, no mail confirmation to follow
78	:	Instruction to pay/accept/negotiate bank Documents to be forwarded to us in one lot by courier
- - - - - - - - - - - - - - - Message Trailer - - - - - - - - - - - - - - -		
MAC : ABCD1234		
CHK : ABCDEFG12345		

- - - - - - -

APPENDIX - 4
FORM A.R.E. 1

Application for removal of excisable goods for export by (Air/Sea/Post/Land)*

To

      Superintendent of Central Excise

      .... (Full Postal Address)

    1.   Particulars of [Assistant/Deputy Commissioner of Central Excise]/Maritime Commissioner of Central Excise from whom rebate shall be claimed/with whom bond/undertaking is executed and his complete postal address.

    2.   I/We .... of ....propose to export the under-mentioned consignment to .... (Country of destination) by Air/Sea/Land/Parcel Post under claim for rebate/bond/undertaking*.

Particulars of Manufacturer of goods- and his Central Excise Registration No.	No. and Description of packages	Gross weight/Net weight	Marks and Nos. on packages	Quantity of goods	Description of Goods
(1)	(2)	(3)	(4)	(5)	(6)

Value	Duty		No. and date of Invoice under which duty was paid/No. and date of bond/undertaking executed under Rule 19	Amount of Rebate claimed	Remarks
	Rate	Amt. (Rs.)			
(7)	(8)	(9)	(10)	(11)	(12)

    3.   I/We hereby certify that the above- mentioned goods have been manufactured.

      (a) availing facility/without availing facility of CENVAT credit under CENVAT Credit Rules, 2001.

      (b) availing facility/without availing facility under Notification 41/2001-CE(N.T.), dated 26th June, 2001 issued under rule 18 of Central Excise(No.2) Rules, 2001.

      (c) availing facility/without availing facility under Notification 43/2001-CE(N.T.), dated 26th June, 2001 issued under rule 19 of Central Excise(No.2) Rules, 2001.

4. I/We hereby declare that the export is in discharge of the export obligation under a Quantity based Advance Licence/ /Under Claim of Duty Drawback under Customs and Central Excise Duties Drawback Rules, 1995.

5. I/We hereby declare that the above particulars are true and correctly stated.

Time of Removal................................

Signature of owner or his
Authorised agent with date.
Name in Block Letters & Designation (SEAL)

APPENDIX - 5
Certification by Central Excise Office

1.   Certified that duty has been paid by debit entry in the Personal Ledger Account No. ....and/or CENVAT Account Entry No............ or recorded as payable in Daily Stock Account, on the goods described overleaf.

OR

Certified that the owner has entered into Bond No. .... under Rule 19 of Central Excise (No.2) Rules, 2001 with the................................[F.No._____], duly accepted by the Assistant Commissioner/Deputy Commissioner of Central Excise_____ on _____(Date).

2.   Certified that I have opened and examined the packages No... and found that the particulars stated and the description of goods given overleaf and the packing list (if any) are correct and that all the packages have been stuffed in the container No. .... with Marks .... and the same has been sealed with Central Excise Seal/One Time Seal(OTS) No. ....

3.   I have verified with the records, the exporter is only availing the export incentives, as specified in box No.6. and found it to be true.

4.   Certified that I have drawn three representative samples from the consignment (wherever necessary) and have handed over, two sets thereof duly sealed to the exporter/his authorised representative.

Place....................
Date ....

Signature	Signature
(Name in Block Letters)	(Name in Block Letters)
Superintendent of Central Excise	Inspector of Central Excise

APPENDIX - 6

CERTIFICATION BY THE CUSTOMS OFFICER

Certified that the consignment was shipped under my supervision under Shipping Bill No_____ dated _____by S.S./Flight No._____ which left on the_____ day of_____ (Month)_____(year)

OR

Certified that the above-mentioned consignment was stuffed in Container No._____ belonging to Shipping Line_____ based on the "Let Export Order" given on _____ day of _____ (Month) _____ (year) on the Shipping Bill No _____ dated _____ and sealed by seal/one time lock No._____ in my supervision and the container was handed over to the Custodian M/s _____ for being shipped via _____ (Name of the Port).

OR

Certified that the above-mentioned consignment has been duly identified and has passed the land frontier today at_____ in its original condition under Bill of Exports No_____ Place_____ Date_____.

Signature
(Name and designation of the Customs
Officer in Block Letters)/(Seal)

EXPORT BY POST

Certified that the consignment described overleaf has been despatched by foreign post to .... on......................day of 200..........

Place ....

Date ....

Signature of Post Master
(Seal)

REBATE SANCTION ORDER

(On Original, Duplicate and Triplicate)

Refund Order No.................... dated .... Rebate of Rs................. (Rupees ....) sanctioned vide Cheque No. ....dated ....

Place ....

Date ....

Assistant/Deputy Commissioner/Maritime
Commissioner of Central Excise

*Strike out inapplicable portions

APPENDIX - 7

INVOICE

Exporter/Manufacturer			Invoice No. & Date	Exporters Ref.
			Buyers Order No. & Date	Income Tax PAN No. :
			Other Reference	
Consignee :			Buyer (if other than Consignee)	
			Country of Origine of Goods	Country of Final Destination
Pre-Carriage by	Place of receipt of pre carrier		Terms of Delivery and Payment	
Vessel/Freight No.	Port of Loading			
Port of Discharge	Place of Delivery			

Marks & Nos./Container No.	No. & Kind of Pkgs. PKGS.	Description of Goods SHIPMENT CODE :	Quantity (in Dozens)	Rate (Per Dozen) (In US$)	Amount (In US$)
MANUFACTURER : DC Location :					

| Amount (In Words)

Net Wt   : KGS
Gross Wt. : KGS.
Ctn. Dim : : | | | Total : | | |

Declaration :
We declare that this invoice shows actual price of the goods described and that the amount indicated represents the price actually charged and that there is no flow of additional consideration directly from the buyers.

Authorised Signatory

APPENDIX -8

SHIPPERS DECLARATION Form SDF"

[See rule 6 (1)(a)]

Shipping Bill No.   Date

Declaration under Foreign Exchange Regulation Act, 1973 :

I/We hereby declare that I/We am/are the *SELLER/CONSIGNOR of the goods in respect of which this declaration is made and that the particulars given in the Shipping Bill No.......
dated ....   are true and that a)* the value as contracted with the buyer is the same as the full export value declared in the above shipping bill b)* the full export value of the goods is not ascertainable at the time of export and that the value declared is that which I/We, having regard to the prevailing market conditions, expect to receive on the sale of goods in the overseas market.

I/We undertake that I/We will deliver to the bank named herein ....

The foreign exchange representing the full export value of the goods on or before   @
.... in the manner prescribed in Rule 9 of the Foreign Exchange Regulation Rules, 1974. I/We further declare that I/We am/are resident in India and I/We have a place of business in India.

I/We* am/are OR am/are not in Caution List of the Reserve Bank of India.

Date ....

                                                                                        (Signature of Exporter)

                                                                                        Name : ....

@ State appropriate date of delivery which must be the due date for payment or within six months from the date of shipment, whichever is earlier, but for exports to warehouses established outside India with permission of the Reserve Bank, the date of delivery must be within fifteen months.

Strike out whichever is not applicable

- - - - - - - - - - - - -

A RELIABLE SHIPPING LINE (Non-negotiable unless consigned to order)				
Shipper / Exporter (Complete Name and Address)	ORIGINAL		Bill of Lading No.	
	Export References			
Consignee (Complete Name and Address)	Forwarding Agent – References			
	Point and Country of Origin of Goods			
Notify Party (Complete Name and Address)	Domestic Routing / Export Instructions (Additional Notify Party Etc.)			
Marks and Numbers	Number of Packages	Description of Packages and Goods	Gross Weight	Measurement

APPENDIX - 9

BILL OF EXCHANGE

INVOICE NO.   DATE :

FOR :   PLACE :

AT _____ DAYS AFTER THE ON BOARD BILL OF LADING DATE :_____, PAY THIS FIRST BILL OF EXCHANGE (SECOND OF THE SAME AMOUNT,TENOR AND DATE BEING UNPAID) TO NAME AND ADDRESS OF BENEFICIARY BANK THE SUM OF_____ AGAINST OUR INVOICE NO._____DATED_____ DRAWN UNDER DOCUMENTARY CREDIT NUMBER_____ DATED_____ISSUED BY NAME AND ADDRESS OF IMPORTER'S BANK

       FOR NAME OF CO.

                          AUTHORISED SIGNATORY

TO :

NAME AND ADDRESS OF

IMPORTER'S BANK

ACCOUNT OF :

BUYER'S NAME AND ADDRESS

APPENDIX - 10

BILL OF EXCHANGE

CERTIFICATE OF ORIGIN			
EXPORTER : Exporters Importer Code : RBI Code : **CONSIGNEE :**		NO. COO/INVOICE NO. DATE :	
Vessel / Flight No. :	Port of Loading :		
Port of Discharge :	Final Destination :		
Marks & Nos. / Container No.	No. & Kind of Packages	Description of Goods	Quantity (IN PCS)
PKGS.			
INVOICE NO. DATED			
CERTIFICATION			
We hereby certify that the GOODS SHIPPED ARE OF INDIAN ORIGIN : Remarks (if any) : 1. Goods consigned from (Exporter's business name, address, country). 2. Goods consigned to (Consignee's name, address, country).		**Authorised Signatory**	

Abbreviation

- **AEN:** Administrative Exception Note
- **AERP:** Automated Export Reporting Program
- **AFESD:** Arab Fund for Economic and Social Development
- **aft:** At or towards the rear of a ship.
- **AFTA:** ASEAN Free Trade Area
- **AGRIS:** Agriculture Information System
- **Agt.:** "Agent, Against, Agreement"
- **AIB:** Arab International Bank
- **AIBD:** Association of International Bond Dealers
- **AID:** Agency for International Development
- **AID:** Agency for International Development
- **AIES:** Automated Information Exchange System
- **AIG:** Airbus Industries Group
- **AIMS:** Agriculture Information and Marketing Services
- **AIST:** Agency for Industrial Science Technology
- **AIT:** American Institute in Taiwan
- **AIT:** American Institute in Taiwan
- **AKA:** Ausfuhrkredit-Gesellschaft
- **ALADI:** Asociacion Latinoamericana de Integracion
- **ALIDE:** "Association Latinoamericana de Institutiones Financieras, de- Desarrollo"
- **AMB:** Ambassador
- **AMCHAM:** American Chamber of Commerce
- **AMF:** Arab Monetary Fund
- **amidships:** At or towards the middle of a ship.
- **AMS:** "Agricultural Marketing Service, Automated Manifest System"
- **AMSC:** African Management Services Company
- **amt.:** Amount
- **AMU:** Arab Maghreb Union
- **ANF:** Arrival notification form
- **AOSIS:** Alliance of Small Island States
- **AP:** Administrative Protective Order
- **APAC:** Auto Parts Advisory Committee
- **APDF:** Africa Project Development Facility
- **APEC:** Asian-Pacific Economic Cooperation
- **API:** American Petroleum Institute
- **Appd.:** Approved
- **ARS:** African Regional Organisation for Standardization
- **AsDF:** Asian Development Fund
- **ASEAN:** Association of Southeast Asian Nations
- **ASEAN:** Association of South-East Asian Nations

- **At. wt.:** Atomic Weight
- **ATFP:** Arab Trade Financing Program
- **athwartships:** Across the ship or from side to side.
- **athwartships:** Across the ship or from side to side.
- **ATI:** "American Traders Index, Andean Trade Initiative"
- **Atl.:** Atlantic
- **ATLAS:** Automated Trade Locator Assistance Network
- **ATMIC:** Agricultural Trade and Marketing Information Center
- **ATOs:** Agricultural Trade Offices
- **ATP:** Advanced Technology Products
- **ATPA:** Andean Trade Preference Act
- **ATPI:** Andean Trade Preference Initiative
- **AUMA:** "Die Ausstellungs- und Messe-Ausschuss der Deutschen, Wirtschaft"
- **Buyback:** See: Countertrade.
- **B & T cl:** Blocking & Trapping clause
- **B. or B/-:** "Bale, Bag"
- **B.B.:** "Bill Book, Below Bridges"
- **B.B.cl.:** Both to blame collision clause
- **B.C.:** Bristol Channel
- **b.d.i.:** Both dates inclusive
- **B.D.I.:** Both days inclusive
- **B.D.S.:** Broker's daily statement
- **B.H.P.:** Brake hore-power
- **B.I.I.B.A.:** British Insurance &Investment Brokers' Association
- **b.m.:** Board measure (timber)
- **B.O.:** "Buyer's option, Branch Office"
- **B.O.T.:** Board of Trade
- **B.P.B.:** Bank Post Bill
- **B.R.:** Builders' Risks Insurance
- **B.R.C.:** "Broker Regulatory Committee (Lloyds's), Brokers Registration Council"
- **B.S.:** Boiler survey. Balance sheet
- **B.S.T.:** British Summer Time
- **b.t.:** Berth terms
- **B.T.U.:** Bow Thrust Unit(s)
- **B.th.U.:** British Thermal Unit
- **B.V.:** Bureau Veritas
- **B/Ch:** Bristol Channel
- **B/D** - "Bank Draft, bar draft (grain trade)"
- **B/E:** "Bill of Exchange, Bill of Entry"
- **B/G:** Bondage goods
- **B/H:** "Bill of Health, Bordeaux to Hamburg inclusive"

- **B/L:** Bill of Landing
- **B/O:** Brought over
- **B/P:** Bills payable
- **B/R:** Bills receivable. Builders' risks. Bordeaux or Rouen (grain trade)
- **B/s:** "Bags, Bales"
- **B/S:** "Bill of Sale, Bill of Store"
- **B/St:** Bill of sight
- **BACAT:** Barge aboard catamaran
- **Bal.:** Balance
- **Bar.:** Barrel
- **bbls:** Barrels
- **Bd.:** "Bound, bond"
- **Bdls:** Bundles
- **Bds.:** Boards (timber)
- **Bg.:** Bag
- **Bg.:** Bag
- **bhp:** Brake horsepower
- **Bk.:** "Back, Backwardation, Book"
- **Bkge.:** "Breakage, brokerage"
- **Bls.:** Bales. Barrels
- **bp:** Between perpendiculars
- **Brl.:** Barrel
- **BTN:** Brussels Tariff Nomenclature
- **bu** – Bushels
- **bow:** Curved forward part of a ship.
- **bulk cargo:** Unpacked dry cargo such as grain or coal.
- **bunkers:** A ship's fuel.
- **BADEA:** Banque Arabe pour le Developpement Economique en Afrique
- **BAGGAGE:** General License - BAGGAGE
- **BANCOMEXT:** Banco Nacional de Comercio Exterior
- **BARs:** Buy American Restrictions
- **BAS:** Caribbean/Central America Business Advisory Service
- **BCEA:** Banque Centrale des Etats de l'Afrique de l'Ouest
- **BCIE:** Banco Centroamericano de Integracion Economico
- **BCIU:** Business Council for International Understanding
- **BCS:** Border Cargo Selectivity
- **BDEAC:** Banque de Developpement des Etats de l'Afrique Centrale
- **BDEGL:** Banque de Developpement des Etats du Grand Lac
- **BEAC:** Banque des Etats de l'Afrique Centrale
- **BEEC:** Border Environment Cooperation Commission
- **BEET:** Business Executive Enforcement Team

- **BENELUX:** "Belgium, Netherlands, Luxembourg Economic Union"
- **BfAi:** Bundesstelle fur Aussenhandelsinformation
- **BFC:** Business Facilitation Center
- **BFCE:** Banque Francaise du Commerce Exterieur
- **BHC:** "Bank Holding Company, British High Commission"
- **BIA:** Best Information Available
- **BID:** Banco Interamericano de Desarrollo
- **BIE:** Bureau of International Expositions
- **BI:** Business Information Office
- **BIS:** Bank for International Settlements
- **BISNIS:** "Business Information Service for the Newly Independent, States"
- **BIT(s):** Bilateral Investment Treaty(ies)
- **B/L:** Bill of Lading
- **BLADEX:** Banco Latinoamericano de Exportaciones
- **BLEU:** Belgium-Luxembourg Economic Union
- **BMWi:** Bundesministerium fur Wirtschaft
- **BOAD:** Banque Ouest-Africaine de Developpement
- **BOP:** Balance of Payments
- **BOT:** Balance of Trade
- **BOTB:** British Overseas Trade Board
- **BRITE:** Basic Research in Industrial Technologies in Europe
- **BSA:** Bilateral Steel Agreement
- **BSP:** Business Sponsored or Between Show Promotion
- **BTN:** Brussels Tariff Nomenclature
- **BXA:** Bureau of Export Administration
- **C:** Consulate
- **C&F:** Cost and Freight
- **C&F Named Port:** Cost and freight. All costs of goods and transportation to the named port are included in the price quoted. Buyer pays insurance while aboard ship up to overseas inland destination.
- **C.:** Collected, Currency, Coupon, Coast
- **C. & D.:** Collected and delivered
- **c. & f.:** Cost and freight
- **c. & i.:** Cost and insurance
- **C. &/or J.:** China and/or Japan
- **C.&I.:** Cost and insurance
- **C.A.C.T.L.V.O.:** Compromised &/or arranged &/or constructive total loss of vessel only
- **C.A.D.:** Cash against documents
- **C.B. & H.:** Continent between Bordeaux and Hamburg
- **C.B.I.:** Confederation of British Industry

- **C.C.:** Current cost, Civil commotions, Cancellation clause, Continuation clause
- **C.C.I.S.G.:** Convention Contracts of International Sale of Goods
- **C.C.S.A.:** Collective company signing agreement
- **C.D.:** Country damage
- **C.D.V.:** Current domestic value
- **c.f.:** Cubic feet. Carried forward
- **c.f.i.:** Cost, freight and insurance
- **C.f.o.:** Channel for orders. Coast for orders. Calling for orders
- **C.F.R.:** Code of Federal Regulations (USA)
- **C.G.A.:** Cargo's proportion of general average
- **C.G.S.A.:** Carriage of Goods by Sea Act
- **C.H. & H.:** Continent between Havre and Hamburg
- **C.I.:** Consular Invoice
- **C.I.E.:** Captain's imperfect entry (Customs). - c.i.f. - Cost, insurance and freight
- **c.i.f. & e.:** Cost, insurance, freight and exchange
- **c.i.f.c.i.:** Cost, insurance, freight, commission and interest
- **c.i.f.L.t.:** Cost, insurance, and freight London terms
- **C.I.I.:** Chartered Insurance Institute
- **C.K.D.:** Completely knocked down
- **C.O.B.:** Cargo on board
- **C.O.D.:** Cash on delivery
- **C.P.A.:** Claims payable abroad
- **c.p.d.:** Charterers' pay dues
- **C.P.P.:** Controllable Pitch Propellers
- **C.R.:** Current rate, Company's risk, Carrier's risk
- **C.R.O.:** Cancelling returns only
- **C.S.D.:** Closed shelter deck
- **C.S.T.:** Central standard time
- **c.t.l.:** Constructive total loss
- **c.t.l.o.:** Constructive total loss only
- **c.v.:** Chief value
- **C.W.:** Commercial weight
- **C/-:** Case
- **C/D:** Commercial dock. Consular declaration
- **c/i:** Certificate of insurance
- **C/L:** Craft loss
- **C/N:** Consignment note. Cover note. Credit note
- **C/O:** Certificate of origin. Cash order. Case oil
- **C/P:** Charter Party, Custom of Port (grain trade)
- **c/s:** Cases
- **CABEE:** Consortia of American Businesses in Eastern Europe

- **CABEI:** Central American Bank for Economic Integration
- **CAC:** Codex Alimentarius Commission
- **CACM:** Central American Common Market
- **CAD:** Cash Against Documents
- **CAD/CAM:** Computer Aided Design/Computer Aided Manufacturing
- **CAEU:** Council of Economic Arab Unity
- **CAF:** Corporacion Andina de Fomento
- **Canc.:** Cancelled
- **cancl.:** Cancelling
- **cap:** Capacity
- **CAP:** Common Agricultural Policy, Country Action Plan
- **Capital Account:** See: Balance of Payments.
- **CAR:** Commercial Activity Report
- **cargo:** Goods carried in or on a ship
- **CARICCM:** Caribbean Common Market
- **CARICOM:** Caribbean Common Market
- **CARICOM:** Caribbean Community
- **CBD:** Commerce Business Daily
- **CBERA:** Caribbean Basin Economic Recovery Act
- **CBI:** Caribbean Basin Initiative
- **CBM:** Conventional buoy mooring
- **CBW:** Chemical and Biological Weapons
- **CCA:** Chambre de Cooperation de l'Afrique de l'Ouest
- **CCC:** Canadian Commercial Corporation, Commodity Credit Corporation, Customs Cooperation Council
- **CCC:** Customs Co-operation Council
- **CCCE:** Caisse Centrale de Cooperation Economique
- **CCCN:** Customs Co-operation Council Nomenclature
- **CCCN:** Customs Cooperation Council Nomenclature
- **CCD:** Conseil de Cooperation Douaniere
- **CCF:** CoCom Cooperation Forum
- **CCFF:** Compensatory and Contingency Financing Facility
- **CCIR:** Comite Consultatif International des Radiocommunications
- **CCITT:** Comite Consultatif International Telegraphique et, Telephonique
- **CCITT:** Consultative Committee for International Telephone and, Telegraphy
- **CCL:** Commerce Control List;, formerly: - Commodity Control List
- **CCNAA:** Coordination Council for North American Affairs
- **CCNAA:** Coordination Council for North American Affairs
- **ccy:** Convertible currency
- **CD-ROM:** Compact Disc-Read Only Memory
- **CDB:** Caribbean Development Bank

- **CDC:** Commonwealth Development Corporation
- **CDI:** Capital Development Initiative
- **CDT:** Center for Defense Trade
- **CE:** Committee of Experts, Communautes Europeenes, Conformite Europeene, Council of Europe
- **CEA:** Chinese Economic Area, Council of Economic Advisors
- **CEA:** Communaute Economique de l'Afrique de l'Ouest
- **CEE:** Commission Economique pour l'Europe
- **CEEAC:** Communaute Economique des Etats de l'Afrique Centrale
- **CEEB:** Customs Electronic Bulletin Board
- **CEFTA:** Central Europe Free Trade Association
- **CEN:** European Committee for Standardization
- **CENELEC:** European Committee for Electrotechnical Standardization
- **CIAT:** Centro Internacional de Agricultura Tropical
- **CICA:** Confederation Internationale du Credit Agricole
- **CIDA:** Canadian International Development Agency
- **CIF:** Cost, Insurance and Freight
- **cif:** Cost, insurance, freight
- **CILSS:** Comite Permanent Interetats de Lutte contre la Secheresse, dans le Sahel
- **CIMS:** Commercial Information Management System
- **CIPs:** Commodity Import Programs
- **CIR:** Center for International Research
- **CIS:** Commonwealth of Independent States
- **CISG:** Convention on Contracts for the International Sale of, Goods
- **CIT:** Court of International Trade
- **CITA:** Committee for the Implementation of Textile Agreements
- **CITES:** Convention on International Trade in Endangered Species in, Wild Fauna and Flora
- **CIV:** Customs Import Value
- **CJ:** Commodity Jurisdiction
- **Ck.:** Cask
- **cld.:** Cleared
- **CLDP:** Commercial Law Development Program
- **D:** District Office
- **d:** Draught
- **D-RAM:** Dynamic Random Access Memory
- **D.:** Delivery, Delivered
- **D.A.A.:** Documents against acceptance
- **D.B.:** Day Book, Deals and battens (timber trade)
- **d.b.:** Deals and battens (timber)
- **d.b.b.:** Deals, battens and boards

- **D.D.:** Damage done
- **D.D.C.:** Damage done in collision
- **D.D.E.:** Direct data entry
- **d.d.o.:** Despatch discharging only
- **d.f.:** Dead freight
- **D.F.:** Direction finder
- **d.l.o.:** Despatch loading only
- **d.l.o.:** Dispatch loading only
- **d.p.:** Direct port
- **d.p.r.:** Daily pro rata
- **D.R.C.:** Damaged received in collision
- **D.T.B.A.:** Days to be agreed, date to be advised
- **D.T.I.:** Department of Trade and Industry
- **d.w.:** Deadweight
- **D.W.A.T.:** Deadweight all told
- **d.w.c.:** Deadweight capacity
- **d.w.t.:** Deadweight tonnage
- **D/A:** Deposit account, Days after acceptance, Documents against acceptance, Discharge afloat, Deductible average
- **D/A:** Documents Against Acceptance
- **D/C:** Deviation clause
- **D/d:** Days after date, Days' date
- **D/D:** Demand Draft, Delivered at Docks, Damage Done
- **D/N:** Debit note
- **D/O:** Delivery order
- **D/P:** Documents against payment
- **D/R:** Deposit receipt
- **D/s:** Days after sight
- **D/V:** Dual Valuation
- **D/W:** Dock warrant
- **DA:** Development Assistance
- **DAC:** Development Assistance Committee
- **DACON:** Data on Consulting Firms
- **DAEs:** Dynamic Asian Economies
- **DBGLS:** Development Bank of the Great Lakes States
- **Dbk.:** Drawback
- **DCM:** Deputy Chief of Mission
- **DCS:** Defense Conversion Subcommittee
- **dd.:** Delivered
- **dd/s.:** Delivered sound (grain trade)
- **Debt Swaps:** See: Swaps.

- **DEC:** District Export Council
- **DF:** Designated Federal Officer
- **DFA:** Development Fund for Africa
- **Dft.:** Draft
- **Direct Exporting:** Sale by an exporter directly to a buyer located in a foreign country.
- **DK.:** Deck
- **DL:** Distribution License
- **dm:** Decimeter
- **DMP:** District Marketing Plan
- **DMs:** Definitional Missions
- **E.:** East
- **e. & e.a.:** Each and every accident
- **e. & e.l.:** Each and every loss
- **e. & e.o.:** Each and every occurrence
- **E. & O.E.:** Errors and omissions excepted
- **E.C.A.:** Economic Commission for Africa
- **E.C.C.P.:** East coast coal port
- **E.C.E.:** Economic Commission for Europe
- **E.C.G.B.:** East coast of Great Britain
- **E.C.G.D.:** Export Credit Guarantee Department
- **E.C.I.:** East coast of Ireland
- **E.C.L.A.:** Economic Commission for Latin America
- **E.C.M.E.:** Economic Commission for the Middle East
- **E.C.U.K.:** East Coast of United Kingdom
- **E.C.V.:** Each cargo voyage
- **E.E.:** Errors excepted
- **E.E.C.:** European Economic Community
- **E.F.T.A.:** European Free Trade Association
- **E.I.:** Each incident
- **E.L.:** Employer's liability
- **E.M.L.:** Estimated maximum loss
- **E.M.P.L.:** Estimated maximum probable loss
- **E.M.S.:** European Monetary System
- **e.o.h.p.:** Excepted otherwise herein provided
- **E.P.I.:** Earned premium income
- **E.P.I.R.B.:** Emergency position indicator radio beacon
- **E.R.V.:** Each round voyage
- **E.S.D.:** Echo-sounding device
- **EAA:** Export Administration Act
- **EAC:** Export Assistance Center
- **EADB:** East African Development Bank

- **EAEC:** East Asian Economic Caucus, European Atomic Energy Community
- **EAI:** Enterprise for the Americas Initiative
- **EAR:** Export Administration Regulations
- **EARB:** Export Administration Review Board
- **EBB:** Economic Bulletin Board
- **EBRD:** European Bank for Reconstruction and Development
- **EC:** Economic Cooperation Organisation
- **EC:** European Community
- **ECA:** Economic Commission for Africa
- **ECAs:** Export Credit Agencies
- **ECASS:** Export Control Automated Support System
- **ECB:** European Central Bank
- **ECCAS:** Economic Community of Central African States
- **ECCB:** East Caribbean Central Bank
- **ECCN:** Export Control Classification Number;, formerly: - Export Commodity Classification Number
- **ECE:** Economic Commission for Europe
- **ECGD:** Export Credit Guarantee Department
- **ECJ:** European Court of Justice
- **ECLAC:** Economic Commission for Latin America and the Caribbean
- **ECLS:** Export Contact List Service
- **ECOWAS:** Economic Community of West African States
- **ECSC:** European Coal and Steel Community
- **ECSC:** European Coal and Steel Community
- **ECU:** European Currency Unit
- **ED:** Export Development Office
- **EDB:** Exporter Data Base
- **EDC:** Export Development Corporation
- **EEA:** European Economic Area
- **EEBIC:** Eastern Europe Business Information Center
- **EEC:** European Economic Community
- **EEC:** European Economic Community, or Common Market
- **EEC:** European Economic Community
- **EEP:** Export Enhancement Program
- **EEPROM:** Electronically Erasable Programmable Read-Only Memory
- **EEZ:** Exclusive Economic Zones
- **EFF:** Extended Fund Facility
- **EFTA:** European Free Trade Association
- **EFTA:** European Free Trade Association
- **EIB:** European Investment Bank
- **EIS:** Export Information System

- **ELAIN:** Electronic License Application and Information Network
- **ELAN:** Export Legal Assistance Network
- **ELVIS:** Export License Voice Information System
- **EMC:** Export Management Company
- **EMC:** Export Management Company
- **EMCF:** European Monetary Cooperation Fund
- **EMS:** European Monetary System
- **EMU:** European Monetary Union
- **EN:** European Norm
- **EOP:** European Patent Office
- **EOTC:** European Organisation for Testing and Certification
- **EP:** European Parliament
- **EPC:** Economic Policy Council, European Patent Convention
- **EPCI:** Enhanced Proliferation Control Initiative
- **EPROM:** Erasable Programmable Read-Only Memory
- **EPS:** Export Promotion Services
- **EPZs:** Export Processing Zones
- **ERLC:** Export Revolving Line of Credit
- **ERM:** Exchange Rate Mechanism
- **ERS:** Economic Research Service
- **ESA:** European Space Agency
- **ESAF:** Enhanced Structural Adjustment Facility
- **ESCAP:** Economic and Social Commission for Asia and the Pacific
- **ETA:** European Technical Approval
- **ETA:** Estimated time of arrival
- **ETC:** Export Trading Company
- **ETC:** Export Trade Company
- **ETSI:** European Telecommunications Standards Institute
- **ETUC:** European Trade Union Confederation
- **EU:** European Union
- **EUCLID:** European Cooperation for the Long-term in Defense
- **EURAM:** European Research in Advanced Materials
- **EURATOM:** European Atomic Energy Community
- **EUREKA:** European Research Coordination Agency
- **EURL:** Entreprise Unipersonnelle e responsabilite limitee
- **F:** Free Out
- **F.P.A.:** Free of Particular Average
- **F/X:** Foreign Exchange
- **FA:** Food and Agricultural Organisation
- **FAAS:** Foreign Affairs Administrative Support
- **FAK:** Freight All Kinds

- **FAS:** Foreign Agricultural Service, Free Alongside Ship
- **FAZ:** Foreign Access Zone
- **FBIS:** Foreign Broadcast Information Service
- **FBP:** Foreign Buyer Program
- **FBSEA:** Foreign Bank Supervision Enhancement Act
- **FC:** Foreign and Commonwealth Office
- **FCA:** Free Carrier
- **FCPA:** Foreign Corrupt Practices Act
- **FCSC:** Foreign Claims Settlement Commission
- **FDIUS:** Foreign Direct Investment in the United States
- **FEMA:** Federal Emergency Management Agency
- **FEMIDE:** Federacion Mundial de Instituciones Financieras de, Desarollo
- **FET:** Foreign Economic Trends
- **FFP:** Food For Progress
- **FGIS:** Federal Grain Inspection Service
- **FI:** Free In
- **FI:** Free In and Out
- **FIAS:** Foreign Investment Advisory Service
- **FIATA:** Federation Internationale des Associations de Transitaires, et Assimilies
- **FIT:** Foreign Independent Tour
- **FMC:** Federal Maritime Commission
- **FMD:** Foreign Market Development Program
- **FMS:** Foreign Military Sales
- **FMV:** Foreign Market Value
- **FOB:** Free on Board
- **FOGS:** Functioning of the GATT System
- **FOMEX:** Fondo para el Fomento de las Exportaciones de Productos, Manufacturados
- **FONPLATA:** Fondo Financiero Para el Desarrollo de la Cuenca del Plata
- **FOR/FOT:** Free on Rail/Free on Truck
- **FORDTIS:** Foreign Disclosure and Technical Information System
- **FOREX:** Foreign Exchange
- **FRA:** Forward (or Future) Rate Agreement
- **FS:** Foreign Service Officer
- **FSA:** Freedom Support Act
- **FSC:** Foreign Sales Corporation
- **FSI:** Foreign Service Institute
- **FSN:** Foreign Service National
- **FSs:** Feasibility Studies
- **FSU:** Former Soviet Union
- **FT:** Foreign Trade Organisation
- **FTA:** Free Trade Agreement/Area

- **FTC:** Federal Trade Commission
- **FTD:** Foreign Trade Division
- **FTI:** Foreign Traders Index
- **FTSR:** Foreign Trade Statistical Reporting
- **FTZ:** Foreign Trade Zone
- **FTZ-SZ:** Foreign Trade Zone-Subzone
- **F. & D.:** Freight and demurrage
- **F. & A.P.:** Fire and allied perils
- **f.a.:** Free alongside
- **F.a.a.:** Free of all average
- **f.a.c.:** Fast as you can
- **F.A.O.:** Food and agriculture Organisation (U.N.)
- **f.a.q.:** Fair average quality
- **f.a.s.:** Free alongside ship, Firsts and seconds (American lumber)
- **f.c. & s.:** Free of capture and seizure
- **F.C.A.R.:** Free of claim for accident reported
- **F.C.I.:** Full container loads
- **F.C.I.I.:** Fellow of the Chartered Insurance Institute
- **F.C.V.:** Full contract value, Full completed value
- **f.d.:** Free discharge. Free delivery. Free despatch. Free docks
- **F.D.O.:** For declaration purposes only
- **f.f.a.:** Free from alongside, Free foreign agency
- **F.F.O.:** Fixed and floating objects
- **F.G.A.:** Foreign general average
- **f.h.:** Fore hatch
- **f.i:** Free-in
- **f.i.a.:** Full interest admitted
- **f.i.b.:** Free into bunkers. Free into barge
- **F.I.C.S.:** Fellow of the Institute of Chartered Shipbrokers
- **F.I.L.:** Foreign insurance legislation
- **f.i.o.:** Free-in-and-out
- **f.i.o.s.:** Free in and out stowed
- **f.i.o.s.t.:** Free in and out stowed and/or trimmed
- **f.i.o.t.:** Free in and out trimmed
- **f.i.t.:** Free of income tax
- **f.i.w.:** Free in wagon
- **F.L.E.:** Fire, lightning and explosion
- **f.o.:** For orders, Firm offer, Full out terms (grain trade)
- **f.o.b.:** free on board
- **f.o.c.:** Free on car, Free of charge
- **F.O.C.:** Flag of convenience, Free ofcommission, Free of charge, Free of claims

- **f.o.d.:** Free of damage
- **F.O.M.:** Flag, ownership and management
- **F.O.N.A.S.B.A.:** Federation of National Association of Shipbrokers and Agents
- **f.o.q.:** Free on quay
- **f.o.r.:** Free on rail
- **f.o.r.t.:** Full out rye terms (grain trade)
- **f.o.s.:** Free on steamer
- **F.O.S.F.A.:** Federation of Oils, Seeds & Fats Associations
- **f.o.t.:** Free on truck
- **f.o.w.:** Free on wagon. First open water
- **F.P.:** Fully Paid. Floating (or open) policy
- **F.P.A.:** Free of particular average
- **F.P.I.L.:** Full premium if lost
- **F.P.T.:** Forepeak tank
- **f.r. & c.c.:** Free of riots and civil commotions
- **F.R.C.:** Free of reported casualty
- **F.R.O.:** Fire risk only
- **f.r.o.f:** Fire risk on freight
- **f.s.l.:** Full signed line (insurance)
- **F.S.R. & C.C.:** Free of strikes, riots and civil commotions
- **f.t.:** Full terms; despatch money, payable on all time saved on the chartered time for loading and discharging the cargo
- **F.T.A.:** Freight Transport Association and Agents
- **f.t.r.r. & i.:** For their repective rights and interests
- **F.V.C.:** Fishing vessel clauses
- **f.w.d.:** Fresh water damage
- **f.w.l.:** Full written line (insurance)
- **F.W.P.C.A.:** Federal Water Pollution Control Act (USA)
- **F.W.T. & G.D.:** Fair wear, tear and gradual deterioration
- **F/R:** Freight release
- **Fac.:** Facultative
- **Fac./oblig.:** Facultative/obligatory
- **FAS:** United States Foreign Agricultural Service
- **FCL:** Full container load
- **FCS:** Foreign Commercial Service
- **FEU:** Forty-foot equivalent unit
- **FIDIC:** Federation internationale des ingenieurs-conseils (International Federation of Consulting Engineers)
- **FIMBRA:** Financial Intermediaries, Managers and Brokers Regulatory Association
- **FLASH:** Feeder-LASH
- **fms.:** Fathoms (timber)

- **fob:** Free on board
- **Frt.:** Freight
- **ft:** Feet
- **Fth.:** Fathom
- **fwd.:** Forward
- **FX:** Foreign Exchange
- **fairway:** Navigable channel
- **G-10:** Group of Ten
- **G-24:** Group of Twenty:Four
- **G-5:** Group of Five
- **G-7:** Group of Seven
- **G-7:** Group of seven: the finance ministers and central bankers of seven leading industrial nations
- **G-77:** Group of Seventy-Seven
- **G-COCOM:** General License - COCOM
- **G-DEST:** General License - Destination
- **G-NNR:** General License - Non-Naval Reserve
- **G-TEMP:** General License - Temporary Export
- **G.A.:** General Average
- **G.A.D.V.:** Gross arrived damaged value
- **G.A.F.T.A.:** Grain & Feed Trade Assoc
- **G.A.S.V.:** Gross arrived sound value
- **G.A.T.T.:** General Agreement on Tariffs and Trade
- **G.F.:** Government Form (chartering)
- **g.f.a.:** Good fair average
- **G.L.:** Germanischer Lloyd
- **g.m.b.:** Good merchantable brand
- **g.m.q.:** Good merchantable quality
- **G.M.T.:** Greenwich Mean Time
- **G.N.E.P.I.:** Gross net earned premium income
- **g.o.b.:** Good ordinary brand
- **G.O.P.:** Gross original premium
- **g.r.t.:** Gross register tons
- **G.S.:** Good safety
- **g.s.m.:** Good sound merchantable
- **G/A:** General average
- **G/A con.:** General average contribution
- **G/A dep.:** General average deposit
- **GAB:** General Arrangements to Borrow
- **GCC:** Gulf Cooperation Council
- **GDP:** Gross Domestic Product

- **GDP:** Gross domestic product
- **GEF:** Global Environmental Facility
- **GEM:** Global Export Manager
- **GFW:** General License - Free World
- **GIE:** Groupement d'Intert Economique
- **GL:** General License
- **GLR:** General License - Return (Replacement)
- **GLV:** General License - Shipments of Limited Value
- **GmbH:** Gesellschaft mit beschrnker Haftung
- **GNP:** Gross National Product
- **GNP:** gross national product
- **GSM:** General Sales Manager
- **GSP:** Generalized System of Preferences
- **GSP:** generalized system of preferences
- **GTDA:** General License - Technical Data Publicly Available
- **GTDR:** General License - Technical Data Restricted by Written, Assurance
- **GTDU:** General License - Technical Data Restricted without, Written Assurance
- **GTZ:** Deutsche Gesellschaft fur Technische Zusammenarbeit
- **HS:** Harmonized Commodity Description and Coding System
- **j. & w.o.:** Jettison and washing overboard
- **J.C.C.:** Joint Cargo Committee
- **J.C.R.A.:** Joint Common Risks Agreement
- **J.H.C.:** Joint Hull Committee
- **J.H.F.:** Joint Hull Formula
- **J.H.I.U.:** Japanses Hull Insurers' Union
- **J.H.U.:** Joint Hull Understandings
- **J/A:** Joint Account
- **JCIT:** Joint Committee for Investment and Trade
- **JDB:** Japan Development Bank
- **JEIC:** Japan Export Information Center
- **JETRO:** Japan External Trade Organisation
- **JETRO:** Japan External Trade Organisation
- **L. def.:** Latent defect
- **L.A.S.H.:** Lighter aboard ship
- **L.A.T.:** Linseed Association Terms
- **L.A.T.F.:** Lloyd's American Trust Fund
- **L.A.U.A.:** Lloyd's Aviation Underwriters' Association
- **L.A.U.T.R.O.:** Life Assurance and Unit Trust Regulatory
- **L.C.:** London clause (chartering), Label clause
- **L.C.L.:** Less than full container load
- **L.C.T.A.:** London Corn trade

- **L.d.d.:** Loss during discharge
- **L.d.l.:** Loss during loading
- **L.H.A.R.:** London, Hull, Antwerp or Rotterdam
- **L.I.B.C.:** Lloyd's Insurance Brokers' Committee
- **L.I.M.:** London Insurance Market
- **L.I.M.D.S.M.:** London Insurance Market Data Standards Manual
- **L.I.M.T.C.G.:** London Insurance Market Technical Co-ordination Group
- **L.I.P.:** Life Insurance Policy
- **L.L.T.:** London Land Terms
- **L.M.C.:** Lloyd's machinery certificate
- **l.m.c.:** Low middling clause (cotton trade)
- **L.M.C.C.:** Lloyd's machinery certificate, continuous survey
- **L.N.G.:** Liquified natural gas carrier
- **l.n.y.d.:** Liability not yet determined
- **L.P.G.:** Liquified petroleum gas carrier
- **L.P.S.O.:** Lloyd's Policy Signing Office
- **L.R.:** Lloyd's Register of Shipping
- **L.R.M.C.:** Lloyd's refrigerating machinery certificate
- **l.s.:** Lump sum
- **L.S. Cls.:** Livestock clauses
- **L.S.H.W. Liab.:** Longshoremen's and Harbor Workers' Liability
- **L.S.T.:** Local standard time
- **L.T.A.:** Long term agreement
- **L.U.A.:** Lloyd's Underwriters' Association
- **L.U.A.A.:** Lloyd's Underwriting Agents Association
- **L.U.A.M.C.:** Leading underwriter agreement for marine cargo
- **L.U.A.M.H.:** Leading underwriter agreement for marine hull
- **L.U.C.R.O.:** Lloyd's Underwriters' Claims andRecoveries Office
- **L.U.T.I.R.O.:** Life and Unit Trust Intermediaries Regulatory Organisation
- **L.W.:** Low water
- **L.W.O.S.T.:** Low water, ordinary spring tides
- **L/A:** Letter of authority. Landing account. Lloyd's agent
- **L/C:** Letter of Credit
- **L/C:** Letter of Credit
- **l/u:** Laid up, Letter of undertaking
- **L/U:** Leading Underwriter
- **La Zone Franc:** See: Franc Zone.
- **Labor Advisory Committee:** A committee of private sector advisors, consisting of trade union representatives and other experts, which advises the Labor Department and the United States Trade Representative on U.S. trade policy matters.
- **LAES:** Latin American Economic System
- **LAFTA:** Latin American Free Trade Association

- **lagan:** Goods that have been jettisoned but are attached to a floating object so that they can be recovered.
- **LAIA:** Latin American Integration Association
- **LIBOR:** London Interbank Offered Rate
- **LPG:** Liquefied petroleum gas
- **M. & D.P.:** Minimum and deposit premium
- **M. & W.:** Marine and war risks
- **m. pack:** Missing package
- **M.A.V.I.S.:** Marine Audio-Visual Instruction Systems
- **M.B.D.:** Machinery breakdown
- **M.C.:** Machinery certificate
- **M.F.C.:** Maximum foreseeable loss
- **M.H.:** Main Hatch
- **M.H.W.S.:** Mean High Water Spring
- **M.I.P.:** Marine Insurance Policy
- **M.L.W.S.:** Mean Low Water Springs
- **m.m.:** Made merchantable
- **M.M.:** Mercantile Marine
- **M.M.A.:** Merchandise Marks Act
- **M.N.S.C.:** Managed Network Steering Committee
- **M.O.H.:** Medical Officer of Health
- **M.P.L.:** Maximum probable loss
- **M.R.:** Mate's receipt
- **M.S.:** Motor ship, Machinery survey
- **M.T.:** Mean Time
- **M.T.L.:** Mean tidal level
- **M/C:** Metalling clause (marine insurance), Machinery certificate
- **M/d:** Malicious damage
- **M/D:** Memorandum of deposit
- **M/s:** Months after sight
- **MOU:** Memorandum of Understanding
- **MPA:** Major Projects Agreement
- **MPP:** Market Promotion Program
- **MPT:** Ministry of Posts and Telecommunications
- **MRA:** Mutual Recognition Agreement
- **MRU:** Mano River Union
- **MSA:** Multilateral Steel Agreement
- **mst.:** Measurement
- **MT:** Multilateral Trade Organisation
- **MTAG:** Missile Technology Analysis Group
- **MTCR:** Missile Technology Control Regime
- **MTEC:** Missile Technology Export Control Group

- **MTN:** Multilateral Trade Negotiations
- **MTO:** Multimodal transport operator
- **NG:** Non-Governmental Organisation
- **OPIC:** Overseas Private Investment Corporation
- **OTM:** Old-To-Market
- **PECC:** Pacific Economic Cooperation Council
- **SED:** Shipper's Export Declaration
- **S.R.&C.C.:** Strikes, riots, and civil commotions
- **S/S [or] S.S. [or] SS:** Stainless steel; Steamship (ocean vessel)
- **SAA:** Standards Association of Australia
- **SAE:** Society of Automotive Engineers
- **SBR:** Styrene-butadiene rubber
- **SC [or] S/C:** Sales confirmation; Sales contract
- **SI:** Système International d'Unités (International System of Units)
- **SIC:** (U.S.) Standard Industrial Classification
- **SITC:** Standard International Trade Classification
- **SKD:** Semi-knockdown
- **SKU:** Stock keeping unit; Stock unit
- **SLC:** Shipper's letter of instructions
- **SM:** Service mark
- **SME:** Small and medium-sized enterprise
- **SO [or] S/O:** Shipping order
- **spec.:** Specification
- **SS:** Svensk Standard (Swedish Standard)
- **St.:** Saint; Street
- **std.:** Standard
- **stk.:** Stock
- **SWG:** Standard wire gauge
- **SWIFT:** Society for Worldwide Interbank Financial Telecommunication
- **3D:** Three dimensional
- **T.P.&N.D.:** Theft, pilferage and non-delivery
- **T.R.:** Trust receipt
- **T/T:** Telegraphic transfer
- **TCT:** Tungsten carbide tip
- **telex:** Teletype exchange (Teleprinter and exchange)
- **TEU:** Twenty-foot equivalent unit
- **TIG:** Tungsten inert gas
- **TIR:** Transit International Routier
- **TL:** Truckload
- **TM [or] T.M.:** Trademark
- **TOFC:** Trailer on flat car
- **tpi:** Teeth per inch; Threads per inch

- **TSUSA:** Tariff Schedules of the United States Annotated
- **TÜV:** Technischen Ueberwachungs Vereine (Technical Inspection Association)
- **tvp:** Textured vegetable protein
- **U.A.E. [or] UAE:** United Arab Emirates
- **U.K. [or] UK:** United Kingdom
- **U.N.:** United Nations
- **U.P.C.:** Universal Product Code
- **UL:** Underwriters Laboratories
- **ULD:** Unit load device
- **UNC:** Unified national coarse
- **UNCTAD:** United Nations Conference on Trade and Development
- **UNEF:** Unified national extra fine
- **UNESCO:** United Nations Educational, Scientific and Cultural Organisation
- **UNF:** Unified national fine
- **UNICEF:** United Nations Children's Fund
- **UNICODE:** Universal digital code
- **UNIDO:** United Nations Industrial Development Organisation
- **UNS:** Unified numbering system
- **UPS:** Uninterruptible power supply (or system)
- **USP [or] U.S.P.:** United States Pharmacopoeia
- **UTC:** Universal Coordinated Time
- **uv:** Ultraviolet
- **V:** Volt
- **VAT:** Value added tax
- **VDE:** Verband Deutscher Elektrotechniker (Association of German Electrical Engineers)
- **vol.:** Volume
- **vs.:** Versus
- **W:** Watt
- **W.A.:** With average (in insurance)
- **W.P.A.:** With particular average (in insurance)
- **W/M [or] W or M:** Weight or measure
- **WAN:** Wide area network
- **WB:** World Bank
- **WHO:** World Health Organisation
- **WIP:** Work in process
- **WIPO:** World Intellectual Property Organisation
- **wt.:** Weight
- **WTC:** World Trade Center
- **WTO:** World Trade Organisation

Glossary

- **Administrative Protective Order:** "An Administrative Protective Order, APO, is used to protect proprietary data that is obtained during an administrative proceeding.
- **Administrative Review:** "Each year, beginning on the anniversary of the date of publication of an antidumping duty order, the Commerce Department's International Trade Administration is required to review and determine the amount of any antidumping duty.
- **ADS:** Agent Distributor Service. ADS provides a custom search overseas for interested and qualified foreign representatives on behalf of a U.S. exporter. Officers abroad conduct the search and prepare a report identifying up to six foreign prospects that have examined the U.S. firm's product literature and have expressed interest in representing the U.S. firm's products.
- **Advanced Technology Products:** "About 500 of some 22,000 commodity classification codes used in reporting U.S. merchandise trade are identified as "advanced technology" codes.
- **Advisory Committee on Export Policy:** "The Advisory Committee on Export Policy, ACEP, is an interagency dispute resolution body that operates at the Assistant Secretary level. ACEP is chaired by Commerce; membership includes the Departments of Defense, Energy, and the Arms Control.
- **Advisory Committee on Trade Negotiations (ACTN):** "A group appointed by the U.S. President to advise him on matters of trade policy and related issues, including trade agreements."
- **Advisory Committee on Trade Policy and Negotiations:** "The ACTPN is a group (membership of 45; two-year terms) appointed by the President to provide advice on matters of trade policy and related issues, including trade agreements. The 1974 Trade Act requires the ACTPN's establishment and broad representation".
- **Advocacy Center:** "The Advocacy Center, established in November 1993, facilitates high-level U.S. official advocacy to assist U.S. firms competing for major projects and procurements worldwide. The Center is directed by the Trade Promotion Co-ordinating Committee.
- **Affiliate:** An affiliate is a business enterprise located in one country which is directly or indirectly owned or controlled by a person of another country to the extent of 10 per cent or more of its voting securities for an incorporated business enterprise.
- **Affiliated Foreign Group:** "An affiliated foreign group means (a) the foreign parent, (b) any foreign person, proceeding up the foreign parent's ownership chain, which owns more than 50 per cent of the person below it up to and including that person which is not owned more than 50.
- **"Affreightment, contract of**: "An agreement by a steamship line to provide cargo space on a vessel at a specified time for a specified price to accommodate an exporter or importer, who then becomes liable for payment even if he is later unable to make the shipment."

- **After Date**: "A term used on a draft, bill of exchange or note indicating the date from which a draft will begin counting days until maturity.

- **Agency for International Development**: "AID was created in 1961 to administer foreign economic assistance programs of the U.S. Government. AID has field missions and representatives in approximately 70 developing countries in Africa, Latin America, the Caribbean, and the Near East. "

- **Agent/Distributor Service**: "The Agent/Distributor Service, ADS, is an International Trade Administration (ITA) fee-based service which locates foreign import agents and distributors."

- **Agreement**: Agreement by one government to accept the accreditation of an ambassador from another government.

- **Agricultural Marketing Service**: "Among its activities, the Agriculture Deparment's AMS is available to foreign buyers to assure that any product shipped overseas meets contract specifications. The service is operated on a user-fee basis. AMS works with the buyers to write a specification".

- **Agricultural Officers**: "Agricultural officers are embassy officials who are responsible for addressing agricultural trade policy issues and preparing reports on agricultural commodities such as rice, wheat, and dairy products.

- **Air Cargo Agent**: A type of freight forwarder who specializes in air cargo and acts for airlines that pay him a fee (usually 5%). The Air Cargo Agent is registered with the International Air Transport Association (IATA).

- **Air Freight Forwarder**: "A type of freight forwarder who specializes in air cargo. The Air Freight Forwarder usually consolidates the air shipments of various exporters, charging them for actual weight and deriving his profit by paying the airline the lower consolidated rate.

- **Air Waybill**: "An AWB is a bill of lading which covers both domestic and international flights transporting goods to a specified destination. Technically, it is a non-negotiable instrument of air transport.

- **Air Waybill (Of Lading)**: "A signed receipt and a contract to deliver goods by air. Such bills are non-negotiable and do not convey title to the goods as do "To Orders" bills of lading used by ocean and land carriers.

- **Airbus Industries Group**: "AIG is a supernational management organisation responsible for design, development, manufacture, marketing, sales and support of selected commercial aircraft. Member countries are France, Germany, Spain, and the United Kingdom. Airbus Industries, G.I.E."

- **Aircraft Agreement (ATCA)**: "Formally known as the ''Agreement on Trade in Civil Aircraft.'' (ATCA), this MTN agreement is the only major sector-specific civil aircraft agreement. It establishes a framework of rules governing the conduct of trade in civil aircraft based on commercial".

- **ASEAN Free Trade Area**: "The Association of Southeast Asian Nations (ASEAN) agreed in January 1992 to create a free trade area (ASEAN Free Trade Area, or AFTA) with use of a common effective preferential tariff.
- **Asia Pacific Economic Cooperation**: "APEC, established in November 1989, is an informal grouping of Asia Pacific countries that provides a forum for Ministerial level discussion of a broad range of economic issues. APEC includes the six ASEAN countries (Brunei, Indonesia, Malaysia, Philippi"
- **Asian Clearing Union**: "The ACU promotes regional trade and economic co-operation, including arrangements to conserve foreign exchange and encourage domestic currencies in trade. Members include Bangladesh, India, Iran, Myanmar, Nepal, Pakistan, and Sri Lanka; Bhutan, Malaysia."
- **Asian Development Bank**: "The ADB helps finance economic development in developing countries in the Asian and Pacific area through the provision of loans on near-market terms, with its Ordinary Capital Resources (OCR), and on concessional terms, through the Asian Development Fund".
- **Asian Development Fund**: "The ADF (or AsDF), an affiliate of the Asian Development Bank, lends funds on concessionary terms to the Bank's least developed member countries."
- **Bill of Lading**: "Bills of lading are contracts between the owner of the goods and the carrier. There are two types. A straight bill of lading is non-negotiable.
- **Balance of Payments Consultations**: The co-ordination between the GATT and the IMF to ensure that trade and payments implications of trade restrictions imposed for balance of payments reasons are taken fully into account.
- **Binding**: "GATT Article 11 provides that signatories may "bind" tariff rates by including them in schedules appended to the GATT. Once a duty is bound, it may not be raised beyond that bound level without compensating affected parties."
- **Booking**: Reservation made by a shipper or his agent with a carrier to carry certain defined goods between locations.
- **Bound Rates**: Tariff rates resulting from GATT negotiations or accession which are appended to the GATT in the form of a 'loose-leaf' tariff schedule and are enforceable under ARTICLE 11 of GATT.
- **Buy American Act**: An act mandating preferential treatment for American products when awarding some government procurement contracts. This act is waived for purchases covered by the government procurement code.
- **Cable Address**: A code word of less than 10 letters, registered annually with the Central Bureau of Registered Addresses, used in lieu of the entire name and address of a firm receiving or sending cablegrams in order to reduce the number of words required in a cablegram.
- **Carriage Paid To**: Carriage Paid To (CPT) and Carriage and Insurance Paid to (CIP) a named place of destination. Used in place of CFR and CIF, respectively for shipment by modes other than water.

- **Cartel**: An organisation of independent producers formed to regulate the production, pricing, or marketing practices of its members in order to limit competition and maximise their market power.
- **Cash Against Documents**: A term denoting that payment is made when the bill of lading is presented.
- **Cash Against Documents (C.A.D.)**: A method of payment for goods in which documents transferring title are given to the buyer upon payment of cash to an intermediary acting for the seller, usually a commission house.
- **Cash In Advance (C.I.A.)**: A method of payment for goods in which the buyer pays the seller in advance of the shipment of the goods. Usually employed when the goods are built to order, such as specialised machinery.
- **Cash With Order**: CWO is a means of payment in which the buyer pays cash when ordering; the order is binding on both seller and buyer.
- **Cash With Order (C.W.O.)**: A method of payment for goods in which cash is paid at the time of order and the transaction becomes binding on both buyer and seller.
- **Category Groups**: Groupings of controlled products.
- **Certificate of Inspection**: A document certifying that merchandise (such as perishable goods) was in good condition immediately prior to shipment. Pre-shipment inspection is a requirement for importation of goods into many developing countries.
- **Certificate of Manufacture**: A document (often notarised) in which a producer of goods certifies that the manufacturing has been completed and the goods are now at the disposal of the buyer.
- **Certificate of Origin**: A certified document as to the origin of goods, used in foreign commerce.
- **Certificate of Origin**: Certain nations require a signed statement as to the origin of the export item. Such certificates are usually obtained through a semi-official organisation such as a local chamber of commerce. A certificate may be required even though the commercial invoice contains the information.
- **Clean Bill of Lading**: A receipt for goods issued by a carrier with an indication that the goods were received in "apparent good order and condition," without damages or other irregularities.
- **Delivered at Frontier**: "Delivered at Frontier" means that the seller's obligations are fulfilled when the goods have arrived at the frontier - but before "the customs border" of the country named in the sales contract. The term is primarily intended to apply to goods by rail or road but is also used irrespective of the mode of transport.
- **Delivered/Duty Paid**: While the term "Ex Works" signifies the seller's minimum obligation, the term "Delivered Duty Paid", when followed by words naming the buyer's premises, denotes the other extreme - the seller's maximum obligation. The term "Delivered Duty Paid" may be used irrespective of the mode of transport.

- **Delivery Instructions**: Provides specific information to the inland carrier concerning the arrangement made by the forwarder to deliver the merchandise to the particular pier or steamship line. Not to be confused with Delivery Order which is used for import cargo.

- **Derrick**: Lifting equipment on board a ship generally used for loading and discharging cargo.

- **Despatch**: An agreed upon amount of money that is paid by the shipowner to the shipper or receiver, when loading or discharging is performed faster than the allotted time.

- **Dispute Settlement**: This refers to the resolution of opposing aims often facilitated through the efforts of an intermediary. In the GATT context, dispute settlement provides opportunities for individual contracting parties to resolve trade problems through negotiated means or with the help Applicants and consignees must establish Internal Control Programs to ensure the proper distribution of items under the DL.

- **Distributor**: A foreign agent who sells directly for a manufacturer and maintains an inventory on hand.

- **Diversionary Dumping**: This occurs when foreign producers sell to a third country market at less than fair value and the product is then further processed and shipped to another country.

- **Dock Receipt**: A receipt given for a shipment received or delivered at a shipment pier. When delivery of a foreign shipment is completed, the dock receipt is surrendered to the vessel operator or his agent and serves as basis for preparation of the Ocean Bill of Lading.

- **Document Collections - Documents Against Payment**: Stipulate that the exporter ships goods to the importer without a letter of credit or another form of guaranteed payment. The importer must sign a sight draft before receiving the necessary documents to pick up the goods.

- **Documents Against Payment (D/P)**: A type of payment for goods in which the documents transferring title to the goods are not given to the buyer until he has paid the value of a draft issued against him.

- **Domestic Exports**: Exports of domestic merchandise include commodities which are grown, produced, or manufactured in the United States, and commodities of foreign origin which have been substantially changed in the United States, including U.S. Foreign Trade Zones, from the form in which they were imported, or which have been enhanced in value by further manufacture in the United States.

- **Domicile**: The place where a draft or acceptance is made payable.

- **Downstream Dumping**: This occurs when foreign producers sell at below cost to a producer in its domestic market, and the product is then further processed and shipped to another country.

- **Downstream Dumping**: This occurs when foreign producers sell at below cost to a producer in its domestic market and the product is then further processed and shipped to another country.

- **Draft Bill of Exchange**: A written, unconditional order for payment from one person (the drawer) to another (the drawee). It directs the drawee to pay a specified sum of money, in a given currency, at a specific date to the drawer. A Sight Draft calls for immediate payment (on sight) while a Time Draft calls for payments at a readily determined future date.

- **Drawback**: A partial refund of duties paid on importation of goods which are further processed and then re-exported, or exported in same condition as imported.

- **Drawback System**: The Drawback System, a part of Customs' Automated Commercial System, provides the means for processing and tracking of drawback claims.

- **Drawee**: The individual or firm on whom a draft is drawn and who owes the indicated amount.

- **Drawer**: The individual or firm that issues or signs a draft and thus stands to receive payment of the indicated amount from the drawee.

- **Dual Pricing**: The selling of identical products in different markets for different prices. This often reflects dumping practices.

- **Dumping**: Dumping is generally seen as an unfair trading practice. It occurs when a good is sold for less than its "fair value", generally meaning it is exported for less than it is sold in the domestic market or third country markets, or it is sold for less than production cost.

- **Duty**: A tax levied by a government on the import, export or use and consumption of goods.

- **Economic Cooperation Organisation**: The ECO strengthens co-operation to improve socio-economic conditions among the populations of members. The Organisation was founded in 1964; headquarters are in Tehran, Iran. Members include: Afghanistan, Azerbaijan, Iran, Kazakhstan, Kyrgyzstan, Pakistan, Tajikistan, Turkmenistan, Turkey, and Uzbekistan.

- **European Community (EC)**: Coming into operation in 1958 and based on the Treaty of Rome, the EC originally consisted of the following countries who joined together to establish a customs union and other forms of economic integration: France, Italy, the Federal Republic of Germany, Belgium, the Netherlands and Luxembourg. The United Kingdom, Denmark and Ireland joined in 1973. Greece joined in 1981, followed by Portugal and Spain in 1986.

- **European Conference of Postal and Telecommunications Administrations**: Refer Conference Europeenne des Administrations des Postes et des Telecommunications.

- **Foreign Exchange Option**: A foreign exchange option is an arrangement in which a purchaser and a seller of foreign currencies agree on a specific rate of exchange at a future date. The purchaser may choose to exercise or pass up the option - thus setting a limit on unfavorable exchange rates. The seller is given a fee for tendering the option. Purchasers may exercise the option at any time - in the European option, currency exchange is made on the originally established date; in the American option, exchange is made within a couple of days of the purchaser exercising the option.

- **Foreign Exports**: Exports of foreign merchandise (re-exports), consist of commodities of foreign origin which have entered the United States for consumption or into Customs bonded warehouses or U.S. Foreign Trade Zones, and which, at the time of exportation, are in substantially the same condition as when imported.

- **Foreign Market Value**: The price at which merchandise is sold, or offered for sale, in the principal markets of the country from which it is exported. If information on foreign home market sales is not useful, the foreign market value is based on prices of exports to third countries or constructed value. Adjustments for quantities sold, circumstances of sales, and differences in the merchandise can be made to those prices to ensure a proper comparison with the prices of goods exported to the United States.

- **Foreign Trade Zone Entry:** A form declaring goods which are brought duty-free into a Foreign Trade Zone for further processing or storage and subsequent exportation and/or consumption.

- **Foreign Trade Zone:** This is also referred to as a "free zone", "free port" or "bonded warehouse: This is an area within a country where goods can be imported, stored, and/or processed without being subject to customs duties and taxes.

- **Free Alongside (F.A.S.) (or free alongside steamer):** The seller must deliver the goods to a pier and place them within reach of the ship's loading equipment. The buyer arranges ship space and informs the seller when and where the goods are to be placed.

- **Free In And Out (F.I.O.):** Cost of loading and unloading a vessel is borne by the charterer.

- **Free List:** A list of goods that have been designated as free from import duties or import port licensing requirements in a given country .

- **Free Of Particular Average (F.P.A.):** A marine insurance clause providing that partial loss or damage is not insured. American condition (F.P.A.A.C.) - Partial loss not insured unless caused by the vessel being sunk, stranded, burned, on fire, or in collision. English conditions (F.P.A.E.C.) - Partial loss not insured unless a result of the vessel being sunk, stranded, burned, on fire, or in collision.

- **Free Out (F.O.):** Cost of unloading a vessel is borne by the charterer.

- **Free port:** Separate area within a port where goods which have been imported may be held without duty payment.

- **Free Trade Area (FTA):** A group of two or more countries that have eliminated tariff barriers among themselves while not applying a uniform external tariff on imports ports from non-participating countries. The European Free Trade Association is the best known example of such an arrangement.
- **Free Trade Zone:** An area to which goods may be imported for processing and subsequent export on duty-free basis.
- **Freight Forwarder:** An agent whose functions are to help expedite shipments by preparing the necessary documents and making other arrangements for the movement of merchandise.
- **Gambia River Basin Development Organisation**: The Organisation (French: Organisation pour la Mise en Valeur du Fleuve Gambie, OMVG) promotes the construction of dams for hydroelectric and irrigation purposes. The organisation was established in June 1978; headquarters are in Dakar, Senegal. Members include: the Gambia, Guinea, Guinea-Bissau, and Senegal.
- **Gateway**: In the context of travel activities, gateway refers to a major airport or seaport. Internationally, gateway can also mean the port where customs clearance takes place.
- **GATT Panel**: A panel of neutral representatives that may be established by the GATT Secretariat under the dispute settlement provisions of the GATT to review the facts of a dispute and render findings of GATT law and recommend action.
- **General Imports**: "General Imports" measure the total physical arrivals of merchandise from foreign countries, whether such merchandise enters consumption channels immediately or is entered into bonded warehouses or Foreign Trade Zones under Customs custody.
- **General License**: These are licenses, authorised by the Bureau of Export Administration, that permit the export of goods and technology to specified countries without the need for a validated license. No prior written authorisation is required and no individual validated license is issued. There are over twenty different types of general licenses, each represented by a symbol.
- **Harmonised System**: The Harmonised Commodity Description and Coding System (or Harmonised System, HS) is a system for classifying goods in international trade, developed under the auspices of the Customs Cooperation Council.
- **Horizontal Export Trading Company**: An export trading company which exports a range of similar or identical products supplied by a number of manufacturers or other producers. Webb-Pomerene Organisations, trade-grouped organised export trading companies, and an export trading company formed by an association of agricultural co-operatives are the prime examples of horizontally organised export trading companies.
- **Import Certificate**: The import certificate is a means by which the government of the country of ultimate destination exercises legal control over the internal channeling of the commodities covered by the import certificate.

- **Import License**: A document required and issued by some national governments authorising the importation of goods.
- **Import Quota**: A means of restricting imports by the issuance of licenses to importers, assigning each a quota, after determination of the total amount of any commodity which is to be imported during a period. Import licenses may also specify the country from which the importer must purchase the goods.
- **Import Quota Auctioning**: The process of auctioning the right to import specified quantities of quota-restricted goods.
- **Import Restrictions**: Import restriction, applied by a country with an adverse trade balance (or for other reasons), reflect a desire to control the volume of goods coming into the country from other countries may include the imposition of tariffs or import quotas, restrictions on the amount of foreign currency available to cover imports, a requirement for import deposits, the imposition of import surcharges, or the prohibition of various categories of imports.
- **Import Substitution**: A strategy which emphasizes the replacement of imports with domestically produced goods, rather than the production of goods for export, to encourage the development of domestic industry.
- **International Chamber of Commerce**: ICC was created in 1919 to promote free trade, private enterprise, and represent business interests at national and international levels. Members include national councils from sixty countries. ICC headquarters are in Paris, France.
- **Letter of Credit**: An instrument of audit issued by the buyer's bank, at the buyer's request, in which the issuing bank promises to pay the seller upon presentation of documents stipulated in the terms and conditions of the audit.
- **Letter of Credit (Confirmed)**: A letter of audit issued by one bank to which another bank added its irrevocable confirmation to pay, thereby obligating itself in the same manner as the opening bank. For example, "we hereby confirm this credit and undertake to pay drafts drawn in accordance with the terms and conditions of the letter of credit."
- **Letter of Credit (Cumulative)**: A revolving letter of credit which permits any amount not utilized during any of the specified periods to be carried over and added to the amounts available in subsequent periods.
- **Letter of Credit (Deferred Payment)**: A letter of credit issued for the purchase and financing of merchandise, similar to acceptance letter of credit, except that it requires presentation of sight drafts which are payable on installment basis usually for periods of 1 year or more. Under this type of credit, the seller is financing the buyer until the stipulated time his drafts can be presented to the bank for payment. There is a significant deference in the bank's commitment, depending on whether the negotiating bank advised or confirmed the letter of credit.

- **Marine Cargo Insurance**: Broadly, insurance covering loss of, or damage to, goods at sea. Marine insurance typically compensates the owner of merchandise for losses in excess of those which can be legally recovered from the carrier that are sustained from fire, shipwreck, piracy, and various other causes. Three of the most common types of marine insurance coverage are "free of particular average" (f.p.a.), "with average" (w.a.), and "All Risks Coverage."

- **Market Access**: Market access refers to the openness of a national market to foreign products. Market access reflects a government's willingness to permit imports to compete relatively unimpeded with similar domestically produced goods.

- **Market Access**: The ability of a domestic industry to penetrate a related market in a foreign country. The extent to which the foreign market is accessible generally depends upon the existence and extent of trade barriers.

- **Market Disruption**: Market disruption refers to the situation which is created when a surge of imports in a given product line causes sales of domestically produced goods in a particular country to decline to an extent that the domestic producers and their employees suffer major economic hardship.

- **Most Favored Nation Treatment (MFN)**: When one country accords another most-favored-nation status, it agrees to extend that country the same trade concessions it grants to any other MFN recipients.

- **Multinational Corporation**: A multinational corporation is a business which owns or controls product or service facilities outside the country in which it is based.

- **New-to-Export**: As defined by the International Trade Administration, a new-to-export action is one that results from documented assistance to a company that assists the client's first verifiable export sale. Either the company has not exported to any destination during the past 24 months or prior exports have resulted from unsolicited orders or were received through a U.S.-based intermediary.

- **New-to-Market**: As defined by the International Trade Administration, a reportable new-to-market export action is one that results from documented assistance to an exporter that facilitates a verifiable sale in a new foreign market. Either the company has not exported to that market during the past 24 months or previous exports to that market have resulted from unsolicited orders or were received through a U.S. based intermediary.

- **Organisation for Economic Co-operation and Development**: OECD provides a forum for discussion of common economic and social issues facing the United States, Canada, Western Europe, Japan, Australia, and New Zealand.

- **Pacific Economic Co-operation Council**: The PECC is a nongovernmental organisation founded in 1980 and aimed at promoting co-operation in the Asia-Pacific region. Members are drawn from 20 countries and territories: Australia, Brunei, Canada, Chile, China, Hong Kong, Indonesia, Japan, Korea, Malaysia, Mexico, New Zealand, the Pacific Islands, Peru, the Philippines, Russia, Singapore, Taiwan, Thailand, and the United States.

- **Port Shopping**: Port shopping is the practice of exporters and importers choosing a particular port on the basis of their assessment of Customs' treatment, rather than on the quality of physical facilities and efficiency.

- **Pro Forma Invoice**: An invoice provided by a supplier prior to the shipment of merchandise, informing the buyer of the kinds and quantities of goods to be sent, their value, and important specifications (weight, size, and similar characteristics).

- **Product Groups**: Commodity groupings used for export control purposes.

- **Profit**: For the purposes of constructed value in an antidumping duty investigation or review, the profit used is the profit normally earned by a producer, from the country of export, of the same or similar product as that under investigation. By statute, the amount of profit shall not be less than 8 per cent of the sum of general expenses and cost.

- **Project License**: The Bureau of Export Administration uses the project license to authorise large-scale exports of a wide variety of commodities and technical data for specified activities.

- **Protectionism**: The use of restrictions to discourage imports and artificially help domestic producers compete with foreign suppliers.

- **Protective Order**: With regard to antidumping cases, a term for the order under which most business proprietary information is made available to an attorney or other representative of a party to the proceeding.

- **Protest System**: The Protest System, a part of Customs' Automated Commercial System, tracks protests from the date they are received through final action. A protest is the legal means by which an importer, consignee, or other designated part may challenge decisions made by a District Director of Customs.

- **Quantitative Restrictions**: Explicit limits, usually by volume, on the amount of a specified commodity that may be imported into a country, sometimes also indicating the amounts that may be imported from each supplying country. Compared to tariffs, the protection afforded by QR's tends to be more predictable, being less affected by changes in competitive factors.

- **Red Clause**: An Authorisation in a commercial letter of credit authorising the advising/negotiating bank to make a limited advance to the seller before the shipment to the buyer is made. Such advances can be made up to 100% of the shipment value. These advances enable the seller to procure supplies for manufacturing or shipment. Negotiations of Red Clause credits are restricted to the bank making the advances in order to assure that proceeds from the shipment are used to repay the advances.

- **Re-exports**: For export control purposes: the shipment of U.S. origin products from one foreign destination to another. For statistical reporting purposes: exports of foreign-origin merchandise which have previously entered the United States for consumption or into Customs bonded warehouses for U.S. Foreign Trade Zones.

- **Revocable Letter of Credit**: A letter of credit which can be cancelled or altered by the drawee (buyer) after it has been issued by the drawee's bank.
- **RWA**: Returned Without Action
- **Sales Representative**: An agent who distributes, represents, services, or sells goods on behalf of foreign sellers.
- **Ship's Manifest**: A list, signed by the captain of a ship, of the individual shipments constituting the ship's cargo.
- **Shipment**: A shipment is all of the cargo carried under the terms of a single bill of lading.
- **Shipper's Export Declaration**: A form required by the Treasury Department and completed by a shipper showing the value, weight, consignee, destination, etc., of export shipments as well as Harmonised Schedule.
- **Shipping Weight**: Shipping weight represents the gross weight in kilograms of shipments, including the weight of moisture content, wrappings, crates, boxes, and containers (other than cargo vans and similar substantial outer containers).
- **Short Supply**: Commodities in short supply may be subject to export controls to protect the domestic economy from the excessive drain of scarce materials and to reduce the serious inflationary impact of satisfying foreign demand.
- **Soft Currency**: The currency of a nation in which exchange may be made only with difficulty. Soft currency countries typically have minimal exchange reserves and deficits in their balance of payments.
- **Soft Loan**: Commonly, a loan from a government or multilateral development bank with a long repayment period and below-market interest.
- **South Asia Preferential Trading Arrangement**: Refer South Asian Association for Regional Co-operation.
- **South Asian Association for Regional Co-operation**: SAARC promotes economic, technical, scientific, and social cooperation among members. The Association was founded in 1985 by seven countries: Bangladesh, Bhutan, India, Maldives, Nepal, Pakistan, and Sri Lanka. The Association plans to establish a South Asian Preferential Trading Arrangement (SAPTA) by 1997 as a step toward creating an economic community in south Asia.
- **South Pacific Forum**: The SPF is a regional arrangement for convening 15 governments and territories for deliberations on issues of mutual interest. The Forum was established in 1971; headquarters are in Suva, Fiji; members include: Australia, the Cook Islands, Fiji, Kirbati, Marshall Islands, Micronesia, Nauru, New Zealand, Niue, Papua New Guinea, Samoa, Solomon Island, Tonga, Tuvalu, and Vanatu.
- **Subsidies**: GATT does not directly define subsidies. The U.S. regards a subsidy as a bounty or grant paid for the manufacture, production, or export of an article. Export subsidies are contingent on exports; domestic subsidies are conferred on production without reference to exports. While governments sometimes make outright payments to firms; subsidies usually take a less direct form (R&D support, tax breaks, loans on preferential terms, and provision of raw materials at below-market prices).

- **Subsidy**: There are two general types of subsidies: export and domestic. An export subsidy is a benefit conferred on a firm by the government that is contingent or exports. A domestic subsidy is a benefit not linked to exports, conferred by the government upon a specific industry or enterprise or group of industries or enterprises.

- **Substantial Suppliers**: If a country supplies approximately 10 per cent of the trade in a given item imported to a second country, the first country is said to have a substantial supplier status.

- **Summary Investigation**: A 20-day investigation conducted by the International Trade Administration immediately following filing of an antidumping petition to ascertain if the petition contains sufficient information with respect to sales at "less than fair value" and the injury or threat of material injury to a domestic industry caused by the alleged sales at "less than fair value" to warrant the initiation of an antidumping investigation.

- **Summit Conference**: A summit conference is an international meeting at which heads of government are the chief negotiators, major world powers are represented, and the meeting serves substantive rather than ceremonial purposes. The term first came into use in reference to the Geneva Big Four Conference of 1955.

- **Tariff**: A tax assessed by a government in accordance with its tariff schedule on goods as they enter (or leave) a country. May be imposed to protect domestic industries from imported goods and/or to generate revenue. Types include ad valorem, specific, variable, or some combination.

- **Tariff Anomaly**: A tariff anomaly exists when the tariff on raw materials or semi-manufactured goods is higher than the tariff on the finished product.

- **Tariff Bindings**: The agreement by contracting parties to maintain the duty rates on specified goods at negotiated levels or below. Bindings are provided for in GATT Article - II.

- **Tariff Escalation**: A situation in which tariffs on manufactured goods are relatively high, tariffs on semi-processed goods are moderate, and tariffs on raw materials are nonexistent or very low.

- **Tariff Escalation**: This term refers to the common situation whereby raw materials and less processed goods are generally dutied at lower rates than more processed versions of the same or derivative goods. For instance, the import duty in most countries is generally higher for petrochemicals than for the petroleum and other raw materials necessary for their production. It is argued by primary commodity exporting nations that this situation confers a higher degree of protection for the processing industries of importing countries than nominal tariff rates would suggest.

- **Tariff Quota**: A tariff that remains at the same level until a certain quantitative limit (quota) is reached. The duty on imports ports in excess of that level will be higher.

- **Tariff Quotas**: Application of a higher tariff rate to imported goods after a specified quantity of the item has entered the country at a lower prevailing rate.

- **Tariff Schedule**: A comprehensive list of the goods which a country may import and the import duties applicable to each product.
- **Technical Barrier to Trade**: A specification which sets forth characteristics a product must meet (such as levels of quality, performance, safety or dimensions) in order to be imported.
- **Technology Transfer**: This term is used to characterise "the transfer of knowledge generated and developed in one place to another, where is it is used to achieve some practical end." Technology may be transferred in many ways: by giving it away (technical journals, conferences, emigration of technical experts, technical assistance programs); by industrial espionage; or by sale (patents, blueprints, industrial processes, and the activities of multinational corporations).
- **Terms of Trade**: Terms of trade refers to the economic factors affecting a country's foreign trade in goods and services, such as dependency on foreign sourcing and relative competitiveness in production.
- **Through Bill of Lading**: A single bill of lading covering receipt of the cargo at the point of origin for delivery to the ultimate consignee, using two or more modes of transportation.
- **Voluntary Export Restriction**: An understanding between trading partners in which the exporting nation, in order to reduce trade friction, agrees to limit its exports of a particular good. Also called voluntary restraint agreement.
- **Voluntary Restraint Agreement**: Informal bilateral or multilateral understandings in which exporters voluntarily limit exports of certain products to a particular country destination in order to avoid economic dislocation in the importing country and the imposition of mandatory import restrictions. These arrangements do not involve an obligation on the part of the importing country to provide "compensation" to the exporting country, as would be the case if the importing country unilaterally imposed equivalent restraints on imports.

Bibliography

(1)   Agarwal O.P., Chaudhuri B.K., "Foreign Trade and Foreign Exchange, Himalaya Publishing House, Mumbai, 2009.

(2)   Balagopal T.A.S., "Export Management, Himalaya Publishing House, Mumbai, 2006.

(3)   Bhalla V. K., S. Shiva Ramu, "International Business", Amol Publication (P) Ltd., New Delhi, 2005.

(4)   Cherunilam Francis, "International Trade and Export Management", Himalaya Publishing House, Mumbai, 2006.

(5)   Chaudhuri, B.K., Agarwal O.P., "Foreign Trade and Foreign Exchange", Himalaya Publishing House, Mumbai, 2006.

(6)   Dr. Jain Khushpat S., "Export Import Procedures and Documentation", Himalaya Publishing House, Mumbai, 2007.

(7)   Mahajan M.I., "Export Do It Yourself", Snow White, 2010.

(8)   Sundaram Anant K., Black Stewart I., "International Business Environment, Text and Case", Prentice Hall of India (Pvt.) Ltd., New Delhi, 2000.

(9)   Khurana D. K., "Export Management", Galgotia Publihsing Company, New Delhi, 2001.

(10)   Kapoor D.C., "Export Management", Vikas Publishing House (P) Ltd., New Delhi, 2005.

☞ ☞ ☞

April 2016
(New 2013 Patter)

Time : 3 Hrs.   Maximum Marks : 80

N.B.

(i) Attempt any five questions.

(ii) Figures to the right indicate full marks.

Q.1. Explain the Procedure of Obtaining IFC and RCMC from DGFT and EPC respectively.

(16)

Q.2. (a) Explain various documents required for imports.   (8)

(b) Explain various payment procedures.   (8)

Q.3. Elaborate the advantages and disadvantages of various modes of transport.   (16)

Q.4. Discuss the exemptions that Government gives to exporters in Service Tax and Income Tax.   (16)

Q.5. Explain the following Duty Remission Scheme.   (16)

(a) DEPs.

(b) Duty Drawback Scheme

Q.6. **Write notes on (Any Two)**   (16)

(a) Deemed Exports.

(b) Mate Receipt.

(c) Concept of Warehousing.

✍ ✍ ✍